A HEART SO GREEN

Not in a thousand lifetimes will I ever let you go.

What did it truly mean, to never let a person go? If Fia never returned to him—if she had already been consumed by Talah's heinous magic—was he honor-bound to grapple with this *thing* wearing her face for the rest of his life? Or was it enough to have loved her so deeply that the sound of her name was etched like a poem upon the parchment of his heart?

By what terrible troth had he—yet again—bound himself?

All his life, Irian had been defined by geasa. His father's curse upon his mother, his enforced link with the Sky-Sword. His invisible bonds to the swan maidens, his marriage covenant with Fia. And now this.

Without his oaths, Irian did not know who he was. He had never bothered to ask. But now he began to wonder: Would the weight of this last pledge be the thing to break him?

Praise for
the Fair Folk series

"Dark and dangerous and teeming with romance. An exhilarating adventure that walks the edge of a blade. Truly enchanting"
Rachel Gillig, *New York Times* bestselling author of *The Knight and the Moth*

"Darkly enchanting and beautifully written. The perfect mix of atmospheric fantasy, heart-stopping action, and delicious romance"
Thea Guanzon, *New York Times* bestselling author of *The Hurricane Wars*

"Opulent and scorching. Selene lured me into her dangerous fairy world, and I never want to leave"
Roshani Chokshi, *New York Times* bestselling author of *The Last Tale of the Flower Bride*

"A beautiful nightmare, an eldritch tale steeped in lore and lush with exquisite prose. By turns seductive and heartbreaking, this enthralling journey heralds a new era of fantasy"
Breanne Randall, *New York Times* bestselling author of *The Unfortunate Side Effects of Heartbreak and Magic*

"Selene makes the world of the fae mysterious, sensual, and enthralling"   *Publishers Weekly* (starred review)

"Readers will get lost in Selene's fairy world; this tale showcases expansive world-building, fascinating political intrigue among the fae, and death-defying love in an epic adventure"   *Booklist*

"Selene expands her lush fantasy setting, bumps the romance from steamy to scalding, and brings new friends and enemies into Fia's path. The prose remains as dreamy and poetic as in the first book, and the ending sets up a dramatic twist that will leave readers clamoring to get their hands on the next volume"

Shelf Awareness

By Lyra Selene

Fair Folk

A Feather So Black
A Crown So Silver
A Heart So Green

LYRA SELENE

A HEART SO GREEN

orbit-books.co.uk

ORBIT

First published in Great Britain in 2026 by Orbit

1 3 5 7 9 10 8 6 4 2

A CIP catalogue record for this book
is available from the British Library.

ISBN 978-0-356-52496-2

Printed and bound in Great Britain by Clays Ltd, Elcograf, S.p.A.

Papers used by Orbit are from well-managed forests
and other responsible sources.

Orbit
An imprint of
Little, Brown Book Group
Carmelite House
50 Victoria Embankment
London, EC4Y 0DZ

The authorised representative
in the EEA is
Hachette Ireland
8 Castlecourt Centre,
Dublin 15, D15 XTP3, Ireland
(email: info@hbgi.ie)

An Hachette UK Company
www.hachette.co.uk

orbit-books.co.uk

*For the ones who believe that "the end" is just
"once upon a time" in disguise*

Part One

Fire in the Head

I am the wind on the sea;
I am the wave of the sea;
I am the bull of seven battles;
I am the eagle on the rock;
I am a flash from the sun;
I am the most beautiful of plants;
I am a strong wild boar;
I am a salmon in the water;
I am a lake in the plain;
I am the word of knowledge;
I am the head of the spear in battle;
I am the god that puts fire in the head.
Who spreads light in the gathering on the hills?
Who can tell the ages of the moon?
Who can tell the place where the sun rests?

—"The Song of Amergin," translated
by Lady Gregory

Chapter One

Within

I had been here before.

A mountain stream slashed down the cliff face and carved out a deep pool in a broad clearing. Spears of moonlight sliced the misty spray into silver prisms. Translucent shallows deepened to midnight near the center of the pond. Glittering flowers spangled sloping banks.

A tall man undressed slowly at the water's edge. His hair was the lustrous, gleaming black of a feather; his powerful body was carved from hard muscle and sinew. And oh, his *face*—sculpted from moonlight and shadow, with plush lips parted faintly in amusement. Silver eyes simmered with desire beneath dark winging brows.

He plunged into the pool. The water swallowed him without a splash as he dived—deep enough for his form to be a star of white in the dark. I inhaled, filling my lungs with humid summer air. And even as I stood transfixed on the bluebell-strewn knoll...I, too, dived into the pool. My hands—clasped as if in prayer—split the dark water. My body knifed down, the cold pond a shock against my sweat-sticky skin. I clawed at the water, pulling myself deeper.

You cannot hide here.

The voice was the whisper of silver ripples lapping rush-lined banks; the susurrus of eager trees bending heavy heads; the sudden pinch of a molten ring wrapped too tightly around my finger; the blinding scream of a collar latched around my throat—

Let me in.

I knew by now not to grab for it. The collar's faint sizzle at my throat was nothing more than sense memory. I could tug until my fingernails shredded. Tear with all my strength. The metal would not give way. Because it was not really there.

Instead, I dived deeper. The man arose in counterpoint, and I watched him as he passed. His sharp jaw was tilted toward the light; his silver eyes were open, fixed on the shadow of a girl standing on the bank.

Me.

Not me. Not anymore.

Part of me longed to turn—to buoy to the surface alongside Irian and let this moment play out the way it was supposed to. To latch my legs around his waist and tangle my fingertips in his damp black hair and press my yearning lips to his. But the rest of me knew—this moment was long gone. It was a dream, a memory. And if I lingered here—if I *stayed*—then *she* might catch me.

Let me in.

I swam deeper. My breath bulged in my lungs, yearning for escape. The moonlight bled away, a last gasp fading into nothing. If this had been real, I would have long ago reached the bottom of the pool.

It was not real.

I thrust myself deeper still, my senses furling away from me like petals from a dying flower. My sight, gone. My breath, stolen. My skin, chilled. I did not know which way was up, down. Whether this was still water, or something colder. Darker. Emptier.

I only knew I had to keep moving.

You cannot hide here.

As if summoned by the words, light appeared—a warm glow green as ivy and gentle as jasmine. Surprise forced my gaze to my chest, where a river stone suddenly hung above my breastbone, pulsing a deep blue-green in the endless dark. A slender sapling of hope grew inside me. I grabbed for the stone, and it hummed between my fingers. Vines clambered up my wrists with tiny sharp thorns.

A forest grew before me. Diamond-barked trunks arched tangled limbs. Branches exploded with serrated leaves scaled green as lizards' bellies. Ferns embroidered lace through teeming underbrush. Vibrant flowers trembled, iridescent as butterflies' wings.

A familiar figure stood amid dappled shafts of moonlight. They wore a crown of silver antlers lofting toward a star-strewn sky. Their muscular limbs were slicked over with russet fur. They had a face like the forest path.

You are mine, they intoned, slow as the seasons and patient as the dusk. Long fingers tipped with claws beckoned me, and I followed without thought. Without fear. Even as the figure turned, disappearing into the darkest part of the wood, I heedlessly ran after them.

Let me in!

The soundless scream chased me, rattling the boughs of the trees until their glass leaves shattered on the path. My bare feet crunched through the litter, pain lancing my calves as blood fletched my steps. Still I ran—as skeleton birds pecked at my eyes and metal trees unfurled into starbursts of violence and my silver crown slipped down over one eye. I jerked it away from my head, and some of my white-blond hair came away with it, silvery strands twining my fingers like wire.

"No," I moaned as my steps slowed. I threw the silver tiara to the ground, but that was no better—gray-fleshed arms punched from the dirt, clawing toward the shining metal with broken fingernails and palms crusted with grave dirt.

You cannot hide here.

I forced myself forward, even as the forest charred to dust at my passing. The ring around my finger burned molten. The scent of scorched metal and bog tar chased me. I swallowed, the sickly sweetness of apple nectar coating my tongue until my teeth began to rot in my mouth.

Still, I ran. Because I was not trying to hide.

I was trying to escape.

Chapter Two

Irian

Every person had a limit to their strength. Irian was approaching his.

This was not the first time in his life his strength had flagged.
Though he had been forced from an early age to make himself a
fortress, he knew hardness and resilience were not the same things.
Endurance was a muscle that weakened as readily as an arm or a
leg. There had been countless times over the years when Irian had
longed to give up. To *surrender.*

More times than he readily cared to admit.

When he had been a little boy rowing himself across a raucous
ocean and climbing clamorous cliffs, only to find his own beloved
mother did not remember him.

When he had been a young man, cast out from the only home he
knew by the only father he'd ever wanted.

When he had been a man grown, and his wife of three minutes
had taken her own life instead of his, leaving him devastated in the
wake of her sacrifice.

Irian looked at Fia now. She lay quiescent in his arms, rocking gently to the motion of the aughisky plodding heavily beneath them. Irian could almost ignore the shifting patterns of metal tracing like lace beneath her skin, the slick scales bulging at her temples before smoothing away, the sharp black pinions spiking her dark hair before softening to sable waves. He could pretend Fia was sleeping in his arms. He could pretend nothing had changed.

But everything had changed. And Irian, yet again, had been powerless to prevent it.

How long since Emain Ablach collapsed? He had lost count. Three weeks—perhaps more.

After the fateful Longest Night, their group had washed up past midnight on a black-sand beach beneath towering crimson cliffs. Irian had been consumed by Fia's transformations—her form rapidly shifting between woman and wolf, girl and goshawk. She had scratched and clawed and beat at him. He had barely spared an ear for the hurried war council carried out by his half-drowned compatriots.

"There will be innocents caught in the destruction," Wayland had ground out when Laoise first suggested retreating to the home she referred to only as *the Cnoc*. "With my father dead, I am king of the Silver Isle. They will look to me—"

"You are king of nothing, Prionsa." Wayland had flinched at the unvarnished truth of Laoise's words. But they had all witnessed the Silver Isle shear away into the hungry waves, had all watched it devoured by silver flames and cold ocean. "There will be some who found currachs or barges or lengths of driftwood. But unless you can command the tide to carry them safely to shore, then I am not sure how you believe you can help."

"If we cannot help them," Sinéad had said, "then we must help those who may be yet caught in the war the bardaí will wage, with Eala dead."

"She is not." Those were the only words Irian had been able to manage as he had wrestled the transforming figure of his magic-warped wife upon the blackened beach.

They had all turned toward him, surprise mingling with denial. Only Wayland had dared approach, reaching to help Irian with Fia. Irian had batted him away, brusque. "Eala lives."

"But I killed her," Sinéad said, with little intonation.

Irian had indeed watched the human girl plunge her twin daggers into Eala's chest a half dozen times before Laoise dragged Sinéad off her swan sister's broken, bleeding body. But he knew too much of the terrible magic of the Treasures to believe it so easy to kill the human princess. Perhaps he might have convinced himself, as the others had done. But he had *seen* her, in the moments before Emain Ablach disappeared beneath the sea. Her gilded head, crowned by a sparkling silver tiara. Her fluttering dress, white as the cliffs at her back. Her sharp smile, ready to carve up destiny and swallow it whole.

"She lives," he had reiterated roughly. Even if he had not seen Eala, smiling like mayhem on that beach, he could *feel* her magic. Just as he could *feel* Fia's, the atonal thrum of it singing in counterpoint to his own. Just as he could *feel* the two ugly points of corrupted wild magic threading darkly over the distant landscape.

The Treasures were all linked. It was as it had ever been. He would know if Eala were dead—if the wild magic of her Treasure had been released.

No—they were not yet finished with the swan princess.

In the end, Laoise's plan had prevailed. The Gentry maiden had surprised them all with the truth of her anam cló. Irian had heard legends of the mythic dragain of the Sept of Scales—from his mother, from Deirdre, even from Wayland when they were boys. But those flying, flaming serpents had been but *stories*, as believable as the colossal eagles or the sea leviathans or the giant elks of the other Septs. To see Laoise transform into a scaled dragan glowing red-gold as she winged toward the clouds had been...impressive.

She was also the only one of them who had a home to retreat to.

Wayland's home was flotsam on the fathomless sea. Irian's a crumbling fort in the heart of bardaí territory. Sinéad had none; if

Balor had one, he seemed unattached to the idea of returning to it. Fia was not in a position to weigh in.

So it had been decided. A few of the aughiskies had abandoned them to dive into the frothing dark sea. Irian's tall black steed, Abyss, had stayed on, if reticently; he thought the stallion's willingness to help had more to do with Fia's mare, Linn, relentlessly harrying him than any genuine desire to help. Sinéad's white mare had also stayed, as had an energetic cobalt yearling whom Wayland had readily taken for a mount. Balor needed no steed; Laoise either flew high above them, scouting the terrain, or rode occasionally upon Linn, though neither Gentry maiden nor murderous horse enjoyed the other's company.

Their strange entourage had trudged over frosted moors, traversed desolate plains where the wind screamed, climbed craggy tors burnished by fleeting sunlight.

And always the sickly thrum of Eala's new-forged Treasure dogged Irian—taunting him, goading him. Surely they had left Fia's sister far behind. But not far enough.

Never far enough.

For the first few days, Irian had barely rested. He did not need much sleep, and what little he had tried to snatch had been plagued by nightmares—so he had stopped trying. Even when they camped and one of the others kept watch, he held Fia. The times he had dared drift off, he awakened to a wolf howling, its fangs in his face; venomous vines climbing his throat; a serpent twining around him with muscular coils. He always managed to fight back his instincts, assiduously kept the Sky-Sword in its scabbard, though it hummed a complaint. Whatever she became, he held her—deer, swan, rock, tree.

Even in the hour before dawn, when Fia transformed into something worse, Irian held her.

This battle he could not fight with weapons; this war he could not win with wrath. He could only pray to gods he had reason to believe were not listening that Fia was still *in there*. Fighting, as he fought. Raging, as he raged.

To think he had already lost her, without even knowing—that was a weight too heavy to hold.

So he held *her.*

It had taken Abyss stumbling and nearly falling to his knees beneath Irian and Fia's joint weight for anyone to challenge this arrangement.

Wayland had watched with worried eyes as Abyss shook his dark mane in frustration. "Any change?"

It had been the same question for three days. The words abraded Irian's bones and made him clench his teeth, although surely his erstwhile foster brother meant nothing but care by them. "Change, I fear, is the only constant. She has not woken, if that is what you ask."

"I think only of you. And of her." Wayland's indigo eyes had been dismayed. His mouth had worked in the moment before he said, "You have held her too long, Brother. Neither you—nor your mount—will survive to keep holding her, unless you rest. Perhaps you will allow me—"

"*No.*" The word had punched out of Irian. He had done many wrong things, had made many wrong choices. Since the Longest Night, he had felt as if he had but one purpose—one vow to uphold. He was not invincible. He was not even as strong as he wished. But he was strong enough to do this one thing. Even if it cost him the last of his strength. "I promised her. *I cannot let her go.*"

"Then she will die," Balor had boomed at him from a great height. "And we with her. *Lord.*"

"Irian." Wayland had kept his tone easy. "Whatever promise she asked of you, surely she did not mean it literally. Fia would never want this for you. In fact, I think she'd be the first to scold you for this madness."

With distant, winged dread, Irian had silently conceded this point. He had not had time to ask his wife, in those last moments before Talah overtook her, whether her request had been literal. Still, he clung to it. For three days and nights, he had carried Fia without respite. Every transformation a new trial, each changing embrace a new way for him to prove how endlessly he loved her.

Was it truly madness, as Wayland said? Or was it valor?

His love might be endless. But he was not. Nor was his mount.

"But who?" His voice had sounded despicably forlorn. He had looked from Wayland to Sinéad to Balor. Up to Laoise's form, streaking like a comet through the dim. "*Who?*"

"No one of us alone can keep the promise you have made her," Wayland said. "But perhaps all of us together...can help."

Still Irian had held her. The distant foothills had been darker than bruises upon the horizon.

"Let me." Sinéad had spoken but a handful of words since she had plunged her ready daggers into Eala's chest. Now she held out her arms. "Together Fia and I weigh less than you and she. My mount is strong. Ride Linn. Let your stallion rest."

Irian had hesitated one last moment before bundling Fia in his cloak and nestling her in front of Sinéad. The other girl had sheathed her daggers, then wrapped her arms around Fia's limp frame. Irian had tensed, every instinct he possessed screaming at him to haul his wife back into his grasp. His time on Emain Ablach had taught him that he could not control everything. Yet if he could not control this, what *could* he control? If he could not hold her, was he not letting her go? "If she transforms—"

"For days we have all watched you care for Fia alone." Sinéad's tone had held exhaustion and dogged determination. "We have all been kept awake by her screams; we have all wept when you wept. This pain does not belong solely to you. Trust us to bear some of it. *Please.*"

So he had, though he feared it had not lessened the pain to share it. His body had found much needed rest. Abyss had regained the strength of his long, elegant limbs. But every moment Fia did not rest in Irian's arms was a moment fletched with fear and sharpened with regret. He might not be able to control the world around him. But nor could he bear to be away from Fia for long.

"Ho!" Now Wayland cantered up beside Irian, sympathy and regret passing over his features as he glanced down at Fia clutched once more in Irian's arms. "Laoise wishes to camp here—where the ground is flat."

Irian's eyes sharpened toward their surroundings. Sunset teased a pale blue sky with bloody fingers; night was not far behind. The broad, flat plain before them stretched toward foothills purpling with dusk. Beyond, rocky ridges cast looming shadows. Nothing grew here but ragged brush and pitiful clumps of grass.

With a flare of fear, Irian recognized this place. A premonition of danger ghosted over his skin and whipped his head back the way they had come. His arms tightened around Fia's motionless form, his fingertips pressing divots into her boiling skin.

Surely Eala could not have followed them all this way.

Then why could he still *feel* her? The same searing power that had blistered from Eala's frame when Gavida's cursed crown touched her golden head rippled toward him across the landscape, raising the hairs on the nape of his neck.

"Laoise." His voice was harsher than he meant it to be. "Why have you brought us here?"

"What, tánaiste?" Laoise—riding now upon Linn—grinned, showing off her fetching dimples. "Do you not wish at last for a flat place to camp? We are only a day's ride from Cnoc Féigleann. But we will not reach it tonight."

"We must not stay here." Irian wheeled Abyss, even as the Sky-Sword began to hum an eerie, atonal tune at his hip. His breath rose haphazardly in his lungs as danger winnowed through him. "Wayland... Laoise—be on your guard. Balor, make ready to run. Sinéad, make ready to ride. We must cross this plain as fast as we can."

Balor seemed unflappable as ever, stomping indomitably forward. Sinéad looked up at her name, her expression hopeless and haggard. Only Laoise's expression betrayed surprise.

"Why, Irian?"

"Because these are the old killing grounds of Mag Tuired," Irian ground out, even as he kicked Abyss into a lurching canter. "This marks the edge of Tír na nÓg, before the Barrens begin. Here the

Tuatha Dé Danann defeated the Fomorians in the battle that would decide their sovereignty. And here every man, woman, and giant is buried where they fell. We have just walked onto an army for Eala to use."

"Surely she could not have followed us this far?" Wayland's question echoed Irian's own concerns.

"We have no idea where she is, nor what she is capable of. Do you wish to risk it?"

Perhaps it was his words that spurred them on; perhaps it was night's sinister promise scraping blood over the slate sky. The aughiskies stretched their sleek legs into a gallop. Balor broke into a thunderous run, his tree-trunk legs propelling him at a surprising clip.

Irian felt the buzzing thrum of magic upon his skin, tasted the sweet-sour sizzle of petrichor on his tongue, heard the mournful discordance of Eala's Treasure entwine with his sword's song.

How?

It did not matter. It only mattered that she was close. Too close.

The first bone-flanged hand burst from the cold, damp earth.

"Ride!" Irian roared. Grotesque shapes birthed themselves in the long, dark shadows cast by the mountains. "If you want to live, *ride.*"

They rode. Irian tallied the distance to the mountains. In the murky dusk, the plain could have stretched half a league. Or seven.

He only knew it was too far.

Another skeletal arm ringed in ancient armor burst from the hard-packed clay and caught Abyss by the foreleg. A glancing blow—the stallion only stumbled. A larger arm reached for the water horse's other leg. Abyss danced out of reach. Yet another rose in turn, pushing mounds of pebbled dirt to one side as it latched around the aughisky's foreleg and wrenched it sideways. Abyss missed a step. The stallion went down.

A precarious tilt, cold winter air streaking sideways. Irian hung weightless above the stallion's back, Fia's limp body lolling against his chest.

The water horse struck the dirt sideways, jolting both riders over his withers. Irian ducked his head and curled himself around Fia, but the impact jarred them apart. He hit hard-packed earth with juddering force, his breath bursting from his lungs as he landed painfully on one shoulder. Lines of black and silver striated his vision. Sharp stones tore his mantle and abraded his cheek as he skidded to a halt on the twisting, heaving earth. He forced himself sideways, rolling onto all fours. He reached for Fia. His hands met only air.

No.

Irian staggered to his feet. There—Fia had rolled ten paces beyond him. She lay with arms and legs tangled between matted clumps of weathered grass, her hair a dark corona around her bruised face. Irian's vision tunneled as he lunged for her, the Sky-Sword already singing free of its scabbard. But the restless earth shifted beneath his feet. Clods of dirt and gobbets of clay rattled his legs as fists of bone punched upward. Skeletal fingers latched around his ankles. He slashed down, his battle metal darkening as sunset kissed rouge along the foothills. The Treasure made easy work of the ancient, brittle bones, but whenever one hand burst into shards, another was rising to take its place.

And another.

Irian lifted his gaze from Fia's prone form, alarm beating dark wings against the back of his head.

All across the plain, the dead were rising. The earth spat them up and belched them out as if it was glad to be rid of them. These were not fresh corpses; the legendary battle of Mag Tuired had been fought in the time of legends, before humans had banished the Folk from Fódla and before the Treasures had been forged. The earth should have long ago reclaimed them. Instead, the boggy plain had mummified the ancient carcasses, rendering them nightmarish in resurrection.

Sword-hacked arms were strung with frayed ligaments and rotted armor. Caved-in skulls sneered with shattered teeth, stared with hollow, empty eyes. Lumbering Fomorians reared to the height of ten men; legless destriers churned in the muck; long-dead warriors reached for maces and axes and swords.

All of them turned toward him.

No. Not him.

Her.

Fia lay so still Irian feared she had died. As if his unrelenting hold on her had been the only thing keeping her alive, and with his promise broken, her soul had simply fled her body. But the blue-green stone fastened above her breast—her Treasure, the Heart of the Forest—still hummed a harmonic counterpoint to his wailing sword. And below that constant murmur, a still-unfamiliar vibration droned in counterpoint too—like molten metal over wet rock, or hot blood kissing iron bones.

The unwelcome melody of the entity to whom Fia had accidentally bound herself on the Longest Night. The deity the islanders of Emain Ablach had called the Year...the Bright One who had named herself Talah.

A circle of space formed between Fia and the rumbling horde of the risen dead. The ancient warriors slammed against a barrier they did not seem able to cross. It occurred to Irian that Talah's terrible power—though he hated what it had taken from Fia—might be the only force keeping the sliding, slithering hiss of Eala's Treasure at bay.

Talah, like the Heart of the Forest, was not eager to let her host die.

Fia's life was threatened by two unknowable Solasóirí of near-limitless power. So, too, was her life *protected*.

The sight of the restless dead's mindless shambling galvanized Irian. He hacked with renewed vigor at the arms clutching at his legs, scattering petrified bones and long-desiccated flesh to crunch beneath his boots. He thrust through the ungainly horde, reaching for Fia—

"*Down!*" The word shattered his eardrum.

He did not turn in time to identify the tall, heavy figure barreling toward him. Only felt the impact as someone tackled him around the chest and bore him bodily to the ground.

Chapter Three

Irian

Irian's already jarred shoulder struck packed dirt a moment before his skull cracked down. He instinctively struggled beneath his attacker's weight, jerking his arms as he fought to free his sword.

"Gods alive, man!" Wayland's voice, ragged with alarm, carved through Irian's aggression like a serrated knife. "Stay *down*."

A surge of flame blasted mere inches from where both men grappled. Blistering heat raked Irian's face; he heaved himself away, and Wayland rolled with him, putting as much distance as possible between themselves and the blaze carving a path through the army of Eala's dead. The conflagration ignited ossified corpses and liquefied time-pitted metal. Irian elbowed Wayland away from him and glanced up.

The red-gold silhouette of Laoise's anam cló was an ardent pennant against the flaming dusk. Sunset kindled scarlet along her sleek scales and silhouetted her wings in ocher and plum. Her sinuous neck curved, molten fury burning from the depths of her gorge to incinerate the wall of shambling skeletons threatening Fia's prone figure. Grudging awe rose in Irian.

From the moment Irian had intuited Laoise's true nature, he had guessed she was formidable. She had proved herself indomitable.

"*Up.*" Wayland's hands propelled Irian to standing. The wall of fire guttered as Laoise moved onward, leaving a trail of smoking skeletons and flaking ash in her wake. Beyond, Fia sprawled, insensate to the chaos. "Laoise is buying us time. Let us not waste it."

Irian kicked through cinders to scoop his wife into his arms. She was whole and breathing, albeit slightly scorched—the right side of her body blackened with ash and a few of her long tresses singed away to nothing. The scent of hot skin and burnt hair withered Irian's nostrils. He fought automatic fury, even as he sheathed his still-humming sword and cradled Fia's head against his shoulder.

"Laoise couldn't have given her a wider berth?" he growled at Wayland. "At this rate, my wife will be bald."

"Scold Laoise later." Wayland's glance was barbed with agitation. "Much as it pains me, we must now heed *your* advice. *Run.*"

The other man set a brisk pace, following the path of Laoise's incendiary carnage. Half-burnt bones caught at Irian's boots; red embers flared up to die on his clothes. Black smoke scrawled over the darkening sky and seared his eyes. It was slow going. And beyond the blackened path, the dead shambled, drawing ever closer.

Irian set his jaw, nestled Fia closer, and drove forward.

At last Wayland burst through the wall of smoke, Irian a half step behind. Beyond, figures writhed. He tensed. But they coalesced into a handful of wheeling aughiskies, Abyss among them—limping but alive. A tall, lithe girl wielding twin daggers. A vast Fomorian blotting out the burn of new stars against the charcoal of dusk.

Irian strode toward Abyss, but Linn moved brusquely in front of him, sliding her slender head beneath Fia's mass of scorched hair and snapping her shark's teeth at him. The picture she burned into his mind was unmistakable: Abyss faltering once more beneath

Irian and Fia's joined weight, before being parceled up and dined upon by the ravening dead.

"But I swore—" The promise Irian had made Fia felt as ancient as this battlefield in his mind, as scorched and desiccated as the corpses marching mindlessly toward their point of dwindling escape. He had relinquished her before. Why did it never get any easier?

Linn shoved her muzzle into his solar plexus.

He took the hint. Lifted Fia in front of Sinéad, who anchored the other woman's frame with her cloak. Grasped Linn's black-oil mane, levered himself onto her back. A conflagration of red flame exploded behind the group, startling them all into a gallop.

They rode for the hills.

Night swallowed them in its toothless mouth. Eventually, Laoise's anam cló swooped in a glittering arc to collapse upon the dirt. She staggered upward in her Gentry form, her limbs trembling and her face gaunt, as if she had aged a century in the span of hours.

Irian had spent a great deal of time in his anam cló, both warped by wild magic and not. Even the simplest shapeshifting took its toll. He could not fathom what it must have cost Laoise to fight off the undead horde, to summon those incredible swaths of fire from her deepest self.

He dismounted. Supported Laoise by her scalding forearms. Interrupted her before she could protest.

"I will walk," he said. "You will rest."

Not even Linn protested the arrangement. Laoise mounted with difficulty, then laid herself over the water horse's withers, twined fingers in her mane, and promptly fell unconscious.

They struggled upward over uneven shale and jagged foothills. At last, the moon rose, bright enough to ease their path.

As it laddered above them, Fia began to change.

She transformed without warning into a wildcat. Pale skin sprouted dense layers of striped fur; vicious claws sharpened on batting paws; her face exploded into a hissing whiskered maw studded with sharp white teeth. Sinéad cried out—Irian thought she must have begun to doze. She struggled to hold on as claws caught her across the temple, raising livid lines of red upon her skin.

Irian lunged for the women. Balor beat him to it, neatly scooping the yowling, scratching creature Fia had become into his massive fist.

"I can take her," Irian growled, relief and worry pounding through him. "Please. Let me have my wife."

"She is perfectly well, lord," rumbled the giant cheerfully as the wildcat continued to strain and shriek in his implacable grasp. "Besides, I love cats."

They trundled onward. When the moon passed its zenith, Irian sent a flurry of zephyrs scouting back the way they had come. They teased over rocky outcroppings, slivered between troughs of still-smoldering flame, brushed over the desiccated notches of scorched spines and blackened bones. Nothing moved—not for three leagues in any direction.

For the first time in nearly a month, the blistering thrum of Eala's magic felt faded. Far away.

"We have not been followed," Irian announced. "Balor—my wife, if you will. It is time we made camp."

He wished he had said it out of concern for them. He had not.

The secret Irian had kept for the better part of the last month blustered through him, suffusing him with dread.

It had happened not on the first night after the Longest Night, nor even on the second, but on the third night, when they camped cold beneath snow-draped trees that cracked and fell beneath the weight of ice. In the hour before dawn, after transforming without respite from hawk to hound to serpent, Fia went deathly still in Irian's arms. Irian's gaze rode the horizon, where faint pink streaked a leaden sky. Worry tangled with relief in the exhausted arsenal of his muscles; briefly, he relaxed.

Fingers too hot for the frigid night trailed up his chest to tangle in his hair. A mouth that moments ago had been fanged glided along the column of his throat to breathe sultry against the shell of his ear. Legs smooth as silk slung around his waist.

Hope pummeled him. Gods alive, but he had *known* not even a Bright One was a match for Fia's strength. "Mo chroí?"

She arched above him, her hips surging over his. His response was reflexive—his body hardening as his hands braced at the divot of her waist, barely sparing a thought for their compatriots slumbering nearby. Reflected moonlight glazed her curves and sharpened her features as Fia leaned down to kiss him. Her fingernails dragged at the ties of his shirt as her mouth met his, lips eagerly parting.

The wrongness of her taste assailed Irian. She savored not of sun-warmed stone or cool moss, but of *bog tar*. Scorched metal. Flesh heated to searing.

His eyes slashed open. His horror caught at her shoulders. His dismay pushed her back, even as she ground on him.

"Fia?"

This time, when metal sparked in her eyes, he knew it was no trick of the moonlight. Her irises were silver threaded through with gold; the pupils, black as an untold future. They were ancient, unknowable. Fearsome. And they *burned*.

With greed. With hatred. With desire.

This was no longer Irian's wife looking back at him. It was something else. And it longed to be free.

Every night, in the hour before dawn, Irian no longer fought with Fia. He fought with himself, and his own treacherous desires. He fought to hold at arm's length the form of the woman he wished never to let go...even as the entity inside her taunted him with her mastery.

That was when he felt his strength begin to crack. His endurance begin to ebb. His hope begin to hollow.

He had promised never to let Fia go. But if she was already gone...then so was he.

Without Fia, there was nothing left of Irian.

At least, nothing good.

Morning blushed behind jagged black peaks striped in lavender and rose. These were not the flowering crags of Ildathach, nor the basalt bastions of Mag Mell—not even the pale silver cliffs of Emain Ablach. They had passed beyond the bounds of Tír na nÓg into the unknown lands Irian had only ever heard called the Barrens. A hard, uncivilized region not even the Fair Folk had wanted to claim.

It occurred to Irian with a burst of irony that in all his years of searching for heirs, the reason he had never found Laoise was simply because she had hidden herself beyond where he desired to look.

Dim rocks came alive with color beneath the rising sun. Veins of sapphire streaked between layers of garnet; seams of emerald reached between geodes bristling with sparkling quartz. A thrill of magic bronzed Irian's veins.

A night's sleep had revived Laoise—dimples quirked in her pert cheeks, and her hair flamed red as the dawn. She grinned infectiously.

"You feel it, don't you?"

"I was always told these lands were naught but desert and despair," Irian growled. The night had been less kind to him than to the Gentry maiden. He curled Fia close so he would not have to regret all the times he had been forced to push her away. "Why would the Fair Folk have steered clear of all this magic if it was free for the taking?"

"Because you can't." Laoise's smile grew. "Take it, that is."

Irian did not enjoy saying *I do not understand.* So he said nothing.

"Don't fret, tánaiste," Laoise said blithely. "You'll see."

Irian tamped down a brisk surge of resentment before forcing his steps onward. It did not matter where they went, what they saw, or how they lived. It only mattered that they survived.

That *she* survived.

Chapter Four

Wayland

Wayland did not enjoy solitude.

He could not remember a time when he had enjoyed being alone. He usually blamed his mother for this indecent character flaw. But then, he had discovered over the past two and a half decades that absent mothers could be blamed for just about anything. It was harder to blame megalomaniacal, narcissistic fathers who defied consequences. Hardest still to blame your deepest, most imperfect, least changeable self. Not that Wayland hadn't done that too.

Still, in those rare, miserable times when he accidentally found himself engaging in introspection, Wayland wore *her* silhouette through his loneliness. As though when beautiful, kind, sad Úna had plucked her heavy oiled pelt from his arms, wordlessly turned her back on him, and dived soundlessly into the glittering ocean, she had left her shadow behind. A mother-shaped lacuna gouged in the fabric of his soul.

Over the years Wayland had found he had a great love for filling holes. (Not only in the most perverse sense, although he enjoyed that too.) When Irian had first arrived on Emain Ablach so long ago—a broken-winged bird—Wayland had shoved him bodily into that mother-shaped gap. Irian had nearly fit; *mother* and *brother* sounded almost alike, after all. In some ways, a brother was even better than a mother—mothers made rules and set bedtimes and forced you to eat your vegetables. A brother dared you to climb salt-rimed cliffs and steal tasty honey-wren eggs, even if it meant a broken wrist and a lashing from your father. A brother made you laugh until you pissed yourself. A brother kept your secrets and trusted you to keep his. A brother never left you alone, no matter if he was smearing frog spawn in your underwear or mercilessly dunking you in the lagoon.

Until he did. Wayland tried not to blame Irian for leaving— unlike Wayland's mother, Irian had no choice in the matter. But Irian's exile had cut something sharper and darker into the gulf yawning inside Wayland, etching a kind of understanding into the emptiness. Wayland began to name the cavernous shape living inside him *loneliness*. It whispered to him, things like *Anyone you ever love will leave.* And *Not that they ever loved you in the first place.*

Wayland found new ways to fill the hole. Bodies were almost always best—sex the finest facsimile of true connection, without any of the risks. He could lose himself in warm flesh and beating hearts and searing touches and snatched kisses and emerge on the other side unscathed. No new holes gouged in his heart, no new rifts carved from his tenderest spaces. When bodies didn't work, there was wine. Or tincture of drualas, sliding bitter beneath his tongue until he was lost in incandescent hallucinations.

Anything to blunt the sharper corners of his loneliness. Anything to drown out the slithering whispers. Anything to light the edges of the shadow waiting to drag him down.

It always caught him, eventually. Just before dawn, when the sex and wine and drugs wore off. When he bolted upright in bed with sweat slicking his arms and darkness collecting in his ragged lungs, grappling with the unrelenting fear that it would *always* be like this.

He would *always* be alone.

For weeks now, there'd been no bodies. No liquor. No tinctures. For the first time in over a decade, Wayland wasn't alone. Somehow, that only made the hole yawn wider—a premonition of returned loneliness. The curse of having *had* something, only to have lost it.

Now, the day after Eala's undead army attacked them at Mag Tuired, Wayland's eyes slid helplessly over their small entourage clambering through a dawn scaled pink as a salmon's belly. The aughiskies, who—despite their reputation for vicious independence—had thrown in their lot with a bunch of reckless bipeds. Balor, the good-humored Fomorian who weathered whatever trials they faced with equanimity. Sinéad, the human girl who had suffered unimaginable loss yet thrown herself into adversity with little care for her mortal frailty. Laoise, the exiled tánaiste of the lost Sept of Scales, with her mythic anam cló. Irian, brother of Wayland's heart, yet again holding Fia, the wife of his own.

They were betrayed and beleaguered, exiled and exhausted. No one was having a good time. They might all die here, skewered between Eala's restless dead and Laoise's merciless mountains.

It was the happiest Wayland had been in thirteen years, at least.

He glanced again toward Irian and Fia, his gaze lingering on *her* longer than was proper.

After the Feis of the Nameless Day, Wayland had thought of the woman he'd known only as Thorn Girl more than he'd ever admit out loud. He still could not say what had prompted him to step in on her behalf with the barda who'd threatened her—he was not in the habit of intruding on Gentry business outside Emain Ablach. He could say even less why he'd placed the geas on her. Something about the angle of her chin, the specific shade of her hair, the color of her strange green blood. Or perhaps it had been something more ephemeral—a significance he could not name. The way her name sat upon his tongue before he ever spoke it. The shape of her mouth, like a promise yet to be kept. He had not given it too much thought—the patterns written in the stars had been his lullabies, his playmates, his bedfellows.

After, he had thought of her an obsessive, unseemly amount. The way her unruly hair had curled around the edge of her mask. The way she'd pooched out her lips, advancing on him like she was marching into battle, so determined to end their connection before it had even begun. The way she'd called *Then I will simply avoid you!* to the terms of their geas, as if the magic of Tír na nÓg could be so easily sidestepped.

And when, a year and a day later, he'd finally met her again... well. She *was* significant.

The patterns in the stars were fixed. They also, apparently, had a cruel sense of humor.

Fia was—then and now—profoundly out of his reach.

Sometimes Wayland replayed their solitary, forbidden kiss against the backs of his eyelids in the moments before he surrendered to sleep. Like a devotion, a sacrilege. The rumpled blankets and tangled limbs. Fia's legs, latched around his waist. Her mass of dark hair spilling damp over his cheek, smelling of cold water and crusted salt and Talah's acrid magic. Her lips, pillow soft and pliant. The way she had gasped against his mouth as the magic of their bargain concluded, her breath tasting like moss and hope and longing—

Wayland's hands tightened on his aughisky's mane. It had been his own longing he had tasted that night—Fia had made that much abundantly clear. She was not his to long for. Never had been, and never would be.

He forced himself to catalog the way Irian's arms cradled Fia's lolling body, the way her sable hair spilled over his calloused fingers. The way Irian's lips moved in silent, constant supplication to absent gods, as if he might persuade the power invading Fia's form to relinquish her through sheer persistence.

Fia had chosen Irian. Of course she had. Irian was steadfast, serious, solid. Dangerous, devoted beyond reason. Protective, respectful. He had offered Fia his love, his very life.

Gods living and dead knew Wayland was none of those things. He was a lush, a libertine. He was lost, incomplete. He had nothing much to offer. Not to Fia. Not to anyone.

The past was proof—Wayland was not the kind of man anyone chose.

"Ho!" He nudged his aughisky, Dubhán. The cobalt yearling gamely trotted toward Irian's stallion, whose limp had returned. The other man barely acknowledged his presence, although Wayland knew he must have heard his approach. "Let me take a turn, Brother. Your mount could use a rest. As could you."

Irian's hands tightened around Fia's shoulders. Wayland knew it was no coincidence that once Irian finally relinquished his mad resolve to quite literally carry her to the ends of the earth, Wayland had held her the least. He also knew it was his fault. He had been too forward with his flirtations. He had shoved the kiss he and Fia had been bound by too cheerfully in Irian's face. Still, threads of guilt woven with resentment twined through Wayland, embroidering the edges of the hole carved around his heart.

His foster brother should have forgiven him by now.

"I have her," Irian said, his voice low.

Yes, he did.

"Then tell me how else I can help," Wayland said. "Surely there is something I can do—"

"Unless you know some novel way to wrangle information from Laoise," Irian said, "then I am not sure what good you are."

Maybe the burr of frustration rasping along Irian's voice wasn't intended for Wayland. They'd endured weeks of hard travel interspersed with altercations with the restless dead. All while Fia transformed with the terrible, unknowable magic coursing through her, and Laoise refused to tell them where they were going. But Irian's words felt barbed, rather than careless.

"I wonder whether anyone's tried kissing it out of her." Wayland forced his tone light. "Historically I'm at my most persuasive when I'm not saying anything at all."

Irian's mouth twitched. His day-blue eyes finally landed squarely on Wayland. "I hate to be the one to tell you this, but I do not think you are Laoise's type."

"Nonsense." Wayland smirked. "I'm everyone's type."

He signaled to Dubhán, and the aughisky cantered up the trail to fall in between Laoise and Sinéad, riding through the humming ravine. Laoise looked tired—dark circles standing out beneath her fiery eyes, worried creases bracketing her full lips. Sinéad looked far worse—her dirty hair limp and dull, her spine curved with exhaustion. The journey had been exacting for all of them; Sinéad, the only human among them, must be near her breaking point.

"I have a proposition for you, Laoise." Despite Wayland's jests to Irian, Wayland had neither the intention nor the desire to kiss Laoise. The Gentry maiden was striking, with her flame-red hair, warm brown skin, and exquisitely curved figure. But there was no spark in their interactions, no heated undercurrent to their conversations. He owed her his life, after she saved him in the catastrophic moments before Emain Ablach plunged into the ocean. But he imagined kissing her would be like kissing a sister. "Tell us where we're going."

"*And?*" Laoise said after a beat. "Usually there is a second part to a proposition. If *this*, then *that*."

"I hadn't gotten that far," Wayland replied breezily. "Perhaps we could call it a favor and decide on the payment later? I think we'd all benefit from a little information. A little direction. I'm beginning to think we might die of exhaustion out here. As pretty as these magical rocks may be, I'm not particularly eager to become one."

Laoise's jaw set. "I have reasons for keeping our destination private."

"Pray, then—share the reasons. If not the destination."

"Because—" A cold breeze whipped from the jewel-smeared bluffs and mussed Laoise's flaming curls. Her ember eyes skimmed the rocky crests hunched like the crooked spines of giants. Wariness, recognition, and then delight tangled over her expression. She pointed at the horizon. "They're all the family I have left."

With his eyes, Wayland followed her finger to where a wildfire glow spilled over the ridge. An answering rill of fear swept his veins. Long years of combat training—though rarely employed—automatically dropped his right hand to his hip. But his weapons were lost with Emain Ablach—down to the ceremonial claíomh he had used in the final battle between the Oak King and the Holly King. Wayland had left it where he'd sheathed it on the Longest Night.

Deep between his father's ribs.

He fisted his hands in Dubhán's mane. The yearling wheeled, thrashing his head as Wayland's growing alarm spilled into him. They weren't alone. Balor planted his huge feet and shielded his eyes as he stared at the mountain. Sinéad propped herself over her aughisky's neck, her mouth parting with fear and awe. Irian cursed, inventively; the Sky-Sword sang out a trilling note as he slung it from its scabbard.

Only Laoise was unbothered by the intensity of the red light blooming above the mountains. She began to smile, a toothy expression of sheer glee.

"Easy, tánaiste," she called over her shoulder to Irian. "If you wave that thing around too much, one of them might take a shine to it. And steal it from you."

Them? Confusion surged through Wayland as the glow resolved into...shapes. Startlingly bright blobs of red-gold hurtling toward their group at a speed he could not fathom. Almost as if they had—

Wings.

A blinding shaft of sunlight blazed above the eastern ridge and illuminated translucent webbed wings and coruscant red scales. Wayland counted six—no, *seven* shapes, although they were not all the same size. Long, sinuous necks; serrated tails spiked with stacked laminae; flexible plates frilling serpentine heads lined with rows of teeth.

Wayland's jaw dropped. They were *dragain*.

"*Oof!*" The first and largest of the flying serpents barreled into Laoise, pummeling her horizontally off Linn's narrow back. She transformed into her anam cló at the instant of impact, clashing with a creature nearly as large as she was. Renewed dread burned through Wayland in the moment before he realized—they weren't fighting. They were *playing*.

Luminous scales chimed against one another. The pair gleefully tussled, grappling with clawed talons as they beat wide membranous wings. A few moments later, the other creatures joined the fracas. Smaller than the first serpent, they clung to Laoise's frilled mane and hung from her plated tail, gnawing at her limbs in playful exuberance. Beneath Wayland, Dubhán wheeled again, understandably unnerved by the wrestling mass of scales and wings.

Wayland would have been able to keep his seat had it not been for the last of the creatures hurtling directly into his chest and knocking him bodily off his yearling. His spine impacted the dirt-strewn rock. His breath gusted from his lungs; he gasped as his vision fuzzed black and white. When he blinked away the blurriness, it was to stare directly into the inquisitive features of a dragan the size of a large cat, perched directly on his chest. It inspected him with glittering red eyes before unexpectedly licking him from collarbone to chin. Its tongue was lightly barbed, rasping like sand against his skin.

"Oy!" he cried, attempting to shove it off. This only entertained the beastling, who latched talons deeper into the leather of his jerkin, barked a shower of red-gold sparks from its snout, and painlessly mouthed his wrists with gleaming, needle-sharp teeth. "Laoise! A little help, please?"

"Nidhoggur! Bad!" Laoise had shifted back into her Gentry

form—her voice collided with the little dragan, who made its ruby eyes huge and pleading as it placed a clawed paw directly over Wayland's mouth, as if to say *shh*. Wayland swore he heard Irian choke on a laugh. Laoise hoisted the now-wailing creature off Wayland's sternum and settled it easily on her shoulder. It gave a disgruntled hiss before nestling around her neck and threading its claws through her curls. "Sorry. Hog's never met a stranger before. But I think she likes you."

Wayland sat up, rubbing his chest where the tiny dragan had burned a hole in his tunic. "What...*are* they? What *is*...she?"

"She's draig goch," Laoise didn't so much explain as cough, in Wayland's opinion. "A red draig. They all are."

"They're awfully small...draigs." Sinéad spoke aloud what they must have all been thinking.

"They're babies," Laoise said, giving Hog's tail an affectionate tug. The biggest draig took offense at this, baring its teeth and snorting twin flames from its flared nostrils. "Except you, Blodwen. You're more of an adolescent."

"Consider me impressed, Laoise." Irian looked like he was trying to stifle laughter. "Dare we ask how you came to be mother of a hefty brood of juvenile draigs?"

"It's a long story, and a long hike to the Cnoc. Shall I tell it as we go?"

Wayland remounted a still-leery Dubhán, turning him to follow the rest of the group. Nidhoggur detached from Laoise's shoulder, taking flight on stumpy wings that seemed too small for her rotund body. She wobbled boisterously through the air to collide once more with Wayland's chest. This time, he was prepared—he had no intention of being knocked from his mount a second time. He tried to fend off the tiny draig, but the creature just happily curled herself around his waist, latching sharp talons through his belt loops and tucking her head beneath the hem of his shirt. Within seconds, Hog was loudly snoring, her plump red body ringing him with heat.

When Wayland was sure no one was looking, he dared stroking a finger along the scaled fiend's ridged spine. Her glass-smooth scutes radiated dry heat. She began to purr, her throat thrumming against the skin of his abdomen.

Wayland hid a smile.

Chapter Five

Laoise

Laoise of the Sept of Scales was born a princess, became a pariah, matured into a warrior, and attained motherhood by neither merit nor fault.

The first draig egg—Blodwen's egg—had belonged to Laoise's own mother. Ceridwen had not been born in Tír na nÓg—she had been raised beyond the Barrens, in the place her people, the Ellyllon, called Annwyn. The egg-shaped ruby had been part of Ceridwen's dowry when she married into the Sept of Scales—an heirloom of her family since the age of legends. If anyone had known it was more than a priceless jewel, they had not told Laoise. But after the tragedy of her thirteenth birthday, no one in her family had bothered to tell Laoise much of anything. Except, in the end, that they were exiling her to Dún Scaith, Lady Scáthach's Fortress of Shadows, where she would not be able to harm anyone else they—or she—cared about. Her banishment felt like a curse. It became a blessing.

Laoise wished she could say her mother had given her the jewel as a parting gift or a token of her love or a pledge of her forgiveness. But she had not.

Laoise found the ruby in the smoldering ruins of her family's apartments in Findias. She had returned too late to save her parents from the Gentry dissidents who would soon name themselves *bardaí*. Blighted wild magic billowed and surged over the black parapets the Sept of Scales had, until very recently, lorded over. Laoise's father sprawled naked in bed, his slashed throat spilling copper blood over ivory bedsheets. Ceridwen had put up more of a fight. Long charcoal scratches smoked from where her fingernails had rent the drapes; starburst scorch marks blazed from the walls; the blackened husks of her would-be assassins slumped against doorjambs. Ceridwen's own leaf-shaped dagger—damasked with sinuous forms in red and gold—sprouted from her throat. Her powerful, beautiful form lay splayed in the center of the room, surrounded by splashes of red hair and redder blood.

With a burst of horrified realization, Laoise knew the placement was no accident.

She lunged for her mother's body, weeping as she rolled the limp, heavy frame from where it had fallen. She did not weep in sorrow, for she had grieved her mother long ago. She wept with desperate hope.

The concealed latch clicked. The blood-soaked flagstones parted like a serpent's hinged jaw. Laoise remembered hiding in the secret compartment as a child, giggling quietly with Elen as their father growled in mock frustration. Now it held her last hope.

Her little brother, Idris, whom she had not seen in seven years, blinked at her from the crevasse. Tears streaked his small face; red light puckered along the old scar. By some miracle their mother's dying gambit had been successful. The bardaí had not bothered to look harder than they wanted to. They had not noticed the secret trapdoor hidden beneath her body. They had not known what it concealed.

Idris was traumatized and dehydrated. But he was otherwise gloriously, wonderfully, impossibly alive.

Hours later—after Laoise had bundled Idris out of the city

and flown like hell toward the Barrens—she'd noticed the ruby he clutched to his chest. A ruby the size of her fist. Their mother's ruby. And for the first time in Laoise's memory...it was *glowing*.

Neither of them had thought much of it for a long time. The business of grief, reconciliation, and healing was slow and all-consuming. Cnoc Féigleann—meaning roughly *sentinel mountain*—had not yet earned its name; it was nothing more than a cave system Laoise had discovered a year or two before when she had nowhere else to go. It seemed as good a place as any to hide from the bardaí, to gather the slivers of all they had lost.

In fact, Laoise came to despise the sight of the ruby. Not because the faintly glowing jewel was the only thing left of their parents, their home, or their legacy. But because it was the only thing her brother would touch, look at, or speak to. When nightmares of bloodshed or conflagration roused Idris, making him scream in the night, the ruby was what he reached for. When Laoise became so frustrated by his distance and silence that she shouted at him, Idris curled bodily around the stone as if he cared more about protecting it than himself. When a hard, dark winter rimed frost through the multicolored caverns and snuffed their meager fires, the ruby was where Idris sought warmth.

Then, in the middle of a chilly spring night, the ruby began to crack.

When a panicked Idris thrust the ruby at Laoise and she saw it was fissured through with expanding veins of jet black and vermilion, a premonition of momentousness thrummed over her skin.

At dawn, when a daffodil sun sprouted above endless jeweled ridges, the ruby gave a resounding crack. It splintered like an egg-shell, yielding to an insistent pressure from within. A tiny claw crept from the jagged stone, followed by another. The draigling struggled from the confines of its embryonic prison, until—with a final, triumphant burst—it emerged. Radiantly red and shockingly iridescent, the tiny creature unfurled its delicate patagia in a luxuriant stretch. Its eyes glowed like the sunrise. With a tentative wriggle of its sinuous neck, it coughed a shower of sparks. Then let loose an ear-shattering scream of horrific intensity, startling both Laoise and Idris into clapping their hands over their ears.

Idris scuttled away and buried himself beneath his furs and his self-pity, his interest transformed to fear. On some level, Laoise understood the reaction. Six months ago, her brother had lost his family—everything and everyone he had ever known—in one scarring act of violence. Now he had lost the last thing he had left of his heritage through a wholly unexpected transformation. The ruby had been his. Whatever had hatched from it...wasn't.

Idris had incubated the egg. Laoise would have to figure out how to raise the draig.

Any awe Laoise experienced upon inheriting a mythic creature from the legends of her ancestors swiftly evaporated. From the moment the draigling hatched, it wouldn't stop shrieking. Barely the length of Laoise's palm and far narrower, the winged serpent made such a racket that Laoise swore it would bring the caverns down around them. Day or night, gleeful or perturbed—the little thing, adorable and astonishing as it was, *never shut up.* Whatever concern Laoise harbored for her truculent brother disappeared on the fourth day, after she'd clocked a cumulative three hours of sleep over two consecutive nights. Her focus narrowed, razor sharp, on keeping the draig alive.

She was not going to let a hatchling born of legend die.

She scoured her memories for the stories her mother had told her growing up. A few had featured Y Ddraig Goch—the Red Dragan. There had been a castle and warring kings and a deadly battle. But the stories had never said where the draig had hatched...how it had been raised...what it had *eaten.*

What did a tiny, noisy, impossible draigling fucking *eat?* Laoise tried to feed it their food—small scraps of the dwindling stores she'd brought with her last autumn from Dún Scaith. But it only mouthed at the dried fruit with utter disdain...licked briefly at the salted meat before caterwauling anew. She held it; it cried. She put it down; it wailed harder. She shifted into her anam cló, but the tiny beast tried to crawl inside her massive smoking mouth, and she was *afraid*. Afraid she would hurt it—afraid the scalding cauldron of her grief and restlessness and hunger would swallow both of them whole. She warmed it upon her chest until they both fell asleep, and awoke in panic to find she'd rolled over in her sleep, nearly crushing the little creature beneath the weight of her body.

By the end of the first week, Laoise was at her wits' end. The draigling had neither grown nor shrunk, only screamed harder. In a fit of irrational desperation, she bared her nipple to its mouth. It stared curiously, licked scorchingly at the mauve areola. Then bit with growing irritation into the smooth, tender flesh of her breast. Its teeth were needle sharp. Laoise cried out, barely suppressing the instinct to bat the dragan away as it began to lap ravenously at the blood pooling like rubies along the swell of her breast. Distaste rose in her. But as the metal tang of her own blood struck her nostrils, so too did an inexplicable intuition.

The stone of the draigling's egg, which had looked like nothing so much as a ruby. The metallic sheen of its tiny, delicate scales. The way it licked the sweat from her throat, slurped the blood from her breast. The way it had hatched *here*, in the Barrens, of all places.

This creature was nothing like her—not warm flesh or tender skin. Why should it require the same sustenance? She did not think it drank only blood—that seemed an unsustainable arrangement for a creature destined to grow to a massive size. She thought it must have more to do with what was *in* her blood.

Laoise strapped her armor on for the first time in months, slid her dozen knives into their cunning sheaths. Nestled the cooing draigling—satiated, on her blood, for the first time since its hatching—on her shoulder. Explained to Idris where she was going, only to have him turn his face to the wall.

She lit a torch, then descended into the caverns. Deep—deeper than she had yet dared go. Multicolored minerals striped the uneven walls. Stalactites dripped endlessly. The infinite weight of the mountain bore down. Laoise wasn't sure what she was searching for. But when her torchlight began to gyrate over massive glowing crystals jutting from the walls and ceilings, she guessed. When the draigling shrieked with joy, propelled itself off her shoulder, and began to gnaw and suckle at the nearest geode, she knew.

This was where they belonged. *All* of them—their strange little family.

Whether they liked it or not.

Idris named the draigling Blodwen the next winter. Laoise thought it an odd name—in their mother's tongue, it meant *white flower*. The draig—grown now to the size of a rotund wildcat—was neither white nor particularly reminiscent of a flower. Her iridescent scales were the color of sunset, shifting from scarlet to rose-gold to crimson with her moods. Her claws and teeth had lengthened, lending her an air of adorable danger. Possibly to herself. She wobbled erratically through the caverns on slowly lengthening wings, claws outstretched to slow her careening passage on nearby stalactites.

Laoise supposed the name must be a private joke. She was glad Idris had chosen one, even if she did not understand it. Or him.

Idris, too, had grown—his frame lengthening, lanky without quite enough food to sustain him. His hair—the same red as hers, although straight instead of curly—swept in a shock over his forehead, hiding his scar as well as the rest of his face. His moods shifted, fretful as the weather above their mountainous home. One moment he would be laughing and loose-limbed; the next he would curl in on himself, tense and tight-lipped; then he would be shouting, railing at Laoise or kicking out at Blodwen. The draig inevitably took this better than Laoise did, spitting a shower of red sparks before tackling the young man into the shadows and wrestling with him until his mood miraculously shifted back to laughter.

Laoise shook her head. She could not remember being so temperamental, so sullen, even as an adolescent. She supposed her volatility had taken a different form.

A more dangerous one.

Visions of scarlet flames licked the backs of her eyelids, mingling with screams she would never forget. Not as long as she lived.

She vowed to be kinder with Idris, more patient with his moods. After all, he was all she had left.

Him...and Blodwen.

They found the cache of blood-red draig eggs the following year.

The caverns extended deep below their mountain—which Idris had taken to calling *the Cnoc*. Far deeper than Laoise had guessed. Blodwen, now the size of a large dog and beginning to grow lean and muscular, had developed a terrifying habit of scuttling away into the dark, chilly vaults for hours at a time, only to return with a burst of incandescent flame and mischief in her eyes. Laoise did not like her exploring so far without supervision. Intrusive visions plagued her—of Blodwen getting lost, or trapped by a cave-in, or devoured by ancient forgotten monsters. But no matter how she scolded, Blodwen never listened.

One day, when Blodwen returned from her explorations, she brought something with her.

Laoise and Idris were busy in the area of the mountain Idris sardonically called the Farm. After a great deal of trial and error, they'd discovered they were able to grow crops beneath the wan but magical light of the minerals thronging the Cnoc. Not many, mind—mushrooms and tubers and a kind of sweet-sour berry that clustered over stones like barnacles. But enough to keep them alive. Laoise was bent over one of the plots when Blodwen unexpectedly curled around Laoise's legs.

"Blodwen. What is it?"

The draig craned her sinuous neck, opened her mouth, and gently dropped something onto the floor. Then looked at Laoise with eager, flaming eyes.

"Egg!" said Blodwen. And then, with a slight lisp: "Sister?"

Laoise and Idris both gaped at the draig, who they had not known could speak, before staring at the stone nestled between her claws. It was the exact size and shape as their mother's ruby. Laoise looked warily at Idris; her brother made a noise in his throat before slowly scooping the egg from between Blodwen's talons. He inspected it, tenderly, then cupped it to his chest.

"Where did you find this?" he asked the draig. "Show us."

They followed Blodwen into the dark. The route was twisting, circuitous—several times, downright dangerous. Laoise feared the young draig had forgotten the way and was leading them into a labyrinth they would never escape from. Anxiety reared fierce inside her, tightening her ribs. She should never have let Blodwen explore; she should never have let Idris come with her; she should never—

A great rush of air smelling impossibly of *outside* gusted into Laoise's cramped lungs and teased the curls from her forehead. Light exploded—red as dawn and brighter than wildfire, though Laoise knew it was night. Stars glinted far, far above—little more than a hint of silver against black.

This was a *sinkhole*, punched deep into the mountain. And as Laoise's eyes adjusted to the light flaring from its center, she saw it was not empty.

Arranged in a loose ring at the heart of the sinkhole were *trees*, though Laoise had never before seen any tree that looked like these. Swooping trunks of gold and vermilion and red, like tongues of draig flame made crystalline. Crimson leaves crackled, flaming from dazzling branches to shatter sparks on the rocks below.

Blodwen squeaked and gamboled forward, gleefully winding her sinuous body around the nearest tree. Laoise opened her mouth to warn her away, even as the unearthly light from the tree seemed to bleed into Blodwen's frame, suffusing her already gleaming scales. Idris followed Blodwen toward the grove, his face slack with awe.

Laoise trailed them. Warmth and wonder and the undeniable thrill of magic painted her bones as she approached the trees, seven in all. This close, molten fire seemed to course below the crystalline bark, veins of light tangling toward leaves bright as comets. Tentatively—almost fearfully—Laoise laid her palm upon the nearest tree. Visions blazed through her, ephemeral as a spark but hot as a bonfire. Red-gold scales crept along her arms; she tasted brimstone and sulfur in the back of her throat.

"Egg!" cried Blodwen, her excitement snatching Laoise's hand from the tree. "Egg! Egg!"

Laoise turned. More rubies were piled in a hollow at the center of the ring of trees. Idris picked one up, cradling it beside the egg Blodwen had carried to the Cnoc. He reached for another, but Laoise grasped his hand. She could almost hear his thoughts, painted in flaming relief against the back of his head. She said, "*Wait.*"

Idris did not have their mother's eyes; he did not have *her* eyes. His eyes were their father's deep, opaque brown. They glimmered with an accusation as he stared from beneath the overlong shock of his crimson hair. "Why?"

"Because there are—" She counted swiftly. Five eggs, including the one Blodwen had brought them. There were indents where more rubies might once have rested, but were now gone. She laughed. *Gone?* Where had they *come from?* "What are we going to do with six draigs, Idris?"

"The same thing we have been doing, Laoise." His voice cracked on her name. Her brother suddenly looked so young Laoise couldn't bear it. He was just thirteen—the same age she had been when she irrevocably destroyed their family. "Surviving."

She stared at him. Stared at Blodwen, who had scuttled into the hollow and was coiled happily amid the eggs, smoke unfurling in tendrils from her nostrils. Stared at the impossible flaming trees.

"If we hatch them," she said slowly, "we will truly be stuck here.

We cannot leave a brood of baby draigs alone. We will not be able to leave this place for a long time. Perhaps *ever*."

"Where would we go?" Hope made Idris's voice eager. "At least this way, we will not be so very alone."

Guilt flooded Laoise's veins, sick and sour. Slowly, almost against her will, she nodded.

"But only one at a time," she commanded, remembering with a shudder those long, noisy nights after Blodwen had hatched. "We will leave the eggs here until we decide we're ready to hatch them. And this time, you will have to help."

A few months later, Barfog hatched. A darker red than Blodwen, he devoured onyx and belched sulfur.

Dwyn arrived a year later, sweet and sly and copper as a coin.

Two years after that came Gwyr and Anwyll, surprise twins hatched from the same egg. The identical male draigs bore freckles of gold along their bellies and were utterly inseparable.

Three years after them Enfys hatched, her scales displaying the broadest range of colors—palest pink radiating toward crimson.

The last egg stayed in the sinkhole, glowing faintly, for nearly four more years. Every time Laoise checked on it, she experienced a burst of longing tempered by a surge of fear. A tinge of melancholy. She wanted one more draig. Feared she could not manage another. Knew that this one would be her last, whether she wished it or not.

"Is it time?" Idris stood abruptly when Laoise gently carried the last egg to the Cnoc, which had been their home for over a decade now. Her brother had long since reached his full height, towering above her. His sleek red hair fell angled over one side of his face, although he could never truly hide the marks of the tragedy that had scarred them. The tragedy that, somehow, had also saved them.

Laoise sighed. "It's time."

Nidhoggur hatched later that year.

When her ruby egg split open, showering splinters of red as she unfurled her delicate, membranous patagia, the flaming trees in the sinkhole began, leaf by leaf, to extinguish.

Chapter Six

Within

I had been here before.

Rath na Mara swallowed me whole, a patchwork of half-remembered hallways and half-imagined occupants. Depleted of happy memories, I had begun hiding from Talah in the places I thought she would not know to look. In the memories I despised; the remembrances I repressed. But forcing myself into my own bitter recollections was its own kind of torture. For I was helpless to change anything.

All I could do was observe as a quartet of trainees in Mother's fiann tormented my adolescent self with garlands of rowanberries and chains made of iron.

"You're just the disposable trash the Fair Folk left behind when they stole the princess," one goaded.

A defiant tilt to my younger self's delicate chin. "And you're a motherless bastard with a slag heap for a face and a stinking privy for a brain."

The trainee backhanded her—*me*—across the face.

When red-hot rock began to drip from the ceiling, I dragged my eyes from the tableau of four overgrown boys beating an underfed changeling bloody for the great crime of being different. The windows above my younger self cracked, then abruptly shattered. Steam unfurled like white wings, barely hiding a pair of livid metal eyes.

Let me in!

I took off at a dead sprint, leaving the memory behind.

I dashed past a fourteen-year-old Rogan, golden torc askew and face contorted with worry as he rushed to rescue me from my attackers. He had indeed chased them off, that day so long ago, but I had barely seen him—my eyes had been swollen shut for a week from the beating I'd endured.

I glimpsed Mother—*the queen*—half hidden behind doorframes and lurking around corners, but when I looked more closely, she was nothing more than faded tapestries or cobwebs. Her voice echoed through the castle: *Only I know how to love something like you. And no one will ever love you more than I do.*

Cathair, slyly watching as I dashed past. He toasted me over the rim of his wineglass, and his mocking laughter chased me. *You must learn to be strong, little witch.*

And always, Talah drifting closer, her regretful but rigid refrain snapping at my heels. *You cannot hide from me here. Let me in!*

Furious tears fell from my eyes, and where they landed, flowers sprouted—white as fallen stars, black as the night sky that birthed them.

I slammed full tilt into a hard frame. I cried out, nearly stumbled. Strong arms sinewed with lean muscle and fletched with severe tattoos caught me, curving possessively around my shoulders. I looked up into the face of the towering man who'd seized me.

Irian's beauty was, as always, a knife to my heart. I inhaled his scent of dawn air and cold metal, fighting the urge to surrender to his embrace.

He, like everything else in this accursed place, was nothing more than memory. Much as I longed for him to be real, he was not. He was nothing but an aspect of myself made manifest.

"You have been here before, mo chroí," he said, rough but gentle. *My heart, my heart.* "Do you hear me? *You have been here before.*"

"I don't know where else to go!" I cried out.

"The pleasure of the losing is in the finding." Sympathy and worry made a battlefield of his perfect features. "Or so I have been told."

"I don't know where to hide so she cannot find me," I bit out. "How can I lose myself in my own head?"

Irian stepped away from me. He stood suddenly at the edge of a cliff, wind snapping his long dark cape. He tilted his head, sending raven strands of hair gliding around his ears. "Your power is part of you, whether you like it or not. And it is *vast*. You are not strong enough to control it. You must find a way to work with it. You must seek the truth of your anam cló—the shape your soul wants to take."

I turned away in frustration, only to halt when I saw who watched me from the moor.

A rack of silver-tipped antlers brushed the sky. Below, their face was inchoate: the shadow-dappled path leading deeper into the forest. Heavy muscle corded over a powerful torso; russet fur glided over legs thick as tree trunks. Behind them, the deep green forest whispered and beckoned, endless and inviting.

"You." My helpless fury pushed me toward them. "Can't you do anything? Aren't you going to *help*?"

What would you have us do? The ancient being spoke like the groaning of oaks in a storm, the sighing of dead leaves settling on cold earth.

"Something. *Anything.*" I had been trapped inside myself for weeks. Perhaps months. Maybe even years, as Talah circled ever closer, following me to my darkest corners. My deepest regrets. Surely the entity to whom I had bound myself beneath the Heartwood could do more than *stand* there. "You are a Bright One, are you not? One of the Solasóirí? You contain within you the magic you brought from the stars. You wield the power of the earth itself. Yet you do nothing!"

We long ago bound our magic to the Treasure you hold. We bound our power to you. They were patient as the seasons and enduring as the millennia. *We can only do what you wish us to do. We can only be who you wish us to be. We can only go where you wish us to go.*

"Go?" I nearly screamed. "In case you haven't noticed, we're trapped inside my head. With *her.* No matter where I try to hide inside my memories, she always finds me. I'm running out of places *to* go."

As if on cue, Talah's fire-fretted voice melted along the cliff face and shrieked from the sky.

You cannot hide here, star child. Let me in.

"No." I jerked my head over my shoulder, but Irian had melted away like a forgotten dawn. I fought a sharp stab of sorrow as I forced myself to remember—he was not here. Had never been here. Somewhere, *outside,* he lived. He had to live.

As long as I was trapped here, I knew he would not let me go. He had made me a promise. And Irian was a man of his word.

But that meant it was my responsibility to free myself from this prison of my own making. To keep Talah from wresting control of my being.

"I thought I had more time."

As long as you run, she will chase you, the antlered figure intoned, with a gesture of their gleaming claws. *But you belong to us. As we belong to you. It is as it has always been.*

Standing preternaturally still with the forest writhing at their back, the Bright One spoke with an air of...invitation. I searched for eyes amid the mottled light and shadow of their face but found only an endless kind of regard that made me feel very small. Very young. Very *other.*

"We belong to each other. Are you saying..." I licked my lips, grappling with the sudden terrible sensation of teetering upon a precipice. "Can you offer me somewhere else to go, where Talah will not be able to find me?"

The figure nodded, unhurried despite the smoking embers curling along the cliffs, the veins of molten metal splintering the sunbright moor. *A long time ago, you were given to us for safekeeping. Three moons ago, we gave you back to yourself.*

The cliffs began to shake; stones rattled toward the seething sea. *You cannot hide here. Let me in!*

"I don't understand." I fought to keep my focus despite Talah drawing ever nearer. "My early childhood is a blank. I have no memories from before I came to Rath na Mara."

You have all you need. The figure turned on their heel, melting into the forest. *Except perhaps the courage to face what you must do.*

My breath accelerated in my throat; my heart thumped an uneven tattoo. Before I could change my mind, I flung myself after the Bright One. The moor dissolved.

The deep forest at dusk. Early frost scribed twigs with glass; leaves flamed in shades of ocher and rouge. A small girl played beside the path—a girl with hair dark as deep water and mismatched eyes sparking green and brown in the low light. She was not alone, although her playmates were wholly unexpected.

Fair Folk clustered around her, playful yet protective. A flock of gossamer-winged sheeries shook the branches until golden leaves fell around her dancing form like lucky coins. Three ruddy-faced leipreacháin hurried the fallen leaves so they chased the laughing girl to and fro. Beyond, a few moss-haired ghillies bent the late blooms—asters and goldenrod and chrysanthemums—to make a bower for the girl to run through.

"Fia!" The shout burst the pleasant hush like a bubble being popped. The Fair Folk immediately hid, slinking behind tree trunks or between dimming shadows. The little girl tried to follow, but in the murky wood her face made a wan moon punctuated by desperate dark eyes. The strident female voice grew louder. "Where are you, you accursed little horror? I told you not to wander off! But do you listen to me? *No*, no, you never do. What does it matter if your nursemaid gets whipped for losing you? You'd rather be off cavorting with your own kind. This ends tonight, do you hear? I'm going to tell the queen where you keep running off to. And then you'll be sorry!"

A russet-haired woman, pretty face contorted with irritation, careened into the clearing through a stand of ash trees. The little girl with the mismatched eyes froze at the sight of her.

"There you are," Caitríona hissed, her eyes narrowing to cruel slits as she lunged for the little girl I had once been. "Just wait until I get my hands on you—"

Her grip was savage. The little girl cried out in pain, and the nursemaid immediately slapped her. The flat of her palm cracked vicious as a whip in the dimming, silent wood. The girl's mouth opened in an O of shock; she began to cry in earnest, gulping in air as huge tears rolled down her reddening cheek. The nursemaid only scowled, yanking on her wrists with unforgiving force.

"Shut up, shut up, shut *up*!" Caitríona hissed between her teeth. "I am so weary of your nonsense. Why don't you ask the Fair Folk to take you back where you came from, willful changeling whelp? No one wants you here. No one *wants* you!"

Night fell with a leaden hush as the young woman and the girl struggled in earnest—a tangle of flailing arms and screaming faces and kicking feet. At last, Caitríona caught the little girl around the waist and hauled her bodily off her feet. But the girl with the mismatched eyes twisted in her arms, her hands forming into claws as she grappled with her nursemaid. Where those claws struck flesh, Caitríona began to change.

I swallowed hard, my ancient guilt transforming into something closer to vindication. The trees at my back reached reassuring branches to brush my shoulders, as if to say, *You were never alone.*

In the deepening gloom, the changeling girl transformed her unfeeling nursemaid into a tree. Her legs became birch saplings;

her hair turned to flowering vines; her face became a staring sun-flower. The little girl fell in a heap, scrabbling backward from the horror she had wrought.

"I'm sorry," she breathed after a moment, her face mottled with tears. "Caitríona, I'm sorry. Please come back. *Please*. I don't care if I get whipped instead of you. Just come back."

The little girl flailed her hands over the young woman's trans-formed limbs, as if she sought to undo the magic she had wrought. But the nursemaid remained a tree. From their hiding places in the undergrowth, the Fair Folk slowly crept forward on stocky feet or lilted through the air on glowing wings. But instead of being com-forted by their presence, the girl now lurched away from them.

"*You*." Her small voice was sour in the dark. "*You* made me do this. *You* lured me away from my home. *You* made me dream of the woods when I should have been learning my letters. *You* are to blame for this. You are wild and wicked, just as Cathair says."

The Fair Folk hesitated. The leipreacháin rustled the dried leaves below the child's feet; the sheeries lifted the ends of her hair with nimble, glowing fingers.

"Go!" Little Fia shouted. She swatted at one of the sheeries; it tum-bled to the ground, stunned. "Leave me alone! Stop bothering me!"

The Fair Folk dispersed swiftly among the shadows, leaving the little girl with the mismatched eyes and the night-dark hair alone. She would stay there until dawn chased her home to explain what she had done to a queen who was not yet a mother.

I forced my eyes from her small kneeling form. The now-familiar figure's antlers glinted silver in the faded starlight.

"Well?" I asked tiredly. "Was this what you wanted me to find?"

They regarded me with the patience of eons. *Was it what you wanted to find?*

"The moment I learned to hate myself?" My throat worked around the taste of decayed leaves. "The moment I rejected the part of me I had not known I needed to accept? The moment I shut away the half of myself I did not know how to love?"

What does it teach you?

The memory felt raw as rough hide, chafing my softest places. "Caitríona was vicious. Cruel. I was not to blame."

You were to blame. The figure's claws lifted toward me. *That does not mean you do not deserve forgiveness.*

"From whom?"

Who do you think? they returned, with infinite gentleness, unyielding firmness.

Somewhere behind me, the trees began to expand with veins of molten silver. Steam floated like fog between the widely spaced trunks. *Let me in.*

I stared at the Bright One's outstretched hand, their palm imprinted with recursive whorls—the striations of untold millennia.

"You have always been with me, haven't you?" I lifted my eyes to their face, formless as the forest path. "Even when I did not know you. Even when I did not want you."

Yes. The figure beckoned me through the gold-and-silver-streaked wood. *Are you ready now?*

I hesitated for one last, aching moment. "I do not know your name."

Ínne, they told me, and it was the sound of trees growing and flowers blooming and stone eroding.

I wrapped my fingers around Ínne's calloused, clawed hand. I followed them deep, deep between the arching trees.

Chapter Seven

Irian

As the diamond-streaked Cnoc reared up before their straggling party, surrounded by circling draigs, Irian finally confessed himself astonished.

Over the past thirteen years, Irian had often believed he had lost the capacity for amazement. That his world, in all its bleakness and boredom and violence, was unalterable; his own destiny, fixed; his story, already written.

Then he met Fia.

Since that fateful night, Irian had been irrevocably disabused of the notion that he could no longer be surprised. His world had cracked open, letting light inside. Bleakness had creaked toward hope. Boredom had spiked toward interest. Violence still sharpened every corner of his life, only tempered now with love—a sword with one edge blunted. His stars had slipped from their alignments, but instead of feeling unmoored, he knew he had been unchained. His story had transformed from a tragedy to a tale with a gloriously unwritten ending.

For a time, it had made him afraid. For so long he had been

tethered to his own doom, the shadow of his death like shackles he could not unlock. While he had not always wanted to die, he had known exactly when he would. It was as it had always been.

Until it no longer was.

Then he had yearned to use his death to save the life of the woman he loved. As she had used hers to save him. But now, gazing at the impossible mountain nest of impossible mythic beasts, he was reminded of all Fia had taught him over the past year.

He could not control the decisions of others. His life did not have to end for it to have meaning. And he could not predict every twist and turn of his own story.

"Oy!" The patter of iridescent pebbles bouncing along the sharply sloping path stole Irian's attention. Wayland, riding ahead, was waving his arms in panic.

The tiniest of the draiglings—more or less the size of an overfed housecat—had awoken from her slumber around the prionsa's torso and was lovingly harassing him, combing her blood-red nails through his sleek hair and repeatedly uttering, "Mine! Mine!"

"Laoise, what is it doing? Is it hungry?" Wayland beseeched.

Laoise flashed an affectionate smile. Irian had to assume it was directed at the draigling, not Wayland. Laoise seemed miraculously immune to his foster brother's impressive arsenal of charms.

"Hasn't a girl ever pulled your hair, Prionsa? It means she likes you." Laoise's smile broadened. "And Nidhoggur has a name. Maybe if you ask her *nicely* to stop, she'll listen."

Wayland grumbled—something about the naming conventions of draigs and keeping control of one's children. But after a few minutes the draigling settled on his shoulder and contented herself with blowing steam in his ears.

The shadow of Cnoc Féigleann swallowed them whole. The temperature dropped, an icy wind slinging down from the peaks to ruffle Irian's hair and shiver between the legs of the aughiskies. Irian instinctively caught hold of it, singing to it in the formless, toneless melodies of his Treasure. It sprinted across the Barrens, reaching in minutes the rough expanse of Mag Tuired, patchworked with brittle grass and scarred by ragged, slumped figures. Irian forced the zephyr to sweep in dogged pursuit of any movement upon the plain. At last, he was satisfied. He released the breeze, which escaped to the south.

He exhaled. Eala either could not or would not follow them into the Barrens, where strange magic had birthed even stranger creatures.

Laoise led their group beneath a vaulted archway into the darkness of the mountain. Sunlight faded to a whisper. Veins of gemstones and metal sheared between the serrated dark stones of the cavern, washing over them in stained glass bands of color and gleam. Crimson bloodied Fia's face; blue glazed her arms like enamel; silver caught on the crown of new metallic streaks in her hair. The glow pulsated, not with the steady, easy throb of a heart but with the syncopation of a sickened organ. The vibration bred unease in Irian's gut—dread birthed by magic gone wrong.

Magic like the corrupted wild power the bardaí had released in their quest for domination of Tír na nÓg.

Irian tightened his hold on the woman lying motionless in his arms.

The jagged cavern narrowed to a pinch point, forcing everyone to dismount. The aughiskies sidled through; Balor wedged himself sideways through the narrow gap, black pebbles raining around his massive head. Irian was not accustomed to being so far away from the air and skies—he felt as though the weight of the vast black mountain squatted upon his shoulders. He inhaled, tasting eons of rock and forgotten magic on his tongue.

All at once, the cavern expanded. And expanded further, the clatter of their footfalls echoing into the distance.

One of the draigs flew by, its leathery wings sibilant, then landed with a thump. Red light bloomed from its gorge; a huge hearth set against one sloping wall ignited with a roar, licking around stacked firewood. Another hearth erupted in turn, casting firelight toward a distant ceiling.

Irian barely kept his jaw from hinging open in amazement.

This deep in the mountain, the Cnoc was no longer rough-hewn stone, but a serpentine dream of black rock sinuously carven into pillars, fluted archways, and vaulted ceilings. Sharp outcroppings meandered into delicate ogees; undulating hallways disappeared into mirror-glass lakes. Multicolored rocks and shining metals caught the firelight and reflected it back, until the whole world seemed to glitter.

"How...?" Sinéad licked her chapped lips, seemingly unsure what she wanted to ask. "Did you find it like this?"

"Sort of." Irian usually found Laoise's smug air charming. In this moment she was positively self-congratulatory. "It wasn't much to look at when we first arrived, nor for many years after. But little by little, the draigs helped us renovate. We had to experiment with what level of heat polished the stone instead of fracturing it, and which of the crystal veins reflected the most light, but—"

Irian tuned out the rest of Laoise's monologue. Night must be approaching—Fia twitched faintly in his arms, her eyelids flickering. Feathers ruffled briefly at her temples before smoothing back into her hair. Her hands clutched reflexively around his arms, but instead of fingernails she had jagged claws that raised red lines upon his skin.

"Laoise." A terrible vision gripped Irian: Fia finally fighting free of his exhausted embrace and flying away in the shape of a swan or a hawk or an owl. Deep into unexplored caverns filled with fire-breathing draigs. "Is there somewhere I can take her? Somewhere safe?"

Laoise dropped her jovial pride in an instant. "This way."

The caverns were almost cozy. A curved hallway flickered with light; grooves in the wall carried flaming rivulets of oil. Open doorways punctuated the stone; Irian glimpsed cushions strewn between carven stools. Glossy tables, sloped bed frames, laddered shelves. Living chambers, all sleekly sculpted from the shimmering stone of the Cnoc.

Laoise waved each of their party into a waiting set of chambers. Sinéad gratefully slumped to her knees in the lush carpeting; Wayland slid through a narrow doorway only to swiftly shut it behind him, leaving a vexed Hog to wail at the jamb, scrabbling her claws and battering her wings. The aughiskies and Balor filed together into one broad, high-ceilinged chamber, looking supremely out of their element, until Laoise sent one of the draigs to show the aughiskies the underground rivers weaving beneath the Cnoc. Balor collapsed on his back and immediately began to snore.

At last, Laoise showed Irian to a room with few furnishings or decorations. One large bed hunched against a wall; beyond was a darkened bathing chamber. Irian set Fia gently upon the bed, swiftly unbuckling his armor before the change fully took hold of his wife.

Laoise lingered by the door. She said, obliquely, "There are more rooms."

Irian fumbled with a clasp, the leather stiff without regular oiling. "Why so many?"

"You may take another, if you choose."

Irian stilled. On the bed, a ruff of golden fur sprouted along Fia's collarbones.

"The doors all lock," Laoise added. "And there is nothing valuable that can be destroyed."

Irian gritted his teeth. "That will not be necessary."

"You have nothing to prove. We all know you love her. She knows you love her."

"I will not leave her."

"You cannot protect her if you drive yourself into an early grave."

"That may be so. But I refuse to cage her."

"As you will, Irian." Laoise exhaled, backed away. "But think on what I said. Consider how well you can look after her if you are not looking after yourself."

The door slid shut, leaving Irian alone for the first time in nearly a month. Somewhere far above these dense stone walls, night was falling over the Barrens. Russet fur licked at Fia's hairline; a scurf of viridian scales surfaced along her shoulders; black feathers prickled her arms before smoothing away. Fia's change would begin in earnest soon, as it had every night since the Longest Night.

Irian gazed longingly at the bed, sloping up from the black rock and covered with a handful of plush pillows and a mound of furs. Exhaustion throbbed along the contours of his bones, making his limbs heavier than they had ever been.

Laoise was right about one thing—Irian needed to rest.

He did not need much sleep; the power of his Treasure sustained him beyond what humans—or even Folk—required. But he needed *some* sleep.

Briskly—as veins of silver-gold stood out briefly along Fia's forearms before her skin was obscured by gray fur—Irian finished undressing, tugging his rumpled, stinking, salt-and-dirt-crusted shirt over his matted hair. Unhooked the belt carrying the Sky-Sword's scabbard, dropped it to the ground. As Fia bared teeth that were lengthening toward vicious fangs, he lifted her from the bed and carried her toward the bathing chamber. He forcefully kicked the door shut behind them. Fia growled, low and threatening, and began to change in his arms.

The wolf was huge and night black. It lunged at him with paws the size of dinner plates and a mouth like damnation. Fangs snapped inches from Irian's nose as he caught the beast around its neck and hauled it sideways, using its own momentum to shove it into the wall beside the tub. The impact jarred them both; Irian's head snapped painfully backward even as the wolf whimpered and convulsed. Irian took advantage of its momentary weakness to wrestle the beast to the tiles, clasping his arms around its furred ruff and pinning it beneath his body. It growled with displeasure, thrashing as it fought to get its limbs beneath it.

"I am sorry, mo chroí," Irian murmured into the beast's tough pointed ears. "But I am not going to let you destroy the bed. I intend to use it. Eventually."

As Irian's transformed wife pivoted beneath him, raking a set of razored claws from his throat down to his navel, he knew: He might let Balor carry her, might let Sinéad ride with her, might let Laoise watch over her. But he'd be damned if he ever left her alone when she needed him. Her cries were his to hear; her pain his to witness; her torment his to feel.

In the depths of Cnoc Féigleann, Irian had no window to the outside. *Time* seemed like a story he had heard as a child, then forgotten. Hours passed like minutes; minutes stretched like years. As mineral stars wheeled close overhead in the nighttime of the caverns, his mind flew, and he could almost imagine the past year had not happened. That he was trapped in a crumbling fort with nothing but shadows and wild magic for company. That *he* was the one who transformed beyond his control—from man to twisted, feathered thing, then back to man. Once, it had been so.

His skin brutally pierced by sharp black feathers, his bones viciously ruptured by grievous changes, his truest self tattered by magic he could not control.

When Fia at last stilled in his arms, Irian felt almost as if he were in a dream.

The dim bathing chamber was gauzy with heat. Irian's sweat-slick skin molded sumptuously against Fia's sleek frame. She clutched at him, her touch finding the ridges of muscles exposed beneath claw-torn clothing. She tangled her slender fingers in his hair as she drew him down over her.

"I don't know where else to go," she breathed against his mouth.

The words startled him back to *here*.

Now.

Fia's lips were pressed to his—her tongue sliding between his teeth, her barely covered breasts tight against his chest, her thighs latched around his hips. In his exhaustion, Irian's body had already begun to respond to her advances—his hands dragging her closer, his desire rising. How he longed for her, how he wanted—

Beneath her dark eyelashes, her metal eyes slashed his heart.

Irian mastered himself with a viciousness he knew he deserved. He pushed Fia—or whoever possessed her—to arm's length with all the strength he had once used to hold her close.

She gnashed her teeth as she writhed in his grip, even more feral in borrowed lust than she had been in borrowed form. And when he met her gaze, he glimpsed not the faintest vestige of his wife.

This, more than anything else, tattered the last of Irian's strength. The promise he had made Fia on the Longest Night echoed in his mind, the litany he had clung to now layering discordant in his skull, like a song he had heard too many times and could not shake.

Not in a thousand lifetimes will I ever let you go.

What did it truly mean, to never let a person go? If Fia never returned to him—if she had already been consumed by Talah's heinous magic—was he honor-bound to grapple with this *thing* wearing her face for the rest of his life? Or was it enough to have loved her so deeply that the sound of her name was etched like a poem upon the parchment of his heart?

By what terrible troth had he—yet again—bound himself?

All his life, Irian had been defined by geasa. His father's curse upon his mother, his enforced link with the Sky-Sword. His invisible bonds to the swan maidens, his marriage covenant with Fia. And now this.

Without his oaths, Irian did not know who he was. He had never bothered to ask. But now he began to wonder: Would the weight of this last pledge be the thing to break him?

Or was he broken without it?

Grimly, Irian set his jaw and waited for daybreak.

Chapter Eight

Wayland

Wayland awoke in darkness punctuated by multicolored glimmers of colored light. For a long, nebulous moment, he had utterly no idea where he was. Then the shimmers grew sharp, piercing his skull with blinding intensity.

Not light. *Claws.*

"Ow!" He jerked upright—or tried to. Smothering weight wrapped around his head and flopped over his neck. He batted at the mass in panic, only half relieved when he felt smooth, hot scales. A low hum vibrated his face.

Hog.

The pain raking his hairline fluctuated as the burdensome draig kneaded at his skin with apparent pleasure. Wayland shoved ineffectually at the creature before letting his arms fall back onto the bed.

Of course—he was deep inside a mountain, being harassed by a toddler draigling who'd seemingly taken a shine to him.

"How did you even get in here?" he grumbled. "I *know* I locked that door."

Hog purred louder, massaging his scalp with her needlelike talons.

"Make yourself useful, at least." He sighed. "I can't see for shite in here."

Hog chirruped in apparent umbrage.

"Light some torches. Please?"

She launched herself off his head. Red-gold sparks showered along the far wall, igniting the tapers embedded in the stone. Wayland sat up in bed as the little draig hurtled back to collide with his bare chest before curling herself possessively around his abdomen. He cradled her form in surrender. She was a strange combination of hard muscle and sleek scales and soft baby fat. He didn't totally despise holding her.

"What am I going to do with you?" he asked helplessly. "Don't you already have a mother?"

Hog rolled onto her back, exposing her velvet underbelly and giving him a sly look. He gently stroked her tummy before groaning at his own weakness and plopping her unceremoniously onto the floor.

"I'm getting dressed now, you leech."

Wayland made a face at the rumpled, dirty trousers and stinking shirt he'd traveled in from Emain Ablach. But he had nothing else to wear. He pulled on the breeches with a grimace but tossed the shirt onto the fire now blazing in the hearth.

The Cnoc's caverns were kept pleasantly warm. And no one—including himself—needed the stench he'd been carrying with him for weeks.

Wayland held out an arm. "Shall we?"

The chubby little dragan gave three jolting lollops of her stubby wings to get herself airborne before landing on his shoulder with a thump. He shrugged to redistribute her weight, then opened the door and strode out into the Cnoc.

Only to collide squarely with the person standing directly outside his door.

Wayland cursed, jerking back even as his stumbling steps tangled his legs with the stranger's. He caught a glimpse of fire-red hair and warm brown skin. Laoise? But Laoise barely reached his chest—this figure easily cleared his shoulders. Wayland lost his balance completely, staggering forward and toppling against the other person. They swayed precipitously in the moment before he caught them both with his hands splayed on the wall.

"Gods alive!" Wayland spat out. "Couldn't you have knocked?" He looked down.

The young man caged between his braced arms was breathing unevenly, his lips parted in surprise. The eyes he lifted to Wayland's face were brown as bark, shot through with filaments of gold from the torchlight and framed in lush auburn lashes. Half his head was shaven; the other half sported sleek scarlet hair spilling over one side of his face. He was a few inches shorter than Wayland, and sparer—his sleeveless mantle displayed the sinewed cut of arms ribboned with lean muscle. He huffed an awkward laugh, and Wayland tasted the other man's breath on his own lips—their near fall had brought them mere inches apart.

"I was about to." His voice was deeper than Wayland had expected it to be. His dark eyes drifted from Wayland's face to his bare chest, then back up.

"Oh." Wayland pushed back from the wall, putting distance between himself and the stranger. He fought the urge to cross his arms over his naked chest, feeling strangely exposed. "Dare I ask why?"

"Someone," the red-haired man said pointedly as he lifted a leather-gauntleted fist toward Wayland's shoulder, "isn't supposed to go sneaking around bothering strangers."

Hog mewled, then launched herself off Wayland's shoulder onto the newcomer's raised hand.

"Kiss?" The draigling did not so much ask as demand, thrusting her fang-rimmed mouth at the man's jaw. The motion ruffled his length of crimson hair, and he readjusted the locks back in place over his cheekbone, the gesture self-conscious but practiced.

"We haven't been introduced," he said as he submitted to Hog's kisses. "I'm Idris."

Of course. Laoise's brother. They did look like siblings—the same smooth brown skin, the same soft, sculpted features. Their eyes were different—Laoise's a supernatural amber, like embers cooling in a grate, while Idris's were opaque brown. So, too, was their hair—Laoise kept her springy curls cropped close to her head, while Idris wore his length of scarlet hair assiduously curved over one eyebrow and cheek, kissing around his jawline before pooling over his chest.

"And I'm Wayland." He fought the urge to reach out and slip the other man's hair behind his ear. The phantom slide of those glossy tresses between his fingertips made Wayland shiver. He shoved his hand in his pocket. "It was no intrusion."

Idris grinned, a sideways flash of humor that was gone almost before it appeared. "Is that why you're not wearing a shirt?"

Wayland flushed, an unexpected flare of heat climbing from his collarbone toward his jaw. He barked a laugh, half in surprise and half in awe.

When was the last time someone had made him blush? He had no earthly idea.

"I meant the draig. She's sweet...when she's not trying to rip my scalp off." Wayland's mouth stretched with the beginnings of a smile. He had never been one to let flirtation go ignored—historically he could give just as good as he got. "But if you enjoyed this chance encounter, I will happily answer my door half naked and pin you against the nearest wall anytime you stop by."

Idris did not blush so much as set himself on fire. Red burned his throat, blazed across his cheeks, and rouged the tip of his visible ear. He ducked his head, his glossy tresses falling farther over his face. When he looked back up, he had composed himself—only the slightest hint of red lurked above the collar of his tunic.

"I came to fetch you," he said with all the gravity he could muster. "Everyone else is awake. And they've all begun to plan."

⌒⌒

As different as the caverns were from Emain Ablach—the silver-hued, wave-strewn, blue-sky island where he'd spent the entirety of his life—Wayland did not dislike them. Their glossy curves and muted kaleidoscope glow reminded him a little of the Year's prison beneath the Silver Isle. But there was something dislocating about being underground—as though he was cut off from some vital part of himself. He had felt the same loss when they traveled inland from the coast—no crash of waves or cries of gulls or salt on the air.

He had never expected to mourn the winter sea. But nor had he expected many of the events he had recently undergone.

The caverns undulated downward. Hog careened ahead of Idris and Wayland, illuminating the caves with sparks of red fire until sunspots danced across Wayland's vision. Soon, he heard the sound of rushing water somewhere nearby. The coursing sensation curling around his bones as his innate magic awoke was both homecoming and affliction. Instinctively, his fingers grazed his throat, where for so many years a thick, heavy collar had choked him. But it was, of course, gone—Wayland had finally taken his power back from the man who had stolen it.

His king. His bane.

His father.

Set me free. Wayland inhaled deeply, remembering the last words he had spoken to the man who had helped create him. Gavida had shuddered, in those final moments, even as his precious isle slid away into the hungry sea. *Let me go, as myself.*

The smith-king's eyes, where they rested upon his only son and heir, had been full of fear. Not of the sword point resting over his ancient, anguished heart, but of an older, greater horror. He had not, in the end, been afraid of his own death. Only feared the method by which he would be dispatched.

"Where are you taking me?" Wayland asked Idris, forcing away his jumbled memories of the Longest Night.

Idris glanced over his shoulder, Hog's patchwork flames turning his eyes molten. "Scared, Wayland?"

The familiar use of his first name inexplicably jolted Wayland. Plenty of people called him by his first name—he had always hated formalities such as *sire* or *prionsa*. Those were roles—personas—he'd been forced into. Perhaps that was what made his name on Idris's tongue sound so strange. This other man knew him only by how he had introduced himself.

It felt like resurrection.

"Not in the least," Wayland responded easily. "Strange men leading me half dressed into unknown places is one of my favorite pastimes."

Idris's gaze dropped unconsciously to Wayland's bare chest before leaping to his face. Wayland's smile crept wider as another flush teased the man's throat. "Laoise warned me that you would try to flirt."

"*Try?*" Wayland laughed. "She underestimates my resolve. I'm not trying. I *am* flirting with you."

Idris looked forward again, hiding his expression behind his spill of hair. "You slept later than the rest. The question of the nemeton was broached. Irian especially wished to see it. But it is a bit of a hike."

The nemeton. Laoise had referred to the grove of flaming trees growing at the base of the sinkhole. Wayland's thoughts flew to the Grove of Gold—the sacred ring of nine ancient apple trees crowning Emain Ablach. A spear of sorrow pierced him, sharp and unexpected. The grove was lost now—he had witnessed the wishing trees being consumed in columns of silver fire before the plunging island devoured them. He had never believed himself particularly attached to the grove. It had simply been *there*, existing, for all his life. But now the knowledge of its destruction carved a hole in his chest—another negative space he felt suddenly unsure how to fill.

"What do you call it?"

"Call it?"

"Many years ago, my king father pithily named our nemeton *the Grove of Gold*."

"Let me guess," Idris said. "The trees were golden."

Wayland laughed. "You're a sharp one."

"When Blodwen first discovered the grove, we had no name for it at all." Idris shrugged. "Only after Laoise began venturing out into Tír na nÓg and Annwyn, collecting stories and books, did we discover the term *nemeton*."

"If it is as impressive as Laoise says, perhaps it deserves an honorific."

"Perhaps." Idris caught Hog—doing flaming loop-de-loops dangerously close to his long hair—by one stubby leg and tugged her onto his shoulder. "Or perhaps not. What is the point of naming something that is dying? Just another piece of it to lose when the time finally comes."

His words struck Wayland like a blow to the chest. The cavern abruptly opened outward. A rill of frigid wind winnowed through the darkness of the cave, and where it gusted along the walls the minerals pulsed brighter: jasper and peridot and tourmaline glittering like colorful stars. A moment later, red-gold light exploded on Wayland's face.

Inside the caverns, he had lost his sense of time. It was late morning, by the angled scrape of sunlight over the high, narrow lip of the impossibly deep sinkhole punched into the mountainside. Beyond, pale clouds scalloped the blue. Below...

Wayland had grown up with the Grove of Gold. As a child he had hidden from infuriated tutors among its gnarled, twisting boughs. As a teenager he had braided garlands for curious paramours from its fragrant blossoms. As an adult he had plucked, then tasted, its devious, tempting fruit, swiftly earning punishment for his heart's desire. A delicious feast resulting in a total loss of appetite; a day of perfect weather in exchange for one horrendous storm. Such proximity ought to have made him immune to the wonders of a mystical grove of magical trees.

Laoise and Idris's nemeton cured him of that assumption with swift and vexing totality. The glade was *incredible*. Blown glass trees molded into fantastical shapes; veins of fire coursing beneath their transparent boughs; roots and branches etched with seams of living gold. Leaves crafted from memories of bonfires; burning blossoms with molten petals.

"Gods alive," Wayland murmured. "It's...unbelievable."

When he finally managed to tear his eyes away from the flaming trees, Idris was watching him with an expression he could not read—curiosity, with a hint of admiration. Or was that disdain?

"Come," said Idris. "They're this way."

Chapter Nine

Irian

Irian had never been the most patient of men. Laoise forcing him to wait for Wayland and her brother before explaining the supernatural grove of flaming trees licking and crackling above his head was making him livid.

"Why is it dying?" Irian asked for the third time.

"I'll explain all I know," Laoise said, also for the third time. "When Idris arrives with Wayland."

Ten paces away, Sinéad—who had been nearly wordless for the past three weeks—was drilling through the forms and variations she'd learned from Fia, taking her aggression out on the air as she kicked and punched and stabbed with her twin daggers. Irian exhaled a frustrated breath, turning in a tight circle as his hand skated toward the Sky-Sword, which hummed a querulous melody beneath his palm. Fia's ghostly weight haunted his arms. Perhaps he should not have left her in the main caverns with Balor, who was too large to easily navigate the smaller caves.

"Leave her with me, lord," the Fomorian had offered. "I will keep her safe. Safer than safe: I will keep her *Balor*!"

Irian had not known what that meant. But it was daytime—his wife was quiescent after the rigors of the night. Though claw marks scored his chest and the imprint of scales pebbled her limbs, he knew she would not transform fully until night fell. So—pushing away his worst misgivings—Irian had conveyed her limp form to Balor, who had handled her with the tender care of a parent holding a newborn.

But as Irian followed Laoise into the bowels of the mountain, the image of the Fomorian cradling Fia's slack body brought him no comfort. He wanted to get this meager council over with.

"Brother." Wayland approached across the curved belly of the sinkhole, trailed by roly-poly Nidhoggur blundering through the cut-glass sunshine. A few paces behind, Idris followed, his face half hidden behind a fall of dark red hair. Irian had met the slender young man briefly before Laoise dispatched him to seek out Wayland, characteristically sleeping in while the rest of the world went to war. Even now, Irian's erstwhile foster brother seemed unconcerned by the conventions of clothing, sauntering boldly bare-chested through the ice-chased morning.

"Wayland." Irian greeted him with a tone he hoped was rough enough to convey his growing annoyance. "Were you having sweet dreams?"

"The sweetest," Wayland said. "For I was dreaming of you."

Irian growled, deep in his chest, but that only made Wayland smile. Irian forced himself not to react further. Wayland had done nothing truly wrong to earn Irian's recent short temper. Yes, Irian's oldest friend and foster brother had kissed his bride—but the geas binding them together had been forged long before Irian had wed her. Yes, Wayland sometimes looked at Fia too long when he thought Irian wasn't watching—but they were all concerned for her well-being. Yes, Wayland had been the one able to remove Fia's collar when Irian could not—but it had needed to be done.

Fia had chosen Irian. He was not jealous of Wayland.

He did not know *what* he was.

"Shall we?" he said, tightly, to Laoise. "Provided the conditions are at last favorable?"

She stalked between the harmonic circle of flaming trees. "We shall."

Irian followed, trailed by Sinéad, then Wayland, then Idris and Hog. At their feet, the dark volcanic rock was pocked with divots approximately the size of Irian's fists. He could only assume this was where they'd found the clutch of draig eggs. Above, a few of Laoise's draigs swooped and swirled, their red-gold scales shifting and flaring in counterpoint to the guttering trees.

"Here is all I have discovered." Laoise's voice held the same resonant gravity with which she'd relayed the tale of her dragain and their upbringing. "Sacred groves are scattered throughout the realms of the Fair Folk. Tír na nÓg. Emain Ablach. Annwyn. They are usually assembled of trees—though not always—but beyond that I can find no pattern. Some groves contain many trees; others only a few." She glanced at Irian. "If Sinéad's stories of your Heartwood are true, some contain only one."

Irian remembered a ribbon of green vines and a ribbon of black feathers, and a much smaller hand clasped in his own. He remembered all that tree had taken from him. And all it had given back.

"The only constant is the magic flowing through and around the nemeta," Laoise continued. "Even then, the magic is variable. I had never encountered anything like the wishing apples of Wayland's Grove of Gold. But nor have I encountered other trees like these. They certainly grant no wishes."

They all gazed at the shadow-flame boughs.

"This is what I have come to believe: The groves are the nodes where magic gathers and flows. Anchors, in a sense, rooting magic into the land even as their branches radiate it through the ether. They are all connected—by lines carrying power and life across our world."

"Like hearts pumping blood through veins," Wayland murmured.

"Where did they come from?" Irian's jaw tilted as he considered this. "Have they always been here? *Will* they always be here?"

"So impatient, tánaiste." Laoise clucked her tongue. "The theory I find most plausible is that the groves are where Solasóirí—Bright Ones—landed when they fell from the stars. Which means they have not *always* been here, but are unknowably ancient. The magic they create, consume, and connect is bound by the same laws as nature—it may even be *the* law of nature. They can consume too much or too little. They can be warped or corrupted or even destroyed. And...they can simply die."

Laoise had alluded to this *dying* before. Irian saw what she meant—though the brightly colored foliage burned like a bonfire, veins of darkness ascended the glittering trunks from the black rocks beneath their roots. The shadows pulsed spasmodically; the sword belted at Irian's waist hummed in protest with every sick syncopation. The minerals gleaming from the walls seemed to darken.

Irian did not know by what rules magic governed this grove, nor this mountain. But he believed Laoise when she said the nemeton was dying.

"Why?" Wayland sounded both bemused and intrigued. Irian was astonished he had not yet made some quip or double entendre—his foster brother had never enjoyed a philosophical puzzle so much as a dirty joke. "You said the grove began to die when Hog—when the last draig—was hatched. Why would that have...triggered... this slow decay? It has been years, has it not?"

"Several." Irian had not yet heard Idris speak, and he was surprised by how deep the quiet young man's voice was. "There are legends among our mother's people—the Ellyllon—that these mountain ranges were once home to Y Ddraig Goch. The Red Dragan. Huge beyond imagining. Powerful and ancient as the stars. Laoise and I have come to believe that this legendary draig existed in truth and was a Bright One. This nemeton was its home—its landing place, its node, its source of cosmic power."

"Where is she—*it*—now?" Wayland demanded, and Irian knew without having to ask that his foster brother was thinking of the

Year. *Talah.* Fia had told him what they had discovered, deep in that tomb where Gavida kept his captive Bright One.

"The Red Dragan has passed beyond these realms. Whether that means death, or some other ending, I cannot begin to say. But they no longer exist in a sense that we understand. They passed the last of their life force into that clutch of eggs." Laoise gestured at the divots hollowed into the dark rock. "We have no earthly idea how long those eggs were here. Millennia, most likely—the ruby passed down through my mother's family was ancient beyond memory. But we believe their existence put the grove into a kind of stasis. Without the Bright One feeding and regenerating its magic, the grove relied on the eggs—which contained some essence of the entity—even as the eggs relied upon the nemeton. A self-sustaining system."

"But when Nidhoggur hatched," Idris finished, "the system terminated. Without the source of its magic—the Bright One or their offspring—the grove is now dying. And all the magic contained in this mountain with it."

Irian glanced at the dying trees, then toward the juvenile draigs shrieking and tumbling through the air near the top of the sinkhole. Their glowing scales chimed like glass bells. "Why are the living draigs not performing the same role? Does the magic not flow from and through them?"

"Apparently not." Laoise gave a complicated shrug. "We know not why."

"Then this tells us nothing." The anger and desperation simmering in the pit of Irian's stomach gnawed at his self-control. His voice rasped ragged between his teeth. "We are exactly where we began. Knowing nothing. Having no path to save Fia's life."

"There is another aspect we have not considered." Wayland spoke up, unexpectedly. "My father did not speak of the Treasures often. When he did, I rarely cared to listen. But I do remember this—he forged the Treasures as conduits between sources and vessels. We now know the sources are Bright Ones. The vessels,

Gentry heirs with affinities toward elemental magic. And the conduits, resonant objects that *must* be regularly renewed lest the cycle of regeneration end and the magic become corrupted."

Irian's thumb skated over the hilt of the Sky-Sword, its metal warm as his own flesh and humming with his own voice.

"We also know," Irian said slowly, thinking through what Fia had told him of her resurrection beneath the Heartwood, "that the sources—these *Bright Ones*—may be bargained with. The cycle of magic regenerated. The Treasures restored."

"The balancing is eternal," Wayland began.

"*But not immutable,*" Irian finished, biting the words to pieces. How many times had Gavida said that phrase? For perhaps the first time, Irian wished he had paid more attention to his foster father's booming prattle about bindings and forgings and the patterns of destiny etched in the stars. But he and Wayland had been boys—they could not have foreseen how complex their own destinies might one day become. "Then there is no rhyme. No reason. Nothing is written."

"Yet all may be possible." A note of excitement thrummed along the contours of Laoise's accented voice. "Think, tánaiste. Perhaps the Bright One who inhabited this grove created their own kind of binding—their own form of balance. They passed their vast elemental magic onward and set themselves free of the cycle in the doing."

"The eggs," Idris clarified, further unraveling the thread Laoise had picked out. "The draigs. They are vessels for the magic of the Red Dragan, in the same way the heirs of the Treasures are vessels."

"Yet surely they are not bound by the same rules of balance as the heirs," Wayland said, sorrow wringing his voice. "Surely they were not born only to die."

"No. It is the nemeton that is dying." Laoise's ember eyes flared with some realization or idea, and she spun suddenly toward the nearest tree in the flaming grove. "Hog, come here."

Hog, who had been sleeping around Idris's neck, abruptly sat up. She gave an aggrieved mewl and flapped her stubby wings.

"Please," Laoise amended.

Hog launched into the air—glazed sharp and gold by the lofting sun—and wobbled precipitously before landing with a thump on the roots at Laoise's feet. She looked at her mother with adoring curiosity.

Laoise bent to the draigling's level and held out her hand. Hog cooed and lifted her taloned paw to gently place it in the maiden's outstretched hand. Laoise folded her other palm over Hog's paw and, without warning, dragged the draig's claw across her skin. The razored point drew scarlet blood, welling luminous as smoldering coals. Hog squeaked in dismay. Laoise gently stroked her snout before stepping toward the closest tree and laying her bloodied palm upon the translucent bark.

Veins of flaming red and smoldering orange and shadowy black seemed to coalesce. The sun crested its zenith, pouring through the aperture in a wave of blinding, molten gold. Simultaneously, the nemeton *flared*, firelight dazzling from every trunk and branch and twig and leaf. Irian instinctively shielded his eyes with a raised arm. Everyone else mirrored the gesture.

Somewhere high above, all the draigs cried out in unison—an ecstatic cacophony of sound that jarred Irian's bones and rattled the Sky-Sword in its scabbard.

When Irian at last lowered his hand, the grove had returned to its prior state—blazing but blighted. The draigs whirled high above, save for Hog, who appeared to have grown six inches in an instant, shedding some of her baby fat as her nose and tail lengthened. And Laoise—Laoise was uncharacteristically weeping as she held her injured hand to her chest.

"Oh," she breathed, almost inaudibly. "*Oh*."

No one dared speak until Hog chirruped plaintively, breaking the spell. Wayland knelt, scooping the still-small draig into his arms with the faintest *oof* of effort. Hog curled herself around his neck and buried her face in his long, rumpled hair.

"I don't understand," Wayland admitted. Laoise was staring at the tree she'd touched with wonder and horror wreathing her expression. "What does it mean?"

Irian's heart rattled with foreboding. Then hardened like a diamond compressed by lingering fear, cut by cold realization, and polished by burgeoning dread.

"It is as it has always been." Irian forced his tone to stay perfectly even. "The first language of the Solasóirí and their sacred groves...is sacrifice."

Laoise lifted her eyes from the fading glow of the trees. "And blood is not enough."

Chapter Ten

Within

The moonlight draped over the clearing was sharp as a blade yet soft as silk. The bare trees glowed with it—trunks bleached to bone on one side, darkened to soot on the other. Frost spangled the undergrowth with tiny winking diamonds; my breath plumed like smoke in the night.

Ínne did not appear to breathe.

"Where are we?" I whispered, afraid to shatter the wintry hush. "What is this place?"

Your true inheritance, they said in my mind. *The memories you thought were lost. But were only hidden away until you needed them.*

The Bright One slowly stepped out into the cold, staring moonlight. I almost followed, but something unknowable bade me to remain in the shadows. I wrapped my arms around myself, trying not to shiver. For a memory, it was brutally and authentically cold.

It's not real, whispered my own voice in my head.

It's real enough to make my tits pinch, I almost replied, before realizing talking to myself wasn't helping my case.

The moonlight chased Ínne's russet fur with silver and incised the powerful muscles ridging their torso. Their face, inchoate as ever, lifted toward the sky, shifting with shapes of things I had no names for—multicolored whorls and spinning wheels and webs so vast they encompassed eternity. Their silver antlers stretched, rearranging stars into symbols I knew I might be able to read if only—

The figure who appeared in the moonlit glade was slight and slender—only a little taller than me. A heavy dark cloak swathed them from head to toe, masking identifying features like species or gender and frankly making me a little jealous. It looked warm. They stood in silence—or perhaps wordless communication—with the Bright One for an excruciatingly long time.

At last, the cloaked figure reached beneath their cloak and drew out a bundle. They gripped the object tightly but carefully, then held it out in a rush. I leaned forward, distracted from my frigid frustration by the intrigue unfolding before me.

Ínne extended their huge hands, claws gleaming like daggers in the moonlight. They accepted the bundle. Which stirred. And began to *wail*.

I clapped my hand over my mouth to stifle a gasp. I flung myself into the glare of moonlight, desperate for a closer look. Creeping knowledge twined through me like vines searching for sunlight, cutting with devious little thorns.

I lurched to a halt a pace away from the Bright One and the hooded figure. The baby—for so the bundle unmistakably was—was now cradled in Ínne's arms, impossibly tiny against their massive eldritch frame. It squirmed within its blankets, tightly swaddled to protect from the chill. It was so, so small. Days—perhaps mere hours—old. Its mouth opened wide and wider, howling displeasure at the indignity of being awoken at such an hour. The hair on its tiny oblong head shone black in the moonlight. Its eyes were wide and willful—one light, one dark.

I stumbled backward as the inevitable realization strangled me.

I might have made a sound, but my voice felt as small in my throat as that baby in its swaddle.

That baby. *Me.*

My gaze jerked to the woman who must be my mother. Deirdre. But before my eyes could dredge the shadows of her mantle, she was turning away, a choked, anguished sound escaping her lips. She fled, the sound of her weeping mingling with the baby's fussing until it—and her dark-cloaked form—disappeared into shadowed forest.

Ínne stroked the tip of their forefinger down the baby's forehead and nose, ever so gently. Once, twice. She quieted, her little lips pursing as her eyes drifted closed.

The moon netted through bare branches, and the crystalline hush remained.

A thicket of questions and accusations prickled sharp and hot in my chest. But the memory—although it could not be mine—was already shifting.

Dawn stroked bloody fingers over frosted grass. Ínne was gone—the babe, nested in her swaddling clothes at the heart of the glade, began squalling once more. Her little face reddened as she fought; her arms broke free, tiny fists balled as she protested the cold air. Her small hungry tummy. Existence itself.

Translucent wings caught the sunlight like stained glass. Sheer-ies fluttered down, coddled in acorn caps and dandelion vests. They clustered around her form, curiosity and concern raising their wispy voices in a council I could not understand. After a few more minutes of alarmed chatter, they zipped away into the forest. A pair of rainbow-plumed ravens, wakened by the ruckus, hopped from their roosts and pecked at the infant with more curiosity than malice. One of the sheeries came zooming back, tossing down an armful of conkers and lifting its fists to threaten the ravens, scolding all the time. The birds flapped away with a few aggrieved caws.

Before long, the rest of the sheeries returned, carrying bowls made of woven petals and acorn cups filled with luminous blue liquid. They tried to pour this down the baby's throat, but she only screamed louder.

Soon, it seemed as if every inhabitant of the forest was gathered around the edge of the glade—fallow deer and darrigs, grumpy badgers and bemused ghillies, wrens and leipreacháin and even one huge, sleepy, shaggy bear.

At midday, when the cold sun stared and made the baby flinch away from the brightness, a ghillie fashioned a little tent from birch bark. In the late afternoon, when the baby's enraged cries gave way to a more horrifying silence, a darrig made a small fire, visibly cringing when the tinder caught alight. Again, the concerned sheer-ies tried to feed the infant their enchanted dewdrops, but her closed eyelids had turned the blue of pond ice; her rosebud lips, the color of new snow.

At sundown, Ínne returned, striding soundless and majestic between the sighing trees. The Bright One took in the scene with a boundless kind of confusion—as though in all their endless wis-dom and infinite grace they had simply never imagined that the animals and lower Folk of the forest would not be able to keep a half-human, half-Gentry newborn alive.

They knelt as the light slipped away, scooping the baby into their massive fur-striped arms. She was too tiny, too still. They bent and—with a face like a forest path, a mouth like an archway of trees—kissed her pale cold forehead. A discharge of energy bulged outward through the glen, then rushed back in. Leaves in summer's full flush rustled in my ears. Green striped my vision. I tasted fresh loam wet with rain in the back of my throat.

Again, the vision shifted, warped, settled.

Springtime. The babe had grown, toddling merrily beneath alders thronged with cottony flowers as her chubby little feet stomped the cool moss. A towering ghillie chased her, its gnarled hands too large and too cautious as it tried to tie the girl's wild dark curls into some semblance of order.

"Be still, child!" Its fingers fumbled and the soft braid fell apart like loose threads of shadow. The girl giggled, clearly accustomed to such clumsy gestures of care.

Summertime. A darrig brought the child—older still and coughing terribly—a draught of muddy water from the deepest swamp, insisting that the rich, fetid liquid would make her strong. She vomited for days until the Bright One was once more summoned. Again, they gathered her in their arms, bleeding their magic into her ailing form until she was hale enough to dance reels by moonlight beneath a halo of singing sheeries.

Autumn. A trio of leannáin sidhe crooned strange lullabies that spoke of thorny embraces and drowning rivers. The girl slept, easily, cradled among their lithe, slender bodies, as they wondered in whispers above her soft dark head, *What exactly makes a mother?*

Winter again. The sheeries plied her with their strange recipes: mushrooms that made her float a few inches off the ground and frog-spawn porridge and fruits that sang melodies to her stomach and butterfly-wing crisps. None of them grasped what it was the child truly needed—warmth, nourishment, safety. These were foreign concepts to creatures born of dew and decay.

Still, the child grew, pale and slight and strange, but undeniably alive. Her laughter now fluted through the forest like wind through hollow reeds. She learned to climb the enchanted trees and speak to the night birds, who never gave straight answers but always made her laugh. She learned to listen to the breezes, though they told her secrets that sometimes made her afraid. Always the Folk watched her and cared for her, enchanted and bemused in equal measures by her vitality, her warmth, her spirit. They loved her, insofar as they were able—the unfamiliar weed blooming in their garden of eternal flowers.

Then, one autumn day, she was...gone. Leaves rich as brocade dropped from black branches. The sheeries fluttered in chaos for half a morning, then simply returned to their routines—painting blackberries and scolding ravens and hanging cobwebs to catch daydreams. A doleful wind rustled the grass. A hedgehog led her sleepy children toward their winter burrow. All returned to how it had been before.

Do you understand now, my child? The voice echoed not in my ears, but in my mind. I whirled to face Ínne as I wiped cold tears from my swollen face.

"Understand?" I repeated, with bitterness. "I understand nothing. Why did my mother leave me with you? With a host of Folk who knew nothing of how to care for a child?"

That is not our story to tell, Ínne told me gravely. *As you have seen, you* were *cared for.*

"*Cared* for? Cared for! That darrig tried to make me drink swamp water!" I shuddered with the grief and resentment of it all, even as the helpless kindness with which I had been raised twined fickle between my ribs. It felt easier to be angry than to be grateful. "I nearly froze to death more than once!"

We would never have let you die, child. Their seriousness was infinite. *You are too precious.*

"If that was true," I blurted out helplessly, "then why would my mother—why would Deirdre—have abandoned me with *you*?"

For long moments, they were still and silent. Their antlers seemed to pierce the dark canopy above us. Again, they said, *That is not our story to tell.*

I swiped more angry tears from my eyes. "Of course not. You're more in the business of meaningless riddles and muddled memories. Tell me something straightforward, for once. Donn damn you, stop telling me stories and tell me something *true*."

The night stretched thin as silk.

Truth is an untrustworthy sovereign, child. For what is a story but a lie? And what is a story but the utmost truth? The Bright One's head swiveled on their neck. *But I will tell you this much. Your seed was planted by a human man and incubated by a Gentry woman. But you grew into childhood primarily nourished by magic. Our magic. Wild magic.*

I stilled. Talah's words from the night I'd discovered her in the caverns below Aduantas thrilled through me, as unnerving and stirring as the night she'd spoken them: *I do not know you. And yet you are known. You are star touched.*

"What does that mean?"

It means you are more than human. More than Folk. You are both. And you are neither. You are more.

The words thrilled through me, tempting and terrifying. I thought of the night of the Ember Moon, when I died, yet was reborn. I thought of the Longest Night, when I semiwillingly opened myself, body and soul, to an entity so far beyond my meager mortality that I could hardly believe she had not yet mastered me. I thought of *now*, traveling through my incorporeal landscapes as if they were physical, unraveling the skeins of my memories.

I was the daughter of a human king who had abandoned his duties. The daughter of a Gentry heir who had unchained herself from her fated path at a terrible cost. Yet also—mythically, symbolically, and practically—I was the daughter of the forest itself. It may not have birthed me, but it had raised me. It may not have nursed me, but it had kept me fed. It may not have understood me, but in its own hallowed way, it had *loved* me. Distantly, calmly, and without judgment—as nature loved all things.

I was made of branches and blossoms and burned-out stars. I had lived my life thinking I was made for only one thing—to be a weapon, honed and used by others. But perhaps I had been made for more. Forged between two worlds and nurtured by a third, perhaps I had been made for so much *more*.

"I am the only one of my kind." Loneliness was a sword in my chest. For as long as I could remember, all I had wanted was a place to belong. A home to return to. A love I did not have to earn. But the truth was, there was no belonging save for what I carved for myself. No home save for one I built. No love save for what I demanded. From myself. And those I chose.

"I am the only one of my kind." This time, instead of a blade, the words were armor.

Yes.

I faced the Bright One. "I am star touched. Because of you—because of how I was raised. Is that the reason Talah chose me?"

Yes. Their antlers chimed. *It is also the reason she has not yet overcome your defenses.*

My unique parentage and upbringing had made me strong enough to sustain her...and strong enough to withstand her. "But not forever."

Their voice rang with untenable sorrow. *Nothing is forever.*

Renewed fear and frustration made a thicket around my heart. "Surely there is something I can do. Some way out."

The only way to escape your body is death, child.

"Some way out for *her.* Some new binding, or—" A thought exploded into my mind with surprising force—a thought echoing from moments ago. All my life I had yearned for belonging. For home. For *love.* What if...what if Talah wanted the same thing? She had been kept trapped in the dark for a thousand years by a devious, selfish king. I had set her free. But truly, my frail body could be nothing but another cage for a being of unknowable power and vast magic. I turned abruptly to Ínne. "Before you were bound to the Treasures, where was your home?"

The Bright One cocked its head with depthless puzzlement. *Home?*

"For the Solasóirí, where is home?" I prompted. "The stars?"

Their laughter—if that was even what it was—was the sound of mountains lofting over millennia; stones eroding beneath the gurgle of fast water. *We have spent eons in these lands. They have shaped us as we shaped them. We are not the same as when we arrived so long ago. We cannot return to the stars.*

"Then where?" Frustration made my tone crisp. "Where is home?"

The Bright One's claw tapped my breastbone, then drew a ragged circle above my heart. Green blood welled, though I felt no pain.

Circles, child, they intoned. *We are all the same. We are all different. Yet by the circles we are all bound.*

Circles. Did they mean...

"Nemeta?" I remembered meeting Laoise on the cliffs and her explanation of the sacred groves. She had said they once punctuated the land, holy places of great magic where miracles could be performed. Talah herself had appeared bound in the dark by the Grove of Gold's deep-reaching roots. But...what if the grove had not been caging her? Gavida had done that with his terrible collars.

What if the grove had been not a prison...but a home?

Somewhere distant, the air shifted. The faint tang of molten metal teased my nostrils. A distant, horrible voice wafted toward my ears.

You cannot hide here. Let me in.

"Can I give her another home?" The words came out rushed, nearly garbled. "Surely I am not the right home for her—this vessel was never designed to withstand two sources. If I give her somewhere else to go, will she leave me in peace?"

Perhaps. Let us venture deeper, child.

Chapter Eleven

Laoise

Gathering and eating with the half dozen strangers she'd brought into her home brought Laoise curious comfort.

Idris was a good cook. He'd had to learn, one of those first long winters at the Cnoc, when Blodwen was a rambunctious juvenile and Barfog an incessantly noisy hatchling. The supplies Laoise had brought from Dún Scaith and scavenged from Findias had long since been used; she could hunt in the form of her anam cló, but the Barrens were not plentiful with game. When her lanky teenaged brother—as relentlessly hungry as the newborn draigling licking sweat from her neck—complained about the lack of food, Laoise had snapped at him, perhaps unkindly.

Lick the walls like Blodwen, Brother, she'd shouted. *If you wish for something with more sustenance, then shift yourself to find it or make it for once in your bloody life!*

Idris had gone terribly quiet for two days, then seemingly taken her words as a challenge. A week later, he'd served a truly horrendous dish of clumsily filleted blind salamanders burned to an utter crisp. Probably by Blodwen. Laoise had choked down the blackened hunks of tough lizard, devouring her own guilt with it. Was this not exactly what she had demanded? The least she could do was accept the effort at face value and pray Idris took the failure as a sign his talents lay elsewhere.

He did not. That, too, he took as a challenge.

The caverns were not rife with life, but nor were they absent of it. Florid yellow lichen climbed the damp walls beside the underground rivers; green geckos and scarlet salamanders and speckled venomous frogs gamboled in the shallows. Tenacious birds with gemstone wings nested high on the walls of the sinkholes; furry burrowing creatures whose calls sounded like wind chimes dotted its floor.

If it could be foraged, Idris learned to forage it. If it could be snared, Idris learned to snare it. If it could be cooked, Idris learned to cook it.

Now—many years after those initial growing pains, which had included a number of accidental poisonings—Idris's culinary talents bordered on the rapturous. Despite Laoise giving him zero warning about the crowd she was bringing to the Cnoc, he'd conjured a veritable feast.

Braised lichen tossed with moonworm honey. Crystal-cap mushrooms steaming on toasted rounds of root bread. Salamander and wild garlic tart. Wine made from twilight berries and deepwood sap.

Each dish was delicious and everyone ate like they were starving. Which perhaps they were. Balor chuckled at the spread before excusing himself, claiming he'd seen a delectable vein of obsidian quartz he'd prefer to sample. Sinéad ate heartily for the first time in nearly a month, and Laoise was pleased to see pink bloom on her wan cheeks. Wayland gamely sampled everything before returning for his favorites. Irian—Fia lying supine beside him, with her head resting in his lap—ate with tense, precise bites. His strict inscrutability refused to hint at whether he was enjoying himself.

Laoise sometimes wished she could tell Irian to take entertainment where he could find it. But she supposed one did not demand the sun shine at night, nor the cliffs bow to the sea.

Before long, the food had been demolished and the conversation began to ebb. The draiglings were all lazily curled between the Folk—or, in Hog's case, stretched languorously over Wayland's lap. Balor had stomped cheerfully back into the cavern and settled himself against a smooth wall, his enormous teeth looking particularly sharp and gleaming. Even the aughiskies seemed sated, having been shown the most plentiful underground rivers by the draiglings.

Laoise cleared her throat, planting her elbows on the stone table before her.

"The magic of the Barrens—and this nemeton at its heart—kept Eala from following us." Laoise jumped straight to the heart of the matter—no point in wasting everyone's time with unnecessary dithering. "But I have received word from my network of...informants. Her withdrawal does not appear to have been a retreat. Quite the opposite—although it has been but a few days since Mag Tuired, she has marched through several Folk settlements, chaos and death upon her heels. The rumors spreading in her wake are concerning. Some call her the Rotten Princess. Others say she has dubbed herself Grave Mother."

"How do you know this?" Irian's hand twitched toward his belt, but he must have left the Sky-Sword in his chambers. He rested his palm on Fia's dark head instead. "Who are these *informants*?"

Laoise did not particularly care to explain her past to the Gentry heir—the long years training in swords and shadow magic at Dún Scaith, the friendships she'd forged and the enemies she'd earned. Nor did she wish to reveal how she and her Twilight Sisters— scattered now across Tír na nÓg, Annwyn, and beyond—stayed in near-constant contact, their messages appearing neatly folded in shadows only Laoise knew how to unfold, sharing joy or warning of danger.

"We call ourselves Twilight Sisters. Women who, like me, trained with Lady Scáthach. Women I trust with my life," Laoise said tightly. "The intelligence is good. Even now Eala approaches the outskirts of the Summerlands—she will likely reach their main city in one, maybe two weeks."

"Perhaps she has given up on us," Wayland said, his tone too light. "On Fia. Perhaps we need worry about her no longer."

Irian barked a harsh laugh. "Eala is mad with power and obsessed with the notion of Fia as her other half. The person who will make her whole, who will somehow cement her position as rightful ruler of both realms. She will stop at nothing until she has her sister by her side, no matter the cost."

Wayland's smile slipped, his broad shoulders tensing. Idris reached out to lay a gentling palm on Wayland's forearm, even as he murmured something below his breath.

Laoise's curious gaze lingered on the men before she addressed the group once more.

"We cannot expect Eala to act logically. In becoming a Treasure, she has undergone a transformation even Folk Gentry struggle with; as a human woman she has been indelibly changed. She no longer is who she once was."

"Or perhaps she is," Sinéad added, in a vicious undertone. "Which makes her all the more terrifying."

Laoise glanced sideways at her friend, who kept her eyes downcast. Laoise knew without having to ask that the human girl was thinking of her actions on the Longest Night—how she had dropped onto Eala from halfway up the cliff without an ounce of hesitation, then brutally stabbed the other woman until she believed her dead. Laoise did not blame Sinéad for her violence—she had witnessed enough thoughtless death to recognize a righteous kill. She only regretted—for Sinéad's sake, if not her own—that the human maiden had not stayed dead.

"We don't know what Eala wants or what she is planning," Laoise said. "But we must find out. And soon, for the specter of destruction haunts her steps. I plan to scout her location in the form of my anam cló—I wish to see with my own eyes where she is going, what allies and armies she gathers."

Sinéad looked up, blue eyes blazing. "I'm coming with you."

"Absolutely not," Laoise said shortly. "When I return, it will hopefully be with enough intelligence to inform our plans for what comes next."

Her words were met with a tense silence. Sinéad rose to her feet and stalked from the cavern. Laoise swallowed the sudden knife in her throat as she watched her go.

Images and memories lapped over her: Blodwen, small enough to carry in her arms, her forked tongue laving sweat from Laoise's collarbones; Sinéad and Chandi, singing off-key with their arms twined through Laoise's, smelling of spiced wine and fresh snow; Nidhoggur—sweet, dear Hog—desperately trying to speak her first word between puffs of acrid, sulfuric smoke.

Mmm. Mmm. Mum!

She still remembered the sunlight slicing through the fog on the morning she approached Fia and Irian on the cliffs by the sea. Irian's words, tense and dismissive: *If chaperone befits your skills, then our camp waits atop the hill.*

Laoise barely understood how she had become a mother to seven unruly draiglings. She understood even less how she had become chaperone, friend, then family for two human girls.

Chandi and Sinéad were both nearly women grown—seventeen and nineteen, respectively. She was not their mother or even their sister. Yet she had come to care for them both. Chandi's betrayal still twisted like a knife in her gut—for Sinéad, the anguish was far worse. Laoise did not wish to cause her any more pain.

"I beg your pardon." Laoise stood, cutting her eyes around the room. "I will attend to Sinéad. Perhaps in the meantime, the rest of you can decide how you will contribute to this stirring war effort."

"I'll plan the valiant retreat," Wayland said glibly.

"I think we've just lived that, Prionsa," Laoise called over her shoulder. "And I'm afraid I'm running out of hidey-holes."

Sinéad sat on the plush carpet in her chambers, toying with her daggers as she stared at nothing.

"Sinéad?" Laoise's voice broke the other woman's reverie—the rhythmic motion of her hands faltered. One of her spinning daggers fell to clatter on the floor. The other dashed against her wrist, blooming red upon her skin. Sinéad hissed in pain, folding her palm over the injury as Laoise cursed and rounded the bed toward her.

"Shite! I'm sorry." She drew Sinéad's hand from her wrist and inspected the cut. It wasn't deep, but the blades were sharp—it was bleeding profusely, the scarlet blood a shocking shade against Sinéad's pallor. "Let me help."

"It's fine." Sinéad jerked her arm from Laoise's grasp and put her already bloodstained hand back over the cut. "It'll stop in a minute."

"There are bandages in the bathing chamber—"

"I said *leave it*."

Laoise stilled at the icy snap of Sinéad's voice. She allowed herself a brief moment of longing for her anam cló—the ripple of hot scales over sleek muscle; the steady, thrilling pump of vast, leathery wings; the singeing blast of fire in her belly.

Draigs did not need to talk about their feelings.

"I'm sorry if I was sharp with you, just now," she began, carefully. "But—"

"Are you?" Sinéad finally looked up at Laoise, her azure eyes blazing like the heart of a flame. "Or were you saying exactly what you meant? That I am useless and you may command me as you please?"

Her vehement words shocked Laoise. "Sinéad—"

"Well?" She glared and glared. "Am I good for anything? Or am I just the weak human girl who tires fastest and eats the most and doesn't know how to fight and—"

"Stop." Laoise reached out and covered Sinéad's mouth with her hand. It was a crude gesture, but effective—Sinéad abruptly shut up. "You know I do not believe you weak. I certainly do not think you are useless. But you are human. And you have spent nearly a month traveling over rough country without adequate clothing or food. Frankly, it is a wonder you are still alive. I will not risk your health for a reconnaissance mission I can perform in my sleep."

Abruptly, tears welled in Sinéad's eyes. She tore away from Laoise, hiding her face as she threw open the sink's taps and scrubbed the cut on her arm with soap and water.

That had been the wrong thing to say. Apparently.

"I would take you with me if I could, Sinéad. But I plan to fly hard and fast. Once I find Eala, I will observe her movements, count her troops, then ideally return without incident. You will miss nothing but another unpleasant journey. I promise."

Sinéad dried the now-abraded cut, then briskly wrapped it with the bloody rag. She fumbled with the ends of the bandage; Laoise pushed her trembling fingers away and tied it for her. Sinéad leaned back against the sink and finally said, "I need to see her. With my own eyes."

"See...? Ah." Sinéad had been distraught when she learned Eala's new Treasure had somehow kept her alive. Laoise had assumed she was simply disheartened by her failure to destroy the wicked princess. But she was forever underestimating how deeply humans could grieve things beyond their meager control. "The Twilight Sisters have confirmed it. She lives."

"But I killed her."

"No," Laoise said in confusion. "You did not."

"I tried. I wanted to. When I plunged those daggers into her chest, I meant it. I wanted her dead more than anything I've wanted in my life." Sinéad passed a bloody hand over her forehead. "Now when I sleep, all I see is *her*. Her blood, arcing over my hands. The surprise on her face, as if until the end she didn't believe I had it in me. The life fading from her eyes."

Laoise listened. She had killed before, and only one of those deaths was something she regretted. Death was a shadow that waited for everyone. No matter how far you ran or how brightly you burned, it came for everyone in time, slipping silently from the dark to claim what was owed. Sinéad's had been a righteous kill; Eala's death, deserved. In Laoise's mind, the only shame was that it hadn't stuck. She could not fathom Sinéad's penitence.

"Don't you see?" Sinéad continued. "In the end, I am no better than her. Than either of them. Eala, who ripped her maidens' hearts out for power. And Chandi. Who—"

Sinéad's voice broke off. And Laoise thought, *There it is at last*.

"Who betrayed you?"

"She betrayed herself. She betrayed her values for an easy solution. She betrayed the truth for a deception—she lost the difference between right and wrong. By killing Eala, I fear I am no better than either of them." Sinéad's fingers curled into tight little fists. "I need to see her. I need to see *them*. I need to see that I am on the right side of this—that they are worse than me. Or rather, that I can be better than *them*."

"Hush." Laoise caught Sinéad's hands, uncurling her fists. "You are nothing like either of them. You saw a chance to end something before it started—you trusted your instincts and fought like a warrior. You have nothing to be ashamed of."

"Except my own frail, human body," Sinéad said with bitterness. "Otherwise you would let me join you."

Laoise relented. Perhaps she was growing soft in her old age. Or perhaps she could not stomach that Sinéad felt so far removed from her own potential because of the way she was made. Iron could hit just as hard as steel; quartz could shine just as brightly as diamond. Strength was forged in the soul, not the body.

"By all accounts Eala's army moves slowly and stops often," Laoise allowed. "Perhaps there is no harm in waiting a week. Two at *most*. You will eat regularly and sleep often. You will regain your strength. If you are fit enough by then, you may join me. But if you are not, you must promise to stay."

"Thank you." Sinéad flung herself at Laoise without warning, throttling her in an embrace. The cut on her wrist broke open, smearing warm blood on Laoise's neck. She was too thin—her ribs pressed into Laoise's torso. Faint human smells Laoise wasn't sure she'd ever grow accustomed to wafted from her hair. "You won't regret it."

"Eat." Laoise laughed a little as she returned the other woman's embrace. "Sleep. And for gods' sake, take a bath."

Chapter Twelve

Wayland

Wayland, Idris, Irian, Balor, and the aughiskies all watched as Laoise strode off to coddle Sinéad, who appeared to be having a tantrum. Linn—who had been deceptively silent lately—sent a blistering vision of Laoise chopping the other girl into bloody pieces with her knives, then serving her up in a delicious-looking stew.

"Ugh!" Idris exclaimed in shock. Clearly he was not accustomed to aughisky humor. "Not in my house!"

"Well." Wayland braced his forearms on the table. "I suppose that concludes our war council."

"Not quite," Irian growled. "There is a matter I would have discussed with Laoise here. But I suppose it mostly concerns you."

"Indeed? I'm flattered."

Irian didn't take the bait. In his lap, Fia moaned, her chapped lips pulling into an O of distress. Feathers rippled suddenly from the crown of her head and ruffled around her throat. Irian's hand curved protectively around her torso; Fia's form responded unconsciously to the touch, her spine undulating as sharp black vanes burst from her skin.

Irian made a noise deep in his throat as his silvering gaze met Wayland's, who had instinctively risen to help, disturbing a disgruntled Hog in the process. He scooped Fia into his arms and rose to his feet in one smooth, contained motion. Irian's sinewed arms barely flexed as his wife began to transform into a black swan, her neck lengthening as dark feathers swept around her body. Wayland expected they would not likely see either him or Fia again until morning. Instead, Irian startled him by striding directly for Balor and stopping a pace in front of the giant. He lifted Fia in surprising supplication.

"Balor, my friend," Irian said. "Would you mind?"

Astonishment mirroring Wayland's own skated across Balor's face. But the giant did not hesitate before his huge hands closed tenderly around the half swan, half woman. A soft smile puckered his broad, jocular face.

"Of course, lord!" Gods alive, but he had *so many* teeth. "I love birds!"

Irian's hands clenched at his sides until Fia was safely nestled against the Fomorian's bulk. He returned to the table, though he did not deign to sit. He loomed in apparent hesitation.

"Speak it, Brother," Wayland urged, abandoning his teasing. "There are no wrong ideas."

"I do not hesitate because I think the idea is wrong. I hesitate because I do not wish you—any of you—to have to do what needs to be done." Irian exhaled and passed a hand over his eyes, roughly brushing away black hair that needed cutting. When he spoke, the words seemed to scald him. "To defeat Eala and restore balance to Tír na nÓg, we will need to reforge the lost Treasures of the Septs." His eyes landed on Wayland, his expression taut with hope, but also immeasurable regret. "*You* are going to have to reforge the Treasures. And become an heir."

For a few long, painful moments, the underground chamber rang with silence. Then Wayland burst out laughing, his incredulous mirth too loud and too raucous in the heavy hush.

He couldn't help it. He had been there that night in Gavida's throne room when Irian had petitioned the smith-king to *unforge* his and Fia's Treasures, and had witnessed Fia's face transform with shock and fury before hardening toward determination.

He jests, Majesty, the strident slip of a woman had pronounced, standing proud and persistent before one of the most fickle and powerful rulers in Tír na nÓg. *Such a natural comedian. Or perhaps madness has struck him.*

In truth, Wayland had thought them both mad. He had never envied his foster brother's fate—life, difficult as it sometimes was, was far better lived than lost. And the Treasures, no matter how powerful, all came with an expiration date. Wayland blamed his father for many things. Shielding his only son from such a fate was not one of them. It had earned Wayland a hazy kind of reprieve he wasn't always sure how to fathom.

But Irian, of all men, ought to have learned not to rail against a destiny carved from the motion of the stars, the movement of the winds, the tilting of the earth.

Fia, of all women, ought to know that powerful magic always came with a cost.

Wayland had seen how the disagreement had nearly torn their marriage asunder. Had watched their quarrel with growing interest from an uneasy distance.

Fia and Irian had mended the jagged rift at the heart of their relationship. Wayland could only begin to guess how they had salved the wound—based on his limited experience of healthy adult relationships, he imagined it had something to do with wholesome communication and robust compromise. Possibly a great deal of makeup sex. But he'd doubted either person's essential position regarding the Treasures had changed.

So for Irian to be standing in front of him, announcing that Wayland must reforge the destroyed Treasures *and* sacrifice his own near-immortal life to inherit one, was...hilarious.

Irian of the Sept of Feathers did not change his mind. Ever.

Except, Wayland supposed, where the love of his life was concerned.

"What," Irian now said, his unforgiving tone slicing through Wayland's continued gales of laughter, "is so fucking funny?"

Wayland forced away his mirth, wiped at his eyes. The rest of the group—sans Laoise and Sinéad—were staring at him with mystification. Balor was chuckling along in a companionable way; Hog was rolling on the floor, giving tiny draigling yips; Idris was watching him closely beneath the fall of his hair.

That, more than anything, pulled Wayland from his hysterics.

"You're joking," he managed at last. "Tell me you're joking."

"Eala wields a Treasure now, her magic vast and frankly terrifying." Irian's head tilted to one side, the glint in his eyes a challenge. It sobered Wayland—he wasn't sure he had ever heard Irian openly admit to being afraid. "With Fia in her current state, I stand the only power to equal hers. We must find a way to even those odds. Or better yet, stack them in our favor. Among us we have two potential heirs. Out there are two warped Treasures that could be resurrected in the same way Fia resurrected the Heart."

"*How?*" The muscles in Wayland's arms bunched; Hog let out a faint whine of distress. Idris once more shifted beside him, his presence silent but supportive.

"You are the smith-king's son, are you not?" It sounded like an accusation. "Heir to his powers? You removed Fia's collar on the beach."

"I inherited my father's affinity for forging magical objects, yes," Wayland replied, a strain in his voice. "But I was collared for over a decade. My father had no interest in schooling me in his ways—the opposite, in fact. He was intensely secretive about his work. Even if he *had* left me instructions, there is no guarantee I could forge new Treasures. Their like has never been created, not before and certainly not since."

"But surely you could figure out how," Irian said intently. "If you had to."

The phrasing sent a shock of familiarity pulsing through Wayland's veins, dragging him abruptly back to the night he and Fia had discovered the Year, in her mountain tomb. The two of them had sat together on the rocky beach after Fia nearly drowned in the underwater caverns—she shivering from shock and cold, he trying not to relish in the physical closeness her mortal danger had afforded him.

Could it be done again? She had asked him the same thing, in almost the same way, there in the darkness. *Could* you *do it? If you had to?*

"Could I teach myself how to forge resonant objects capable of carrying within them the vast elemental magic of bound deities?" Wayland said, a little helplessly. "Perhaps, with enough time and research and experimentation. But what of the corrupted wild magic? What of the heirs—what of Laoise and me? How are we to renew magic that has been warped? To inherit objects that have been destroyed?"

"Fia did it," Irian said, blunt.

"And I've never met anyone else like Fia." Instantly, he regretted the phrasing—Irian's eyes scathed his own, raw and resentful, and Wayland felt suddenly claustrophobic in his own facile manner. He had woven his philandering reputation so seamlessly that it now clung to him like a second skin. Did he ask too much for his oldest friend—his *foster brother*—to see more to him than that? Could Irian truly not understand that Wayland was drawn to Fia not just by attraction, but by genuine care? That he was capable of an emotion more complex than lust? "I only mean that she is... extraordinary. She is not fully Folk; she is far more than human. In the caverns below Aduantas, Talah called her *star touched*. I don't know exactly what she meant by that, but it aligned with all my father feared about Fia. That her presence changed the patterns of the stars, that she carried within her the capacity to bend destiny to her will."

"How do you know *you* are not star touched?" Idris softly asked from beside him.

Wayland laughed. "I've been touched plenty, Red, and enjoyed every moment of it. But I think I'd remember if a star had done any of the touching."

Idris hid behind his veil of hair.

"So you will not do it?" Irian asked, with an air of menace that made Wayland think if he said no, he might soon be experiencing the edge of the Sky-Sword at his throat.

"I did not say that." Wayland lifted his palms. "I am willing. I may even be able. But if this is our chosen way forward—forging new Treasures and binding the wild magic let loose over Murias and Findias—I fear I simply do not know where to begin."

For a few moments, the only sounds were the crackling of the hearth and the faint anguished growl of the large Fia-wolf Balor was rocking in his arms like a baby.

"Time, research, and experimentation," Idris said slowly. They were Wayland's own words from moments ago, repeated back at him. "You have time—at least until Laoise scouts your princess and ascertains her movements. Perhaps not months, but weeks at least. As for research, we have a fairly impressive library, full of the materials Laoise and I have collected over the past thirteen years. We sought information only about the nemeta, but the books and scrolls are rife with uncanny spells and fell magic. Perhaps there is something of forging in them."

Wayland lifted an eyebrow. "Please tell me you're also open to experimentation."

Idris smiled, a broad, fetchingly dimpled confection. "Well... we do have draigs."

"For?"

"Your new forge, of course."

Chapter Thirteen

Within

The forest grew deeper, dusky with the colossal shadows of ancient trees. The silence was profound, heavy with millennia of unsung songs and carefully kept secrets. My breath fogged as I exhaled, although the air kissing my arms no longer felt cold.

"What is this place?" My words jangled through the air, a profanity in this undeniably sacred space. The wood stilled even further, rebuking me with faint attention.

Do you not remember? Ínne seemed so perfectly at ease here, I half expected them to have grown roots.

"I've never been here before." I would have remembered this wonder and awe leafing through my chest. I would have remembered these widely spaced trunks, this canopy dense as a night sky. If this was a memory, it wasn't mine. "Perhaps, for once, we could do away with the riddles."

As you wish. Ínne stepped through the gloaming toward the nearest vast tree. *What do you see?*

The gnarled trunk and lofting branches spoke to the tree's age; its serrated leaves and draped yellow catkins told me it was some form of hazel. My eyes followed the undulations of growth, the whorls and burls and faces—

Shock pumped ice water through my veins. It *was* a face—a woman's, Folk Gentry, embedded in the trunk a few inches above my eye level. No, not embedded—for she was *made* of wood, though I could not guess whether the tree had grown around her or she had somehow *become* the tree. I stepped closer as my fear subsided, and saw the subtle outline of the rest of her form, merged effortlessly with the tree's bark.

She was…arresting. Her figure seemed poised in motion—one pointed foot stepping off the ground while her other knee bent. Her torso twisted as she reached, reached, a subtle flow of fabric falling over her generous breasts. And her *face*. She gazed outward as if bewitched by some sight or sound I could neither see nor hear. A glimmer of emerald flashed from the center of her breastbone.

"Who is she?" I could not take my eyes away from her exquisite face.

Her name was Eibhlín, said the figure, with tenderness. *She was the first.*

I searched for meaning in the Bright One's shrouded expression. "The first *what?*"

The first heir to the Treasure of the Sept of Antlers. They lifted a hand, clawed and furred, and gestured expansively toward the forest spilling out around us. *This is your birthright, child. Your legacy. And your last resting place.*

A chill ghosted over my skin, raising a shiver in its wake. I glanced again at the frozen maiden, then peered deeper between the trees. Now that I knew what to look for, my eyes snagged on the suggestions of more figures entombed in the trees. An outstretched arm. A reaching hand. An upturned face. My unease intensified, pebbling my arms with gooseflesh as I began to understand.

This was no mere forest. It was a mausoleum. A necropolis of trees.

Every trunk a gravestone, every sighing breeze an epitaph.

Although they had to die for the magic of our Treasure to be renewed, their memories live on. Emotion, deep and heart-wrenching, threaded Ínne's voice. *Here. Forever.*

"But...where *are* we?" I had forgotten Talah for long moments, but now the thought of her encroached. I imagined her molten metal and scarlet flames wreaking havoc upon the sacred stillness of this grove. The thought turned my stomach. "Is this inside my memories? Or yours? Or—"

You. And they. And it—the Bright One reached out and tapped the Heart of the Forest; the stone flashed emerald in the dim, belling a note like homecoming—*are we. Something borrowed. Something shared. Something taken. Something taught.*

I frowned—the words echoed through me with a formless familiarity I could not name. I struggled to make sense of them.

"You're saying this place exists both inside and outside of me?" I wrapped my palm around the Heart, as much for comfort as for understanding. "But only because I inherited this Treasure?"

I took the neutral weight of their silence as assent.

"Show me, then." If Talah had not found me here yet, then I did not mind lingering. I was curious about all these fallen heirs—had been curious about them from the moment I had learned of the Treasures. From the moment I had learned who I truly was. "If the memories of these past heirs are a part of me—if they live on inside me—then I want to know their stories. I want to know them. I want to know *you.*"

The Bright One's regard was infinite, compelling. Somehow both seeing...and seen.

When the first chieftains ordered the Treasures forged, Eibhlín volunteered to carry the weight of this immense burden, to shoulder the responsibility of such power. She was brave and honorable and kind. She went to the first tithe in ecstasy and gratitude. We loved her. As she loved us.

For the length of a heartbeat, Eibhlín seemed to move within the tree, like a child stirring in sleep. The Bright One paced onward, ducking beneath the low-sloping branches of a huge oak with gemstone leaves and pale gray bark. The figure interred in this tree was male, with a handsome, brazen face and a stark, muscular figure.

Cuan. Our little wolf. Affection blossomed in Ínne's psychic voice. *He, too, volunteered. In the beginning, all Folk were potential heirs for the Treasures. Magic was so plentiful then. We were as legion as the forest. As endless as the plains. As strong as the ancient oaks.*

I stared at the face of a man who had died for magic nearly a millennium ago yet who somehow lived on in me. Or...through me? I wasn't sure I understood. "What happened?"

We began to weaken. Sorrow touched the Bright One's voice. *All four of us who bound ourselves to Treasures began to weaken. We thought channeling our wild magic through conduits into Folk vessels would protect it from the voracious greed of the humans who sought to bleed our resources dry. But we should never have agreed to bind ourselves to the Treasures. The cycle was not robust enough. The balance, uneven.*

I knew parts of this story. But this was my first time hearing it from a source.

The Bright One moved on, weaving between thick trunks. There were more figures growing from the wood, more faces blindly watching us pass. Ínne paused beside each; sometimes, the compassionate touch of their clawed hand seemed to shift the expressions of the old heirs. Unclenching a frown long held, turning a smile more serene.

Clodagh. They spoke the names of the long dead with reverence. *Aodh. Bradan.*

They stopped at last before a tall, weighty sycamore swaying in an invisible breeze. The woman entombed in the tree looked older, with graceful lines bracketing her smile and endless, unseeing eyes.

It soon became clear the magic flowing to and from the heirs was not as strong as it once had been. The number of those fit to inherit the Treasures dwindled. We all knew something was wrong. The Bright One touched the woman's hand. *Her name was Líadan. Through her, we begged to be set free of our prison. We had been enslaved once before, an age ago; we never thought those who had set us free once would themselves, in turn, keep us enslaved. The Folk said they did not know how to free us, and perhaps that was true. But they never sought to learn.*

A terrible pity rose in me at the Bright One's words, and I abruptly remembered what Gavida had said to me after Rogan and Irian battled in the arena: *I know not how to unforge the Treasures. I am not even sure it can be done. Not the right way—not without warping the source by destroying the conduit or the vessel.*

But the truth was, the Bright One continued, moving slowly onward through the stillness of the grove, *the power of the Treasures was too great for the Septs to relinquish. Even as it slowly diminished, they clung to it all the harder. Year after year. Tithe after tithe. Heir after heir. In time, they retreated to their strongholds lest anyone steal from them what they claimed as birthright. Until the dynasties they guarded so jealously were themselves felled.*

I knew the rest of this story. Heirs like Irian and Deirdre were hidden away by their Septs as the magic of the Treasures found fewer and fewer potential vessels. Dissident Gentry began to grumble about the balance of power wielded by the Septs. In the human realms, a high king and his queen began to wonder whether the Folk's precious Treasures might be the answer to the wars, plagues, and famines tarnishing their lands. It was where my own story began.

The Bright One paused beside one last tree, a mighty yew with swirling gray bark that looked purple in the dim. I glanced at the figure sepulchred in the trunk, only to startle away. I stumbled over a root, nearly falling. Shock brambled fear against the inside of my skin. I squinted at the figure in the tree—a young woman with waving dark hair and slender limbs, her eyes gazing upward and her palms lifted toward the sky as if in supplication.

A young woman who looked exactly like *me*.

"But she's—" I swallowed, hard, and wrapped my hands around my arms as if to ensure I was truly standing here. Warm and breathing and *alive*. I remembered a frigid night a year ago, when I'd stood dripping and bleeding on a beach and a tall Gentry heir had looked at my face and said, *It's you*. I glanced sharply at the Bright One. "Is this Deirdre? Is this woman my mother?"

No. The Bright One, boundless and benign, placed their clawed paw upon the neighboring tree, a pale-boughed ash with an unblemished trunk. *Deirdre lives*.

The revelation ricocheted through my chest like a rogue arrow glancing between shadowed trees. Irian had shared that same belief when he'd revealed his suspicions about my parentage. I'd rebuffed the notion, saying, *People do not return from the dead. Tragedies do not have silver linings*. But part of me had hoped. Of course I had. What child growing up without a mother does not secretly yearn for one, even when they have outgrown tall tales?

"How?" I demanded, longing and bitterness tangling inside me. "And if this woman trapped in the tree is not Deirdre, then who is she?"

Do you not know, child? Their voice held both warmth and sorrow. *Do you not remember?*

My memories of the night of the Ember Moon, when I'd tithed myself beneath the Heartwood, slid over me. I had chosen myself, accepted my birthright, and promised my heart to the Bright One before me. Then I had flung myself into their embrace, in ecstasy and ascendancy. I had fallen through an endless sky, unmade and remade in the same breath. My roots and branches had both scraped the stars.

"Then..." I had not wanted to accept it. "Then I truly died, beneath the Heartwood."

You did.

"How am I standing here?" The question was plaintive, and I grappled with a sharp thorn of regret for all that had passed. All who had truly lost their lives. All who had not had the privilege of resurrection. "How did I come back to life?"

Circles. Cycles. Balance in all things, my child. The Bright One reached out and, with its thick, sharp claw, again drew a circle above my left breast, where my heart solemnly throbbed. Dark green blood once more welled; again I felt no pain. The Heart of the Forest glowed. *We are all connected. We are all the same. We are all different. When we die, we return to the place we were born. Every ending is its own beginning. Time comes and time goes. Hearts break and hearts heal. Balance is not voluntary. It is essential. And endless.*

As they spoke, the forest faded—the smaller, featureless trees melting away as if in a dense mist, leaving behind only the majestic trees marked by the figures of the long-dead heirs. The trees made a circle a hundred trunks strong, each with a silent face staring inward. The look of arrested wonder I had seen on Eibhlín's face echoed across every expression. I turned to see for myself what they gazed at, in their final rest.

At the center of the grove was a vast tree. I had thought the Heart-wood colossal. It was but a sapling compared to this eldertree—little more than a shadow cast upon the ground from a far greater essence. I fought to comprehend the immensity of its breadth, the profundity of its existence. I could *hear* it, a soundless singing like stars screaming through vast empty spaces. Its trunk—a monolith of ancient knotted wood—swirled with intricate patterns tessellating in a million fractal forms. Its branches soared endlessly high before curving back down around us, jeweled with multicolored leaves. Its roots drove impossibly deep, thrusting not through dirt and loam and clay and stone, but through the very fabric of reality—twining through the memories of long-dead kings and the dreams of sleeping children and the hopes of pregnant mothers. When the roots entwined with the stretching branches, they wove the warp and weft of...*everything.* A hundred million stories, spoken in husky voices over crackling campfires and carved in ocher clay upon dark cavern walls and etched in ink upon parchment and thrilling to life inside hopeless, hopeful hearts.

One story. One vast, expansive, enduring story.

I swayed toward that unknowable tree, hardly noticing the cool tears on my cheeks or the trembling of my limbs or the song of wonder spilling unbidden from my throat.

Ínne caught me with a hand upon my shoulder. Drew me gently away. Embraced me when I struggled.

Not yet, my child, they murmured softly in my ear. *Your part in the story is not yet finished. There is more you must do before your saga can be etched upon these boughs. Battles you must win before your ending is whispered between these leaves.*

It broke my heart to turn away from the godhead at the center of everything. Yet the moment I faced away, the tree of life slid gently from my mind's eye, until it was little more than a distant, perfect promise. I knew I would return here, in time.

We all would.

I turned my tearstained face to the tree that bore my likeness, some small part of me trapped even now in this necropolis of trees.

"Would we go free?" I asked Ínne, haltingly. "Would all the heirs be freed to their true rest if the Treasures were unmade?"

Yes.

A thread of light stitched over her breastbone, sliced the center of her stomach, and split her down the middle. The tree—my tree—yawned open. Beyond, in dense, dusky shadows, a doe stood in the undergrowth, so motionless she might have been a statue. Her dark, depthless eyes seemed to swallow me.

All my strange dreams from the past few months rippled hazily through my mind, mingling with everything I knew or suspected about my mother. Dread and hope beat twin pulses between my temples.

The deer flicked her tail, white in the dim. Then turned on her delicate limbs and bounded away into the evening shadows.

Go, said the Bright One when I hesitated. *There is one place still for you to visit. Your future will wait for your past. Unless you do not wish to know it fully.*

For as long as I could remember, I had wanted nothing more. Yet now, confronted with the deep forest of my mind, I was afraid. I had already seen so much. *Felt* so much. Could I bear to do this?

Could I bear not to?

Chapter Fourteen

Wayland

The Cnoc's library—and Wayland felt exceptionally generous dubbing it that—was not huge. It covered one wall of the medium-sized cavern Idris led him to. But a mere glance told Wayland all he needed to know about how precious these books, scrolls, parchments, and tablets were to Laoise and Idris.

He had heard it said dragain hoarded treasure. Treasure, he supposed, was not always gold and jewels. It could as easily be knowledge. Stories. *Books.*

He could not relate. Wayland hated reading. He could hardly remember a time in his life when he didn't loathe the sight of a book. In his admittedly limited experience—since he had avoided the damned things since childhood—books were designed to convey one of two things: truth or escape. But he had long since found truth was best discovered at the bottom of a wine bottle, and *escape* was just another word for *falsehood*. Wayland was too accustomed to living a lie to relish in the prospect of reading one.

His mother had adored reading. In one of his few distinct memories of her, she was clad in her coziest nightgown, practically hidden beneath mounds of blankets, curled around a book, utterly absorbed by its contents. He had climbed beside her and snuggled in close, reveling in the warmth of her frame, the heavy sweep of her long brown hair, the press of her lips on his forehead.

But when he looked at the book in her hands, it had been... words. He had not taken to his letters yet, much to his tutors' constant scolding, and this book had no pictures.

"What are you reading, Mama?" he had asked her.

"A story, rónán beag." *Littlest seal*, she had always called him. Her voice had been like sea silk.

"Will you tell it to me?"

She had laughed, a secret kind of chuckle. "No, rónán beag. This story is only for grown-ups. But when I'm done with this chapter, I promise to read you one of your picture books."

He supposed, if he was being brutally honest with himself, that was where the trouble began.

The Cnoc's collection, although not plentiful, seemed exquisitely curated—sorted and ordered using a system Wayland could not fathom. Fat jewel-spined tomes sat beside crumbling stone tablets; carven blocks etched with foreign symbols propped up shredded volumes of vellum and tar. It was not the grandiose splendor of the archives at Aduantas; it was not even the uncontrolled chaos of Master Blink's bookstore, where Wayland had ventured once in his youth, in pursuit of a rare collection of enchanted pornography.

"This looks...complicated." Wayland folded his arms over his chest as Idris moved around the room lighting torches and candles to supplement the faint glow from the minerals. The light turned the young man's red hair molten and made his brown skin soft as gold. Hog wobbled up to flop onto the mantel above the hearth, stretching her frame along the warmed stone. "Am I to be favored with a tour?"

"I'm afraid it won't be much of a tour." Idris laughed low. "And I don't see it as much of a favor."

Wayland quirked an eyebrow. "Why do you say that?"

"Because I can already tell you see research as punishment."

"Gods alive." Wayland sent his eyes to the ceiling and sighed theatrically. "Why do the pretty boys always assume I'm illiterate?"

Idris flushed, hot and fast, his cheeks going visibly—and fetchingly—pink. "I don't think you're illiterate! There are simply some for whom scholarly pursuits come easily."

"And some for whom they do not." Wayland hid a smile as he stepped next to Idris, in front of the bookshelves. "You have me correct on all counts but one."

"Oh?" Idris had conquered his blush. "What, pray tell, is that?"

"That I don't enjoy being punished." Wayland grinned, broad and blinding—a smile that had felled many a lesser adversary. "It all depends on who's bending me over their knee."

This time, Idris's flush was a conflagration, and Wayland felt an answering surge of warmth course his spine to settle below his belt. It was too easy. If Idris responded like this to mere words, imagine how he would respond to Wayland's touch. His kiss. His—

Wayland mastered himself, roughly. Had he learned nothing in this past month of forced marching and dreadfully sober self-reflection? Just because he could didn't mean he should.

Even if it would be so, *so* much fun.

"Can I ask you a serious question?" Wayland asked, taking pity on Idris.

Idris turned his attention to the books, pulling a few from the shelves. "As long as it's serious."

"Why have you and Laoise stayed here all these years? Surely you could have settled somewhere less..."

"Isolated? Lonely?" Idris finished for him. His expression hid behind the screen of his hair. "The bardaí slaughtered our parents—would have killed us, too, if they knew we survived. We thought for a time to return to Annwyn, whence my mother hailed—she was a princess among the Ellyllon. Had she not defied her family's wishes and married into the Sept of Scales, we would have been raised there as hereditary royalty. But then the draigs came along."

Wayland waited for him to elaborate. "I don't understand."

"Long ago, in the times of legends, draigs were an irreplaceable resource to the Ellyllon. Valuable beyond gold or jewels or even magic." The words seemed to pain Idris. "They were trained in combat and ridden into war; their shed scales were harvested and forged into armor; their eggs, passed down through generations as treasure until everyone forgot what they really were. A family in possession of a draig was guaranteed political and social ascendancy. Laoise and I came to realize that the repatriation of Ceridwen's wayward children in Annwyn... would likely come at the cost of our draigs."

Hog rolled over on the mantel, letting out a faint, steamy huff accompanied by a shower of golden sparks.

"We may someday still try our luck with our mother's people, when the draigs are grown," Idris murmured. "When this nemeton dies and the veins of minerals lose their magic, the draiglings' sustenance will be gone. They must go *somewhere*. Once their existence is known, they will be coveted by whoever encounters them. At least in Annwyn, they will be protected. Cherished. Laoise and I might have a say in where they go, how they are treated, and who has access to them."

"But they would not be free."

"No." Idris's voice was nearly inaudible. "I've read the old tales, seen the old engravings. The Ellyllon will saddle them, chain them, collar them."

Reflexively, Wayland's hand floated toward his neck. Idris's eyes tracked the motion; Wayland tried to make the gesture careless, brushing his length of mahogany hair over one shoulder.

"I've distracted you." Wayland cleared his throat, tried on a smile. "You were about to be my tour guide."

"Yes—of course." Idris looked relieved by the change of topic. "The books. Over here is Laoise's collection of histories. There's *Whispers of the Forgotten Courts*—that's mostly a genealogy of the Ellyllon royal bloodlines. That stack of bark cloth there is, of course, the *Redbark Histories*, although I think those were written before the Treasures were forged. The big jeweled volume there is *The Shattered Throne: Saga of the Winter Kings*, and— Oh!" Idris struggled with a heavy lock binding the pages together. "There's an exceptional chapter about Gavida in here—although technically he is not considered a winter king, some scholars argue—"

But with his mind already fettered by thoughts of collars, the unexpected name of Wayland's father spoken in Idris's lilting voice roared up and dragged him down. He wrapped his palm around his throat, as if the memories themselves could strangle.

On the Longest Night, Wayland had hunted his father with the intent to kill him. The island he had so rarely departed roiled beneath him in its death throes, wrenching and throbbing and howling, but his steps had never been so sure. He had not seen where his father had fled in the aftermath of Eala's unholy coronation, but he knew.

Aduantas was a nightmare made real. The citadel was imploding, sheets of pale stone smashing to shards from the high, curved ceilings; seashell candelabras and nacre chandeliers shattering to crunch beneath Wayland's boots. The veins of silver and gold the Year had named *her metal* were melting, dripping from the walls and forming molten rivers on the floor. Great rifts opened in the sheeny polish of the flagstones, burping more slag from the deeps. Fear sent an unsteady ripple through the bloodthirsty roil of Wayland's veins, but he pushed onward, sidestepping crumbling statuettes and fissuring marble.

Gavida's forge was nearly unrecognizable. Dense white vapor plumed the throne room, stinking of sulfur. The ceiling had been damaged—howling winds whistled in and out, swirling the smoke into phantasms. The far wall was blank—the smith-king's crucible had been moved to the Grove of Gold for the Longest Night. And—as the mist swirled away, then back—Wayland saw his father's commanding throne of rough-hewn stone had split in two, one half crumbled on the floor.

Wayland had almost laughed. It was too on the nose, even for him.

Then he'd glimpsed his father amid the gusting white. Gavida had a thousand moods, each more fickle than the last. He could be wrathful one moment, riotous the next. Cruel, compassionate, composed. But Wayland wasn't sure he'd ever witnessed Gavida's current unhinged chaos. The smith-king circled the room like a captive wild animal, clawing at the walls. Ripping priceless fine tapestries, knocking magical artifacts from their plinths, thrusting whole stacks of books from their shelves. There was a knapsack laid open at his feet, but Gavida wasn't packing anything in it. He seemed to be *searching*. But for what?

A few of the king's blank-eyed battle puppets stood guard over their creator; at Wayland's approach they lowered their helmed heads and charged. Gavida turned at the sound of their footfalls, flicked his meaty hands with choleric impatience. The puppets did not just stop—they collapsed, tumbling bodily to the floor before exploding into their component parts. Metal armor and rivets and wires jangled away across the slick floor, joining the cacophony of groaning stone and screaming winds.

Gavida took one look at Wayland, lowered his grizzled head, bunched the muscles of his shoulders, and charged him like a bull. Wayland drew the sword at his waist in one smooth, sweeping motion—although the blade was ceremonial, it was finely forged and sharply honed and, Wayland reckoned, long overdue for its first kill. The smith-king shuddered to a stop beyond the reach of its gleaming tip. He stared at the claíomh, breathing hard, before looking up at his son. His deep blue eyes—so like Wayland's own—were lit with a terrible, furious, vengeful light. The smile creasing his weathered face was downright psychotic.

"So, my son—it has come to this." His words were hammers, heavy and blunt. "The Oak King and the Holly King, in truth. One must fall for the other to rise."

"This is not your grand pageant, old man," Wayland spat,

forcefully. He was horrified to realize both his voice and his hands were shaking. He clenched the hilt of his ceremonial blade until the carven metal was imprinted onto his palm. "This is your heir, finally in a position to demand what ought to have been given to him years ago."

Gavida barked a brusque laugh. "What's that?"

"My freedom. My destiny."

"The damned *pattern*." Gavida shook his grizzled head, then flung himself back toward the walls, continuing his dismantlement of the space that had once been his sanctum. "Marban said this would happen. He said the balancing would find me, in the end. He warned me that the cost would be high—too high to pay. But that blasted fool never knew—well, I never told him—"

Wayland watched as his father careened from one wall to the next, his ramblings becoming more and more disjointed. A treacherous finger of pity stroked the rigid spikes of Wayland's vengeance until it began, horribly, to wane. The tip of his sword came to rest on the shaking floor.

Gavida had lived over a thousand years. Wayland had never once, until today, thought of his father as old.

"This is all her fault!" Gavida's huge, meaty fists splintered a graceful credenza with the force of his destructive rage. "I never should have allowed her to come."

"She manipulated us all, Father." Abruptly, the ground beneath them lurched several inches to the right. Both men stumbled, fought for their footing. "But *you* never should have forged her a Treasure."

"Not the human princess, you fool!" Gavida staggered to face him, his face like a rictus of death. "That changeling bitch ruined everything! I tried to control her, but she just had to shove her starry little fingers into the warp and weft of the pattern and *pull*. And now everything is ruined—ruined!"

Just as abruptly as he had raged, Gavida groaned and sank to his knees on the rocking flagstones. Mortar fell like rain around his head, coating his hair in white dust. Another section of the ceiling sheared away, swirling the seething vapor. When the king looked at Wayland again, he appeared composed, his deep blue eyes serene as a summer sea.

"I have always known I would not die an old man in my bed, my dear Way."

For a moment, Wayland saw him only as the beloved father who had dandled him upon his knee as a little boy, delighted by his son's cleverness and wit. The beloved father who had sung him endless lullabies in his awkward baritone after Wayland's mother had abandoned them both. *Rest now, my Way, where the black waters creep. The sea knows your name, and she calls you to sleep.*

"There are but two honorable ways for a man to die: in battle, or by his own hand. I fear, even amid all this destruction, that I have not the fortitude for the latter." Gavida gestured toward his ruined throne. "So give me my hammer and my steel, Son. Then send me on my final journey. I know you want to."

For a brief, ungenerous moment, Wayland wanted to do nothing of the sort. If his father wanted a clean death, then let him do it himself. Better yet, let him go down with his precious island—let all the terrible architecture of his power be the thing to destroy him. Let this crumbling white stone crack his skull, let this sharp-edged palace grind his bones to dust, let this devouring magic drown him forever.

"I will grant your last wish, Father," he ground out. "In return for mine. Remove my collar, and you shall have your death."

"But why, my son?" Something sharpened in Gavida's eyes. "We both die here today. Or did you think you had time to enact vengeance on your father *and* escape this island before it falls into the sea?"

The words sent an icy wave of realization crashing over Wayland. An hour, Irian had said. How long had it been? The time seemed to yawn behind him, a curse not yet fulfilled. He would never make it. He had doomed himself. And for what?

"Set me free," he said, more forcefully. "Let me go as myself. Then you may die a penitent father, and I may die a free man."

Gavida hesitated, then lifted his hands to Wayland's face, cupping his son's cheeks with surprising gentleness. His calloused palms were rough on Wayland's skin. He stared deep into his eyes, searching for something. What, Wayland did not know—as much a mystery as what he had been ransacking his throne room for.

"I know you hate me for what I have done," Gavida murmured. "But perhaps someday, when you have a son of your own, you will come to understand. Destiny is a bastard who longs to kick you in the balls. But if you really want that pain, then you shall have it."

His huge hands dropped to Wayland's throat, clasping around the heavy, carven metal stretching from his collarbones to his jaw. Veins of silver light flared around the metal before twining Wayland's face and tangling in his hair. Pain screamed down his back and up into his skull, whiting his vision and rattling his teeth. He was flayed alive—every inch of Wayland's skin sliced away, torn bodily from tendon and bone, exposing all the blemished meat of him. The charming, choking revulsion of him. The laughing, lacking wretchedness of him.

The collar crumbled away in his father's hands, silver as sand in the moonlight. Father and son stared at each other. High above, another piece of ceiling screeched and slid. Far below, the island bellowed a warning. Gavida reached for his tools, hefted them in his beefy arms.

Wayland grasped the Holly King's ceremonial blade, flipped his grip on the hilt, and drove the steel between his father's ribs.

The old man collapsed against him, and Wayland caught him in his arms. Hot, dark blood jetted out over his hands and his tunic as he lowered them both to the pale tiles. He smoothed his father's wild hair from his face as his eyes went wide, then far away, then gray, gray, gray. Below the tumultuous anguish of the Silver Isle tearing itself apart, Wayland sang, brokenly, "Rest now, old man, where the black waters creep. The sea knows your name, and she calls you to sleep."

A moment or a lifetime later, Wayland remembered Irian's last request: *Fia needs her Heart.* It wouldn't matter now, he supposed. But perhaps, with his collar removed, he was no longer immune to miracles. He reached below the collar of Gavida's tunic and slid the chain over his head. A spark of heat passed between his fingers— sharp, stinging silver. Wayland drew the chain over his head, and when the cool blue-green stone settled over his breastbone, he experienced a burst of solace, green as a Midsummer forest. He glimpsed a path cloistered with long-boughed ash trees. And in the distance, a glade crowned with sunlight—

He jerked his head, even as a touch, like pollen-dusted fingers, ghosted over his cheek. And he knew, with distant horror and creeping hope, that it was *magic.*

For the first time since he was a boy, he could sense magic again.

Wayland left Gavida in a pool of his own blood, sprawled with his tools and a sword splitting him in half. He climbed onto the remnant of the throne of Emain Ablach—he was king now, after all. He sat. And he waited. The wind howled and the sea churned and the Grove of Gold ignited in a great roaring sheet of ardent flames.

When Laoise's anam cló came soaring over the crest of the island, shimmering red-gold like coins or autumn leaves or burning coals, Wayland did not think to be afraid. He had simply known— he was truly free.

But destiny could be its own kind of collar.

Now he realized with a lurch and lollop of his heart that Idris was staring at him. Curiously. Sympathetically.

Pityingly.

"Where did you go?" Idris asked gently. "I fear I must have been boring you terribly."

Wayland almost told him. About the night he committed both patricide and regicide. The night he lost a past and gained a future.

The night he both relished and regretted. Instead, he said, "Somewhere long ago and far away. But it was not your doing at all."

Both men turned back to the bookshelves. This time, it was Wayland who spoke first.

"Prince Marban." Wayland still did not know what his father had been searching for in the throne room on the Longest Night. He feared he might never know. But that name—a name his father had mentioned in passing many times over the years—stuck in his throat. He could not ask his father to teach him magical forging. But his father in turn must have learned from somewhere. Or someone. "In all your research, have you ever come across accounts of a man named...Marban?"

Chapter Fifteen

Laoise

It took two weeks for Sinéad to regain her strength. The human girl ate like a woman possessed—devouring everything Idris cooked as fast as he could cook it. She slept like rest was a competition she could win. She trained with fervor, throwing herself back into her strengthening exercises. When Laoise refused to drill her further for fear of overexertion, Sinéad went behind her back and asked Irian. After catching them sparring together in the Armory, Laoise had scolded them both.

"Are you her mother, Laoise?" Irian had shrugged, bemusement plain on his stark features. "If she wishes to train, it is surely her decision."

Laoise had to bite her tongue to keep from pointing out that just six weeks ago, Irian had gone berserk at the slightest whiff of danger toward his precious wife. She supposed if he had revised his stance on that, it was none of her business.

But as the promised two weeks drew to a close, Laoise had to admit to herself that she was *worried*. Not for herself. She was the last heir of the Sept of Scales, mercilessly trained by the lady

Scáthach; her anam cló, a mythic draig. She had faced opponents more fearsome than the human princess and prevailed.

No, not for herself. She worried for Sinéad, so determined yet so fragile. She worried for Idris, so curious about the world she had sheltered him from yet so naïve of its dangers. She worried for her draigs, growing so quickly yet still so young.

The Cnoc was safe—the safest place she knew. She had made it that way—carving a home out of a literal mountain so everyone she loved could be safe. It was her fortress, her haven, her sanctuary. As long as her draiglings and her brother and her friends just *stayed* here, no harm could come to them.

Was that too much to ask?

At last, Laoise could put it off no longer. More shadow missives had arrived from the Twilight Sisters, detailing Eala's inexorable progress through Tír na nÓg. Laoise could hardly fathom the destruction they spoke of—the burning forests and ruined settlements. The risen dead. Like Sinéad, she knew she had to see it herself to believe it. To truly understand what they—all of them—faced.

She briefly considered leaving in the night without telling anyone. But she knew Sinéad would never forgive her for breaking her promise. And if she had learned anything from witnessing Fia and Irian's explosive dramas during the Tournament of Kings, it was this: Betraying those you loved for what you believed to be best for them never ended well.

On a bright blue morning shivering toward spring, Sinéad met her in the sinkhole, near the nemeton. She was dressed in fighting leathers beneath a heavy traveling mantle, with her hair tightly braided to her head and blades strapped to her waist. When Laoise caught her eye, she scowled, as it anticipating some rebuke.

"I am quite recovered," she stated, without preamble. "I'm coming with you."

Laoise sighed. "So I see."

Above, two of the draiglings wheeling against an azure sky detached from their siblings and swooped down. Blodwen curved an affectionate wing around Laoise's shoulders; Barfog butted his large head into Laoise's hip, nearly knocking her over.

"Come too," lisped Blodwen, smoke curling from her nostrils. "Please?"

Laoise's heart might have been a stone for how heavily it settled between her ribs.

"Come! Come!" Barfog's eyes, gleaming onyx, were alight with excitement.

Laoise had always known the draiglings would not be babies forever, would not need her for long. But she had hoped for longer than this. She glanced helplessly at Sinéad, then back to her eldest children, trying to find the words to tell them all no. To tell them that she could protect them better if they stayed where they were, if they stayed *how* they were. She could protect them best if they never grew up.

But that was a fractured kind of truth—comforting only in subtraction. To ask them not to mature would be refusing them growth. What kind of mother would that make her?

"I should have expected an ambush." Laoise made her tone rueful so they would not hear how her voice wanted to shake, then shifted into her anam cló so they would not see her tears.

Her skin rippled along her collarbones, deepening to a burnished red-gold before pouring along her arms like molten gold. Her limbs lengthened, undulating with seams of muscle. Claws, long and wickedly sharp as swords, burst from her hands as she fell on all fours. Her massive wings came last, erupting from her shoulders and stretching wide, the translucent membranes shimmering with all the hues of a blazing sunset. Sinéad rocked an instinctive step backward, and Laoise grinned, baring her rows of razor-sharp teeth. A curl of steam escaped her nostrils as she said, "Climb on."

Laoise had let someone ride her only once. She'd asked Idris whether he wanted to, when they were both younger. He'd thought about it, then shaken his head no: *I don't love heights.* Wayland, of all people, had been her first passenger, when she rescued him from a crumbling Aduantas on the Longest Night. It had been unpleasant for the both of them—he hadn't known where to put his hands, awkwardly gripping the spikes serrating her long, agile neck, and she'd hated the way he'd clamped his legs around her ribs.

Sinéad was different. Her mettle barely wavered before she ascended onto Laoise's back, instinctively settling her weight in the hollow at the base of Laoise's neck. She tucked her legs neatly behind Laoise's wings as she laid herself nearly flat, her hands sliding into the grooves between Laoise's jutting spikes. It struck Laoise as strangely intimate—a shared secret or a quiet understanding. It was comfortable in a way Wayland's ride had not been, both physically and otherwise. Laoise felt perfectly at ease with Sinéad on her back.

"Hold on," she hissed in the moment before she lofted toward the sky, Blodwen and Barfog launching themselves behind her. She was larger than they were—she had to pump her wings hard to cast herself skyward, raising clouds of dust and pollen to swirl around them like mist. Her belly skimmed the tops of the flaming trees as she fought to climb above the lip of the sinkhole. Then—wind and sky. A thermal updraft filled her wings and gusted her steeply upward in a rush. As she banked hard to the south, the remaining four draiglings (save little Hog) soared close to graze the edges of their wings against hers, familiar and affectionate. *See you soon.*

On her back, Sinéad whooped, her voice nearly lost to the wind and the wild lands sweeping out below them.

Insofar as a draig could smile...Laoise smiled.

Laoise needed no map. She had flown over these regions a thousand times. Wings stretched taut and wide, she swept high above the glittering patchwork tapestry of Tír na nÓg, Blodwen and Bar-fog keeping easy pace behind her.

They left the mountains behind as the sun dipped, passing beyond Mag Tuired over mist-swathed valleys. Laoise flew until she spied a silver thread of water, then tucked her wings and dived for the ground, the draiglings squawking and whistling as they explored the glade she'd chosen for the night.

Sinéad climbed off Laoise's back, stretching stiff limbs in a way that made it clear she was trying not to offend. Her face was bright red from the wind whipping it all afternoon; her honey-blond hair was an absolute disaster, her undone braids matted and coiffed in an astonishing helmet atop her head. Laoise shifted back into her Gentry form, pressing her lips together so she wouldn't laugh.

"What?" Sinéad patted her head as she lowered herself gingerly onto a rotten tree stump. "Surely it's not that bad."

"It's that bad," Laoise confirmed. "Here—let me."

She straddled the tree trunk to sit beside Sinéad, slowly finger-combing through the snarled strands and tangled braids.

"I suppose this is why you keep yours so short," Sinéad observed, with a note of apology.

"Something like that." In truth, it had been more about slicing away the parts of herself she no longer wanted to look at, excising a life she had lost. Her long hair had reminded her too much of Elen. "Idris is a real bore about his hair. I figured one of us ought to be practical. If it was up to me, I would have chopped his all off in his sleep—alas, I sacrificed my vanity instead."

Sinéad choked on a laugh. "Spoken like a true sister."

"Siblings are beastly," Laoise said genially as she began to rebraid Sinéad's hair. "Although I suppose you'd know even better than I."

Sinéad stilled, and Laoise cursed her fool mouth. Sinéad had spoken of her human family only once, on the Silver Isle, and they'd all been in their cups. Laoise, Sinéad, and Chandi—a pleasant, intuitive triangle. Before Chandi had done the unthinkable.

Sinéad had been born a shepherd's daughter—the seventh of nine children, and one of only two girls. By the age of seven, when she'd been spirited away by the Folk, she'd already taken on the bulk of the family's laundry and cooking and was expected to look after her two younger brothers while her parents herded the flock or drank themselves into a stupor.

"They bred sheep." Sinéad had laughed into her wine. "And people. The latter far more successfully than the former."

Now Sinéad wasn't laughing. She looked discomfited, and a pang of guilt sliced Laoise like a sword.

"I had a sister, you know." The words spilled over Laoise's lips like something bad she'd eaten that did not want to stay down. Funny, considering she had not spoken about Elen for two decades.

Sinéad looked up. "You did?"

Laoise bit her lip and tried to decide whether to recount the whole awful tragedy. It had been a long day and she wished to rest, not exhume ancient memories that would surely bury her in grief and regret. Perhaps someday, when all this conflict had ended, she would tell her friend the sordid tale. She thought she might even like it—she could picture how Sinéad would listen to her words without judgment, quietly absorbing the gravity of what had passed. After, she would not try to hug her—no, neither Sinéad nor Laoise were women of easy embraces. But she would say something compassionate and unvarnished, and Laoise would be glad to be seen. To be heard. To be understood.

"I did" was all Laoise said, in the end. "Relationships are fraught and tangled. But it's normal to miss the pieces of our past that felt like home. Especially when they're gone forever."

On the third day they saw the smoke.

Laoise's intelligence must have been outdated—they had flown nearly to the ever-flowering fields of Ildathach before she realized they ought to have crossed Eala's path by now. They traveled south along the coastline, then crossed back inland, scouring the valleys for signs of the princess. Where *was* she?

Sinéad smelled it first, rearing back on Laoise's neck to shield her face with her sleeve.

"What *is* that?" she called, above the shrieking of the wind across Laoise's back.

A suffocating reek of filth, decay, and dense, oily smoke struck Laoise's nostrils. And she knew: It was death.

She had experienced her fair share of destruction. She recognized—all too well—the stench of skin crisped by fire and bodies laid to waste, the carrion call of blood and guts spilled over heaving earth. But the horrors of the battlefield never grew easier to bear. Trepidation cleaved her sense from her body, and she saw herself as if from a distance. Laoise, all of thirteen, as flames engulfed the warehouse, devouring flesh and hair like brittle kindling. Laoise, seventeen, vomiting bile after a skirmish with renegade gruagaigh in the Altaír stole three of her Sisters' lives. Laoise, twenty, rolling her mother's heavy, fetid body off the trapdoor that had protected her brother from slaughter.

She snapped back to her senses. Slanted her wings, banking hard. Wind rippled over her back, nearly unseating Sinéad, who yelped and clung harder to her spikes. Beside her, Blodwen and Barfog barrel-rolled, easy in the air without the terrible weight of knowledge Laoise carried.

She had to protect them from that.

"What are you doing?" Sinéad howled over the wind whipping past them. "Eala's that way—just beyond the ridge!"

No—no. Laoise could already envision what lay beyond that last range of hills, as if prescient—the blight and ruin, the waste and havoc. She did not want to see; she did not want *them* to see.

"Please, Laoise!" Panic touched Sinéad's voice, and it was not for what lay beyond the ridge. "We've come all this way. *Please.*"

Inwardly, Laoise cursed. Sinéad's words from two weeks ago

threaded through her hesitation. *I need to see that I am on the right side of this—that they are worse than me. Or rather, that I can be better than* them.

Sometimes, the best way to protect someone was to give them what they needed. Even if it caused you pain.

Abruptly, Laoise banked again and pointed her nose toward battle.

The scene beyond the ridge was worse than she had imagined. The fianna of the dead were vast—Laoise struggled to understand how Eala had amassed such an army in the time since the Longest Night. As they swooped lower, she began to. Some of the soldiers were waterlogged and bloated, still clad in Gavida's pale blues and lambent silvers. Still more were ancient and bog parched—desiccated corpses strung with rotting flesh and armed with weapons from a forgotten age. But the bulk of them were fresh—blood still oozing from slit throats, hollow eyes gazing from lopsided heads upon recently broken necks.

They advanced in eerie silence, heavy steps trudging over early-blooming snowdrops. The air should have been crisp with the gossamer scents of frosted pine and waking earth; instead the putrid reek was like a grave split open—rotten flesh and mold and damp carrion, underlaid by the acrid tang of burnt hair, scorched marrow, old blood turning to rust. Where they marched, the land withered—green grass blackening, yellow daffodils curling into ash, crystal streams turning to inky sludge. The last rows of dead warriors carried torches; eager flames devoured whatever life remained. Behind them stretched the wasteland of their passing, a stark wound slashed through the serene beauty of late winter's landscape.

"Your fire!" Sinéad's shouted in Laoise's ear. "We have to destroy them!"

Laoise did not relish adding more destruction to the desolation already scarring Tír na nÓg. But Sinéad was right. This was war—Eala's army could not be allowed to march onward. And if Mag

Tuired had taught them anything, it was that draig fire destroyed dead warriors better than anything else.

Laoise dived, folding her massive wings as she plummeted toward the cavalcade. Fire erupted from her maw—a searing torrent of molten gold that bathed the undead horde in cleansing flame. Bone and rusted steel melted like wax; soundless mouths parted in Os of distress as empty lungs incinerated. Laoise soared lower, her talons lashing out to cleave through brittle skulls and snap spines like dry twigs. In her wake, a scorched trench marred the earth, the smoldering remains of Eala's army little more than ash swirling in her furious updraft as she climbed back into the sky.

She descended again and again, screaming fire out of the blue to decimate the horde. To her right and left, Blodwen and Barfog followed suit, their draig fire less powerful but no less destructive. Within minutes, the cool morning sun was hidden by stinging smoke and sifting ash, accompanied by the searing stench of burnt bodies.

"There!" Sinéad was laid low along Laoise's neck—her voice raw from shouting. "Up ahead! I see her!"

Laoise did not know how the girl could see anything through the smolder. Still, she swooped toward where Sinéad indicated, her wings slicing the smog into wafting specters like the souls of the dead warriors below. There—through the shifting smoke, she spied the tangled sprawl of a hazel wood, buds still curled tight in the chilly grasp of late winter.

Figures wove through the wreckage with swift steps, their silhouettes flickering between the twisting branches. A golden-haired human man led the group, hacking with his sword at the grasping boughs hemming them in. Behind him, a slight blond-haired woman moved with silent urgency, her shredded cloak billowing amid the death-scented wind. A tall, slender girl with long black hair followed, her spine hunched as she glanced repeatedly over her shoulders. A score or more heavily armed warriors brought up the rear, though Laoise could not determine whether they were living or dead.

Her stomach contracted, not with belching fire but with curdled relief. Chandi lived.

So, too, did Eala.

Upon her back, Sinéad's legs tightened. She leaned precipitously along the length of Laoise's neck, forcing her to rear back and bank her wings to keep the human girl from sliding off.

"I know this place!" Sinéad shouted. Between the hazel trees, past the haze and ruin, a glade beckoned—a patch of untouched green bathed in distant sunlight. The human prince was cutting a path directly toward it, Eala and Chandi at his heels. "Geata Coll—the Hazel Gate!"

The Hazel Gate. The Gates had never been of much concern to Laoise—she had little interest in the human realms and even less in the stolen domains of the bardaí. But she knew enough. Only a Treasure could open a Gate. Eala was now a Treasure.

Perhaps this had always been Eala's route—the human realms her deadly target. Perhaps this was the promise of escape within reach, with a fire-breathing assailant at her heels. It mattered not—the princess knew these territories as well as Sinéad did. There could be no doubt about where Eala was heading.

"Lower!" Sinéad screamed, her fingers digging into the tender spaces between Laoise's spikes. "You have to fly lower!"

Laoise hesitated. Despite Chandi's betrayal, she did not wish to harm the girl. She could not kill Eala—not unless she wished to unleash wild magic over these lands. Nevertheless she obeyed, descending from the heavy bank of smoke.

"Lower!" Sinéad urged.

Hazel branches scratched Laoise's belly and grasped at her scales. Sinéad tilted sideways. Panic threw Laoise in the same direction. But the girl's legs were unlatching from her shoulders, her hands unhinging from her spikes.

Sinéad threw herself down into the hazel grove.

Shite. Laoise banked, rolled, and tucked her wings tight. She flung herself after Sinéad, transforming from her anam cló as she plummeted. Hazel branches bent and snapped, scratching Laoise's fragile Gentry skin and showering her with pale catkin pollen. She hit the ground hard, her knees thunking on cold, muddy ground. Her eyes swam over a confusion of tangled branches and lurching figures and skeining smoke.

Where was Sinéad?

Laoise shoved forward, careless of the thrashing branches catching at her hair and clothes. A heavy, reeking warrior wildly swung a sword in her direction; she neatly sidestepped and rolled beyond his reach before flinging herself back to her feet. Panic made her dizzy—her heart beating too fast as she dragged smoke-stained air into her gasping lungs.

Where was Sinéad?

There. Her slender form had found the path the human prince had cut through the wood—she dashed swiftly through gusting smoke, twin daggers gleaming from her fists. Laoise swerved sideways, seeking the same path even as her fear flamed higher. She silently cursed her friend. What was Sinéad *thinking*? She had already tried to kill Eala once—surely she knew better than to try again.

The glade opened up, green and gold glowing through the smoke. Eala had nearly reached a natural archway created by two huge ancient trees leaning toward each other, framed with shivering catkins and spiky new hazel leaves. Sinéad pushed herself even faster, but the human prince abruptly turned. Drew his sword. And slammed bodily into the human girl, knocking her off her feet. She fell onto her back in the loam, the breath visibly gusting from her lungs. She gasped and flailed, struggling backward as the human prince slowly bore down on her, his steel gleaming over Sinéad's bared throat.

Laoise pumped her legs harder, longing for her draig flight. She was never going to make it in time; she wasn't close enough; she wasn't—

A stripe of red-gold slashed her vision as Blodwen hurtled into the smoky glade like a shooting star. She collided with the human prince's shoulder and slammed him into the dirt, the impact knocking them apart. Barfog landed a moment later, lowering his head as he spread his black-striped wings protectively in front of Sinéad, who lay choking on the ground. Sparks glowed from his hissing mouth as Blodwen joined him, unfurling her own wings like a shield.

Laoise finally caught up to them, skidding to her knees in the dirt beside Sinéad. She helped the younger woman—still gasping and shuddering—to her feet.

"Stupid," Laoise said, voice low but vehement, as she handed Sinéad the daggers that had fallen from her hands in the tussle. "That was so incredibly stupid."

But Sinéad didn't seem to hear her. Her eyes—glittering with smoke and terror and venom—were fixed beyond where the draiglings hissed and spat sparks. The human prince had climbed back to his feet beside Chandi in front of the Gate, both of them smoke smudged and dirty but otherwise unharmed.

Sinéad wasn't looking at them. Princess Eala stood beneath the ancient hazel trees, the boundary of the Gate a silver susurrus behind her. Her pale blond hair stirred in the smoky breeze, a gilded halo turned ghostly in the charcoal smog. Her face, once serene as sculpted ivory, now seemed to bear faint fractures, like cracks in a broken mask. Her hands and arms bore more of the markings, pale as glass and delicate as lacework. Barely leashed power thrummed beneath her skin and flickered in her ice-blue eyes—Laoise sensed the vast, unrelenting stirring of her magic. Raw. Unfettered.

Wild.

Laoise fought the urge to step back, instinctive fear roiling in her chest. As a child, she had been taught the power of a Treasure was immense—too great even for some Folk to bear. Humans were never designed to wield such monstrous magic. Eala's fragile mortality suddenly seemed less a limitation than...a danger.

If she wasn't controlling it...then it was controlling her.

"Hello, Sinéad." Eldritch glamour and seeping bitterness threaded Eala's voice, raising the hair on Laoise's neck. "Come to finish the job you neglected to complete?"

Delicately, Eala drew down the collar of her ruined gown—the same fluttering concoction she'd worn on the Longest Night, now shredded and filthy and smoke stained from traveling. Yet the princess wore it like the raiment of a queen. Her narrow breastbone was ridged with seven long, ragged marks—reminders of the places Sinéad had viciously stabbed her.

"Seven scars," Sinéad spat. "For the seven sisters you stole from me. It is less than you deserved."

"I forgive you," Eala said, in a way that made Laoise suspect it was not remotely the truth. "Surely you know I have never meant you any harm. I loved you. Yet you defy me. Defile me. Destroy my children."

Sinéad's eyes flew wide, then snapped narrow. "Your *children*? Is that what you are calling . . . *them*?" She gestured toward a hulking Gentry warrior Laoise could now see was dead—half his throat had been ripped out, making his head loll strangely. "They are an abomination."

"They are a *miracle*." Eala's face contorted with emotion, and again Laoise glimpsed those strange markings spiderwebbing her skin. "Until you killed them."

"They were already dead."

"They were more alive than you can fathom," Eala argued, even as a flicker of uncertainty scathed her expression. "But now they are gone. You have left me no choice. I must make my way to somewhere I will be more appreciated."

"You mean you are fleeing in defeat," Sinéad spat. "To rain your destruction upon the human realms."

"Call it what you will." Eala turned toward the Gate before looking back over her shoulder. Her eyes shone like diamonds. "Tell my sister she has one moon to join me at Rath na Mara. Then I will start killing the people she loves."

"Eala!" Chandi's cry of distress startled Laoise; beside her, Sinéad also stiffened. It was the only sound they had heard the other girl make, and it was a wretched thing—shrill as the wail of a wounded animal.

"Fine." Eala visibly composed herself, concealing a frenetic energy that suddenly struck Laoise as *panicked*. "*Two* moons—no longer. I need my sister, my other half. My patience is not infinite."

With a deft, forceful gesture, Eala grabbed Chandi's wrist, then looped her arm through the human prince's elbow. She dragged them both through the Gate.

Silver flashed. Sinéad lunged forward as the draiglings shrieked. Bodies thumped to the earth as the revenants lurching through the wood collapsed. They were suddenly alone—the Gate nothing more than an empty circle of sifting smoke between budding hazel trees.

Sinéad fell to her knees in the dirt. When Laoise crouched beside her, she saw wet tracks cutting through the soot staining her face.

"We should have stopped her," Sinéad said furiously. "We should not have let her escape. She will do to my world what she has done to yours."

"How?" Laoise said gently. "We cannot kill her. We cannot bring her home with us, lest we put those we love in more danger. We protected ourselves—for now, it must be enough."

For a time, they crouched there beneath the hazels. Blodwen and Barfog crept close, nuzzling their sleek, scaly heads against Sinéad's cold, wet cheeks and bumping Laoise with their wings. Finally, Sinéad sighed, rose to her feet, and sheathed her daggers.

"You're right," she said. "The only person who can end this is Fia."

Laoise smiled, though the expression felt forced. "Then we'd better go home and tell her to wake up."

Chapter Sixteen

Irian

The Cnoc bored Irian beyond belief.

Since he had become entombed a thousand feet deep in dense black rock, his sense of time had deserted him. He had nothing but the time-telling contraption Laoise kept in the library to go by, and Irian had been avoiding the library. Instead, he had begun trekking every day to the sinkhole with its flaming nemeton, if only to stare at the oval of open sky and breathe in fresh air and listen to the draiglings' leathery wings.

A moon had come and gone since Laoise and Sinéad had returned, soot striped and disconsolate. Their group had all silently listened as Laoise recounted their encounter with Eala and her undead horde. Irian wished he had been surprised by their news. But he was not shocked Eala had fled to the human realms. He was only shocked she had not gone there sooner.

"Well," Wayland had said boisterously. "Who's going to go wake Fia? Has anyone tried *shaking* her? Loud noises? Irian, you have *kissed* her, haven't you? That always works in the stories."

Irian's jaw had clenched as memories of his nightly struggles needled him. Yes, he had kissed her. But Fia was no pale princess entombed in ivory and glass. Nor was she a briar rose surrounded by thorns. She was his wife, a woman of sharp wit and stubborn pride and irritating grace and impeccable violence. And yet she lay before him, caught in a state deeper than dreams and more dangerous than death. Beyond his reach, although he stubbornly held on to her.

If Irian had thought kissing would wake Fia, he might have even let Wayland take a turn.

Since then, the days had taken on a depressing routine. Irian stayed with Fia through the nights as she endlessly transformed. When dawn arrived and she fell still, he left her with Balor or Linn and descended the winding stairs to the new forge Laoise and the draigs were excavating beneath the living quarters. He chiseled stubborn veins of metal and hauled loose scree until his shoulders screamed, then wolfed down a cold lunch of last night's leftovers. Afternoons he spent in the Farm, working beside Sinéad, while Idris and Wayland pursued lore about forging magic.

Irian knew Wayland too well to believe knowledge was his primary pursuit.

"You don't have to do that," Laoise had told Irian as he carried water from the underground river and harvested moon mushrooms and weeded lichen beds. "I'm sure the boys could use your help in the library. There are many texts to wade through, and Sinéad can't read our tongue."

But Irian did not want to help in the library, occupied as it was by Wayland flirting relentlessly with Idris, who seemed to be the only one inclined to perform any real research.

Irian supposed this boredom was, in a sense, a novel sensation. He could not remember a time in his life when his boredom had not been fraught with fear or self-loathing. There had certainly been hours with little to do after he'd been exiled from Emain Ablach. Crouching for long, torturous days beneath the tall multicolored flowers of Ildathach while Folk hunted him like prey had been supremely boring, yes. But it had also been utterly terrifying.

He had not known whether he would survive. He had sometimes wished he would not.

The years he'd spent in the crumbling fort beyond the Willow Gate had been little better. Cursed to spend his days as a winged horror, damned to spend his nights plagued by all the harm he had done to those he should have protected. Whether he lurked close by or watched from afar, the swan maidens' existence mocked and punished him. He had been obsessed with keeping them safe—his presence both shelter and damnation. He had followed them to every full moon feis and midnight party. That long line of girls trailing behind their swan princess through nights like mouths waiting to swallow them whole.

He had loathed every repetitive party. Hated standing like a statue at the edge of the revelry. Despised the watching eyes wringing every ounce of familiarity from him until he was as sharp and bitter as a measure of bad whiskey. Detested the constant frisson of danger—his enemies just out of reach, just out of sight, just waiting for him to drop his guard. Yet those nights had kept him strong, made him stalwart.

Now, after months of mourning, then fretting over, then fighting with, then protecting his beautiful, beloved, and captivatingly troublesome bride, Irian was simply *bored*. Not even Eala's threat inspired fear. He cared little for the humans who had tormented his wife. He would not mourn when Eala executed them.

"Ho." Wayland didn't bother knocking—he swung the door to Irian's chambers violently inward. Or maybe that was just Hog— the little draig never seemed far from her new chosen companion. She trundled cheerfully toward Irian as Wayland's deep blue eyes scanned briefly over the room. "Where's your pretty sea snake?"

Seated on the edge of the bed with the Sky-Sword's hilt rolling restively between his palms, Irian bristled. Sinéad had taken a morning watch over Fia while her changes were dormant so Irian could sleep. Not that Irian was sleeping.

And not that it was any of Wayland's business.

"Surely you have something better to do than bother me." Irian's voice rasped in his throat, as if rough from disuse. "Like determining how to reforge the Un-Dry Cauldron and the Flaming Shield?"

"Every day brings me closer." Wayland stopped an arm's length from Irian. "Have you ever heard tell of a man—a human man—named Marban? My father spoke of him as an authority on bindings."

"No." The name sounded vaguely familiar, but Irian could not place it. "Why?"

"I found mention of him in the *Silverwing Annals*."

"A heavily biased pseudohistory." Irian snorted. The book Wayland named recounted a contentious period of the Sept of Feathers when two feuding Gentry families nearly tore the Sept apart. "I would not take it as truth."

"Yes, yes." Wayland waved a hand. "He appears but once—on a list of tributes offered at a feast."

"So?"

"The annals were compiled, what? Two, three hundred years ago? When my father spoke of Marban, he led me to believe it was during his youth. Not long after the Treasures were forged."

"But that was a thousand years ago."

"And Marban was said to be human."

"That is a Folk lifespan. And decently long, even for one of us." Irian straightened. He had read the annals, a long time ago. He did not remember this Marban. "What was the tribute?"

"Something called the Songbird's Heart."

Irian's pulse throbbed. The Sky-Sword, clasped between his palms, hummed a strange little melody.

"There is a story," Irian said, with a touch of perturbed curiosity. "A story I have not heard since I was a child. It was a favorite of…" He could still hardly bear to speak her name—the friend he'd lost so long ago. "Of Deirdre's. Fia's mother. A legend about a human prince and a Gentry woman, their true love cursed by a bargain gone terribly, terribly wrong."

Wayland frowned. "That seems…significant."

"Your father's gods-damned pattern." Irian shook his head, rueful. "But I cannot see how it pertains to the Treasures, nor their forging."

"No," Wayland agreed. "It is likely a fruitless avenue, and I should admit defeat before I embarrass myself further."

"You have never been one to yield for embarrassment's sake," Irian pointed out, with some asperity.

Wayland just looked at him.

"Was there something else?"

Wayland hesitated, then extended his hand. "May I hold it?"

Irian stilled. The request slid under his feather-fletched skin and made him shudder, as intrusive and presumptuous as...well... kissing someone else's wife and having the audacity to *like* it. Just as an example. The Sky-Sword did not just *belong* to Irian—it was a part of him. An extension of his being, an avatar of his soul. In all the years he had wielded it, he had let only one other person in the world handle it. Fia.

Somehow, he managed to furl the dark wings of his fury and bite out, "*Why?*"

Whatever Wayland heard in Irian's voice made him drop his hand.

"Because I have no idea what I'm doing." A thread of frustration pulled Wayland's voice taut. "Small forgings are simple—little geasa strung together. Creating resonances between disparate objects. But in truth, I know not how to craft the larger geasa necessary to bind new conduits—new Treasures—to the sources. Especially not if the sources have been warped. Perhaps if my father had not collared me..."

Wayland's hand twitched toward his throat, an unconscious gesture. Irian's anger veered vexingly toward sympathy. He well remembered when Gavida first collared his only son. Wayland had just turned eighteen—Irian was not yet fourteen. Wayland had been summoned one morning into his father's forge. When he emerged, the silver collar glared from his neck, so thick and heavy it seemed to cow him. Irian's jaw had dropped, wrath writhing swiftly through him.

But Wayland had never raged like Irian wanted him to. Never complained. Barely participated in Irian's increasingly frenzied attempts to free him from the magical contraption. Finally, Wayland had stopped him with a brotherly clap on the shoulder.

"Come, now." His broad face had creased with an affable smile. "Perhaps my father has done me a favor. I'm far too soft to spend all my days hammering over a forge."

Now Irian exhaled, flipped his grip on the Sky-Sword, and offered the weapon to Wayland. The other man hesitated before curling his tanned fingers around the inlaid hilt.

The blade screamed, furious and atonal. Energy crackled around the length of metal; the pressure of the air abruptly shifted, popping Irian's ears. Wind whipped the blankets off the bed and lifted the hair off the nape of his neck. Hog dived under the bed with a shriek. Wayland's eyes fluttered shut, his hand reflexively curling even tighter around the Sky-Sword. Then, with what appeared to be preternatural effort, he unhinged his fingers and dropped the blade to clatter onto the flagstones.

The Sky-Sword went silent as death. The air in the room abruptly returned to normal, popping Irian's ears again. He bent, palming his Treasure as it hummed a self-satisfied chord, then slowly rose to his full height. He had only a few inches on Wayland; he grappled with a decidedly mean instinct to lord them all over the other man. Perhaps it was because he had spent so long being younger, shorter, and weaker than Wayland. Or perhaps it was some other reason.

"Well?" Irian canted his head to one side, well aware of how intimidating the gesture was. "Did you discover aught of interest?"

"Yes." Wayland's eyes were downcast, focused on the powerful shard of metal dazzling from Irian's grasp. He rubbed absently at his wrist. "Fight me."

Irian's head jerked back, his surprise like a slap to the face. "*What?*"

"You're angry." Wayland's cobalt gaze slashed up, darkening with hesitation, then something like hurt. "At the world, mostly. But also with me."

Irian's lips thinned. "I am not."

"You're a bad liar, Ree. Always were." Wayland gestured toward the Sky-Sword. "It's worse. I could *feel* your rage. All of it, like a storm painted over a blackening sky. And I—I am one of the clouds. So come and fight me."

"I am not going to fight you, Wayland."

Wayland folded his heavy arms over his chest. "Then I'm afraid we'll have to kiss instead."

"You disgust me." The faintest breath of mirth coiled in the corner of Irian's mouth. He stood. "A fight it shall be."

Irian's and Wayland's shadows stretched long in the light of the torches as they entered the Armory. Carven from black rock and striated with pulsating threads of garnet and malachite, the chamber was indistinguishable from the many other rooms honeycombing the Cnoc. Save, of course, for the array of weaponry displayed against the far wall.

Laoise's arsenal surpassed her library. There were massive double-headed battle-axes forged from bronze, with edges gleaming like molten gold and intricate knotwork spiraling around heavy shafts. A long, elegant silver-ash spear—light enough to wield with precision, yet powerful enough to pierce the thickest armor. Longbows crafted from yew heartwood, resting beside quivers of iron-tipped arrows fletched with raven feathers.

Beside Irian, Wayland whistled in appreciation. He inspected each weapon with interest, occasionally reaching out to graze the bevel of a blade or touch the tip of an arrow.

"But this—" Wonder brightened Wayland's voice as he brushed the haft of a triple-pronged trident too large for any ordinary man to wield. "This is Fáilsceim. In the hands of a worthy bearer, it is said to part seas and split mountains."

"Wielded by Fiachar of the Sept of Scales in the massacre of

Geata Ruish, during the Gate War," Irian growled, by way of agreement. "Laoise must have looted it from Findias in the wake of the bardaí's uprising."

"Better her than them." Wayland slid a fingertip over the polished cabochon of blue amber inlaid where the long prongs diverged. "Once, it was said to belong to the Sept of Fins. They called it Scepter of the Flood for the way it sliced through water."

Irian inclined his head. "Pick it up."

"Me?" Wayland jerked his greedy hand from Fáilsceim's haft. "I think not. One legendary, enchanted weapon between us is enough." Wayland's mouth twisted into a broad wry smile. "Besides, the stories say when in the hands of an *unworthy* bearer, the trident taints your shadow and whispers vile notions in your ear. I would hate to accidentally murder you in the grip of a warp-spasm, Brother."

The idea of Wayland besting him, even in the throes of a battle rage, made Irian's jaw clench. He watched his foster brother move away from Fáilsceim to select a simple, blunt practice sword, and said, simply, "Why would you think you are not worthy?"

Wayland hefted the practice blade, testing its balance. "Why would I think I am?"

He gave the claíomh a few experimental swings, moving through the basic forms both men had learned a lifetime ago. Step, step, swing, parry. Sidestep, feint, thrust. Then Wayland flipped his grip on the hilt, lunged sideways, and attacked Irian without warning.

Instinct alone shoved Irian from the path of the blade, curving his spine to one side as his back foot pivoted. He heard the whine of blunt metal an inch from his face, felt the whistle of wind shadowing its path. The Sky-Sword sang free from its scabbard with an eager note, meeting Wayland's return swing with a clang. Impact vibrated Irian's arm to his elbow as steel on steel echoed through the cavern.

"What was that?" Irian parried Wayland's blows with ease, now that he knew to expect them. To any other opponent, Wayland would be formidable. To Irian, he was predictable. They had sparred so many times as boys that Irian knew every cascade of movement, every feint and slash and riposte. Fighting Wayland was like fighting himself. "I thought you said you did *not* want to murder me in a warp-spasm of rage."

"Just checking you haven't gotten slow with age." Wayland's deep blue eyes locked onto Irian's face, a flicker of some emotion glinting like metal in dark water. "Little brother."

Irian answered with a more forceful swing than the casual rhythm of good-natured sparring required, his knuckles white around the hilt of his blade.

"If anyone has gotten slow, *older* brother," Irian said, "I would imagine it has to be you. All that wine. All those women."

"And men!" Wayland grinned as he rained a flurry of short, fast blows around Irian's head. "Time was, you might have joined me. Sharing bedroom partners, bottles of wine, and ensuing headaches alike."

Irian feinted high, then slashed low. "We were little more than boys then. Maturity has brought me an appreciation for quality over quantity."

"Indeed—you have become a one-woman man," Wayland mused as he danced back. His eyes sparked suddenly with a wild humor Irian remembered. A wiliness he mistrusted. "Although the woman in question is not, perhaps, strictly a one-man woman."

His words struck Irian like lightning. Deep in his chest, the cold fury he had harbored since the Longest Night roared to life in a tempest of jealousy, heartache, and anger. His breath rasped as he lunged at Wayland once more, the Sky-Sword bellowing the thunder of his rage.

"There he is." Wayland's smile twisted with bitter humor as he met the strike with his ill-forged practice blade. "There's the wild, wrathful boy I remember."

Irian bared his teeth, his strikes growing ever more savage. In Wayland's hands, the practice sword chipped, its softer metal splintering beneath the enchanted steel of the Sky-Sword. "I. Am. Not. *Angry.*"

"Learning to talk about your feelings is a valuable skill, Brother," Wayland chided between swift breaths. "If you won't tell me why you're so mad at me, I'll have to guess."

"Or you could learn to shut up for once in your gods-cursed life," Irian ground out.

Wayland sidestepped, ducking under Irian's guard before driving his elbow sharply into his ribs. The unexpected feint sent Irian staggering back. Wayland pressed his advantage, forcing Irian to cede all the ground he'd gained.

"It's not just that I kissed her, is it?" Wayland's words were sharper than either sword, shredding the remnants of Irian's careful composure. "It's not even that you know she must have enjoyed it. I am, after all, renowned for my tongue."

Irian roared, cleaving the Sky-Sword down. The practice sword shattered in Wayland's grip, shards of metal scattering to the stone as the blade sheared away at the hilt. Wayland staggered back in surprise, struggling to keep his balance. The black blade met his sternum before Irian could reconsider, pinning Wayland to the wall. Knives and hanging shields clattered down from the impact. Irian jerked the Sky-Sword up to aim where Wayland's collar had once rested. Irian's breath rasped in his throat; his blood rang in his ears; the sword sang out a bloodthirsty little threnody.

"You are angry." Wayland tilted his jaw away from the blade, but his gaze held no fear. Only a careful kind of consideration—as if he were measuring Irian, weighing him, assessing him. *Seeing* him. In a way Irian did not wish to be seen. "You're angry because you know, deep down, that had the timing been a little different— had the stars aligned differently—that *it would have been me.* Me, by her side. Me, in her bed. Me, in her heart."

Irian's knuckles ached from the force of his grip on the Sky-Sword, which trembled in his hand.

Not the sword. *He* was trembling.

He did not trust himself to move a muscle.

"But I'm not." Wayland's voice rasped raw. "I never was. I never will be. Do you know why?"

Still, Irian could not speak. Could not move. Could barely think.

"Because she chose *you*, Ree. Even with the magic of Tír na nÓg twining us together—the magic of a kiss owed—she chose you. With a thousand flirtations falling from my tongue, she chose you. With my hands on her waist and my lips on hers—" Irian flinched. Wayland laughed, but the sound was hoarse, hollow. "Yes, even then— she chose *you*. There may be patterns—destinies—etched between the stars, Brother. But our choices are more powerful than any fate. When it comes to Fia…Irian, you know I never stood a chance. You don't have to trust me. But you can trust in that."

"You think *that* is why I am angry?" Irian demanded, terse. "I know Fia chose me. She has never betrayed me. She made mistakes— near fatal errors—because she did not know the customs of our people. But she never betrayed me. *You*, however." He inhaled, as though a full breath might make the words easier to speak. "When Gavida forced me from Emain Ablach, I thought I would never see you again. I mourned you and foolishly believed you mourned me too. For a long time I did not know who I was without you. But when I returned to the Silver Isle, it was like I meant nothing to you. Like you had cast me off to the fates thirteen years ago and never spared me a second thought. And when you began pursuing *her*…" Irian spat the words between his teeth. "You keep calling me *Brother*. But you have acted like anything but family."

Wayland's eyes lightened, from fathomless blue to indigo shallows.

"You believed *you* were the castoff?" His nostrils flared, all that challenging humor leaking from his expression. "You abandoned *me*. You left Emain Ablach flush with mythic power while I stayed behind, alone. With a collar around my neck. I heard the tales of your empire of desolation, your fortress of vengeance. All that magic and you could not find a way to send word? To visit me?" Wayland's throat bobbed beneath the scrape of Irian's sword. "When I saw her, I knew. Whatever space I'd once occupied in your heart had been filled. And you had no need for me anymore. *Brother.*"

Irian forced in a slow, controlled breath. His hand suddenly went limp, and the Sky-Sword dropped from Wayland's throat to clatter on the stone floor.

"For many years, you were the only person who bothered to love me," Irian said, simply. "A brother cannot be replaced. Do not forget that again."

He turned away from Wayland. Then pivoted back on his heel and slammed his closed fist into Wayland's face. Cartilage crunched beneath his knuckles as Wayland's head snapped back against the wall; blinding pain shot up Irian's wrist to his shoulder. Hot dark liquid burst from Wayland's nose, spattering Irian's skin.

"Fuck me!" Wayland cursed, clutching at his newly rearranged face with both hands. Skeins of blue-black blood dripped over his mouth and stained both his palms. "What was *that* for?"

"For kissing my wife," Irian growled, forcefully. "And for baiting me. I could have killed you."

Wayland choked out a laugh. "I suppose a broken nose is my consolation prize?"

"Maybe next time you will think twice before provoking the Sky-Sword with nothing more than a practice blade." Irian turned away, leaving Wayland breathless, battered, but inexplicably grinning. "Idiot."

"You needed a scapegoat," Wayland called after his retreating back. "And I've never been one to refuse a good consensual whipping!"

Irian glanced back, incredulous.

Wayland smiled wider, his gleaming teeth rendered gruesome by the deep blue blood oozing steadily from his bruised nose. "Although next time, I'll thank you to buy me dinner first."

Chapter Seventeen

Wayland

Wayland meandered toward the library, cursing as he tried to stanch the blood oozing plentifully from his damaged nose. His first thought upon Irian's fist colliding with his skull had honestly been *Oh no, not my pretty face.* But since approximately one split second after that, all he'd thought about was how much his pretty face fucking *hurt.*

Despite all his bravado in the aftermath of their tussle, Wayland felt strange. As the adrenaline leaked from his veins, rendering his limbs weak and his heart hollow, he couldn't help replaying some of the horrendous words he'd thrown at Irian and the dreadful wrath that had come crashing back on him.

He'd thought a physical battle might scour a slate so grimed with years of grief and guilt that neither man knew how to wipe it clean. The clash had certainly brought animosities to the surface. But had it resolved them?

A brother cannot be replaced. Do not forget that again.

He supposed only time would tell.

Wayland wasn't sure why his footsteps were carrying him to the library, of all places. Gods only knew he'd spent enough time on those uncomfortable draig-stone chairs with his nose crammed in a book. But although he had his own chambers in the Cnoc—complete with piping-hot water, mountains of pillows, and precious little else—they felt far less like home than this library now did. Maybe it was the honeyed glow of a hundred beeswax candles reminding him of his bedroom in Aduantas, sunken now to the bottom of the sea. Maybe it was the way Hog liked to drape herself along the mantel above the hearth, belly up, wheezing little puffs of smoke from her nostrils. Or maybe it was—

The door to the library shoved outward with the force of Idris's shoulder. Between the hair falling over his face and two leather-bound tomes clutched in his arms, the younger man's vision was obscured, and he didn't see Wayland until he was nearly on top of him. He jerked in surprise, then gasped when he took in the sight of him, sweat-stained and bloodied. Idris's face blanched white. He dropped the oversized volumes dangerously close to Wayland's toes, even as he reached out gingerly for his face.

"Gods alive, Wayland," he breathed. "Your nose, it's—"

"Destroyed?" Wayland's voice came out thick. "Mangled? Mutilated?"

"Broken." Idris's cool fingertips were faintly scented with dust and ink as he very gently prodded the screaming contours of Wayland's nose. Wayland fought the urge to push him away—for what might be the first time in his adult life, he had no desire to be touched. "Not badly. Laoise's had worse—those Twilight Sisters at Dún Scaith are *notoriously* vicious. Come on—let's get you cleaned up."

Wayland prepared to march into the library, but Idris planted his feet and gripped Wayland around both biceps.

"Oh, no." He pushed Wayland bodily down the hallway in the opposite direction. "I'm not going to explain to Laoise how someone got blue blood all over her priceless scrolls. And you don't want to either. Or did you not hear what I said about the Twilight Sisters?"

Wayland laughed, but the movement dislodged whatever clot had formed in his nostrils. Fresh blood splattered over his lips and his already ruined shirt.

At first glance Idris's chambers were more or less identical to Wayland's. But as he looked around in interest, he noticed small differences. A wall of hanging cavern plants arranged in a gradient of umbers and ochers and reds. Pots of brightly colored paints arranged in neat stacks beside hand-stretched canvases with their faces turned to the wall. Pallets of tiny button mushrooms growing in orderly rows beside a beveled window cut into the stone. Beyond, Wayland heard the sound of water rushing somewhere far below.

"Sit." Idris pushed him. Wayland reeled back, caught his heel on the platform of the bed, and obliged with a thump. The bed was, perhaps unsurprisingly, meticulously made, each pillow fluffed and all the coverlets carefully tucked. Normally, this degree of orderliness would have compelled Wayland to disturb it by any means necessary. Preferably involving a great deal of disrobing and rolling around naked between the sheets.

Perhaps it was the blood loss talking, but when it came to Idris, Wayland couldn't help but find such neatness charming.

He kept his bloodstained palms carefully upturned as he listened to Idris move around the rooms, rummaging in the bathing chamber and clattering in the wardrobe. After a moment, he returned with a bowl of steaming water, a stack of frayed rags, clean bandages, ointments, and a few long, narrow sticks.

"I know I said I enjoy some light punishment from time to time." Wayland raised his eyebrows. "But I'm not sure about being whipped twice in one day."

Idris flushed, but barely. He dipped one of the rags in the steaming water and leveled a no-nonsense gaze at Wayland. "Shut your mouth. If you even know how."

Wayland obeyed, surrendering himself to Idris's ministrations. The rag felt blisteringly hot on his skin, but Idris was gentle as he cleaned crusted blood from Wayland's chin and lips. Wayland winced when Idris wiped the tender, swollen flesh of his nose, but even that became tolerable after a few moments. Idris uncorked a few of the unguents, sniffed them speculatively, and selected one to pour onto a bandage. It smelled like cedar and spiced wine, and between the soothing scent, the sound of rushing water, and Idris's cool, deft fingertips on his skin, Wayland felt suddenly and completely at ease. His eyes drifted closed, and he relaxed.

Idris closed his forefingers around the bridge of Wayland's nose and shoved the whole structure back into place.

Renewed pain screeched from jaw to temples. Wayland's eyes flew open as he grunted in pain, but Idris just smiled, calmly holding a new rag beneath Wayland's nose to catch the latest gush of dark blood.

"Sorry," Idris said, not looking even the slightest bit apologetic. "Just a mild sedative so you wouldn't fight me. Unless you wanted a crooked nose?"

Wayland huffed. "Are you calling me vain?"

"I suppose I am." Idris's smile was the perfect level of crooked, giving his handsome face a haphazard impishness. "Very vain indeed."

When the bleeding stopped, Idris broke one of the long sticks into shorter lengths, rolled narrow bandages around them, then gently splinted Wayland's nose. He finished by affixing the whole contraption to his face with some kind of adhesive.

"Finished." He sat back on his heels, his eyes lifting to collide with Wayland's own gaze. Wayland inhaled. Despite all their hours together in the library, he could count the number of times he'd actually made eye contact with Idris. The other man so often kept his gaze downcast, his features hidden behind his spill of hair. But his eyes were beautiful—a deep, rich brown shot through with tiny threads of amber. Wayland had originally thought Idris did not share Laoise's ember eyes. But while the heat in his gaze might be buried deeper, it simmered with an intensity that conjured an answering blaze in Wayland's stomach.

"Now. Are you going to tell me who did that to you?"

"Irian." Wayland shifted his weight and made a rueful face. "I deserved it. Although he didn't have to hit me quite so hard."

"Irian?" Surprise punched a fetching dimple in Idris's cheek. "Isn't he your...brother?"

"Foster brother," Wayland corrected. "And if you don't think brothers fight, then you clearly don't have any."

"No—only sisters." *Sisters...plural?* "Why were you fighting?"

"Because—" Wayland almost told Idris about Fia, about the bargain they'd made. About the kiss, and the swift rejection that followed. About the blade-sharp sting of being second best. Runner-up in every race he'd ever run, every contest he'd ever competed in, every battle he'd fought. But with startling prescience, he knew how Idris would react—disgust at the whole sordid drama and then, most likely, pity. Wayland wasn't sure he could bear seeing that kind of condemnation on Idris's face. "Family is a funny thing, Red. Blood family is the tether we're born with, but that rope is not always woven with love. Chosen family, though—some people stitch themselves into the gaps left by blood, and love by choice instead of duty. Even then, it's a gamble. Those who choose to love you can just as easily choose to stop. And the ache of love unreturned is the most profound wound."

Idris stared at him with surprise verging on wonder, as if he hadn't realized Wayland knew so many big words. Gently, Idris dipped another rag in water, then took one of Wayland's blood-stained hands.

"You believe the people who choose to love you are your real family," Idris said carefully as he wiped away more spatters. "I believe they are the people *we* choose to love—those we seek out as mirrors for ourselves. Those who reflect our best qualities back at us and let us forgive ourselves the worst. If someone chooses to stop loving us, it is not the measure of how undeserving we are of love. Rather, it must be the measure of their own lack."

It was Wayland's turn to stare. "You are wise for one so young."

"I'm four-and-twenty." Idris lowered the rag, but his hand lingered on Wayland's wrist. "I'm not that young."

Wayland shouldered through the brief, buzzing apprehension of *dangerous territory* into the glossy, sugar-coated paradise beyond. The land of desire was a place he was intimately, gloriously familiar with, and it felt unspeakably good to return. He forgot the pain thudding in his face, forgot Irian and Fia, forgot the Treasures. His blood roused in his veins, throbbing and eager, and he slid his hand along Idris's wrist, grasping him below the elbow and pulling him closer. The other man swayed toward him, steadying himself with a hand on Wayland's thigh. When Idris looked up at him with those deep, burning eyes, Wayland dared to touch him—his thumb grazing over the elegant point of his chin, then ghosting over the soft pillow of his lower lip. Idris's mouth parted, his breath warm on Wayland's knuckles. Blood hammered at his temples and blotted out all rational thought, and he settled deeper into the tantalizing sensuality of touch. He lifted his other hand to Idris's jaw, sliding back the curtain of hair—

Idris jerked, whipping his head away and throwing himself backward. "Don't!"

Wayland froze, both arms arrested in midair. Confusion and alarm gushed over him like ice water. The imprint of Idris's hand on his thigh felt like his own dashed hope—fading so swiftly it might never have existed in the first place.

"I'm sorry." He meant it. "If you tell me what I did wrong, then I promise never to do it again."

Idris, flattened against the wall and breathing hard, unconsciously smoothed the long side of his hair more securely over his face. Wayland began to understand.

"I'm sorry, Idris," he said again, with more significance. "But you don't need to hide from me."

Idris hesitated for one more moment, then ducked his head and began gathering his scattered medical supplies.

"This was a bad idea." He grabbed for the bowl of bloody water;

it spilled, sloshing aquamarine fluid over Wayland's boots. Wayland tried to help; their hands collided. Again, Idris shied away, reaching for the soiled rags strewn on the floor. "You should go."

Wayland levered himself off the bed. He paused by the door, slinging one arm up onto the doorjamb, to watch Idris gather bandages to his chest, his shoulders hunched protectively and his hair swept over one eye.

No, Idris was not particularly young. He was older than Fia, older than Sinéad. But he had spent the past thirteen years entombed in this mountain with no one but his sister and a brood of baby draigs for company. He was clearly inexperienced. Vulnerable. Possibly traumatized.

And Wayland could not bring himself to mind. He rubbed a still-bloody palm over his aching head and wondered whether he had shite for brains or just the worst luck in the entire world.

"Idris." He pitched his voice to be heard over the rushing water far below.

Idris turned in surprise, as if he had expected Wayland to be long gone. Wayland met his eyes and chose his words carefully, fighting tooth and nail for a sincerity that did not come naturally.

"Whatever might have happened to you." *Don't make a joke.* "Whatever you look like." *Don't make a fucking joke.* "I think you're beautiful."

Idris stared at him.

"I'm not afraid to see you, Idris. Whenever you are ready to be seen."

Then Wayland shut the door and wobbled off toward the kitchen in search of a bottle of mushroom whiskey to dull the pain.

To dull all the fucking pain.

Chapter Eighteen

Within

The doe set a brisk, nearly unmatchable pace through the wood. This forest was dense with undergrowth, and there was no path to speak of. I squinted between the vast old trunks and heavy canopy, trying to get a sense of my bearings. The light was dim and murky in places, yet shafts of pale sunlight slanted through others, as if both dusk and dawn were occurring simultaneously. The trees' foliage was also strange—lime-green shoots and frothing white flowers peering between brittle yellow leaves painted red at their tips; waxen green fronds nudging between grasping black branches.

I hacked my feet through tough brambles and thorny bushes and tried to keep sight of the doe's twitching white tail amid the gloom.

We walked for hours. Or perhaps mere moments. Time felt ghostly amid the vaulting buttresses of the eternal forest—a sepulchral parade not of minutes or even hours, but of years and centuries and millennia. Even the tallest tree here would one day be brought low by decay or storm or hungry beetles, and that was all right. From their fallen trunks mushrooms would nudge red spotted caps; ants would bore infinite highways; seedlings would sprout new fronds.

Time was rot and rebirth. Time was death. It was nothing to be afraid of.

I glimpsed clearings beyond the path, sometimes—glades suffused with light and ringed with powerful trees. No—not always trees. Branching tongues of flame, or sentinels of pitted igneous rock, or reaching fronds of multicolored coral. I peered at these circles as we passed by, but they were hazy and undefined, as if seen through smoky mirrors.

The doe finally stopped, poised where the forest's shadow gave way to the light of a clearing. I raised my hand to shield my eyes from the spill of sunlight, harsh after the gloom of the forest. But the light did not warm my skin and seemed more silver than gold. Behind the sun, stars were stenciled sharp against a laminate sky.

Day...night. Both...neither.

I kept forgetting—this place was not strictly real. It was as real as I was, I supposed. But none of this existed outside my own mind.

Still, I couldn't help but wonder exactly *where* inside my mind I had now managed to wander.

"What is this place?" I asked the doe out loud. The delicate shells of her ears flicked forward, then back. She trotted a few steps, hesitant, then pawed one hoof through the long grass. My eyes twitched toward where she indicated.

Across the glen sat a strange, sturdy little cottage. Familiarity breathed a shiver down my spine—I had been here before. I had dreamed it. Or something similar to it. Half-remembered images layered over the scene before me—rough-hewn stone walls the color of river stones, a roof thatched with a multitude of birds' wings, wildflowers like a kaleidoscope path designed only for me. I hesitated, then began to walk, my steps unspooling toward the door.

A figure sat in profile beside the wall, basking in the silver-gold light. I slowed. I was not afraid—not precisely. I did not think the doe had brought me here for harm. But after so long hiding from

Talah within the labyrinth of my memories, then wandering with the Bright One through time and space, I had become well and truly lost. I glanced over my shoulder in the hopes that my guide would be shadowing me. But Ínne had left me to walk this path alone. I felt suddenly ill-prepared to confront whatever lurked here, at the heart of all I knew.

Would it be damnation? Or deliverance?

The figure turned as my footfalls neared, surprise etching his fine-boned features. His hair was light—a paler gold than Rogan's. I could not tell his height from the lanky stretch of his legs flung out before him. His eyes were pleasantly brown, a warm counterpoint to his angular features and blond hair. He could not have been much older than me. Five-and-twenty, perhaps. Thirty, at the most. And he was...human.

Untethered familiarity rushed through me once more, vertiginous. I stumbled, and the man rose as if to catch me, before subsiding back into his chair among the wildflowers. He gazed at me, and I stared back in return, trying to shackle his image to some memory, some understanding beyond this piercing sense of *knowing* him.

"There you are, little deer," he said.

My eyes jerked automatically to the doe who had led me here. But she was gone, and the strange man was not looking at her. He was looking at *me*. His smooth tenor unhinged something vital inside me, a memory buried so deep I could not be sure it was mine.

Ba dum dum dah dum...ba dum dum dah dee. The sound distant, muted, mottled—sung in counterpoint to the endless, exquisite throb of a pulse. A rush and roar like the sea all around me.

"Who are you?" I demanded, although part of me already knew.

He did not quite smile. "I am exactly who you think I am, little deer. I am Rían Ó Mainnín, last high king of Fódla. I am your father. And I have been waiting for you."

He hummed: *ba dum dum dah dum...ba dum dum dah dee.* Except this time, it was not muted beyond the tides of my mother's womb. It was rich, and real, threading through my veins like gold or glory or hard-earned love.

"This isn't real." A single traitorous droplet squeezed from my eye and slid down my cheek. I had cried too much already. This man did not deserve my tears. "I couldn't possibly remember that. I couldn't possibly remember *you*. My father died before I was born."

"Yes, I did." He turned his suddenly anguished gaze from me, staring toward the dark line of the forest. "What is real, little deer? What is a memory? Perhaps your mind does not remember. But something inside you does. Your bones bear the imprint of love as surely as they do loss. Your heart throbs with my blood as surely as it does your mother's." He reached out and touched my cheeks, almost too gently to feel. Once below my right eye, once below my left. "We are both a part of you, little deer. We always were and always will be."

I jerked back, fighting another wave of treacherous emotion. Even if this were real, Rían had been a villain. He had seduced a Folk maiden for her Treasure, even as he betrayed his pregnant queen. He had been power hungry and unprincipled—a symbol of everything wrong with humanity. Because of him, both realms had suffered through years of war and lingering enmity. His character, I had no doubt, lived on in Eala.

If it lived on in me as well, then it was something to deny. Not embrace.

"You are no part of me." I mustered malice to mask my pain. "And if you are, then I rebuke you. You are no father to me."

Torment pulled his fine features into a rictus of despair. He made a strangled, wordless sound of dismissal, as if he wanted to argue with me but did not know where to begin. "Why?"

"*Why?*" My voice punched from me, shrill and accusing. "Which betrayal to start with? I suppose the betrayal of my mother is the most egregious. She knew nothing of men—not to mention perfidious humans. You led her astray, ravished her, and kidnapped her—all for magic you could not even wield."

The specter of the last high king of Fódla—this ghostly memory living in my lineage—opened his mouth. But I slashed a hand between us, silencing him.

"But that was not your only betrayal. What of your queen, keeping your hearths lit and your kingdom tended while she grew your firstborn daughter in her womb? What of that daughter, raised without a father in a war-torn kingdom while her mother grieved and raged? What of your people, flung in battle against the Gates of the Folk? What of—" My voice broke, disloyal. "What of me? Raised without parents? Without love? Without anyone?"

For a long moment, beneath the numinous not-sky, Rían sat perfectly still and achingly silent.

"I do not know what stories you have been told," he said at last. "And perhaps whoever told them believed them to be true. I see that *you* believe them. But I, too, have a story. May I tell it, little deer?"

Fury blistered my soul. I did not want to give this man—alive or dead—any more power over me. My time here was short. Talah had found me in my oldest memories—surely she would find me here too. "Why?"

"Because we will never have another chance," he responded gravely.

I hesitated. I had already learned so much of my past—and perhaps my future. Things I had yearned to know, and things I now wondered whether I ought to fear. I had never—not even once—desired to hear from my blackguard father. I glanced over his shoulder at the cottage, thatched with birds' wings and shadowed despite its position in the middle of the slaked-silver sunlight. I thought I spied movement behind the fogged glass windows, but when I squinted, I saw nothing.

"I think I'm meant to go in there." I gestured at the little house. "I don't have time for you."

He almost smiled. "He cannot see you yet."

"He? *Who?*" Frustration scalded me. "And why not?"

"This is the Deep-Dream," Rían said, by way of explanation. "Where nothing is real, yet anything may come to pass. Save, of course, what cannot be."

"Morrigan help me," I growled. "But if I hear one more obtuse riddle, I'll scream."

"Then let me tell you something plain, little deer." Rían's pain was evident on his face. "I beg of you."

Despite my best intentions, curiosity corroded my misgivings. "Tell me why you keep calling me that name. *Little deer.*"

"Because I did not live long enough to give you any other ones." Misery arrowed over his aristocratic features. "Tell me your true name, my daughter."

I clenched my fists. "Fia."

"You see! *Little deer.*" Gladness brightened his face before he frowned yet again, as some new emotion ghosted over his features. A memory, a premonition. "Who gave you that name?"

"Eithne Uí Mainnín. My adoptive mother. And your widow. Unless you forgot about her?"

"No." The name triggered visible horror in Rían. He paled, his skin ashen beneath his light golden hair. "Then you have truly been a pawn of destiny. An instrument of the stars. And I am sorry for it."

"Did you not hear what I just said about riddles?" I growled. "Tell your tale, sire. Then leave me in peace."

For an aching moment, the specter-king—my dream-father— was silent.

"Once, in a time of warring chieftains and mounting plague and gnawing famine, a young king and queen wondered how to save their people." As Rían spoke, the metal sky began to shift and blur with colors and images. I saw a human wedding, a fort beside the sea. A beautiful maiden with dark golden hair and ice-blue eyes leaned to murmur in the ear of a serious blond man with warm brown eyes. Both wore royal torcs around their elegant throats. "Theirs was not a match born of love, but of ambition. The king had been born to rule but longed for his books and his poetry. The queen had been born to weave and breed but longed to lead armies and gird herself with power. They both thought they could sacrifice a little happiness in order to gain all they desired. But the stars tend to punish those who deny their destinies."

A chill rippled over my skin. My eyes were glued to the sky as the picture shifted to the young queen—Eithne—slyly clasping hands with a young, clean-shaven Cathair before turning back to her husband.

"A druid blessed with visions of the Fair Folk told the queen of a path toward power—*magic*. But the Folk Gentry were wary of diplomacy. They would treat only with the high king of Fódla—no emissaries, no generals, no underlings. And so the reluctant king traveled into Tír na nÓg alone."

I glimpsed wild revels, devious plotting, councils that went nowhere.

"Defeated, the king returned to his queen and told her all that he had seen. When she heard of the Treasures, both her imagination and her ambition were inflamed. Surely even one of these magical Treasures would turn the tide of wars, cure plagues, solve famines. And though the king told his wife how jealously the Treasures were guarded by their heirs, this only made the queen more eager to possess one. She placed her hand upon her stomach, still flat beneath the bodice of her kirtle, and begged him to bring back the magic they needed to cure their ailing realm, to make their kingdom a home safe enough to raise a child in.

"Together they hatched a plot—to steal one of the Treasures of the Folk and bring it back to Fódla. The king returned to Tír na nÓg with new determination, ingratiating himself into the Sept of Antlers. He bided his time, attending revels and war meetings alike under the guise of seeking counsel from the Folk. And then—then he met *her*."

The young woman whose image splashed across the sky was Deirdre—there was no one else she could have been. She looked like me; or, I supposed, I favored her. Not in the way I resembled Eala, with our twin features we'd inherited from our shared father. I echoed Deirdre like a candle does a bonfire, like a raindrop a waterfall. Through Rían's eyes she was luminous and breathtaking and terrifying as she approached him beneath a long-ago moon. Dark hair cascaded like shadow down her back. Her green eyes were lush as wild, ancient forests. Her frost-pale skin gleamed as if woven from starlight. Her smile was enchantment and ruin.

"At first, the king intended to seduce the young woman, new heir to an ancient Treasure. He assumed her an easy mark, a naïve target. But as he sought to bring her under his spell, he found it was he who became swiftly seduced—by the maiden's exquisite grace, her quiet power, and her deep, devastating sorrow. For she was in mourning—for her only friend, whom she'd lost; for an unwanted life, thrust upon her; for her foretold death, creeping closer with every day she lived."

The two handsome figures—Gentry maiden and human king—walked slowly in the woods. Their hands brushed. Flowers bloomed behind them, dark and bright as night pierced by falling stars.

"She told the king how she had been born to a destiny she never asked for. How she had been born to die. How the magic she inherited longed to be freed, and she with it. How she yearned for a life beyond the bounds of her Sept. With every word she spoke, the king began to yearn for the same things. He saw how trapped he himself had become, although he had never thought to rail against his silken prison. He began to dream of a destiny beyond the high walls of his fine castle, the tight bonds of his duty, the brittle charade of his loveless marriage. He began to dream...of *her*."

My heart squeezed, a vicious throb I wished I were immune to. How many times had I heard this story lurking at the beginning of my own? In how many ways? I did not know which version to believe, yet the soft pith of me wanted it to be *this* version. The story where I was not a product of treachery or betrayal or seduction... but of *love*.

Images flashed by, the yarn of my parents' destinies winding tighter on the spindle of their own destruction. I watched them kissing beneath jewel-spangled trees; passing letters beneath barred doors; stealing away to watch the sunrise; tangled together in rumpled sheets as bells tolled in distant towers. Part of me wanted to look away—this felt too intimate to intrude on. But another part of me could not bear to abandon even a glimpse of the people who had made me. For so many years, I had longed to know my own story: where I came from, who I was, *why* I'd been created. Though I knew this would not make me whole, it was a sliver of something jagged coming home—a shard of broken mirror glass pressed gently back into its shattered frame.

Abruptly, they were running, swathed in heavy cloaks against the chill of late winter. Slush gnawed at their boots and made their steps laborious; crushed crocuses cried out a lament as they passed. Their eyes were wide with fear as they fled unseen pursuers; their gloved hands gripped each other tight enough to bruise.

"The king and the heir made plans to escape the stories written for them in order to write their own." Rían's voice was choked with emotion—I wondered what it must be like to witness the last moments before your own death. "They wanted to live their own lives, nurture their own love, raise their own family. They made for the Deep-Dream. Deirdre had heard tales of others who had fled there—a place where everything was possible, even if it wasn't strictly real. But they were discovered." A tear glistened upon Rían's cheek. "The king was cut down where he stood. And as the lifeblood gushed from his body, he watched the only woman he had ever loved fling herself from the cliffs in sorrow."

I, too, was treacherously crying. I swiped at my face as the images all faded, mastering my emotions. "Is that really what happened? Is what you have told me true?"

"What is truth, little deer?" Rían did not try to wipe away the sorrow furrowing his noble face. "Every story changes depending on who tells it. I have told you my truth. Is it enough?"

"Enough for what?" My fury returned, though softer than before. "To absolve you? You may not be the villain I believed you to be, but you are not blameless. You still abandoned your queen for another woman. Abandoned your unborn daughter for a family who existed only in your imagination. Because of what you and Deirdre did, the Gate War decimated both Folk and human realms. The bardaí learned of the Septs' weaknesses. As a result of your selfishness, the heirs of the Treasures and all their kin were slaughtered."

"The cost of free will is the burden of choice, and the terrible weight of consequences," Rían said gravely. "Those who choose their own destinies will forever be cursed by uncertainty and plagued by regret. Those who choose love above duty will forever be tormented by all they have forsaken. But those who are not willing to sacrifice their hearts for the prospect of truly living may never learn what it is to be alive."

His words hollowed the marrow from my bones. "Why are you telling me this?"

"Because you will have to choose." A sudden wind blew in from the forest, harsh and hot. Rían's hair lifted off his shoulders, and his eyes flashed dark with new fear. "And soon."

Dread yanked my gaze over my shoulder. The trees beyond the grove were lashing with the force of a growing storm; the air corroded my nostrils with the scent of bog tar and scorched metal. The sky was hammered too thin, veins of red spiderwebbing its surface. Wildflowers sighed in warning around my knees.

Let me in.

Not Talah. Not here. I clenched my fists. How did she find me?

"Choose what?" I ground out, turning hastily back to Rían. But he was retreating toward the strange cottage thatched with feathers. I chased after him, alarm quickening my steps. "Why am I here? Why are *you* here?"

Rían rounded on me at the threshold of the cottage. His hands fell on my shoulders; his eyes bored into mine.

"He is to blame for your troubles, little deer. Not I."

I frowned—the words echoed strangely inside me, conjuring a distant kind of familiarity I struggled to place. Someone had said that to me before. Here?

"Who?" The ground beneath my feet lurched. The forest whispered words that sounded like *You cannot hide here.* A figure moved beyond the blurred cottage windows—a shadow in the dim. "Who is to blame?"

"Find your sister. You are her balance. Only you can bring her to the light."

"Eala?" Hatred and hope were twin pulses in my galloping heart. "*How?* How do I bring her to the light?"

"I must say goodbye now." His eyes were panicked, pained. "I am sorry for all I have done. But I am sorrier still for all I never got the chance to do. I would have liked to have held you. I would have liked to have known you. I would have liked to have…to have loved you, little deer."

His hands fell from my shoulders. He stepped away. Reached for the door to the cottage. I tried to lunge after him, but the wind shoved me backward. The ground bucked, making me stumble to one knee.

"Don't leave me!" I screamed. "Tell me what I must choose! Tell me who to blame! Tell me how to save my sister!" He turned the knob. Opened the door. "*Father!*"

The word shattered over him, curving his spine and unearthing a sound from the depths of his chest. But he uncurled as he turned, and when he spoke, it was as if he channeled someone else's voice—a voice so inhuman I hardly recognized its speech.

"A feather so black will rise from pain." Rían's frame seemed to expand, filling the entryway of the hut as his hair blossomed around him. "A crown so silver will rise to reign."

I froze. I had heard these words before—Corra had spoken them to me the last time I was at Dún Darragh. I had thought them meaningless drivel. But now I was rapt—the weight of importance clung to Rían like a shroud. I suddenly knew, in the depths of my soul—these were the last words my father would ever speak to me. I crawled toward him over the rocking earth, coughing against the billows of acrid smoke.

"A heart so green must bleed once more," intoned Rían—or whatever father-shaped thing he was becoming. "For light and dark to one restore."

Talah screamed into the glade. I covered my head with my hands as the glass sky shattered, raining sooty diamonds around me. When I looked up, everything had vanished—the forest, the wildflower fields, the cottage. My father.

"No." The word emerged as a whisper, but as the tempest of Talah's fury roared around me, it became something to cling to—a buoy in the dark. There was more he'd been meant to tell me. More to the poem—the prophecy. And now he was gone. Forever. "No! *No!*"

Talah reared behind me, colossal in this strange, liminal space between living and sleeping, dreaming and dying. Her hair was a million strands of swirling darkness, ever shifting as the dance of time; her skin shimmered with the molten glow of a thousand suns. Her metal eyes burned with ancient stars; every breath she took shuddered through the cosmos, as if her presence was both creation and destruction. I shielded my eyes from her visage. But it was no use.

She was not truly here, expanding and contracting before me. She was *inside* me.

Come, child. Her voice reverberated in my skull. *It is time. There is nowhere left to hide. Let me in.*

No. This was all wrong—this was not how my story ended.

Trapped in my own mind, I had experienced a hundred different emotions, relived a thousand different memories. I had witnessed my own conception, glimpsed the beautiful ending at the heart of all creation. I had heard the Bright One to whom I'd bound myself speak longingly of home, heard my dead father speak of the terrible sacrifices he had made for love. All this had occurred in the space of a heartbeat, or perhaps years. Everything crashed over me like the felling of an ancient tree, bludgeoning me with half-remembered facts and confusing rhymes and opaque pronouncements.

My fear and frustration merged into a primal force that burned hotter than reason and darker than doubt. Ínne's words thrilled through me, birthing echoes to swirl around me.

We are all the same. We are all different. Yet by the circles we are all bound.

I suddenly knew what I had to do.

"You're right," I screamed at the molten endlessness of Talah, relentless and unstoppable. "There is nowhere left for me to hide. I am going to let you in."

I registered her faint surprise as I climbed shakily to my feet amid the shattering spell of the Deep-Dream.

You are?

"I am." I mustered all my dreadful determination and buckled it over my uncertainty like armor, until I stood ironclad before my psychic oppressor. "I'm going to let you in. Then I'm going to shove you out."

Again, Talah registered a remote kind of astonishment. *How?*

I had no earthly idea whether my plan was going to work. I had no idea whether my friends were even alive, or where they had brought me while I fought my internal battle. Perhaps we were still on Emain Ablach as it sank into the sea. Perhaps I was moments from my own true death.

But if there was one thing I had learned over the last year, it was this: There was a pattern embroidered among the stars. I was tangled in it—and had been since before I was even born. And I could either let it take me where it pleased... or wrap my fists in its gods-forsaken threads and steer it where I wanted to go.

By the circles we are all bound.

"My name is Fia Ní Mainnín. First daughter of Deirdre, heir of the Sept of Antlers. Last daughter of Rían, high king of Fódla.

Wife of Irian of the Sept of Feathers." I climbed slowly to my feet on the glass-strewn emptiness below me. I began to run, my boots finding purchase on dying dreams, on scattered stars. "I was made of unscrupulous kings and sorrowful heirs and forbidden love; of burned-out stars and deep green magic and unruly thorns." I flung myself at the Bright One, expanding until I matched her in size and magnitude and will. We circled each other in the endless dark. I smiled as I wrapped my arms around her. "And I want my body back, you bitch."

Chapter Nineteen

Laoise

Laoise felt spring in the cool air as she soared over the Barrens. The sun lofted higher and brighter over the glittering fangs of the mountain ranges separating Tír na nÓg from Annwyn. The faint scents of turned earth and new leaves wafted from the south. She performed a showy barrel roll for the thrill of it, reveling in the warmth of the sun glossing her scales and the vertiginous rush as the world kaleidoscoped around her.

At last Laoise spotted Gwyr and Anwyll sunning themselves on the lip of the sinkhole, nearly camouflaged against the mineral gleam of the rock. She tucked her wings along her back and dived, her neck stretching long as her tail streamed sinuously. Both draiglings rose to greet her, chirping and spiraling alongside her.

She caught her descent at the last possible moment, her fanning wings buffeting the scrawny trees and shrubs clinging to the walls of the sinkhole. A few rockjays lofted from their nests, cawing with irritation. Enfys chased them toward the lip of the cavern, eyeing their nests for eggs to steal. Only the vast fire-lit trees of the nemeton did not move—they stood in their eternal ring, glowing fitfully as threads of darkness slowly climbed their twisted trunks.

Laoise shifted into her Gentry form, her boots striking the ground as her arms shrank, her body became more compact, and her scales molded softer until they became skin and curling hair. There was always a moment of disquiet after Laoise relinquished her draig form—a terrible heaviness combined with parched longing for something left behind. She knew some other shapeshifting Gentry felt the same—an anam cló was, after all, the form of one's soul. But it never failed to strike her as strange that her truest shape was not the one she had been born into.

She strolled toward the caverns leading into the Cnoc. Only to nearly collide with Irian, ducking out into the indirect morning light filtering in from above.

"Oh!" Laoise stepped out of his path. "I didn't see you."

"Nor I you." Irian rocked to a halt, lifting his hand to shield his cavern-dim eyes from the harsh natural light. Upon his skin, he bore evidence of his nightly struggles with his transformed bride—livid scratches scouring his cheeks and throat; a bruised eye purpling the already sleepless hollows of his sculpted face. Laoise knew that by noon, his Treasure would heal him without any scars to speak of. But for now, he looked battered. Exhausted. Halfway to broken. "My apologies."

He cut her an exquisite little bow, then swerved to move past her. Laoise hesitated. Irian was a man of few words at the best of times. In the past few months, he had grown downright taciturn. Laoise did not particularly mind—she had little she desired to discuss with the tánaiste who for years she had known only through violent rumors. Anytime she ventured from her self-imposed exile into Tír na nÓg—for supplies or books or a brief respite from the noisy chaos of seven draiglings—she had encountered whispers of the shadow heir, the vicious Irian, who had cursed twelve innocent human girls to the forms of swans only to dangle them over the heads of the bardaí. Beautiful, deadly, deceitful. She had heard many dark tales she was now inclined to disbelieve—stories where he hanged enemies by their own hair, tricked maidens into his bed by wearing the faces of their old lovers, slaughtered innocents for the pleasure of their screams.

Laoise had never witnessed Irian be needlessly cruel. But she had watched him bloody his own wife in the interest of saving her life. She had seen the broken nose he'd inflicted on his own foster brother. She had felt the menace of his unflinching regard. She had witnessed him walk the edges of his own control, like a brewing storm that could break at any moment. Carefully passionate, violently calculated. For months he had lived beneath her roof, and she still did not know where his limits were.

"Irian." Her voice reached out and stopped his progress.

He tilted his head like a bird of prey. "Laoise?"

She hesitated. "You know we are all doing what we can to protect and revive Fia."

Irian blinked. "If I have not expressed it sufficiently, then let me extend my gratitude for all your hospitality. Without this haven, we would not have survived this trial."

Gods alive, but the man spoke as if he were reciting a historic epic from the times of legends.

"The forge is nearly complete. But though the boys have spent a great deal of time in the library—"

Irian grumbled something under his breath that Laoise gathered had to do with at least one of Wayland's errant extremities.

"We have discovered little about the process of forging Treasures," Laoise finished. "Spring rises on the wind. Despite Eala's threats before quitting Tír na nÓg, Fia has not awoken."

Irian's shoulders bunched. "Your point?"

"Whatever arcane struggle is playing out upon her bones cannot last forever," Laoise said, as gently as she could. Irian was no fool. But thinking a thing and hearing it spoken aloud were two different things. "Soon she must either triumph over Talah...or Talah will triumph over her. Soon Fia will either awaken...or she will die."

Irian stiffened, his hands fisting at his sides. His black hair fanned out over his stark brows as he stared at the stone beneath their feet. "Do not mince words on my account."

"We are tánaistí," Laoise said. "We were not raised to soften our blows. Nor expect them softened for us."

Irian was deathly silent.

"I need to know what you will do," Laoise said. "I know you bear our group no great love. So if the unthinkable happens, and Fia is gone, I deserve to know what you will do."

Irian released all his tension on an exhale. "What do you mean?"

"Come, Irian." Laoise shrugged. "You are loyal to us because Fia chose us—each of us, in one way or another. And you are promised to her. But what are we to you? Sinéad is like a younger sister you barely know. Balor is a mystifying if occasionally helpful stranger. I am an ally you never wanted. And Wayland—sometimes I think you'd rather punt Wayland off a cliff than spend another moment in a room with him."

"I knew you did not think much of me, No-Oath Laoise." Irian's eyes flashed, brilliant as the trees flaming behind him. "But I did not realize you thought so little."

"I do not mean this as an insult," Laoise clarified. It was probably true. "There are worse things than being bound by the love of a woman. I cannot fault you your commitment to Fia these past months. But I also cannot help but wonder what happens to you when—if—she dies." Laoise hesitated. Words had a way of bringing reality to life. Blessings and curses could be spoken in mere whispers and still carry to the ears of the gods. "What will your grief make of you? Who will bear the brunt of your vengeance? Will I be forced to stand as the shield to your sword?"

When at last Irian spoke, his voice was fraught as a distant rumble of thunder.

"You say I do not love any of you, and that makes you afraid. You are right—I do not love you. But that should not make you afraid. Rather, it should be a comfort—loyalty is a blade less sharp than love, and more easily hefted." Irian ran a helpless hand through his black hair. The gesture swirled discomfort around Laoise's spine—as if in asking for honesty, she had received vulnerability. "I am bound and defined by my oaths—the promises I have made more potent than any geasa. So long as you—and everyone else in this mountain—continue to align your goals with mine, you have nothing to fear from me. Love is far messier. Whether Fia lives or dies or exists somewhere in between, I must love her. Desperately. Indecently. Ingloriously. Whatever I would do for her now, I will do for her always. She would never wish anyone but our enemies to bear the brunt of my wrath. Even if I do sometimes long to punt Wayland off a cliff."

It seemed like an attempt at a joke, so Laoise smiled. But Irian looked away, his profile stark.

"As for vengeance? The only person I blame for Fia's fate is myself."

It was not what Laoise expected him to say. "Why?"

"She has been my salvation; I have been her ruin," Irian said without inflection. "Her love saved me; my love has destroyed her. Without her, I am nothing. Without me, she could have been far more."

"If I understand the story correctly," Laoise said, fighting to keep a note of condemnation from her voice, "you saved each other. She has gained far more than she ever lost."

Irian's expression spasmed, hope and bitterness and longing winnowing over his fine features before smoothing away. He turned on his heel and paced away from her.

"If you truly could go back to the start—back to the beginning of your story with Fia—would you truly undo it?" The question spilling unbidden from Laoise's lips wore Idris's face. From the moment she had decided to bring her new friends here, to her home, to her family, she had worried for her brother. She worried for her draiglings too, but they were, well, *draigs*. They might not be able to take care of themselves now, but give them a few years and they would be indomitable. Idris, on the other hand, had been but a child when she rescued him from the ruins of Findias. He had spent the bulk of his life closeted from the world, growing food and reading books and cuddling draiglings. He was soft, in a way that made Laoise hope he never discovered what it meant to be hard.

But she had seen the way he had changed these past weeks. How he had straightened into himself, thrown off the last tatters of his childhood. How he glanced at Wayland when he thought no one was looking, with wonder and hunger and something like hope. How he seemed poised on the precipice of a new story, barely begun—only Laoise did not yet know whether it would be a triumph. Or a tragedy.

She wanted Idris to have the chance to live. To love.

But she had already hurt him so much. And she did not wish him to experience any more pain. "All that love lost, in return for pain avoided?"

"For my sake? Never," Irian said vehemently. "I would trade a thousand days of torment for a single day with her. To hear her laugh. To touch her skin. To taste her lips. But for her sake? If I knew my sacrifice would bring her peace?" Irian broke off, his eyes flying far away. "I think perhaps it is good it is not my choice to make."

Laoise could have traversed the caverns blindfolded. Fortunately, she didn't have to—her eyes adjusted as Dwyn came gamboling behind her, her scales gleaming copper. Laoise could hardly believe how large she'd become—another few years, and her eldest three draigs wouldn't be able to fit inside the Cnoc anymore.

The thought sent a spark of agony to lick at Laoise's heart. She doused it before it could devour her, and stepped into the library.

Idris and Wayland were bent over the same large tome, ostensibly doing research but clearly doing anything but. Idris had his eyes locked on the page in front of him, but he had his lips pressed together like he was trying not to laugh. Wayland wasn't looking at the book at all, but had his chin propped on one hand as he gazed at the other man. He was speaking in an undertone, and the blush rising steadily on Idris's face made Laoise think he wasn't discussing the properties of metallurgy.

She shut the door with a click. Both men startled. Idris had the grace to look faintly guilty; Wayland grinned as he sprawled back in his chair.

"How goes the research?" Laoise asked, a little tartly.

"Excellent," Wayland said. "Assuming you're looking for a method to imprison your enemies' souls in crystal orbs, perfect for shattering when you grow tired of them staring at you from their glass prisons."

Disgruntled curiosity made Laoise ask, "Who did *that*?"

"Lady Saorla of the Sept of Scales had quite the penchant for inventive punishments," Wayland said, his smile exposing too many teeth. "An ancestor of yours, perhaps?"

"Alas, my ancestors were far more efficient." Laoise grinned back. "Why waste time with anything but the classics? Thumbscrews... hot coals...a good whipping."

Wayland put a hand over his heart and sighed theatrically. "Don't tempt me."

"That's enough, you two." Idris slapped the book shut and glared at Wayland before his eyes landed on Laoise. "Anything amiss topside?"

"Mercifully, no." She'd scouted as far as she could easily fly in a morning but seen little more interesting than tufts of grass and nerve-weed. "Eala remains in the human realms, but a moon has come and gone. Spring is upon us. We are running out of time."

The smile fell from Wayland's face. But as Laoise turned back to the door, she heard him whisper to Idris, "Better read faster, Red. Or it's the thumbscrews for you."

Laoise rolled her eyes and shut the door behind her.

The Farm was empty. Laoise followed the sound of loud crashing to one of the lesser-used passageways—a straight, flat hallway between the dining hall and the latrines. There she found Balor, his huge bulk obscuring the corridor. Laoise peered around his massive frame as he rolled enormous boulders to crash into stalagmites sticking up from the floor.

"Balor?" she called over the reverberating noise. "What in the gods' names are you doing?"

"Boulder bowling, lady!" He cheerfully hurled another massive stone. "Would you like to try?"

Laoise looked askance at the massive pile of rocks. "No, thank you. Any idea where Sinéad and Fia are?"

Balor pointed down the hall toward the bedchambers, and Laoise left him to his thunderous game. She'd nearly reached Irian and Fia's bedroom when Sinéad came hurtling out, her hair half-braided and her knives unsheathed. They nearly collided; Laoise put gentling hands on the human girl to keep her from stumbling over her own feet.

She took in Sinéad's twitching mouth, her wild eyes. "What's the matter?"

She was answered by a coughing moan emanating from the open door behind Sinéad. Laoise pushed by the other girl to stare inside. Fia, as usual, was laid out on the bed like a corpse, with her singed hair fanned out around her and her arms crossed over her chest.

The sound came again, half a gasp, half a sob. Laoise stared over at Sinéad. Sinéad said, strangled, "*That's* what's the matter."

Without warning, Fia's body began to jerk violently atop the sheets, the stillness of her daytime slumber shattered in an instant. Her chest heaved, ragged breaths tearing through her as her limbs convulsed, twitching with a wildness that made Laoise's stomach twist.

As one, both women wordlessly lunged for the bed. Laoise grabbed Fia's shoulders, bracing her against the mattress. Beside her, Sinéad sheathed her daggers and steadied Fia's shuddering legs, even as she glanced instinctively at the ceiling.

"It's not yet noon," Laoise confirmed, her voice tight. "She does not usually transform until nightfall."

"We should fetch Irian." Sinéad's eyes were wild with panic.

Laoise shook her head. "He's at the nemeton. It's too far."

On the bed, Fia's fingers clawed at the sheets, opening and closing as if for purchase. Another low, guttural sound escaped her lips. Beneath her eyelids, her eyes darted back and forth. Laoise held on to her, although she did not know what was happening—every time she had witnessed Fia transform, there had been warnings beforehand. Feathers rippling over her arms. Claws bursting from her fingertips. Horns nubbing her forehead.

"Go," Laoise said. "Bar the door behind you. I'm stronger than you, and heal faster. I'll do what I can to keep her safe."

Sinéad did not move a muscle except to slowly unsheathe her daggers again.

Fia's eyes flew wide, locking onto Laoise's with terrifying intensity. Filaments of silver shattered through her green eye; veins of gold glittered from the brown. Before Laoise could react, Fia's hands shot out and seized her wrists with an iron grip, her fingertips scalding on Laoise's skin. Fia's body convulsed again, but her gaze never wavered, as if she were dragging herself upward from some abyss and using Laoise as her anchor. For a brief, terrifying moment, Laoise couldn't tell whether Fia was fighting her way out of a nightmare...or pulling Laoise in with her.

Then she opened chapped lips and croaked, "The circle. Take me to the circle. *Now.*"

Part Two

The Ninth Wave

Not of mother, nor of father was my creation.
I was made from the ninefold elements:
From fruit-trees, from paradisal fruit;
From primroses and hill flowers,
From blossom of the trees and bushes;
From the roots of the earth I was made;
From the bloom of the nettle;
From water of the ninth wave.

—"Battle of the Trees," attributed to Taliesin

Chapter Twenty

Fia

I awoke to a confusion of glimmering black. For a bleak, blistering moment I thought I had failed—thought Talah had swallowed me in fire and fury.

Then I saw a face swimming before my unfocused eyes. Brown skin, curling auburn hair, ember eyes. I stared past the filaments of metal fracturing my vision, blocked out the strangeness of whatever dark glow surrounded us. I grabbed Laoise's wrists as tightly as I could. Partly to make sure she was real—not another figment of my dreamscape—and partly to anchor myself here.

Wherever *here* was.

"The circle." Morrigan, but my throat was dry—speaking felt like dragging fingernails through sand. How long since I'd had something to drink? Heat and sulfur rose with my fear, threatening to overwhelm me. I heard Talah's voice inside me like a silent scream. Whatever strength I'd found in the Deep-Dream was keeping her at bay—for now. I doubted I had much time. "Take me to the circle. *Now.*"

Laoise's eyes widened with a potent mixture of shock and

confusion. I shook her a little—although perhaps I was shaking myself as I fought through the same blend of emotions. I had no idea where I was. No clue how long I'd been trapped inside my own mind. I knew only that everything I'd learned in the Deep-Dream pointed to one thing.

"The...*nemeton*." I dredged the word from somewhere deep inside me. "It's here, isn't it? Tell me it's here."

My mention of the nemeton—or perhaps the urgency grating harshly in my voice—jolted Laoise from her befuddlement.

"It is. But not close. A half hour's walk, through the caverns."

Caverns? I didn't have time to question it. Talah undulated inside me with slow but unstoppable force, her molten might scraping the inside of my skin with terrible promise.

"Then we must run." My breath tasted of brimstone and ozone. "Show me the way."

Still Laoise hesitated. I didn't understand why until I glanced past her shoulder at Sinéad lurking a few paces away. Her azure eyes blazed with unalloyed fear. Two gleaming daggers were braced in her hands. Pointing toward me.

It hit me like a punch to the gut—they were afraid of me. Or rather, they were afraid I *wasn't* me. They were afraid I was Talah.

Not yet. Not fucking yet.

"We run." I stared into Laoise's flaming eyes and prayed for understanding. "We run like the last time we found ourselves in caverns. We run like we've got Gáe Bulga lighting our way. We run like we've got a fucking dobhar-chú snapping at our heels. But it has to be *now*."

My words eased something in Laoise. She heaved me up off the mattress in one smooth motion.

I'd forgotten what it was to have a real body. In the Deep-Dream, I'd been a creature of pure thought, a denizen of memory. Sundry concerns like hunger, thirst, and exhaustion had been immaterial to my cosmic struggle with Talah. Now I felt how weak I'd become—my knees practically buckling beneath my own weight, my stomach cramping with hunger, my throat parched with thirst.

How long had my Treasure been forced to keep me alive without any other sustenance?

I girded my limbs with the strength of my certainty; the power of my will; the magic that had birthed me, raised me, saved me.

In the moment before I followed Laoise from the room, I reflexively pawed at my hips for absent skeans.

"Here." Sinéad was by my side in an instant. Although her eyes were wide and wary, she flipped her grip on her knives and handed the hilts to me. "Take mine."

They were not my skeans. They were longer and the balance was different. But I smiled at Sinéad, gripped the blades, and followed Laoise.

These caverns were vastly different than the caves below Aduantas. Instead of pale stone, there was black rock inlaid with glittering veins of gemstones and metals. Rather than dripping with moisture, the stalactites were formed into chandeliers and lanterns blooming with candlelight. Delicate archways thronged with shadows; narrow staircases flickered with firelight.

I forced my eyes to Laoise's retreating back. Talah's presence rammed inside me like a reminder: I would have time to sightsee later.

The Gentry maiden set a brisk pace, her booted feet pounding an easy rhythm on the stone floor. I was regrettably barefoot—my feet slapped noisily on the slick rock. I cursed as my blood slowly awoke in my veins—a battlefield of sluggish green and furious silver, fighting for dominance.

I held Talah at bay by will alone. And she was putting up a fight.

"Faster," I panted at Laoise. "Faster!"

She glanced over her shoulder at me as if to say, *You're barely keeping up.* But she took me at my word. And began to sprint.

She was *fast.* I nearly lost her as she accelerated into the dim. Skidding through an intersection, I almost missed when she turned left. My feet slipped on the slick stone; I scrabbled for purchase on the wall and flung myself after her. I shoved all my flagging will into my pumping lungs. Pushed all my fear and loathing for Talah into the quivering muscles of my thighs. Forced the slow throb of the Heart of the Forest to pound faster, keeping time with the rabbit patter of my mortal pulse.

Donn be damned, I wanted to *live*.

I caught Laoise, drawing abreast of her as we half slid down a steep descent. She shot me a glance, flashed me a suggestion of a dimpled smile. And ran even faster.

The caverns streaked by, gems and metals gleaming like fallen stars in a black night. I stopped thinking—I knew only the screaming burn of muscles that had been dormant for too long, the scraping hiss of breath in my atrophied lungs, the terrible battle of green and molten silver throbbing below my skin. Heat suffused me, and I felt suddenly too small to contain all the magic living inside me. I whimpered a little and ran even faster, as if I could outrun Talah's inexorable advance.

"Almost there!" Laoise shouted toward me.

Faster.

There—a breath of sky-fresh wind. A shadow not soft with torchlight, but crisp and harsh with sunlight. A sound like bells chiming.

Or, perhaps, an enchanted sword singing.

We burst out into a blinding noon. My eyes narrowed to slits against the brightness, even as my too-fast steps skidded over uneven rocks and stunted scrub. I stumbled; pain streaked up my leg as my shin rasped over stone. I cried out but shoved myself back to standing. Laoise's hands wedged beneath my arms. She pulled me upright, slung me forward. The impression of scalding red flames swam before me. A bonfire?

I blinked.

Trees.

Another figure stood nearby. Tall—devastatingly tall. Black hair swept over blue-gold eyes as he whipped his head around to look at me.

"...*Fia?*" Irian reached for me, trembling and desperate, my name like a prayer upon the wind. I longed for his touch—yearned for it as if it were the only thing that might anchor me to this world.

But it wasn't. I sidestepped him neatly. Achingly.

Sorry, mo chroí.

The flaming trees reared before me, intricate and awesome. I had no time to be impressed by them—Talah was a curse inside me, buffeting the last of my will with her furious strength. My feet were going soft—slurping like molten lava against the rock. My limbs were beginning to burn, my veins no longer metal but slag. My hair singed, the acrid stench mixing in my nostrils with the tang of petrichor and bog tar.

I struck the closest tree with my palms. Its bark was smooth as blown glass, whorled with strange patterns. I nearly lost my grip as I skidded to my knees, rock and dirt and dingy plants scraping my limbs. I wrapped my arms around the trunk as far as they would go—the tree was *massive*. Energy scythed through me, dragging a gasp from my blistered throat. Flaming leaves in a hundred shades of red and gold scattered around me, kissing my skin with even more heat.

"Get out." I was coming apart, fusing together. I couldn't withstand her for even one more minute. *"Get out!"*

You have no idea what you are asking, star child. Talah's voice was the roar of collapsing caverns; the thunderous birth of magic; the bending, twisted growth of a thousand-year-old tree. *This is not my home.*

"Neither am I," I roared back. "You cannot have me!"

But you bound me, Talah argued. Reality itself bent to her words. My spine crumpled. My head bowed. Wayland's ring flashed triumphantly around my finger, a circle of Talah's metal binding me to her. And her to me.

Circles. My head snapped up. My fingers flexed against the smoldering bark of the flaming tree. Ínne's voice once more echoed through me, throbbing in time to the Heart of the Forest. *We are all the same. We are all different. By the circles we are all bound.*

I had bound her to me. But she had been bound before. By Gavida. By the Oak and Holly Kings. By the Fomorians.

Again and again, Talah had been bound. I might not be able to *unbind* her from myself. But that didn't mean I couldn't bind her anew.

I drew one of Sinéad's daggers in a rush. I jerked the collar of my tunic to one side, exposing my breastbone. Somewhere, distantly, I heard an agonized male roar reverberate through the canyon, answered by inexplicable chiming shrieks high above.

Irian had nothing to fear. I had no intention of sacrificing my life for Talah. The opposite, in fact.

I drew a clumsy, jagged circle over the place where my heart beat. Emerald blood welled, as it had in the Deep-Dream. But so too did pain, sharp and visceral. Talah felt it, and she paused.

That will never work, star child.

Maybe not. But I had to try.

I slapped my hand over the uneven circle of blood, transferring it onto my palm.

The cost will be high. A sacrifice will be due. A bare note of dread touched Talah's resounding voice.

I smiled in triumph. She was afraid it *was* going to work.

I slammed my hand, bloodied with a ragged circle of my heart's blood, onto the tree.

For the briefest of moments, the only sensation was one of suspension, the opposite of Talah's grinding, grueling domination. A shimmering spider's thread, taut and delicate and poised to unravel.

The fire coursing below the translucent bark of the trees flickered. Flashed. The grove began to shudder like a beast in its death throes. The trunks swayed and lashed, shedding flaming leaves as they bent double. Rocks pelted and clattered from the high walls. The strange, chiming shrieks intensified, and I swore I heard the beating of leathery wings upon the wind. Impossible shadows sliced between shards of sunlight, but I dared not look up. Dared not do anything but hold my bloodied palm to the writhing tree and *concentrate*.

"Every ending is its own beginning!" The words slammed out of me. I could barely hear my own voice over the roaring in my ears, the pounding of the rocks rattling from the cliffs, the clamor of the bell-like calls. "I bound you to me. But your beginning demanded an ending I cannot abide. So our stories must diverge."

The grove flailed and jerked as if caught in an invisible storm.

All magic comes at a cost, Talah warned, but I heard only her fear. *It may break your heart to pay it.*

"Our hearts were made for breaking—that magic made for mending." The fire from the tree felt as if it was beginning to leak into my flesh—a blinding incandescence that illuminated my skin from the inside. But I could not have drawn my palm away even if I'd wanted to. "The balance is not voluntary. It is essential. Eternal. But mutable. By these laws I bind you, O Talah."

My skin thrummed. Throbbed. Shone. Somewhere deep inside me, Talah thrashed.

"Before, you were bound by threes. Three shackles, three kings, three elements. Thrice three trees." The words juddered out of me, hasty. Uneven. "We bound you anew with fours. Four heirs. Four shackles. Four elements." I dared take my eyes from the flaming tree in front of me long enough to sweep my eyes around the grove. I had counted six other trees, had I not? I could not falter. "Now I bind you by seven. Seven flaming trees." What else? My mind raced, unsteady. I glanced at Laoise, gripping Irian as if she had any hope of holding him back, should he truly wish to shake her. I had glimpsed Sinéad back in the caverns. Who else had made the journey with us? Balor? Wayland? Linn? I had to hope it was enough. "Seven companions, their friendships forged through hardship." Inside me, Talah loosened, as if the invisible strings binding us together were snapping, one by one. "Seven—"

"Dragain!" Irian's roar shattered my concentration—I whipped my head around to look at him. The word shuddered through me, evading my full understanding.

"Irian—" Laoise cried in protest, glancing up at the shadows whirling above my head.

"Seven *dragain*!" Irian repeated, adamant.

Wonder and bewilderment beat wings around my head.

"I bind you, O Talah, with seven mythic dragain." My palm, connected to the tree, was on fire—heat and light bleeding into my veins. Inside me, Talah had almost stopped struggling—as if she, like me, realized this moment was inevitable. Whatever I had set into motion—for good or ill—must now be completed. "By earth and by sky, by fast water and by ancient flaming trees, I bind you, O Talah!" My rising voice was echoed by the cacophonous shrieks of the creatures winging overhead. The words crackled along my throat, throbbed along my bones. Talah began to slip away from me at the same rate she had once colonized me—slowly but irrevocably. Her molten consciousness sluicing hot between my ears, her flaming force slurping through my marrow. I held myself still, although I was shaking. I stared at the hand connecting me to the flaming tree, the skin unblemished despite the tumultuous pain making me sure I was burning alive.

That is not the price, Talah whispered as she was dragged away by her new binding. *The night you freed me from Gavida, you ate of my apples. I could not grant the wish you spoke, for I had already been torn from the network of groves I have heard you call* nemeta. *Now I am returned to the source of my elemental magic. This is not my home. But it is...home.*

I could barely focus on her words. I remembered biting into the last morsel of the wishing apple, swallowing its tender, sweet flesh. What had I wished for? *I wish to become whatever I must be to withstand her.* Sudden fear rose in me, white-hot. Surely that wish had already been granted. Surely all I had become in the Deep-Dream—all I had done to withstand her—had been because of that magic.

Have you learned nothing, star child? Talah murmured as the last of her consciousness ebbed away like a falling tide. As always, she sounded vaguely regretful, as if her actions were beyond her control. As if she were simply performing a role already scripted for her by the patterns etched between the stars. *The cost and the reward are the same—both a heart rended and a heart mended. It is as it has always been. Now you have become truly star touched.*

The grove exploded with light. Fire screamed from all seven sacred trees, light and heat lofting in magnificent columns of gold and red and smoking black. I snatched my hand away and scrambled back. The energy coursing upward abruptly changed direction. The frenzied flames swirled into the ground. The stones shook, deep and deeper. The caves Laoise and I had sprinted through groaned. I braced myself against shattered memories of Emain Ablach on the Longest Night, suddenly terrified that whatever I had done to free myself from Talah had doomed me instead.

Doomed all of us.

With one last heaving shudder, the earth stilled. I slowly looked up. The trees were *alive*, breathtaking and brilliant, their blown-glass trunks and crystalline branches coursing with molten firelight. Veins of silver and gold now joined the red and yellow, plunging into the earth where the roots stretched. High on the branches, tucked between red leaves embossed with metal, I swore I saw apple blossoms, pink and gold as a long-awaited dawn.

A tall black-clad figure hurtled toward where I crouched. Irian's arms gathered me; his hands fluttered at my shoulders, swept over my hair, cupped my cheeks. His lips parted as if he meant to speak to me. Or perhaps kiss me.

Instead, he *roared*.

The raw sound tore from him, born from an instinct so extreme it could only be physical pain. His head dropped, his spine convulsed—and then he wrenched away from me. His hands did not so much lift from my skin as *peel* away. His palms, when he spread them in shock between us, were blackened and smoking, the skin destroyed.

Burnt.

"Fia?" His voice warbled with desperate uncertainty, as if he was not sure who I was. His eyes, when they lifted to mine, were harrowed with pain and wide with creeping shock. "Gods alive, Fia. You are—"

Surprised, I glanced at myself, barefoot and barely clothed, smeared with cave dirt and tree soot and stone dust. I was *glowing*. Shining. Not in the way all the Folk Gentry did—as if they were lit from within by soft, luminous candles. But aggressively. Astonishingly. Incandescently.

My skin shone white-hot, concentrated and cold and fierce. I ran my hands instinctively over my arms, braced for whatever scathing pain had injured Irian. But to my own hands, my skin was cool. Pliant. *Normal*.

Horror wavered through me, chasing away the triumph of Talah's new binding. I was not normal. Not anymore.

Irian was still staring at me as if I had fallen from the sky. "You are—"

"Star touched," I breathed.

Chapter Twenty-One

Wayland

The mood in the Cnoc was like someone had accidentally kicked a hornet's nest and now waited for the inevitable sting. Tense, heavy anticipation haunted the halls with unspoken fears. Wayland had barely been here for five minutes and already he was tired of it.

News of Fia's awakening had buzzed swiftly through the caverns. Mere moments after Fia and Laoise had begun their race toward the nemeton, Sinéad had slammed into the library where Wayland and Idris were working, wild-eyed and spouting gibberish. Once Wayland had worked out what she was trying to say, he'd left the library at a dead run, leaving Idris to stare open-mouthed after him.

In the end, he had missed all the excitement. He had met Laoise, Irian, and Fia returning from the sinkhole, preceded by a pungent waft of burnt skin and molten metal, both odors unpleasantly familiar to him after a lifetime as the son of a smith-king. Laoise led the way, her half dozen draiglings scampering boisterously ahead. Hog bobbled off her shoulder and made a beeline for Wayland, slamming into his chest before sagging into his waiting arms.

Her scales seemed to gleam a touch brighter in the dim, but he didn't think twice about it. He peered over Laoise's shoulder, trying to catch sight of Fia. He saw Irian first, towering at her side, his arms bare and his face barren. Worry spiked through Wayland when he noticed the careful distance his foster brother was keeping from his bride. He didn't seem to know what to do with his hands.

Then Wayland saw Fia.

"Thorn Girl?" The nickname spilled from him before he thought better of it, hammering Irian's expression hard with menace. But Wayland only had eyes for Fia—he wasn't sure he could have looked away from her if he'd tried. Although she was mostly swathed in Irian's overlarge dark mantle, and her pale skin wore half-moons of purple beneath her eyes, and she had grown thinner, she was... radiant.

He did not mean it as hyperbole. Fia had always been beautiful. Now she was terrifying—luminous as the moon and just as untouchable. Her skin literally glowed, rays coruscating between the tangles of her uncombed, half-burnt hair. The gleams at her hairline that had once been Talah's metal were now the silver-gold of starlight. He remembered the words Fia had repeated when they'd first encountered the Year trapped far beneath Aduantas.

Star touched, she had said, frustrated but wondering. *What does that mean?*

Wayland had not known then. He did now. It made him afraid. Just as the power of a Treasure had seemed too overwhelming for Eala's fragile human form, so too did the volatile ancient magic radiating from Fia's skin.

It was one thing to be held hostage to the pattern in the stars.

It was another thing to *be* a fucking star.

He had been staring too long. He forced his eyes away from Fia, landing on Irian. He saw now why he was holding his hands awkwardly crossed, palms up. They were injured—nearly blackened. Horror flashed through Wayland as he realized what must have happened.

Irian had tried to touch her, to hold her, to comfort her. And Fia had hurt him. Gravely.

"Gods alive," he said out loud. "What happened?"

Laoise held out her hands for Hog. The little draigling reluctantly vacated Wayland's arms. Again, Wayland noticed some alteration in her. Not nearly as grievous as Fia's transformation. But her scales seemed brighter. The flames of her eyes sharper.

"Let's get everyone together," Laoise said tiredly. "And tell it once for all."

They gathered in the Cnoc's dining hall. Idris busied himself with laying out food and drink, clearly discomfited by the whole ordeal but nevertheless wishing to be helpful. He pressed a steaming cup of something medicinal into Fia's shining palms, ignoring her curious glance of unfamiliarity.

Wayland thought she needed a stiff dram of whiskey, not tea. He thought they all did. But he wasn't going to be the one to say it.

Then everyone sat in stilted, awkward silence. And he realized he absolutely was going to be the one to say it.

"How about something stronger, Idris?" Idris gave him a startled kind of look before diving toward the sideboard and uncorking a jug of his deepwood sap wine. Glasses were passed; alcohol was poured. Still, everyone simply sat there, trying not to stare at Fia radiating like a fallen star. Idris shot Wayland a dolorous look.

"Gods alive." Wayland lofted his glass. "Are we not celebrating? For months, this is all we have talked of. All we have hoped for." Perhaps not exactly like this. But Wayland knew, perhaps better than anyone else, that wishes granted rarely came true in the way you expected. Stories always changed in the telling. And most people wouldn't recognize a happy ending if it spat in their open mouth. "Fia, the fierce. Fia, the fortunate. Fia, triumphant."

Everyone echoed his sentiments, albeit wanly. Fia sat a little straighter, shrugging out of Irian's cloak and reaching for her own glass. She hesitated in the moment before picking it up, as if afraid the black cup would shatter. It did not, only seemed to take on a pale aura as she lifted it to her shining lips.

"Good," Wayland said. "Now, *what* exactly happened?"

Irian opened his mouth. "She—"

"Please, Brother." Wayland held up his palm. "I would hear it from her."

Irian glowered but fell silent. Fia looked into her wine, her fingers playing over the ragged edges of her hair where Laoise's fire had scorched her two months ago. When she spoke, her voice was faintly hoarse.

"When Talah overtook my body on the Longest Night, she and I were cast into struggle in a place I've come to know as the Deep-Dream." Fia's words were stilted, as if she was not sure how to tell her tale. "We were not the only ones there. Our battlefield was my memories; the fianna, everything and everyone I have ever known. The only reason I survived the struggle was because I was already linked to another Bright One—the elemental source of my Treasure. Ínne. They showed me—" Fia trailed off, emotions tangling over her features before sifting away like dried grass. Fear... ecstasy... sorrow... determination. Wayland could not help but wonder what she had experienced, trapped in the winding halls of her own mind. "They showed me many things. How I was conceived, and why I survived. Who came before me in the lineages of the Treasures, and how the magic has, over the centuries, slowly begun to degrade. How everything—the Solasóirí, the Treasures, all magic—connects back to the nemeta. The sacred groves."

"The nemeta?" Laoise did not so much ask as demand. "What of them?"

"They are where the magic of the stars—and the Solasóirí—exist in perfect balance. Where there is neither too much given nor too much taken. Where all magic coincides and collects. The closest things a Bright One might have to a home."

Laoise and Idris shared a loaded glance, and Wayland remembered that had been one of their pet theories—that the groves were places to which the Solasóirí had descended from the stars. Wayland had thought it a convenient explanation. But all of this seemed to be veering rather terrifyingly into bedtime story territory.

"Is that how you knew to bind Talah anew?" Irian asked. "Did your Bright One tell you?"

"Irritatingly, no," Fia said with a little laugh. "Solasóirí seem upsettingly allergic to speaking in anything but riddles. It was more of an impulsive, if slightly educated, guess. I did not know it would work until it did."

Silence stretched out as everyone absorbed Fia's words.

"And what, exactly," Sinéad asked, "*did* happen?"

"The Grove of Gold was once Talah's home. But in time it became her prison—in the same way the Treasures have become prisons for others of her kind. She was bound first by twos—by the Oak King and the Holly King. After, Gavida bound her by threes. Three elements, three shackles, thrice three trees. Then we bound her by fours." Fia's eyes slid far away, and Wayland knew she was remembering that night beneath the glowing apple trees of Emain Ablach. They had all been so certain something was going to happen...and then utterly sure nothing had. They had been wrong on both counts. But Fia had been the one to pay for that foolishness. "Gavida once told me, *Bindings are always easier than unbindings. All the pieces of the cosmos want to be connected, even as they fall apart.* Perhaps that means the natural state of balance is... *binding.*"

The words clattered against the inside of Wayland's skull. He'd heard those words before. Many times, in fact. Unless he was much mistaken—

"Did my father say who told him that?" Wayland asked sharply.

Fia's brow creased as she studied him as if for the first time. Her mismatched gaze widened when she focused on his throat, curious and canny and unflinching. Wayland experienced the same forced unveiling as he had on the Longest Night, as if Fia had torn off his skin and stared into the unmasked meat of him. There was no judgment in the recognition—only kinship. Maybe even solace, green as a well-trodden path through a sunlit wood.

"He mentioned a man named Marban," Fia said after a beat. Satisfaction chased away Wayland's less convenient feelings, and he shared a loaded glance with Irian. "And he said he had never met a human who had not changed the course of his life. Do you know of whom he spoke?"

"It can wait. I interrupted your tale—please continue."

Fia lifted one shoulder in an eloquent shrug. "When I saw the flaming trees of the nemeton, I hoped Talah might find a new home and leave me in peace. But I was forced to bind her anew. Seven trees. Seven…friends."

"And my dragain," Laoise said, in a clipped tone that made Wayland think she was trying not to sound as furious as she was.

Fia's chin came up an inch. "Seven dragain. And a price, levied in counterpoise to the magic performed."

"What exactly *was* the magic performed?" Laoise had surely noticed how the minerals embedded in the cavern walls suddenly appeared more silver than gold, like Talah's metal veined through Aduantas. How the draiglings' red-gold scales all seemed glossier than they had before—as if embossed with hammered silver. "And what was the price?"

"The girl is glowing, for gods' sake," Wayland scoffed. "And nearly burnt her husband's hands off, if I'm not much mistaken. Is that a high enough price for you?"

Irian reflexively curled his palms, though his skin had nearly healed over, pink and smooth as a babe's arse. Wayland almost pitied him—it would be hell to earn his sword calluses back.

No—Wayland did pity him. Swordplay was likely not Irian's first concern in this unlikely scenario of his wife's touch burning the very flesh from his bones.

"But why?" asked Sinéad softly.

"I don't fully understand." Fia looked at her hands. Her glow had dimmed but not disappeared. "I must think on all I've learned. Now—will you tell me what has happened since the Longest Night? What happened to the Silver Isle? Where is Eala? Where are *we*? Who else is here with us?"

Her gaze fell on Idris with this last question, and Laoise's brother dipped his head behind the screen of his hair, struck inexplicably shy by Fia's direct gaze. Everyone was silent as the past few months arose like a monumental mountain in their midst. No one seemed to know how to traverse it.

"Come, mo chroí," Irian finally said, his voice pitched low. "You will wish to bathe and eat and perhaps sleep. Then I will tell you all that has passed."

Chapter Twenty-Two

Fia

The wine tasted strange on my tongue—like bitter mallow or soured wort. I had a feeling food would be similar. I was reasonably certain I never wanted to sleep again.

But I would commit gross acts of treason for a bath.

So I gathered the folds of Irian's overlarge mantle around my frame and stood from the table, feeling the eyes of the group follow me. I knew they had questions. So did I. But I could read Irian's careful stoicism better than any book. I had seen the way his hand had lifted toward me, then dropped away. I had heard the hurt hollowing his rough burr.

Irian was in pain. And not just because I'd charred the flesh from his hands.

But as I followed him toward what I assumed were our chambers, I could not summon my own emotions. I, too, should be feeling something. Triumph or horror or heartbreak. But all I felt was a strange tranquility. After everything I had experienced in the Deep-Dream, it was a relief to feel numb. Distanced.

Talah had left my body. For now, that was all that mattered.

We entered the same room in which I'd awoken an hour before. Just an hour? It felt like a lifetime. The walls, bed, and ceilings were all carved from the same black rock as the rest of the caverns, pricked through with gemstones and veins of metal. I dallied in the center of the room while Irian ran a bath, skimming my eyes over the unfamiliar surroundings. My gaze snagged on deep scratches cut into the stones; shredded tapestries; a shelf that had been crushed, then hastily mended. Something twinged in my stomach.

"Who did this?" I pitched my tone lightly over the sound of running water. "You haven't been letting Linn into our chambers, have you?"

"You did." Irian did not laugh. "During your transformations."

My eyebrow crept up my forehead. "Transformations?"

"Did you truly have no awareness of the outside world?"

I slowly shook my head. "What did I become?"

Irian seemed at a loss for words.

"Everything," he said at last. "A swan. A deer. A wolf. A serpent. By day, you seemed to sleep. By night, you took on the shapes of a hundred animals. Scratching, howling, pecking, screeching. And in the hour before dawn—"

He trailed off.

"Tell me," I prompted, impatience chafing at my pleasant calm.

Irian would not meet my gaze. "Talah peered from your eyes and experimented with your body's...pleasures. Or tried to."

"Truly?" A tendril of sharp, searing horror threatened to pierce my calm. I stared at the deep, broad scratches marring the stone, then gazed at the rumpled sheets of the broad bed. Within the Deep-Dream, Ínne had defended my most profound self from Talah's inward advance. But I suddenly recoiled from the thought of what a heavy burden Irian must have carried in protecting my physical self from her outward attacks. "And you? What did you do, while I transformed?"

"I held you," Irian said, simply. "As I promised I would."

His last words to me on the Longest Night settled, delicate as snowflakes, on my tongue. *Not in a thousand lifetimes will I ever let you go.* Affection rose in me, hot and fierce—the first complete emotion I'd felt since waking up. I longed to throw myself at him—to crush my arms around his neck and crash my lips to his and remind myself what it meant to have a body. Instead, I wrapped my arms tighter around my chest and willed myself to stop glowing.

"Irian," I chided with a laugh. "Of all the things to take literally!"

"Did you mean it some other way?" His eyes were grave. "What does it mean to you to never let a person go? Should I have set you down when my arms began to tremble? Should I have dropped you when my back began to ache? I took you at your word. And I held myself to mine."

Another deep pulse of tenderness surprised me. I did not have to look at myself to see I was glowing a little brighter. "I cannot fault you for that, mo chroí. But I did not intend for you to single-handedly carry me to the ends of the earth."

"I did accept help when it was offered." The smallest smile touched his plush mouth. "Eventually."

For a long moment, we both looked at each other. Then he surged toward me—not with the heedless intensity of before, but with anguished precision. As if he had tallied every inch of distance between us and found each one intolerable. As if he were a lodestone drawn inexorably to me, his guiding star. Irian gazed down at me from a hand's breadth away, energy searing the space between us.

"Oh, Fia. This is too cruel." My light flared, fracturing his perfect face into shards of brightness and shadow. "This is worse than absence. This is presence turned to suffering. For months I have waited—I have wanted—" The words choked him. He lifted a fist to his mouth, as if to steady himself. "So many times over the past months, I believed you returned to me, only to have the press of your skin be a taunt, the brush of your hands a mockery. Yet now that you are indeed returned, I am denied even that."

"Is that all I am to you?" The words emerged without the lightness I had meant for them. "A body to be held?"

My words conjured some horrified mordancy onto his features and, strangely, seemed to calm him.

"No. It is but a perverse irony that all the nights I held myself back from you were bitter practice for now, when I truly cannot touch you." He lifted his still-healing palms toward my cheeks, cupping the air around my shining face. "Have we two not sacrificed enough? Death and pain and twisted magic and separation? When do you and I earn a moment of peace, mo chroí? I would trade a thousand years of torment for one day with you. But I do not know what we have done to deserve this fate."

I gazed up at him, his desolation marring the veneer of eerie calm I'd carried with me from the nemeton. This *was* cruel. He was right to rage—right to seethe and storm over the injustices etched into our stars. But I could not join him in it.

I knew that if I started, I would not be able to stop.

Abruptly, Irian turned away, spinning the taps on the bath until water no longer gushed. Steam wafted temptingly from the tub. He scraped hair back from his face, visibly mastering himself. He forced lightness into his demeanor as he gestured toward the rows of vials and unguents.

"There is soap. I believe this one is shampoo? Whatever it is, it is heavily perfumed. And—"

"Irian," I said gently. "I know how to take a bath."

I stepped toward the large tub, dropping his cloak to the floor before sliding my thumbs under the straps of someone's borrowed shift. Laoise, most likely. Irian turned on his heel, angling his head away from me.

"Really?" It was easier to tease him than it was to rage with him against our fate. I smiled up at him as I slid languorously into the warm water. "You have seen me without a scrap of clothing before, and in far more compromising positions. One might think you human with all this overwhelming modesty."

"Just being considerate of your tender sensibilities," he growled.

"Whatever my sensibilities are, I doubt them tender." I loved him for making this easy on me. "More like well seasoned, to handle the likes of you."

I leaned back and ducked my head under the water. When I surfaced, water sluicing from the crown of my head, Irian had moved to the floor. Propped against the tub, he dangled one arm over the side, trailing nearly healed fingertips in the warm water. He watched me as I wiped water from my eyes and smoothed wet hair down my back, his eyes golden and blue as an afternoon sky.

"How I have missed you, mo chroí."

I believed him. Oh, how I believed him—his longing for me blurred the air between us with heat. I could not fathom what he must have experienced these past months, could only imagine all he had done to keep me—and possibly everyone else—alive. But I knew this. Knew *us*.

"And I you," I whispered.

"Where were you that you could miss me?"

"Says the man who's been hauling my unconscious body around for months."

The brief flash of his smile was like a diamond—something I wished to polish until it shone, then cherish forever. "In truth, colleen, I *would* like to know where you went. For it is something that has troubled me greatly."

"I—" Beneath the water, our hands lingered mere inches apart. Too close. Yet immeasurably far. I wished I could touch him. Instead, I laid my cheek on the cool edge of the tub. Irian mirrored me, until we both leaned against the stone, faces inches apart, eyes locked. "The Bright One called it the Deep-Dream. But it mostly seemed like the inside of my own mind. My thoughts, my memories. That was where I hid from Talah, for a while."

"Hid?" Irian's plush mouth formed the word like a curse.

"She was...hunting me. I think she had to catch me, consume me, before inhabiting my body." Remembered fear reared inside me. "So I hid. In my memories. Good ones, at first, then banal ones. But eventually I realized it took her longer to find me in memories I was too young to recall, memories so harsh I'd repressed them. Still she came. Until at last I had to confront parts of myself even more consequential and terrifying than my worst memories."

Irian's eyes flicked between mine, searching. "Do you wish to tell me?"

Somehow it seemed almost sacrilegious to speak of all I'd seen, all I'd learned. "Perhaps someday. But I have spent too long inside. Will you not tell me of outside?"

He told me of all that had happened after the Longest Night. Eala, standing on the beach as Emain Ablach crumbled. Wayland removing my collar. My transformations. Weeks of hard travel over harder land as Eala's pursuit grew ever more terrifying. The Barrens, the Cnoc, the draiglings. The group's decision to reforge the Treasures that had been lost. The slow research and frustrating failures. When he related the events of Laoise and Sinéad's confrontation with Eala at the Hazel Gate, I sat up straight in the tub.

"She said *what*?" Although my eyes never strayed from Irian's face, I knew without looking that my glow had intensified, turning the bathwater to quicksilver.

"Laoise or Sinéad should recount this," Irian said, reluctance slowing his words. "But Eala threatened you. She swore that if you did not join her in the human realms in two months, the lives of those you loved would be forfeit."

"I see." My fingernails tightened on the edge of the bath, digging into the smooth stone. Fury lashed the inside of my skin, molten as Talah's metal. "How long ago was that?"

"About six weeks."

Panic joined my fear, whittling away my uncanny calm until I prickled with sharp thorns of agitation. I remembered my father's words to me in the Deep-Dream, moments before he'd disappeared forever into the cottage thatched with birds' wings.

Find your sister. You are her balance. Only you can bring her to the light.

I stared at my hands, glowing like stars beneath the frothing surface of the bath. Then I curled them into fists.

I had just defeated one enemy. Surely I was owed a single afternoon with the man I loved before plotting to defeat another.

I lifted my hands to a hank of my sopping hair, forced my tone easy, and said, "And how in Donn's hell did *this* happen?"

Irian took one look at the damp, ragged tress of burnt hair I was holding and threw his head back. Before I knew it, I was giggling too, our joined laughter echoing through the bathroom.

"Draigs are apparently not as precise as they could be when it comes to mowing down legions of the undead with living fire," Irian finally managed, rueful. "I did scold Laoise."

"Good." I crooked my finger at him. "Now go find me a sharp knife."

He froze, all his humor evaporating. "Surely not—"

"Cut to it!"

He reluctantly obeyed, moving into the sleeping chamber. The Sky-Sword mewed a traitorous little complaint as Irian unsheathed it.

I stared, askance. "Are you cutting off my hair or my head?"

"I know no sharper blade." He looked downcast. "May I speak in defense of your hair?"

"You may." The water was starting to get cold. I quickly finished my bath, scrubbing my body and face and kneading my scalp with my fingertips. "But I may not listen."

"I like your long hair."

"So did I." I stood, the air bracing after the relative warmth of the tub. Irian handed me a towel, which I used to gently dry my hair. I once more indicated the burnt patch, which stretched from one of my ears halfway down my back, a mess of crimped, blackened frizz. "I don't like this. So go on."

Irian's distress was plain as I turned my back to him, hiding a smile. The man could battle a ravening ollphéist or a dozen armed Gentry warriors but couldn't bear the thought of cutting my hair? He hesitated one long moment before gathering my hair in his fist, firmly but gently. The Sky-Sword kissed the back of my neck, cold and humming. In one swift jerk, Irian pulled the keen blade through the hair gathered at my nape.

The first sensation was one of perfect lightness—as if a thousand pounds had been lifted off my shoulders. I sighed at the short strands brushing my neck and falling along my jawline, then turned to Irian, who was holding the discarded ends of my hair like a wet animal carcass.

"Well?" Sudden shyness cast my gaze to the floor. "Has this made me unbearably loathly?"

Irian's eyes grazed my face, my hair, my collarbones. He twitched his finger, and a concentrated burst of air swirled around my head, ruffling my hair until it settled dry above my shoulders.

"Quite the opposite. I fear it is unexpectedly fetching." Simmering anguish glinted deep in his dazzling eyes. He hid it once more beneath humor. "Do I have your permission to keep these cast-off strands?"

"Why?" I narrowed my eyes at him. "Is it not unwise to gift the Folk even a single strand of your hair? A whole handful must be downright dangerous."

"You are correct," he mused. "I could command you to dance reels until dawn. Or sing out all your deepest secrets."

"You've heard my singing voice." I raised my eyebrows. "That would be a punishment for us both."

"But worth it. For all the delicious secrets." He plucked out a hair and held it to the light, considering. "What shall I ask you first?"

"Oy!" I swiped for the tresses, but Irian jerked them out of my reach. "Give it back!"

As I chased him briefly around a room carved from black rock glinting with silver and gemstones, I allowed myself to forget, for a few moments, that I could not touch the man I loved.

It was harder to forget that somewhere—far beyond these walls, these lands, this realm—my sister was going to war.

Chapter Twenty-Three

Fia

I could not fall asleep.

Irian and I had spent the rest of the afternoon talking, acquainting ourselves with all that had passed over the past few months. Acquainting ourselves with our new physical dynamic, achingly different from what we were accustomed to. Acquainting ourselves with each other—for in some ways, he and I were still strangers.

At what I assumed to be suppertime, Laoise's brother had stopped by our chambers with an array of strange foods and a pitcher of wine. Irian conversed with him in low tones; the younger man had avoided looking at me, hiding his eyes behind his sheet of hair. I'd sampled the food but found I had little appetite. Just as the wine had tasted sour and flat earlier, so too did the provisions taste bland. I craved something older. Wilder. I wished not to eat, but to consume.

Or, perhaps, be consumed.

Eventually, Irian's physical exhaustion could no longer be ignored. I gathered that he had not rested much over the past months, standing sentinel over my nightly transformations. His Treasure glossed over hollow cheeks and bloodshot eyes. But it could not stop him from yawning.

I gaped. I didn't think I had ever seen Irian yawn.

Now he slumbered deeply beside me, face down on the mattress, limbs outstretched as if in his dreams, he was flying. I rolled to face him on the pillow and smiled a little. I could not begrudge him the rest, even if my own felt impossibly distant. Every time I closed my eyes, shapes clattered against the inside of my eyelids—patterns sharp as silence and vast as eternities, imprinted in living starlight upon my innermost reaches. In the dark and silence, my sister's last words to me on the Longest Night reverberated between my ears, mingling with the echoes of prophecies I'd heard in my dreams, spoken by ghosts.

You are my sister. My other half. Only together can we be made whole.

Find your sister. You are her balance. Only you can bring her to the light.

Eventually I sighed and sat up, running a hand through my unfamiliar short tresses. I padded to the wardrobe, which—fortunately for me—contained more than Irian's too-large clothes. Earlier, Laoise had thoughtfully stopped by with some sundries, including clothes for both day and night. She was close in height to me, if not proportions, and I easily laced myself into a soft, simple kirtle before toeing on worn leather boots.

I opened the door and slipped out into the Cnoc.

Grooves set in the stone walls carried rivulets of flaming oil to supplement the gleaming minerals and gems studding the walls. I had no idea how anyone told time in these caverns, but I judged it to be late—along the corridor, doors were shut, and no voices or sounds echoed. I followed the lights to the vast dining chamber we'd met in earlier. Balor slept in one corner, his bulk like a fallen tree and his

snores like the scraping saw that felled him. The hearths guttered
with red flames; a few of the larger draigs were clustered close to
the heat, their leathery wings wrapped protectively around their
scaled bodies. I gave them a wide berth as I skirted through the
chamber. Irian said Laoise had raised them as her children...but
even children got hungry. I wasn't positive either my Treasure or
my new radiance could protect me from toothy draigs.

Beyond, a single door stood ajar, spilling honey-gold light across
black stone. I glimpsed chairs, a table, stacks of books. A library?
That seemed as good a place as any to bore myself to sleep.

I wasn't the only one with that thought.

Wayland sat at the large table in the center of the room. A few
candles illuminated him in gold against the dark rows of books at
his back. He looked up when I entered, then stood abruptly, the
legs of his chair scraping.

"Sit down, Wayland." Morrigan, but everyone was acting
strange toward me. Wayland subsided back into his chair as my
pale, unearthly glow joined the homey light of the candles. "Up
late reading when everyone else is in bed? That doesn't sound like
the prionsa I know."

Wayland did not so much smile as bare his teeth. "Does it not?"

"The prionsa I know would himself be in bed. His, or someone
else's." I continued past him to the bookshelf, skimming my eyes
over gilded spines and scrolls curled like fiddleheads. "Although
likely not sleeping."

"Perhaps I have changed, Thorn Girl." His voice was like a hand
on my shoulder, turning me toward him. "At the very least, I am
prionsa no longer. My father is dead. Which makes me a king."

"King of what?" In the dim, his cobalt eyes glittered like an
ocean at midnight. I could not tell whether he was joking, and I felt
abruptly guilty for teasing him. "I am told Emain Ablach fell into
the sea. What makes a king if not his kingdom?"

Without missing a beat, Wayland said, "You mean *besides* his
very large—"

"Shush!" I almost reached out to smother his ridiculous, incorrigible mouth before remembering what I'd done to Irian. Wayland's smile grew with my shock—he always loved to provoke.

"I was going to say *throne*, Thorn Girl. What did you think I was going to say?"

"Stop it," I chided as I turned back to the shelves. "You aren't allowed to flirt with me anymore."

"Why not?" He rose from the chair, leaning his hip against the shelf. "Because you don't like it? Or because Irian doesn't?"

I glanced up at him—his smooth golden-brown skin, his deep blue eyes, his half smile and heavy musculature. To be honest, I'd never really minded the flirting—it had been a constant undercurrent tugging at us since the moment he and I had met. It meant nothing—there was little between us but friendship, as far as I was concerned. But I knew Wayland's familiarity bothered Irian. Perhaps it ought to bother me too. So I said, "Both."

"Then I shall endeavor to cease any and all flirtations with you from this moment until the end of time."

I faced him. "That was shockingly easy."

"That's what most people say about me." He winced, pulling a face. "Sorry. Was that flirting? Old habits."

"That was solidly self-deprecating. We'll let it slide." I cocked my head. "Speaking of your father—"

"We weren't."

"You said he died. What happened?"

Wayland's easy stance hardened, his good humor evaporating like smoke. "I killed him."

"Good." The word came out venomous. I bit my tongue, for Wayland's sake. "I'm sorry."

"Don't be." He lowered his head, spilling sleek mahogany hair over one shoulder. "Mothers leave. Fathers die. It is as it has always been."

Horrified sympathy choked me. I thought again of Rían Ó Mainnín. His words to me in the Deep-Dream: *I would have liked to have loved you.* And I thought of Deirdre, the last missing puzzle piece of my shattered past. I thought perhaps I understood a little of how Wayland felt, grieving a dead father and an absent mother.

"But he set you free, in the end." I gestured to Wayland's throat, where the outline of his heavy collar stood out pale against his skin. "You have your magic back."

"And my destiny." Wayland's hand curled around his neck in a gesture that was at once violent and vulnerable. "Do you know what he said to me, in the end? *Destiny is a bastard who longs to kick you in the balls.*"

"That sounds like him." I glanced down at where my visible skin glowed faintly in the dim. "I daresay he was right. But surely it's better to have a destiny and an aching arse than be cut off from your stars entirely."

"Do you think that's true?" Wayland had always looked at me like my words mattered—something I still wasn't used to. Now his deep blue eyes glowed with an intensity I wasn't sure I liked. "Is it truly preferable to be destined for adversity than chained to happy mediocrity?"

"I think the cost of free will is the burden of choice." I could not seem to banish Rían's specter, his words in the Deep-Dream cutting furrows through my wakefulness. "Those who are not willing to sacrifice their hearts for the prospect of truly living may never learn what it is to be alive."

"And do you feel alive?" Wayland asked gravely. "With all you have already sacrificed?"

"I don't know." I fought the urge to pull the sleeves of my tunic over my glowing skin. "But at least I know the choices I've made were my own to make."

"Were they?" Wayland shook his head, then gestured at me. "Your...starshine. Is it harmful to all? Or just your husband?"

I shrugged, discomfited. "It seems a foolish thing to test."

Before I could react, Wayland reached out and gripped my lucent hand. Light flashed in the space between us, searing my vision.

"Wayland—!" I jerked away, and he released me, inspecting his palm with curiosity in the waning brilliance. I stared, horrified, then relieved when I saw no blackened skin, smelled no seared flesh. "You gods-cursed idiot! What were you thinking?"

"That you deserve to know how much others ought to fear you." Wonder touched his voice as he continued to stare at his unblemished palm. "It...saw me. It tasted me. And it told me...*soon*."

His words sent a shudder spiraling down my spine. "What does *that* mean?"

"What did she say to you?" Wayland's eyes bored into mine, devouring as a midnight sea. "The Year. Did she tell you why she... cursed you with this?"

I closed my hands into fists. "She told me she was granting my wish from the Longest Night, when I asked to become whatever I needed to be to withstand her. *The cost and the reward are the same*, she said. *Truly star touched*."

"Then you burned Irian." Wayland once more reached for me, tentative. Though trepidation fluttered like moths between my ribs, I let him touch the tips of his fingers to my arm. Yet again, my glow flared but did not harm him.

"But not you." I frowned. "What if it is because you are not yet a Treasure?"

Wayland cocked his head. "Go on."

"The Solasóirí came from the stars. Their magic flows through the Treasures but is bound by Gavida's geasa—the laws of the tithes." The words came slowly, then faster as my theory grew. "If I am indeed *truly star touched*, then maybe whatever power now flows through me is pure wild magic? Light, instead of dark. The counterpoint to the warped wild magic released from the destroyed Treasures."

"And this *pure* star magic wants to, what?" Wayland looked skeptical. "*Destroy* Treasures?"

"Or perhaps...just the vessels." A thrill and a threat wended through me. "Ínne told me, *Balance is not voluntary*. Perhaps the pure wild magic was forcibly trying to set the magic of Irian's Treasure free when it burned him."

"But you're a Treasure too," Wayland pointed out. "Why isn't it harming your...*vessel?*"

The radiance bathing my skin seemed suddenly perilous—less a benediction than a curse. *A heart rended and a heart mended.* "How do you know it's not?"

The door creaked open. Wayland and I jumped nervously apart, although we had not been standing particularly close, nor discussing anything untoward. It took me a long moment to recognize the stranger in the doorway. But when the golden candlelight caught on his long auburn hair and glinted in his dark brown eyes, I remembered. Laoise's brother. Idris. I wasn't sure why he had come to the library in the middle of the night, but he was probably wondering the same thing about Wayland and me.

"Idris!" Wayland braced his miraculously uninjured hand on the table and gazed at the other man. "It's late. What are you doing here?"

"I could ask you the same thing." He hefted a lopsided tome bound in hairy leather by way of explanation. "This kept moaning at me while I was trying to sleep."

Wayland grinned. "Are you sure you finished it properly?"

Idris didn't smile in return, simply strode purposefully toward the shelves. His gaze flicked toward me as he passed, his dark eyes cold. I flinched, offended. Until I saw his eyes continue on past me to settle with confused concentration on Wayland.

Ah.

"Well!" I said brightly. "This has been anything but illuminating. My bed summons. Good night to you both!"

I fled the library. Listening to Irian snore would be far preferable to intruding on this brewing lover's quarrel.

Chapter Twenty-Four

Wayland

Wayland watched Fia slide out the library door, her short hair fanning around her glowing shoulders, then turned hesitantly toward Idris.

The other man's presence buzzed with waspish energy. He kept his back slanted toward Wayland as he reorganized the stacks to accommodate the thick, heavy tome he'd ostensibly brought from his room. Wayland sighed, trying to decide whether to lean in to the impending conflict... or lean well away from it.

"Moaning, you say?" He kicked a chair's legs out from under the table and sat down heavily. Might as well get this over with. "It's a sad day when hairy old books are getting more action than me."

Idris picked up the book. Paused. Then slammed it back down, the huge volume shaking the shelves. A few lightweight scrolls bounced to roll away across the floor. Still, he did not turn to face Wayland, bracing his arms on the ledge and keeping his head bent.

"You should have told me you loved her," he muttered after a long, tense moment.

Wayland straightened in his chair, the words curling around him like the lash of a whip. Memories puddled along the painful grooves left behind—memories of hopeful dreams and shared secrets and one impossible, unbearable kiss. Damp dark hair tangled between his fingers, the taste of her like moss and mint and new beginnings. He shoved the thoughts away. Kicked his legs out in front of him.

"She is my friend," Wayland said carefully. "And my foster brother's wife. Of course I love her. We all love her—it's why we're here."

"You are *in* love with her," Idris clarified. "And if you think we can't all see it, then you must think us all blind."

Wayland swallowed, confusion peering through the uneven slats of his careful facade. The truth was, he'd nearly forgotten the feelings he'd once harbored for Fia until she came wandering through the caverns shining like a fallen star. He'd spent the last two months flirting with Idris and Idris alone. As much good as *that* had done him.

Unless—

"Surely you are not jealous," Wayland said softly. "Are you, Idris?"

At the sound of his name, Idris finally turned. His expression— glossed golden by candlelight—was turbulent, an unsteady combination of anger and fear and terrible loss. Shock rippled through Wayland. He abandoned his louche, easy demeanor, shoving from his chair to approach the other man.

"Idris," Wayland said again as he lifted one hand to the shaved side of Idris's head. His skin was warm to the touch. A shivering spark passed between them, forcing Idris's gaze to Wayland's. "I hate to point this out, but for the past two months, you have shown me very little interest. When I flirt with you, you ignore me. When I try to spend time with you outside the library, you make yourself scarce. And when I tried to kiss you, you pushed me away." Idris frowned and opened his mouth, but Wayland interrupted him. "As is, of course, your prerogative. You owe me nothing. But forgive me for assuming it also meant...you felt nothing."

Idris looked at Wayland as if he wished to carve something nameless from the space between them. A promise, perhaps. A certainty. A known from the unknown.

"It's not that I feel nothing," Idris finally murmured. "It is more that I feel everything. But cannot make sense of what is real. What is *true*."

Wayland was quiet, even as guilt frothed through him. He knew he should have been more careful with Idris. He was sheltered, inexperienced. Heavily marked by the whims of tragedy. And for all Wayland's faults, he never wished to cause anyone pain. But in the turmoil after the Longest Night—the loss and uncertainty and introspection—Wayland had wanted something easy. Something familiar. A heady flirtation, a frivolous dalliance.

Real had not entered the equation. For it had been a long time since anyone had cared about Wayland's truth.

"Let me tell you about Fia." Idris's eyes shuttered in surprise, then wariness. Wayland barreled onward. "When I first met her, at a full moon revel at the Elder Gate, we shared only a handful of words. We wore masks—I could not see her face, nor she mine. I safeguarded her against a predator and, in return, stole the promise of a shared kiss. I don't know why I demanded that bargain. My father would say the pattern of the stars required it. Regardless, when we parted, she stole something of me in return—a tendril of whatever magic brought us together. I became...*infatuated* with the mystery girl at the revel who refused a kiss at the cost of her life." Idris's shoulders lifted toward his ears, a protective gesture. Gently, Wayland laid his palms on Idris's collarbones, forcing his posture to ease. "But infatuation is the easiest kind of love—all spark and shimmer, like catching fireflies in the dark. Bright. Brief. Weightless, before it slips through your fingers. It never lasts—eventually, it either dies in the darkness of forgetfulness, or pales before the terrible dawn of reality."

Idris's gaze trembled.

"Fia swept back into my life like a winter tempest wrapped in thorns—untamed and unstoppable, trailing glorious destruction in her wake. But she arrived not as a fantasy, but as a whole person, complete with thoughts, opinions, and desires of her own. And oh—let us not forget—one inconvenient husband." Wayland grinned. Idris did not smile back. "My infatuation burned out like a morning star before a rising sun, even as the magic of our geas drew us closer. As Fia and I circled each other, I saw glimpses of myself in her—as well as the impossible promise of what she saw in me. That was the real intoxication. Love like that is a mirror, not of your reflection but of how they see you—brighter, braver, more *whole* than you ever imagined. And in that light you can't help but want them—because no one else has ever shown you yourself quite like *that*."

Idris stilled. "She showed you your best self."

"She seems to have a way of doing that." Wayland huffed a laugh. "But that's no better than infatuation, in the end. A love built on borrowed reflection shatters when they look away. And you are left searching for yourself in the dark places they never illuminated."

"And now?" Idris's voice was nearly inaudible.

"Now let me tell you about *you*." Wayland's voice dropped. "I understand how hard it is to be vulnerable. To be honest. To bare something of yourself you have never bared before. I understand more deeply than you know. But I have also learned this: Love is neither fixed nor perfectly malleable. It is neither lodestone nor shifting tide. It does not grow in isolation; it cannot be nurtured in solitude. Words like *real* and *true* are but meaningless fog until you cut through the haze. I have made my interest in you abundantly clear."

Idris's pulse fluttered in the hollow of his throat. "I am...afraid."

"We're all afraid, my darling man." Wayland dropped his hands from Idris's shoulders. He leaned over and blew out the candles, one by one, letting darkness dampen the spaces between them. "What shall it be? The safe shadows of a sheltered heart? Or the cold, uncertain light of possible heartbreak?" He snuffed the last candle and made for the door. "It will always be your choice."

Chapter Twenty-Five

Fia

Despite my unsettling theories about the new starshine slicking my bones, I finally slept, curled a safe distance from Irian on the bed with a pillow propped between us.

Only to dream of Eala. She strode toward a feather-thatched cottage in the middle of a field of wildflowers, her white dress and pale hair blowing in the wind. She turned when she heard me approach. I jerked back from her. Black mold veiled her eyes, spreading like rotten veins across her porcelain face; ribbons of green lichen braided through her hair; a crown of pale mushrooms sprouted from her head. She smiled when she saw me; her mouth was full not of teeth, but of white wriggling maggots.

"There you are, Sister," she lisped. "Shall we go in together?"

The door wheezed open as a shadow moved within—

I jerked awake, sweating in the ambient warmth of the caverns. A swift glance showed me Irian's side of the bed was empty; his sheets were cool to the touch. A note slid from the pillow—I snatched it. Irian's spiky, restless handwriting stared up at me.

Did not wish to wake you. Find me in the Armory.

My dream spurred me out into the quiet, dim halls of the Cnoc. Morrigan, I hated it here. Irian once told me I was as connected to rocks and minerals as I was to trees and plants, but I had never believed it. Perhaps I had tied my awareness too closely to the fleeting cycle of growth and rot and rebirth to truly commune with the ancient unchanging life of a mountain. The connection felt too heavy—an unbearable weight I did not care to shoulder.

The sound of steel on steel was the map I followed. The Armory was long and broad, with glittering ceilings and walls glinting with an impressive arsenal—long claimhte and unstrung bows and pikes and daggers and axes. In the center of the training mat was Irian, sparring with—to my immense surprise—Sinéad.

"And kick. Again. *Again.*" Irian's low voice, stark with command, sent delicious warmth skeining through my belly. But his intensity, for once, was not intended for me. He held his palms angled at chest height while Sinéad landed a flurry of targeted kicks, her feet smacking with concentrated force against his hands. Irian shifted his weight backward, urging the human girl to rock onto the balls of her feet while rooting herself with her core. "Find power in your hips. Keep your shoulders square. *Again.*"

I shoved away the plague of apprehension my dream had seeded in my mind, leaning one shoulder on the doorframe to watch them. They'd already been training for a while, judging by the sweat darkening the back of Irian's tunic and dripping off Sinéad's brow. Sinéad had visibly improved since the last time I had trained with her—new muscles stood out along her bared upper arms, and her footwork was far steadier. She fought with a dogged determination that spoke more to her mental resolve than any innate talent for combat.

And Irian? He was flawless, effortless, and fluid, even as he ducked and parried Sinéad's sometimes unstudied strikes. His compassion for Sinéad's skill was evident—he corrected her mistakes with ease if not humor, instructing without punishing.

I thought, with a pang, of something Chandi had said to me last year. *Irian was like a strict older brother. When he was kind, it felt like too little; when he was cruel, it felt like too much.*

Maybe he had found a way to be a little softer toward one of the maidens he had once treated so hard.

Irian finally noticed me lurking in the doorway. His eyes fastened on mine; his sudden inattention earned him a hard kick in the gut from Sinéad.

"Oof." He grunted and doubled over, holding out a hand to Sinéad, who looked less chagrined than triumphant. "A moment."

I met him halfway across the room. His hands lifted toward me; I swayed toward him. We both remembered at the same moment, the distance between us less an arm's length than a chasm. I swallowed brambles as I thought of Wayland staring at his unblemished hand.

It saw me. It tasted me. And it told me... soon.

"How are you?" Irian asked softly.

"Fine." *Except for the celestial radiance that means I can't touch you.* Only *you*, I added silently. "When you're finished here, I wish to speak to Laoise about her encounter with my sister. Will you help me find her?"

Irian glanced at Sinéad, who was letting down her damp hair and peeling off her sweaty wrist guards. "We are finished. Shall we go now?"

Something about Sinéad's demeanor snagged my awareness. Her eyes were downturned; her posture, stiff. She reminded me of—

"Give me a moment." Eala be damned.

Irian followed my gaze. Understood. "I will change my tunic."

I sank onto the ground beside Sinéad. She looked up from tying on her boots, faint surprise ghosting over her expression.

"How are you feeling?" she asked, dropping her eyes.

"Fine." I supposed I was going to have to get used to people asking me that. And lying about the answer. "Irian told me how you helped care for me, watch over me, when I was... Well. I'd like to thank you."

"It's nothing." She inspected one of her daggers, reached for the polishing rags heaped beside a stack of old greaves. "Everyone pitched in."

"Sinéad. I made a mistake, with Chandi." The other girl visibly flinched at the name of her sister. But she finally looked at me, her gaze bleak. "I was so consumed with my own dramas and difficulties that I refused to see what was staring me in the face—my friend, hurting. Maybe it wouldn't have changed anything if I'd shown more care. But maybe it would have. And I intend to learn from my mistakes."

Sinéad's mouth made a flat, unhappy line. "I didn't see it either."

"Neither of us is solely to blame." I reached to touch her arm, but despite Wayland's experiment, I couldn't risk it. "But we should try to be better nonetheless. In both directions."

Sinéad's eyes burned cold as a winter morning, less in defense than in consideration. "I killed her. Eala. Or thought I did. Did he tell you that?"

Her vehemence took me aback. Irian *had* told me, though I had felt little save passing regret that the slaying hadn't stuck. Sinéad's bloodthirst toward my sister seemed well earned and eminently rational. I myself had imagined brutally murdering Eala more than once. But Sinéad had not been raised a warrior. I wrapped my arms around my knees and carefully considered my next words.

"I killed for the first time when I was eight." I could still hear Caitríona's cruel words, still feel her hard slap on my cheek. What I'd witnessed in the Deep-Dream had changed my perspective; it had not lessened my regret. "I didn't mean to. But my nursemaid died nonetheless, her human form sprouting branches and roots and vines, because I could not control myself. The guilt made me so wretched I blocked away my truest nature for over a decade." Sinéad slowly resumed polishing her daggers, but I knew she was listening. "Before too long, killing became quotidian. My—the queen and her druid made me murder rats in the kitchens, then a brùnaidh who wished for nothing more than to tidy bedrooms in return for scraps of food or milk. Soon, I was executing púcaí who terrorized farmers in the borderlands; slaughtering leipreacháin for the terrible offense of stealing sips of ale from taverns. Every death became easier. At least, that's what I told myself."

Sinéad jerked her daggers into their scabbards. "So I must simply kill more, until I grow inured to it?"

I shook my head. "When I was sixteen, I accompanied the high queen on a diplomatic mission to a neighboring kingdom. We were ambushed on the high road by bandits stupid enough to think they could take on the queen's fianna. One of the thieves broke through the shield wall. Charged straight for me, where I rode beside the queen. I had no time to think. My training took over—I flung myself from my horse, tackling the bandit to the ground as I plunged my blades into his neck. It was a bad miss—instead of severing his artery, I tore his tendons. He screamed as he slowly bled out, reaching for me as if I could save him, when I was the one who had mortally wounded him. He cursed me, begged me, wept at me. In the end, the queen had to climb from her horse and sever his head with her own blade."

Sinéad blanched ashen, all the pink in her complexion draining away.

"For months, I dreamed of him. Nightmares where he again cursed me or bled all over me. Where I was the one dying in the dirt instead of him. I never even knew his name, but he held a power over me that took a long time to shake. When at last I confessed all this to Cathair, the queen's druid, he told me, 'Death is easy. Life is hard. We carry all those we have hurt inside us. They do not grow weaker; we simply grow stronger.'" I still often wondered whether he was right. "So you tried to kill Eala. So you failed. It is less important what you did than how you feel about it. Your penitence does you credit. I hope you never lose that."

Sinéad sat perfectly still. In my periphery, I saw Irian stalk back into the Armory, wearing a fresh tunic. I ignored him, keeping my focus on my friend.

"Did you?" she asked, at last. "Lose it."

"I lost it a long time ago. And I fear it is not something that easily returns, even if I wanted it back." I stood. Sinéad stood with me. "I *will* kill my sister. Soon, I hope. And the only regret I will have is that I did not do it sooner." I hesitated, then added, "You saw her, did you not? At the Hazel Gate."

She gave a brusque, unhappy nod.

"Do you think she meant it?" The words bloomed dark with all my unspoken fears. "When she threatened the lives of Chandi and Rogan?"

Sinéad's eyes yawned dark as hollow graves. "Not only did she mean it, Fia, but she meant it as a...benediction. She believes what she's doing is holy. I dread the toll Eala's magic will take. I only hope those I once called friends will survive her reign of death."

We wove through the labyrinth of the Cnoc in search of Laoise.

"You slept a long time," Irian said, from a step ahead of me. "I had begun to worry."

I glanced at the changeless rocks. "How late?"

"Well into the afternoon, I fear." Irian paced in silence before adding, "It was good of you to speak to Sinéad. She has been troubled."

"It was good of you to train her," I responded. "If not speak to her about her troubles."

"Mo chroí." The glance Irian threw over his shoulder was faintly amused. "You should know talking is not my greatest talent."

"Your *greatest* talent?" I laughed. "No, I daresay it is not."

He turned on his heel, walking backward as he lowered his gaze to mine. He opened his mouth, but whatever he might have said was drowned out by the sudden sound of arguing.

"...Are you mad?" Wayland's usually merry tenor was tight with irritation. The hair on the back of my neck lifted—I was not used to audible aggression from the prionsa of Emain Ablach. "That is the last thing we should wish to do!"

The response was quiet, but I thought it must be Laoise's cool, accented voice. I widened my eyes at Irian; we both walked a little faster.

Unlike the rest of the Cnoc, the forge was still rough-hewn. The stone bore the divots of chisels and hammers, and scorch marks where draig fire had smoothed the masonry. Wayland and Laoise faced off over a workbench. Behind Laoise, a large red draig hovered, her pellucid wings glowing faintly in the silver glow permeating the walls; between them on the table, a fat little baby draig rolled around, her soft tummy a strange counterpoint to whatever conflict was winging between them.

"Nothing has changed!" Laoise was arguing. "Unless you simply do not know how?"

"My knowledge is irrelevant. I am not my father."

"Oy!" My voice's harmony joined their discord. Both turned toward me, faintly guilty. "What's the problem?"

"Why have we built this forge, if not to forge things?" Laoise swept her arms broadly. "We all agreed it was the best path."

"That was two months ago." Wayland pointed to one of the veins of silvery mineral threading through the dark rock. "Now *she* is here. It changes things."

"How?" Laoise's screech of frustration rattled the draig at her back. The creature stretched its wings, the hard ridges nearly touching the roof of the cave.

"Because I am not my father!" The repeated words scraped abrasively. "He kept her enslaved for a thousand years. Now that she is here, I will not use her in the same way!"

"It is metal, Wayland. This is a forge. You, presumably, are a smith. Albeit an inept one."

Wayland glowered. "Do not try to shame me into abandoning my values."

"A convenient value indeed. For I have not heard you voice it before."

"That's enough." I wasn't sure I understood the argument, but it was clear Laoise and Wayland were going around in circles, and both were likely to hurt themselves on the barbs they were slinging. "Surely there is a way to resolve this without shouting at each other."

"There is," Laoise said, with sharp impatience. She turned to the draig at her back—bigger than a horse, with fiery red-gold scales and wings scraping the sides of the forge—and pointed at a dense vein of silver-gold metal bisecting a wall. "Blodwen, melt!"

Wayland lunged around the table. "Blodwen, don't—!"

The draig—Blodwen, I gathered—had already reared onto her hind legs, fanning out her wings as she inhaled deeply into her barrel chest. A blaze sparked deep in her gorge, shining between her rufous scales like light through chinks of armor, then rose swiftly along her sinuous neck. She opened her delicate muzzle, studded with distinctly *undelicate* teeth. Snaked her neck. And breathed fire.

I instinctively jumped back from the white-hot conflagration roaring from Blodwen's mouth, nearly colliding with Irian at my back. Immediately the broad vein of metal began to smoke, then melt, droplets of gold-streaked silver beading the black rock below. Wayland turned away in dismay, scooping the much smaller baby draig off the worktable and clasping her to his chest. I was so surprised by his easy familiarity with the draigling that I almost missed Blodwen's head shudder. Her flame stuttered. Her wings flared wider, as if she was trying to lift off inside the cavern. There wasn't room—the unfinished forge was narrow, the ceiling barely taller than Irian's dark head.

Slowly, as if fighting some resistance, Blodwen turned her head, still breathing a ragged sheet of flame. The fire scorched along the wall, scathed the floor. Laoise cried out, jumping back and beating the edge of her tunic where tiny cinders alighted on her clothes.

"Blodwen!" she scolded, her voice touched with the barest note of alarm. "That's not funny."

But the juvenile draig was not engaged in caprice. The conflagration blazing over the forge workbench ignited my own alarm.

I stumbled back another step. Both Wayland and Irian retreated with me.

"Blodwen!" Laoise cried out again.

But the draig didn't seem to hear her—her graceful legs moving ponderously but purposefully across the floor, her neck coiling as she belched great gasps of sizzling red and gold throughout the forge. Heat blossomed, unbearable in the closeness of the room. Through the curling skeins of black smoke clouding the cavern, Blodwen's eyes stared, glossy yet somehow unfocused.

Eyes suddenly gleaming silver. Silver...veined with filaments of gold.

Fear stampeded my heart, and I almost dropped to my knees, coughing as black fumes invaded my lungs. I squinted through the sheeting flames and opaque smog as another hulking serpentine creature with scales of shimmering red-gold joined Blodwen, screening us from the conflagration with broad, membranous wings.

Irian threw his heavy black cloak over my shoulders and wrapped his arms around my torso. The world stretched thin as silk before snapping inside out, yanking us away from the rampant wildfire.

Chapter Twenty-Six

Fia

The endless jet-black weight of the mountain swallowed me whole before spitting me out. I stumbled to my knees on more smooth, dark stone, bracing myself as I retched against familiar nausea.

I hadn't experienced Irian's peculiar mode of transportation in months. Time had not eased my opinion of it.

Worry and panic picked me up from the floor. I whirled on my heel, throwing off Irian's cloak as I searched for him. He stood a pace away, glancing at his untarnished arms. Covering me with his cloak had seemingly shielded him from the worst of my starshine. I looked past him—to my surprise, Wayland stood beside him, one of his hands resting on Irian's shoulder. Another surprise—Irian had flown us not out of the Cnoc, but simply back to the vaulted dining chamber, where all the hallways and caverns converged.

"Find Sinéad," Irian commanded, simply, with a gesture toward the Armory. "Wayland, warn Idris and Balor. I shall try to find the aughiskies. Then meet outside—I do not think any of us should linger here."

I nodded—the roar of flames echoed through the twisting caverns, and the thunder of serpentine bodies colliding with stone shuddered beneath my boots. Or perhaps that was Talah, testing the bonds of the new home I'd given her.

"Laoise?" I hated how my voice trembled.

Irian's jaw tightened.

"Laoise can take care of herself," Wayland answered as he wrestled the rotund baby draig, hissing like a furious cat, into his own mantle. Her needlelike claws were extended as far as they could go, and tiny sparks ignited in the air as smoke curled from her nostrils. Her pupils were hugely dilated and noticeably silver. "Irian's right—we're not safe here."

As if to punctuate his words, another of the juvenile draigs—smaller than Blodwen, but not by much—came shrieking into the main cavern, swinging turbulently from the arched ceiling to the floor as the points of its wings scraped the rocks. Erratic flames rocketed from its mouth, sending light and heat to blossom like captive suns in the black night of the caverns. I hurled myself out of the draigling's unsteady path, diving down one hall as Wayland veered the opposite way. I did not see Irian, but the singing of the Sky-Sword vibrated along my bones, humming in counterpoint to the soundless throb of the Heart of the Forest.

Confusion and fury puddled in my gut as I dashed along the halls. No matter what Talah had done to Laoise's draig family, I did not wish to see these creatures harmed.

Sinéad was in her bedroom—if her wet hair was any indication, she'd been bathing. She looked up when I flung open the door without knocking, surprise swiftly turning to alarm when she noticed my soot-striped skin and scorched clothing.

"What's wrong?"

"The draigs," I gasped out. My lungs felt congested with acrid smoke. "Something's wrong. They're...*attacking*. We need to get out of the Cnoc. Now."

Sinéad did not hesitate, shoving her feet into boots, snatching her daggers, and whipping her mantle around her shoulders before dashing after me. Smoke snaked a terrible warning along the ceiling. We slammed our fists on the closed doors as we passed back through the hall. No one exited.

The main cavern was a thunderous cacophony of roaring fire and splitting rock and scales colliding with stone. Another two draigs—these with patterns of gold scales on their red bellies—had joined the first. They circled one another in volatile spirals, the unsteady beating of their wings buffeting the smoke into great stinging sweeps. I swallowed as tears sprang to my eyes, wetting my lips against the ominous taste of char.

"The exit!" I screamed at Sinéad, who was staring in shock at the draiglings. "Do you know how we get out of here?"

"There!" She gestured toward a sharp, narrow crevasse cut into the far wall. Renewed panic pulsed through me—we'd have to cross beneath all three frenzied draigs in order to reach it. We could skirt around the edges, but we were both already coughing and retching from the stench of smoke and burnt metal.

"On my count, we run!" I screamed, yanking the collar of my tunic over my nose. "One, two—"

"*Three,*" Sinéad shrieked.

We flung ourselves forward, fire bombing around us.

I feinted left. A ball of fire slammed inches from my foot; I spun right, nearly colliding with Sinéad. I leapt over a smashed decanter of mushroom whiskey; flames guttered hungrily along the spill. Another sheet of fire arced over my head; I ducked and nearly stumbled. The narrow gap in the stone Sinéad had indicated wafted, inchoate, between phantoms of smoke—I tried to keep it locked in my vision, even as my eyes and lungs and muscles burned. Just ten more paces—

I tripped over something large on the floor, my knees giving out as I catapulted onto the slick black ground. The breath whooshed harshly from my chest; my elbows screamed where I caught my fall. Instinct forced me to my feet; I almost didn't register what had made me fall. The exit was temptingly, tantalizingly close—

It was a…*person*. Panic spiked my veins—was it Irian? Wayland?

A gust of air formed and re-formed the shifting smoke, and I glimpsed straight hair the color of draig fire; lean, muscled arms curled around himself; eyes shut tight as if to block out the chaos. I reached for him. Hesitated when I remembered what I'd become.

Wayland had been able to touch me without injury. I took a chance—laid my palm on his shoulder. He flinched but did not move save for his lips, mouthing words I couldn't hear. I lifted my hand away.

"Idris!" I shouted. That was his name—wasn't it? Around us, bursts of fire lashed, shrieking through the air to explode near our heads. I ducked and winced, staring after Sinéad as she disappeared down the aperture. "Idris, you have to get up! There isn't much time."

Somewhere, the Cnoc's supplies of oil and wine must have caught fire—muffled blasts rocked the caverns, the smoke fuming from the deeps. The walls dripped with molten silver metal, as if the mountain were weeping. I had lost count of how many young draigs bellowed and flapped and rained fire upon our heads. I prayed to gods I had reason to believe weren't listening that my friends had found a way out of this conflagration. Sinéad, at least, was safe. Irian was a ruthless warrior who wielded a Treasure. Wayland was an obstreperous reprobate with an uncanny knack for weaseling into—and out of—trouble. Balor and the aughiskies had likely survived worse. Laoise could take care of herself.

Which meant there was only me. And Idris.

I couldn't leave him here.

I crouched beside him, cursing myself for barely speaking to him yesterday beyond cursory introductions. The only salient thing I knew about Laoise's brother was how he'd looked at Wayland last night in the library. Like the prionsa was something rare and forbidden—a sweetness he could hardly resist, or a poison that might linger long after the thrill.

That didn't help me now.

"Listen," I rasped, my voice choked by smoke. "Fear is the body's armor. It can be a shield. But it can also chain you."

Again, Idris's lips moved inaudibly. My patience was as shattered as the rocks crumbling from the vaulted ceilings high above. "What?"

"Not...a...fighter. Not...strong."

"You're alive, Idris. That makes you a fighter," I choked out. "You don't need a blade in your hand to be strong. Strength comes in standing, even when fear grips you. All it takes is one step. Then another. Be your own shield. Don't let yourself die chained to your fear."

He uncurled. Slowly—painfully slowly. I fought with every ounce of my self-control not to harry him, hurry him. Grab him bodily by the arm and haul him toward safety.

"That's it," I encouraged, my voice disappearing beneath the booming blasts and crackling fire. Idris levered himself to his feet. He was surprisingly tall—I had to slant my face to look at him. Half his face was shadowed by the fall of his hair. The other half was utterly petrified.

"Go on," I screamed, pointing toward the crevasse where Sinéad had disappeared. "I'm right behind you! I won't let anything happen."

He moved as if he were made of stone. But he moved. Shadows swallowed us; a few steps later, fresh air swirled around my face, sweeping fumes from my lungs in one relieved gasp. I urged Idris forward, my flame-roasted gaze dredging the darkness for scraps of light. After what felt like eternity, pale blue filtered in. Daylight. We spilled out onto the mountain.

The landscape unfolded with rugged, desolate beauty—a vast expanse of windswept dark rock and craggy mountains stretching toward the endless horizon. Sparse patches of velveteen moss clung to crevices, defying the harshness around them; pale, slender wildflowers pushed through fractured stone as if holding vigil in the solitude.

"You made it." Sinéad had her hands planted on her knees as

she sucked in breath after breath of fresh mountain air. Behind her, the aughiskies sallied and stamped, their aquatic beauty at odds with the stark strangeness of the Barrens. "Thank the gods."

Linn sent me a blistering image of myself, so blackened and sooty that I crisped away like ashes upon the wind.

"Missed you too, fiend," I grumbled.

My momentary relief at having escaped the caverns faded before my mounting worry for everyone else. A huge craggy head appearing above the rise swiftly alleviated at least one fear; behind Balor were Irian and Wayland. Soot was smeared across Irian's face, and half his tunic was burned away; Wayland was still wrestling with the baby draig.

At the sight of Wayland, or the draigling—or both—Idris shook himself from his lingering stupor.

"Hog!" he cried, holding out his arms. The baby draig launched herself at him—but instead of whatever welcome he had been expecting, she attacked him. Her little mouth spat sparks as she snapped at his face; her diamond claws raised livid scratches along his throat. He jerked back, horrified, even as Wayland reached out and recaptured his wayward charge, bundling her back into his mantle.

"She is not herself," he said somberly.

Without warning, one side of the mountain burst open. Rocks groaned. Stones clattered. Black smoke plumed, even as a pennant of rose-gold hurtled through the opening. Vast wings snapped open, catching afternoon sunlight and glowing vermilion. I gasped—Laoise's anam cló was astonishingly huge and impossibly graceful and exquisitely menacing. Primeval instinct seeded panic through my veins. I could not stop myself from retreating a few steps down the mountain as she flicked her tail to the sky and hurtled down, her vast form arrowing straight toward us with her shining wings outstretched.

Had Laoise fallen prey to whatever terrible force gripped the draiglings?

If she had, we were all dead. Of that, I had no doubt.

I was not alone in my fear—Idris crouched, as if proximity to stone would protect him from an attacking draig; Wayland angled his body so Hog was protected behind the curve of his chest. Balor stared upward, his massive palm shading his eyes, his fearsome features slack with resigned terror. Only Irian did not cower before the advancing draig, planting his singed boots on the slope and drawing his glittering blade with a song of warning. Sinéad hesitated, then stomped over to stand beside him, drawing her own twin daggers in dauntless solidarity.

I loved them both for it. I wished I had my skeans so I could stand beside them.

In lieu of that, I simply tried not to flee in fear.

Laoise rocketed down the crumbling side of the mountain. Moments before colliding with our trembling group, she opened her mouth. I expected fire to gather in her gorge, as it had in Blodwen's. Instead, her voice—strangely guttural and unbelievably loud—poured over us on the force of her violent exhale.

"Up!" she roared, the word echoing through the gorge in fading triplicate. "*Up!*"

She banked sharply around the ridge of the mountain as, high above, a half dozen draig shapes in various sizes spilled from the hole she'd made. Laoise performed a complicated barrel roll in midair, snapped her wings wide, then climbed vertically. Wind buffeted us, flinging my hair across my face, stinging my eyes, and dragging the breath from my lips. When I looked back up, I saw the draiglings had all spun to follow her, their forms disappearing in the boundless blue.

All...except Hog.

The rotund baby draig was still struggling with Wayland, scrabbling at her swaddle as she hissed and spat with venom. When she flung her head to and fro, her eyes gleamed as deadly silver as the new streaks laddering my hair, and the circle of metal fused to my finger where Wayland's mother's ring had once sat.

I stared at the sky, where the draigs were little more than min-iatures. Heard Laoise's strange command echoing in my ears. *Up.*

"Up," I cried, lunging toward Wayland and ripping the bundle containing Hog from his arms. Laoise was trying to lure her draig children outside the sphere of Talah's influence. The Bright One might be able to control them while they were inside the mountain that was her new home. But she had no control over the air, the winds, the sky. "She needs to fly!"

But the little draigling, upon being freed from her bonds, simply flung herself with renewed vigor at her captor. Wayland threw up his hands as she bashed his head with her stumpy wings, clawing at his face and spitting sparks into his hair. I whirled on my heel, searching for Irian amid the chaos.

"Mo chroí," I screamed. "Wind!"

A stiff breeze smelling of late frost and split stone shrieked to life, whipping my hair around my ears. The draigling—possessed as she might be—squeaked in alarm, digging her claws into Way-land's flesh. Stared at us with vexed silver eyes as the updraft caught her squarely beneath her outstretched wings and launched her ver-tically. Hog keened as she soared unwillingly after her siblings and Laoise, the noise slowly fading as the clouds swallowed her.

We all watched in silence as the eight tiny dots that were Laoise and the draigs circled, their paths erratic. At last, the largest shape—Laoise—banked her vast wings, scooped the smallest dot to her body, and took off toward the west, flying toward the setting sun. One by one, the other draiglings fell in line, following their mother.

We watched until they were specks on the horizon.

Behind us, the ruined mountain belched skeins of black smoke. Rumbled in horrible agitation. Then exploded, soot and rock and gemstones arcing upward in a disastrous plume before billowing down. We dashed for what cover we could find, sliding into crev-ices and sheltering behind boulders as we shielded our heads from the smoldering detritus.

At last, it was over. We slowly crawled from our hiding places.

"Well," drawled Wayland, brushing flakes of snow-white ash from his sleeves and hair. "I don't think the Year appreciated being rehomed. And now I daresay she has returned the favor."

I glanced over my shoulder. The red sun slipping behind the ragged teeth of distant mountains summoned sudden regret. Not for myself—it hadn't been my home destroyed by the Bright One's fury. But for Laoise, who had opened her haven to us when she knew danger dogged us like a curse. And for Idris, who was staring at the ravaged Cnoc in silent devastation.

I had never had a home I would have minded seeing reduced to a pile of rubble. Except, perhaps, Dún Darragh.

"We should follow Laoise," Sinéad suggested.

Wayland made a face. "Are we sure she wants to be followed?"

After a long, fraught moment, Irian sheathed the Sky-Sword in a liquid motion. "Better start walking. The nights here get cold."

Chapter Twenty-Seven

Fia

We made little conversation as we tromped through the dimming Barrens. After a while, a waxing moon sailed over the range. A hazy veil of color—unusual pinks and greens—wafted across the stars from the north, tremulous and fantastic. But below the splendor of the heavens, the Barrens were black and bleak.

The night grew cold—I could not feel it, but Sinéad began to shiver despite the mantle she'd worn from the Cnoc. Irian said nothing, only unclasped his own cloak and layered it over her shoulders. She hesitated, then nestled gratefully in the warm fabric. Warmth of a different kind surged along my spine, even as shadows of regret coiled in my darkest spaces.

How many belongings had been lost in the Cnoc? All those tomes and scrolls in the library—burned to ash. The gardens I'd glimpsed—swallowed by flames. The stores of grain and wine carefully hoarded over the years—fuel for the conflagration. The vast array of weapons and armor stored in the Armory—now molten metal.

At least Irian had the Sky-Sword. Sinéad had her daggers. Balor had his colossal fists. The aughiskies had their shark teeth.

I glanced back at Wayland walking beside Idris in terrible silence and noticed a polished haft protruding from above the collar of his mantle, as if he had a weapon strapped to his back.

I hadn't noticed before, but it was good he was armed. We were going to need all the fighters—and weapons—we could get.

An hour later, Balor spotted something. His whole demeanor lit up—he pointed with a fist the size of a wine barrel toward the shadows of a distant ridge.

"Fire, lady!" he rumbled, with a large smile for me.

I saw it. A streak of blood-red embossed with gold, arcing across the sky. Distant but unmistakable.

Draig fire.

"Laoise," Irian said.

Hope and lingering horror burned through me in quick succession. Had Laoise survived the trials of the afternoon intact? Had her draiglings? "It has to be."

"Dragan Mother is giving us a signal," Balor agreed, his booming voice chattering the pebbles beneath my feet. "She wishes for us to meet her."

"Or she has encountered new enemies and is warning us away," Irian said, encouragingly. "Let me scout."

His silver eyes flew far. His thumb ghosted over the hilt of the Sky-Sword, belted at his waist. And I knew he had flown away, in mind if not in body. I counted my heartbeats.

Ten. Twenty.

His metal eyes flicked back into focus. He smiled—or perhaps it was a grimace.

"It is indeed Laoise," he confirmed obliquely.

"The draiglings," Idris asked. "Are they all well?"

"They are all well." Irian abruptly sank onto the ground. "We should rest."

"The flames appear no more than a few leagues away," Wayland said, after a moment. "If we continue walking, we shall surely reach her by morning."

Irian settled his spine against a rocky outcropping, rested the sheathed Sky-Sword across his knees, and closed his eyes. "For once, time is not of the essence."

"She is my sister," Idris said, a little hotly. "She may need our help—"

"She needs time." Irian's expression was strange—neither amusement nor understanding nor even sympathy, but somehow all of them at once. "That flare was meant neither as warning nor beacon. I am not sure we were meant to see it at all."

"Then what?" Idris demanded.

"Laoise is very, very angry." Irian cracked one eye open. "In my admittedly limited experience, angry fire-breathing draigs should be left to work out their feelings in peace."

Irian was, as usual, correct.

We all slept badly, if we slept at all. Balor snacked upon a few quartz outcroppings, then stretched out on his back and snored thunderously at the sky. In perfect counterpoint, Irian kept a still, silent vigil, his eyes closed and his palms resting on his sword, although I knew he did not sleep. Sinéad huddled a few feet away beneath her cloak; Wayland and Idris leaned together, but uneasily, as if their frames did not fit close enough for comfort. I was too restless for sleep.

Dawn came with frigid fog and a palpable wave of hopelessness wafting over the group. Hunger descended on me with swift and unexpected force, hollowing out my stomach and twisting my insides. I glanced with sympathy at Idris, Sinéad.

If I was hungry, they had to be famished.

The sky turned pale and glossy as a pearl as we walked south.

Soon, the sun rode higher; mist burned off and warmth blossomed. Sinéad threw off Irian's extra cloak; Wayland gratefully turned his face—paler now than when I'd first met him—toward the warm blue expanse.

We smelled smoke before we glimpsed the fire. A plume the color of charcoal bloomed from a narrow valley, unfurling like a greedy, glowering rose. It stank of incinerated things—wood and scorched earth and broken rock.

What must have once been paradise had been reduced to fire and ash. Towering skeletons of scorched trees twisted starkly against a smoky sky. A curving river was a blackened scar, choked with charred debris. Wisps of smoke curled from the ground, filtering muted, eerie stripes of sunlight. Against a wall of black rock, Laoise's anam cló curled amid her brood of draigs, the eight of them looking like the dying embers of an extinguished wildfire.

Hog squealed with glee as we approached, launching herself from the spikes on Laoise's back. But Laoise shifted back into Gentry form with one smooth, practiced motion and grabbed Hog from midair, unceremoniously plopping her between her siblings before turning on her heel and stalking toward our group. Her hair was a flame; her eyes were bonfires; her expression could have destroyed worlds. I heard Wayland take a sweeping step backward, heard Irian draw the Sky-Sword, heard Sinéad exhale a shaky "*Laoise?*"

But Laoise's fury was reserved for me. I knew it without having to ask—understood it on a visceral level. The truth was, I blamed myself too.

For all of it. I had *seen* it—that tree at the center of everything. Every story, every legend, every myth. Every action, every reaction, every twist of fate. Every hero, every villain. Irian, Rogan, Wayland. Eala, Gavida, Talah.

Me.

With every step I had taken, every action I had made, every choice I had chosen, I had manipulated the stories of those around me. I had dug my thorny fingers into fate's tangled vines and *pulled.*

Some things had gone my way; others had decidedly not. But after all I had learned in the Deep-Dream, I could no longer pretend to be a hapless pawn in my own destiny. I was rooted deep in all our stories—no maple seed spinning on a breeze, but a taproot wedged firmly in dark soil.

I just was no longer sure whether I was the hero.

Or the villain.

Perhaps that was why I did not retreat as Laoise plunged toward me with violence and venom. Perhaps it was thoughtless bravery. Perhaps it was resignation.

Or perhaps I knew—a friend incinerating me on the spot was not the way my story ended.

"You!" she screamed, the word igniting like a match on her lips. "This is your fault! Do you ever think about the consequences of your reckless, half-baked plans? No—*you* decide and then you drag everyone else into the mess you created! Emain Ablach is at the bottom of the ocean because of you. The Cnoc—*my home*—is nothing but smoke and ashes because of *you*!"

In the blink of an eye, she shifted back into her anam cló, her scaled form massive and sinuous. Flames blossomed in her gorge. Maybe she wanted me to flee, to cower, to beg. I did nothing, just held my ground and lifted my chin. Her long neck swiveled; her eyes flickered like coals. She hissed, spat. Then breathed fire a pace to my left. Heat roared over me, crisping the hair on my arms and flushing my skin. Irian stepped in front of me, shielding my form with his larger, taller figure.

"A little late, mo chroí," I breathed at his back.

"Not really." Over his shoulder, his mouth quirked with the tiniest smile. He pitched his voice loud enough for everyone to hear. "I am not trying to protect you from her. I am trying to protect her from *you*."

I huffed, but amazingly, the jibe had its intended effect. Wayland laughed; Sinéad made a sound of relief. Laoise shifted back into her Gentry form, although she still vibrated—every muscle along her arms and shoulders clenched. She glared at me around Irian's forbidding figure but did not try to attack me again.

"You should not have bartered my draigs in your unholy bargain, tánaiste," she snarled. "They were not yours to trade."

"I was the one to suggest it," Irian said. "If you wish to rage at anyone, Laoise, let it be me."

This deflated Laoise, unleashing the last of her anger like ashes on the wind. She sank to her knees in the ruined ravine. Hog once more squeaked, lofted into the air, and bumbled across the ravine. Laoise gathered her into her arms.

"She turned them against me," Laoise cried, so softly I could barely hear her. Idris knelt beside his sister, nesting both woman and draig within the embrace of his larger frame. Laoise bowed her head into the crook of his neck, the most vulnerable gesture I'd ever seen the Gentry woman make. It shattered something inside me. Their home—their *life*—had imploded with a blaze, the years they'd lost glowing for a fleeting moment before fading to cold ash.

This was not a thing that could be mended. This was an end.

And I might not have been its sole cause. But I had certainly precipitated it.

I did not blame Laoise for her vitriol. All of this had happened because of me.

It was going to get worse before it got better.

There was no reason to stay in the valley—Laoise's fury had destroyed anything that might have been worth staying for. Water…food… shade. But as the draiglings lofted skyward, expressing our group's growing restlessness in ever-expanding circles, an idea grew inside me.

This little valley—almost like the miraculous sinkhole in the Cnoc, save for its nemeton—had everything we needed. Earth, albeit blackened with hours of draig fire. Seeds, albeit charred and split. Water, albeit little more than a trickle.

And four tánaistí of four essential elements.

"Let's stay." I interrupted Wayland and Irian, discussing our next steps in hushed undertones. "Not forever. Just for the night."

"We have no supplies," Wayland helpfully reminded me, as if I could have forgotten the disastrous events of the past day. "No food, water. Clothes. Bedding."

"Besides," Irian added, "this place smells like a charnel house. I fear the insides of my nostrils are already coated in soot."

A buried acorn—dropped from its tree in the autumn and left to overwinter as the seasons changed—rested a few inches below the topsoil in a corner of the valley relatively untouched by Laoise's draig fire. It responded to my gentle nudging, unfurling from the blackened soil in a curlicue of green before rapidly shooting to my height. But then it slowed, even as I poured my energy into it.

"The soil is too dry—Laoise's fire dehydrated the moisture. Can either of you—"

Irian understood. He glanced at the sky, which was clear and blue as an enamel bowl.

"If there were a storm gathering nearby, I could bring it closer. Lower the pressure to hasten the rain. But I fear there is nothing."

"What if there were—" Wayland licked his lips with uncharacteristic nervousness. "I think there's a spring. The stream fed off it, though it's blocked now."

"Can you call it?"

"I—" He looked almost shy. It did not suit him. "I don't know."

"Try."

Wayland closed his eyes. At his sides, his hands curled into fists. I watched him, sensing his focus.

Droplets of water seeped from the earth, gathering like diamonds on the blackened soil. Wayland swayed, stumbled. Irian's hands twitched; moisture misted upward from the earth to hang over the valley in an eerie fog.

"Where do you wish it, mo chroí?" he asked. "For the roots? Or for the leaves?"

"Both, ideally." I glanced at Wayland, who was visibly weakened from the effort. His innate magic was not yet bonded to a Treasure. "But I wish it were warmer."

"I can help with that." Laoise had come up behind us, silent as a cat.

"Don't you think you've done enough?" Wayland quipped, with his hands on his knees.

"Making jokes?" Laoise drawled. "In your state? Careful—you might use the last of your energy trying to be clever." She faced me. "I was able to raise the temperature a few degrees in the caverns for Idris's garden. I could do the same thing here, if there was a way to keep it from evaporating."

"I can keep the climate contained to the valley," Irian said, matter-of-factly.

Laoise's feat was less visible than lofting fire between her palms or shifting into a giant draig with scales and teeth, yet just as impressive. The fog grew heavier and warmer. My skin flushed, a bead of sweat collecting at my hairline to dribble along my collarbone.

"That's very good," I said.

I closed my eyes, sending my awareness descending along the brutalized root systems spanning the valley. The trees had been old, well established. Laoise had utterly destroyed their trunks. Branches. Leaves.

All but their roots.

They wanted to grow. They wanted to live.

Everything did.

I sowed all my power—my Treasure and starshine alike—into the earth. Every tree in the valley regenerated in a heartbeat, unspooling along the thread of my consciousness. My magic made it possible; the heat and moisture held static in the air of the valley made it effortless. Within moments we stood in a jungle—trees towering over us as ferns nudged our boots and flowers scented the air with rich perfume. A few of the draiglings came diving from the sky to land in a perfect ring of mushrooms, which they proceeded to stomp on with their sharply clawed talons. Linn pawed at the earth, then sent me a greedy image of her mane and tail growing to absurd lengths and turning rainbow colors.

"Well." Wayland looked like he was trying not to be impressed. "I'm not sure we've solved the problem of food, water, supplies, or bedding. But it *is* more pleasant here than it was before."

Laoise rolled her eyes. "You know, Wayland, I have heard it said one can perish from being too clever."

"Oh?" Wayland said airily. "Then it's no wonder you're still with us."

Laoise launched herself at Wayland with a growl. As they tussled good-naturedly amid the seething, expanding growth of the newly regenerated valley, I allowed myself the tiniest smile.

Things were going to get worse. But for now, they weren't so dire.

Chapter Twenty-Eight

Fia

The unnaturally warm, verdant afternoon faded into a pleasant dusk. The valley felt primeval now, ancient as the earth itself—dense, lush, heavy with life. We gathered beside the stream, which Wayland had managed to coax from a trickle to a laughing brook. A few of the trees grew fruit—pear-shaped clusters hanging from branches. I bit into the violet skin of one, despite Irian's protests—the soft, marbled flesh was savory, like figs and roast chestnuts.

"Not poison," I confirmed to the group. "Although it would be tastier with bread and cheese."

"Everything's tastier with cheese," Wayland said sadly.

Idris found mushrooms and declared at least half of them edible. We spitted them on bendy twigs and had the draiglings roast them with uneven bursts of flame. Everyone was famished—we ate the strange fruits and tender mushrooms until our tongues were stained violet and our fingertips tingled from pulling apart the flame-seared caps.

Stars wheeled overhead as we relaxed, sated, upon pillows of lime-green moss draped with blankets of woven vines.

Irian—never one for pleasantries or patience—asked the question we were all pondering.

"What now?"

The question chafed me like a badly forged shackle. The Cnoc was dust and ashes. We had no shelter, little food, barely any clothes, no more books, no weapons, and no forge to make new ones. We had no allies and no plans, save for the one still echoing through my mind, spoken in my father's voice.

Find your sister. Find your sister. Find your sister.

"We could throw ourselves upon the mercy of the Ellyllon and quit Tír na nÓg for good." Laoise's fury toward me had burned lower, but I feared it had a long wick. "Or we throw our lot in with the Summer Twins and anyone else who stands against Eala, and join the fight that is surely coming."

"There's a third option: join Eala's dread army." Wayland inspected his fingernails, his expression deadly serious. "I hear the retirement plan is to die for."

Sinéad silently walloped him on top of the head.

I waited for someone else to chime in, before realizing everyone was waiting for me to speak.

"From the madness Eala spoke to me on Emain Ablach, I believe she wishes to unite the Folk and human realms into one. Through conquest, for I cannot believe she desires peace." *Under my guidance, both realms could be better, stronger, more powerful than either stands alone.* "If she has indeed returned home, then she will conquer the human realms first. Wrest Rath na Mara from M—the high queen—and crown herself in her stead. Only then will she march back upon Tír na nÓg and bring it to heel."

"What does she want with you?" Sinéad asked, her voice faintly hoarse from smoke inhalation.

"She believes Fia completes her," Irian growled from beside me. He had heard Eala's dire philosophy on the Longest Night. "And wishes for her to swear obeisance—to stand beside her in conquest. Their power joined in balance."

"Clearly that's not going to happen," Wayland said. "But it means we have a little time, does it not? Surely the human realms cannot be conquered in a handful of months. We can consolidate our power, reforge the lost Treasures—"

"With what forge?" Laoise words were so hot she might as well have breathed fire. "What magical volumes and rare grimoires collected over a decade of searching?"

"To be fair," Wayland muttered, looking only slightly chagrined, "we weren't getting on particularly well with any of those things before, either."

"You're both right." This earned me surprised looks. "And you're both wrong. We must plan to stand against Eala...but we do not have time to spare. And we must reforge the Treasures... but I doubt we will find the answers in books or scrolls."

I had been thinking about the Treasures since Wayland and I had discussed my starshine. In the Deep-Dream, the Bright One had told me how the magic of the Treasures had begun to dwindle with time, despite heirs' regular tithes to the nemeta. But Irian, Wayland, Laoise, and I had just worked together to regenerate the valley, even without two Treasures.

"What if the Treasures were always supposed to be used together?" I earned myself blank stares. I backtracked. "On the Longest Night, Eala surprised me by naming nine dúile—nine elements of magic. I knew only of the four contained within the Treasures—earth, water, air, fire. Why did the original chieftains—and Gavida, presumably— choose those four to focus their power? Perhaps they were simply the most common or the easiest to manipulate. Or perhaps it's because in nature, those elements are designed to operate in balance." Somehow the looks I got were even blanker. "A tree cannot grow without air, sunlight, or water, no matter how fertile the earth may be. Rain clouds cannot gather or move without heat and wind. Fire cannot spread without air, is bound by water, is fed by organic matter. Our four elements are the building blocks of nature. Each element is both nourished by and bound by the others. *Counterpoise*."

Slowly, Irian nodded. "Together, we are balance."

"Eternal, but not immutable," added Wayland. "It does make a kind of sense, Thorn Girl."

A glow of pride ignited in my chest, and my starshine responded. But then I remembered the theory I'd spoken to Wayland—*How do you know it's not?*—and dimmed once more.

"The balance was broken a long time ago—the moment the Treasures were forged," I continued. "The magic should never have been parceled up and hidden away—it was always meant to work together. But it was broken again—and more deeply—when the Treasures were destroyed by the bardaí during the Gate War. Wild magic cannot exist outside the regenerative cycles of nature. To restore balance, we must first reforge the Treasures. Then, and only then, can the Treasures be safely unmade and the elements returned to their natural state."

"We reforge the lost Treasures," Wayland repeated. "Then... unforge them?"

"Yes." My hand found the Heart of the Forest as a sudden wave of anticipated loss surged through me. I could not fathom losing it—this *thing* that had entwined with my very being. It did not just live within me; I, somehow, lived within it. A world, vast yet intimate, both within and around me. My *heart*. "After we use them together to defeat Eala."

"But how?" Laoise said this slowly and clearly, as if talking to a particularly dim-witted child. "We do not know how to reforge the Treasures. Much less how to safely unforge them, once this hazy defeat has been accomplished."

"I have some ideas."

"You're full of them today," Laoise muttered.

"Hush," Irian growled. "Let her speak."

I shot him a tiny smile before returning my focus to Wayland and Laoise. The heir of fire was the one I was going to have to convince of this plan.

"The Treasures are composed of three components. The source

of the magic—the Bright One, an elemental entity." I grabbed a nearby mushroom and placed it on the ground before me. "The conduit—a resonant object forged by Gavida." I plucked a blade of grass and placed it near the mushroom. "And the vessel—a tánaiste. A living heir powerful enough to channel the magic." I placed a rock next to the grass and the mushroom, creating a triangle. "For a thousand years, the source and the conduit were fixed, while the vessel was tithed anew every twelve or thirteen years." I plucked up the rock and replaced it with one of approximately the same size. Then I swiped the blade of grass, leaving only the rock and the mushroom. "Now we have two warped sources. Two willing, powerful vessels. But no conduits."

Wayland stared at my little diorama, his eyes narrowed. Laoise looked like she was restraining an eye roll.

"Resonance exists between the source and the vessel, because of the innate power they wield. I glimpsed Ínne, my Treasure's Bright One, long before I bound myself to the Heart of the Forest." I drew a line between the stone and the mushroom, then extended another at a perpendicular angle. "If we could harness the existing resonance between source and vessel, could we not *create* a conduit—completing the natural circuit?" I returned the blade of grass, forming the missing point of the triangle.

"Create? No." Wayland stood, manic light dancing in his eyes. He looked briefly—and terrifyingly—like Gavida. A shiver of fear, laced with excitement, coursed through me. "Echo? Yes." He plucked up another mushroom, another blade of grass, another stone. Placed them directly atop mine. "Nature is a great mimic, is it not? Tides rise and fall so precisely, so regularly, that they can be tracked and predicted."

Irian's silver eyes gleamed. "Migratory birds follow ancient inherited routes, journeying across vast distances they have never seen yet somehow know."

"Trees root and leaf in the same fractal sequences, although they cannot see what their neighbors are doing," I added.

"Yes, *yes*. The fucking pattern!" Laoise threw up her hands. "But *how*?"

"We have everything we need." Wayland was alight with excitement. "We just need to arrange it in the right order. Irian, Fia—your Treasures."

The Sky-Sword hummed an eager chord as Irian drew it. I pulled the chain holding the Heart of the Forest over my head.

"Just hold on to them," Wayland said. "Now, Laoise." Wayland faced the redheaded Gentry maiden, who seemed perilously close to exhausting her patience. "Is there anything physical—an object or keepsake—that matters a great deal to you *and* might somehow connect to the element of fire?"

"In case you weren't paying attention," Laoise said acidly, "my home of the past decade just burnt to the ground. So no, I don't have any keepsakes."

"Actually." Idris—who, like Sinéad and Balor, had been silent during the past few minutes of increasingly impenetrable dialogue—leaned back. We all glanced at him in surprise as he fished in his pockets, then drew out a craggy jewel. It glinted in the firelight, ruby red and opaque as spilled blood.

Laoise blinked. "Is that—"

"Part of Blodwen's egg." Idris flushed, pink blooming on his brown cheeks. "I kept fragments from all the draiglings' eggs, over the years. But this piece always stays with me. It's become something of a ... talisman."

"The fucking pattern," Laoise repeated, but this time there was a note of wonder in her tone. "But, Idris—that's yours."

"It was always yours." He slid the draig egg fragment into Laoise's hand. "I was just keeping it for you."

Laoise gazed at it before bowing her head and clasping it to her chest.

"And you, Way?" Irian asked, his voice low but curious. "You, too, have been divested of your home and most of your belongings. What is your emblem?"

Slowly, Wayland drew the weapon I'd glimpsed earlier, poking above the collar of his cloak. A massive trident slid free from its binding on his back, carving an arc in the air that gleamed with iridescence—like the shifting hues of an iris or a rainbow. I gasped. Irian raised an eyebrow. Confused recognition flickered in Idris's eyes while fresh anger darkened Laoise's.

"That's—that's *Fáilsceim*!" she hissed, enraged. "Did you *take* that from the Armory?"

"Should I have left it to melt?" Wayland returned. "I found I could not leave it as I fled the flames."

"But it's not yours," Laoise protested.

"Whose is it, then?" Irian's cutting voice was its own weapon. "Fáilsceim was said to be forged so hot its metal could only be quenched in the deepest, darkest seas. It was wielded by Mannanán Mac Lir, first chieftain of the Sept of Fins, until he was betrayed by his kin and it fell into the hands of the Sept of Scales. The trident already chose Wayland. He simply was not ready to accept it."

Laoise blinked but subsided. Wayland could not hide a flush of pride.

"Then it is decided," Irian said. "It appears one enchanted weapon between us was *not* enough."

"I have never been known for my moderation, Ree." Wayland smiled, then sharpened his focus back onto our group. "I have handled both the Sky-Sword and the Heart of the Forest—one was like touching a storm, the other like being kissed by a forest. Although my innate magic is tied to the element of water, I could sense the elements Irian and Fia wield—high winds and distant skies; damp earth and twisted roots. The conduits must be constantly channeling the energy of the source, even when the heir is not wielding it.

"What if we can layer the resonances of the existing Treasures atop these new objects?" Wayland continued. "*Show* them how to connect to our sources?"

"What's the worst that can happen?" I was fairly certain that was what I'd said before inviting Talah inside me, but now didn't seem the best time to bring up that particular mistake. "Let's try."

Wayland set Fáilsceim gently onto the ground at the center of the circle and motioned for Irian to set the Sky-Sword parallel to the other weapon. I lowered the Heart of the Forest between them so that the smooth blue-green stone touched both the haft of Fáilsceim and the cutting edge of the Sky-Sword. Laoise lowered her shard of draig egg opposite the Heart of the Forest.

The Sky-Sword began to keen, a wordless melody of exultation... lamentation. A flurry of emotions blew across Irian's usually stoic expression. Surprise...scorn...heartache.

Nestled beside the blade, the Heart of the Forest beamed cool radiance. My own body responded, my blood throbbing eagerly along the inside of my skin as my starshine slipped, glancing in rays from my skin. The hairs on the back of my neck lifted as my flesh pebbled. Thorn-studded vines slithered from my Treasure and embroidered outward over the Sky-Sword and Fáilsceim, embossing the pale trident and dark blade with filaments of bright green, then threaded over the glossy, uneven edges of the ruby shard.

Flowers grew, tiny and delicate, with petals sharp as daggers. White as glittering stars. And black as the night sky between them.

"I think you should touch your Treasure, Fia," Wayland said, his tone wondering. "You too, Irian. Think of your Bright Ones. Complete the circuit—source, conduit, vessel. Perhaps it will show the new conduits how to link to Laoise and me...and our sources."

I laid my palm on the Heart of the Forest. At the same time, Irian touched the hilt of the Sky-Sword.

The Deep-Dream lingered, near as my own shadow. Ínne was there, waiting for me. Their imposing figure now brought me nothing but comfort. The burnished fur slicking their shoulder blades was leaf mulch on a forest path; the planes of their golden torso were the smooth bark of an ancient oak; their face was the dimming closeness of a shaded wood. Antlers pierced the sky and smeared blood upon the blue.

In that blue, I saw another figure. This one was not so well known to me, though I had glimpsed them before. In a faded memory, a dream I'd forgotten, a story I'd heard long ago. They resounded inside me, not in my human veins or even my Folk heart, but in the starry marrow lining my bones.

The Bright One of Irian's Treasure was colossal as a cyclone, thunderous as a tempest. Their eyes were dark as burned-out stars and bright as struck lightning. They were the endless night and a clear cold morning. They raged, in the space where all the skies of the world met, yet they were also perfectly calm. They were the wilds of the weather and the silence between the notes of a song.

Their name rippled through me, ineffable and inexhaustible and irate: *Geth.*

The wordless sound of it tangled with Ínne's name and somehow, distantly, with Talah's. And there were other sounds, too—other *names*, syllables and contours I had never heard, never imagined. They were the whispers of the universe carrying eternal secrets: the endless song of starlight, the deep groan of continents shifting, the murmur of seas unfurling, the susurrus of stories unraveling. As foreign as a stranger's dreams, yet as familiar as my own name spoken by someone who loved me.

And two of them were *rotten.*

Not a vow but a curse. Not a blessing but a blight. Not a memory but a *haunting*—beauty and bounty, now twisted and defiled. The syllables of their names came to me in the same way that Ínne's and Geth's had, but they floundered slick as slugs between my teeth. If I tried to speak them, they would come out wrong—guttural and gluttonous and warped. And the figures lurking beyond were just as corrupted. Bloated, shrunken. A sucking tide, a smoking ruin. Wrongness clung to them like a dead hand.

Solasóirí corrupted by violence and greed and destruction. Wild magic turned in on itself. The sources of the two lost Treasures.

"They're here," I breathed. "I can...sense them."

"As can I," Irian said, his low tone touched both by awe and misgiving. I suddenly remembered the first time he had showed me the blighted wild magic billowing above an abandoned Folk city. What had he told me, that night on the moor? *I might not mind oblivion, if you were the one to deliver it.*

Perhaps Irian had known exactly what he spoke of. Oblivion suddenly seemed very close by—terrifying yet tempting.

"Try to maintain the connection." Wayland's voice—so real, so warm, so *physical*—was like a shock. The sensation dragged me back from the edge of the beckoning corruption. "Laoise? Are you ready?"

I heard her reedy inhale. "As ready as I'll ever be."

Chapter Twenty-Nine

Fia

As Wayland and Laoise touched the objects they hoped to forge into Treasures, their psyches flickered to life in the endless depths of the Deep-Dream like tremulous candles in the dead of night. Wayland was cool and deep as a midnight tide, with a ripple of humor frothing like foam. Laoise was a sharp red flame, staunch but brittle enough to extinguish.

Against the undulating mass of the corrupted Solasóirí, the two Gentry heirs looked small. Fragile, even. Fear clutched me. How could they possibly face such odious, overwhelming power? They would be consumed. Devoured. Unmade.

"I don't think—" I almost snatched my hand away from the glossy, clinging surface of the Heart of the Forest.

Stay the course, child. It was Ínne's voice, strong as an oak and ancient as a stone. *We are all the same. We are all different. By the circles we are bound.*

I fought my instinct to stop this before one of my friends got hurt. They had both already lost their homes because of me; I did not wish to be the architect of any more pain. "I'm afraid."

I was speaking to Ínne, but it was Irian who responded.

Together, mo chroí. He did not speak out loud. In the endless dark and blinding light of the Deep-Dream, his voice rang steady and true as the Sky-Sword's song. As the wailing wind. As the drumming stars. *We go forward together. And not in a thousand lifetimes will I ever let you go.*

Together. We reached toward the blighted wild magic.

Touching it was like biting on something rotten—bitter and cloying, the metal taste of decay sharp as rust on my tongue while the dense residue of rot seemed to cling to my skin.

I wrapped tendrils of the wild magic around my hand like the reins of some terrible beast, then *yanked.* I shoved all that wrongness along the tether of my physical senses, pouring it into the Heart of the Forest and beyond. It thrummed like a blight along the vines my magic had grown over Fáilsceim and the draig egg. Veins of black embossed over the Treasures, releasing bursts of toxic spores. A nauseated heartbeat of terrible magic throbbed outward. Around us, the creation we had wrought abruptly reversed, life dying away in an instant as the soil was poisoned, the air clogged, the spring ran dry, and the fire died in a puff of sour smoke. A dull ache reverberated through me as I forced my hand to lift from the Heart of the Forest; the once-emerald vines binding the Treasures together sifted away to gray ash.

"It's done," I whispered.

"I know." Laoise wept as she brought the fragment of draig egg to her chest, great gulping sobs warping her usually pristine features. "I can see them. I can feel them. I did not know they were so...so *broken.*"

Wayland was not crying, but his motionlessness was somehow even worse—beyond anguish, toward numbness.

"So can I," Wayland said, almost swallowing his words. "I can feel their pain. Yet also their hunger. For more. More power, more decay, more deterioration. Like a rabid animal chewing on its own limbs, they are ravenous for that which destroys them."

"Wild magic." Irian's tone was taut with old shame. "It is a hunger that feeds as it devours. Darkness disguised as pleasure. Depravity and delight."

I shivered, remembering the shadows that had once wreathed my husband like great black wings; the corruption above Murias, slicking danger along my bones even as it beckoned me close. I looked at my glowing hands and thought of what I'd guessed about the nature of my starshine. Could it truly somehow be the counterpoint to the warped wild magic?

"Depravity and delight?" Wayland said, with a ghost of his usual insouciance. "Just an average weekday for me."

Idris made a sound in his throat, but I laughed. "If anyone can overcome this trial armed with nothing but wit, I have no doubt it will be you, Wayland."

"High praise, Thorn Girl." Wayland smiled but quickly sobered. "But you're the only one who has actually reforged a Treasure. How did you do it? If we are to succeed, we need to know what you know."

Laoise had stopped crying, but her eyes glowed like lit coals in the darkness.

"The nemeta are key. The blight is tied to where the Treasures were destroyed, but the Solasóirí are tied to their nemeta. The groves are like homes to them." I glided a thumb over the Heart of the Forest, thinking of all I'd learned from Ínne. "And there will be a ... sacrifice demanded."

"Surely you mean a death?" Laoise asked harshly. "We have heard the stories, Fia."

I flinched, glancing at my palms: the tracery of green veins embossed over faintly glowing skin. I thought of that shard of my own soul entombed within a tree within a glade within a dream. I thought of all that my friends had already lost, all they would yet be forced to sacrifice. And I thought I finally understood why Irian had wanted so badly to unforge the Treasures on Emain Ablach— to divest ourselves of this destiny before the great burden of it destroyed us.

I met my husband's silver eyes in the dark. It had been months since the Ember Moon, but tatters of Irian's grief still clung to him like cobwebs. Yet his fingers twitched closer to mine on the soft green moss, and I saw my own determination reflected in his gaze.

Together.

"I *may* have been, ah, overzealous."

Sinéad gave an indelicate snort. "You? Shocking."

"Death is not the key. Life is," I clarified. "Although you will be promising both. The next thirteen years of your life. And the tithe of your death at the end. In truth, it is a balance paid twice."

Everyone was grimly silent.

"If we have our way, you will not be bound long. Nor will you need to tithe the Treasure in thirteen years." I clenched my glowing palms and hoped that was true. "We will find a way to unforge the Treasures, set the magic of our Bright Ones free ... and set ourselves free in the doing."

Irian's hand ghosted over the Sky-Sword, laid across his lap. "I hope it will be that simple."

Blindingly, I remembered his blackened palms, his face contorted by pain, his roar of agony.

So did I. So did I.

"Murias lies to the west. Findias to the south," Laoise pointed out.

"You and Wayland should separate," I agreed. "The sooner the Treasures are reforged, the better."

"Who goes with whom?" Sinéad asked.

Some harrowing emotion passed swiftly over Wayland's face before smoothing away.

"We'll decide in the morning," Irian said, with paternal certainty. "It has been a long few days. We should try to sleep."

As life slowly crept back into the valley, we tried. Water trickled down the rise; mushrooms fruited in the dense moss between the roots of the trees. A warm breeze rustled the green leaves, and the fire sputtered back to life. But the memory of the warped wild magic lingered like a bad smell.

Balor finally began to snore, laid out on his back with his limbs lofted like mountains. Sinéad nodded off in the shadow of his knee; Hog nested in the warmth of her cloaked body. Idris rested his head in his sister's lap. The aughiskies stood guard atop the distant line of rocky hills, their belling cries restive and eerie in the gray of false dawn.

I did not sleep, restless for dawn's rosy fingers reaching westward across the lightening sky. Time felt fleeting, slipping like words over hasty lips, unmeasured and misspent and impossible to recover.

Somewhere, a world away, Eala was raking her greedy fingers through the patterns etched in the stars. Manipulating, coercing, or killing her way to more power. And I was beginning to think I might know how to stop her.

As the sun edged over the lip of the valley, we gathered.

"Today, our paths divide." I met everyone's eyes in turn. "Wayland and Laoise, respectively, seek the sources of the Treasures they hope to reforge."

"And you, lady?" boomed Balor.

I twined my glowing fingers together and opted for the simplest explanation. "I must heed my sister's threat. I travel to a Gate in order to cross into Fódla."

"Why?" Laoise asked bluntly. "Before the Treasures can be renewed? Without allies or draigs? You have no hope of defeating her alone."

How could I explain what my father's specter had told me in the Deep-Dream? *Bring her to the light.*

Those words were no coincidence—I had tasted enough of destiny to know that.

"Before I plunge both realms into all-out war, I must give my sister one last chance to set things right."

Irian looked unconvinced by this reasoning but folded his arms over his chest. "I travel with Fia."

"You don't say," muttered Wayland, who had a sleepy Hog slung around his neck like a court lady's mink shawl.

Linn snaked out her long sea-foam neck and chattered her shark teeth while burning a brief sharp image of her diving after me into a seething sea.

I assumed that was her way of saying, *Through hell or high water.* I grinned—the mare and I hadn't had much of a chance to reunite. I was glad to hear her complicated affection for me stood.

She snapped her teeth at Abyss's mane, and the tall black stallion reluctantly pawed at the moss, as if to say, *Where she goes, I go too.*

The last two aughiskies, a rangy yearling and a white mare, flicked their tails and sent us all visions of distant lakes teeming with fish. *This is where our paths diverge.*

"I will accompany Laoise," Sinéad said. "Someone's got to hold the map and carry the rations."

Laoise's cheeks dimpled. "Not sure you'll be able to carry enough food to keep Idris satisfied."

We all chuckled. Except Wayland, who cast his eyes downward as he brusquely slung Fáilsceim over his broad back and fastened the straps across his chest.

"I'm not going with you, Laoise," Idris said, clearly and simply. "I shall be accompanying Wayland."

I couldn't tell who looked more stunned—Wayland or Laoise.

"You can't." Fear surfaced in Laoise's gaze, an unpredictable smolder that threatened to burn anything in its path. She yanked her brother close, conferring with him in rushed, hushed tones. I thought I heard the words *ingrate* and *mistake* and *ill-suited* before Idris recaptured his arm from hers.

"I can," Idris said, with a sweeping flicker of his sister's offhand bravery. "And I will."

Relief rippled over Wayland's features—a pebble tossed in still water. "Are you sure?"

"I am." Idris smiled a little and held out his hand to Hog, who batted at his fist with a clawed paw. "Without adult supervision, you two are liable to bring the whole realm down around your ears."

Laoise's smoldering anger flashed into a conflagration. "If you think you're taking one of my draiglings *anywhere*—"

Hog yawned broadly before poking one slim claw into Wayland's dimpled cheek and cooing, "Mine."

"And me?" Balor's massive frame seemed to sag beneath its own weight. His barrel-sized hands fidgeted at his sides. "I wish to be of help to whoever needs it. But I would not like to follow where I am not wanted, lady."

I hesitated, remembering his words to me on the Silver Isle: *Every year for twenty years I come to this island. This was the first year I made a friend.* But I wasn't sure how to make him useful.

"I have a special task for you, Balor," Irian interrupted. I glanced at him, surprised by the rogue sparkle in his gilt-blue eyes. "Should you choose to accept it."

Balor's vast shoulders straightened perceptibly, a spark lighting in his eyes. He grinned, revealing numerous teeth in a horrifying yet homely smile. "Gladly!"

"You will travel to the Summerlands as swiftly as you are able," Irian commanded. "You will declare yourself to the Summer Twins, Siobhán and Seaghán. If they still stand against Eala, you will tell them all we seek to accomplish. You will tell them we shall all join them there in one month hence, should the living gods allow it. And you will demand their hospitality in my name."

"Verily, lord," said Balor, in agreement. "I have but one question: What *is* your name, scary husband?"

We all laughed, Balor's easy humor popping the formidable bubble of Irian's words.

"Well then." I smiled to mask the cold, creeping dread strangling my spine. "Let us all embark upon our springtime vacations."

"Let's," Wayland agreed sardonically. "Nothing says a quick getaway like charging headlong into danger. Really clears the mind."

Chapter Thirty

Fia

It was decided that Linn and Abyss would travel with Irian and me to a Gate before awaiting our return with Balor in the Summerlands.

"The Willow Gate may not be the closest Gate, but it is the only one I know that is not buried or guarded in the human realms," I told Irian.

He inclined his head. "Once we pass beyond the Barrens, it should be but a few days of riding to reach my domain. I know many folkways to shorten the distance."

Last spring, Chandi had shown me some of these folkways—mystical gateways throughout Tír na nÓg and beyond that bent the fabric of distance and blurred the lines between spaces. They appeared without warning in natural places—between two ancient trees, in a circle of mushrooms, or in the fog of a moonlit meadow.

Linn chattered her teeth and sent me a friendly vision of one of these gateways closing as I strode through it, slicing me neatly down the middle.

I sighed and quelled a shudder. "Shall we?"

We rode. Jeweled canyons slowly transformed into a broad, flat plain Irian named Mag Tuired. He told me of Eala's ambush; I stared at the blackened craters and scorched weapons scattered among contorted remains of long-dead warriors, hardly believing I had been senseless to all that chaos and violence.

Linn sent us a gleeful recounting of Abyss being dragged down by a skeletal hand, only for Irian and me to go somersaulting through the air a ludicrous number of times before flopping comically onto the ground. Irian colored and almost pouted.

I nudged Linn with my heels. "He rarely appreciates being teased."

We camped that night in a dense glade of towering fungi, caps dripping bioluminescent ooze. For supper, the aughiskies caught soft, succulent fish from the glass-bright ponds dotted throughout the grove. Their glittering bones hummed with unearthly melodies that made my teeth ache.

We traveled the next two days through dank marshlands that had Irian buzzing with silent apprehension, then beneath shimmering waterfalls misting the air with giddy rainbows. An hour after sunset on the third day, when exhaustion began to weigh on me, a river cut a broad swath through a forest just coming alive with spring, its banks dotted with tender green shoots and quivering aspens. Irian instantly relaxed, swinging down from Abyss's broad back.

"This is the boundary of my domain," he said. "Abyss, Linn— this channel cuts straight through the Summerlands to the ocean. Follow it, and you will find Balor."

Linn tossed her head as I, too, dismounted. Then the water horses were gone, sifting their finned fetlocks over the spray of the water until the night swallowed them.

"The Willow Gate is not far," Irian said, with the strange hesitation that had dogged our interactions since I'd awoken from Talah's curse. As if every sentence he spoke was underlaid by an unspoken, more anguished phrase. "We can cross into the human realms tonight. Or I can fly us to the fort if you would rather."

That idea made me queasy. So, too, did hiking all night to reach

Rath na Mara. I walked a little ways between the trees, considering. Branches of oaks and rowans sifted the silver light of a newly risen moon between unfurling leaves. Beneath them, carpets of bluebells and wood anemones trembled in the cool evening air. The scent of fresh growth and loamy soil mingled with the sharp sweetness of new blossoms, and I felt suddenly at home.

"The night is balmy." I brushed my fingers over the earth. Moss deepened, rounding soft and thick over the roots of trees. Vining clematis and wallflower whispered down in a fragrant screen. "Come. Let us rest here tonight. The Gate will wait until dawn."

The smallest smile tugged at Irian's mouth. "As you wish, my sylvan queen."

Night exhaled a last gray breath before dawn, and I awoke to find Irian watching over me.

He sat as close to me as possible without touching me. His crossed knees nearly brushed my shoulders; his broad leather-clad fists rested close to my head. I did not need to sit up to see him, only tilt my chin upward and open my eyes.

"Sky-Sword," I murmured, my voice pliant with sleep. "What do you think you're doing?"

Irian barely moved at the sound of my voice, his eyes jerking down to meet mine. In the faint mist sifting ghostly between the trees, they shone unearthly as the moon netting low between new leaves. After a moment, they flicked back up to continue their alert perusal of the silent forest.

"Keeping watch." Irian's low burr rasped pleasantly in my ears, raising a shiver along my nape. "As you see."

But the silence in the wake of his words felt frayed, like a tapestry with threads pulled. As if there was something he wished to say but couldn't find the shape of. Ever since I had woken from Talah's curse, it had been like this. Irian, ever stoic—yet now without the private smiles and searing glances meant only for me. I longed to speak to him, to weave new threads where the old had unraveled. But all my words seemed either too much or not enough.

I, too, grieved the months stolen from us, time lost like stones dropped down a bottomless well. I, too, ached for his touch, like a flower yearns for the sun. I, too, felt untethered without the steady, wordless language of our bodies.

"I doubt we are in any danger," I said softly. "We are both Treasures. Additionally, I carry within me the great, ghastly power of a dying star. I should think anyone who dared stumble upon us in the night should be more afraid of us than we of them. I wish you would rest."

"Do not scold me for safeguarding your slumber, mo chroí." He quirked an eyebrow at me. "And I was resting."

"You were looming. *Brooding.*"

"I neither loom nor brood, mo chroí." The barest smile touched Irian's perfect face—little more than a glint of a canine beneath his lush lips. "I stand sentinel."

"Handsomely, I might add. But I wish you would sleep."

"I will sleep when I am dead." The broad line of his shoulders shifted as his gaze dropped to me. His eyes lingered on my face, tracing the plane of my cheek and the bow of my lips. Against my breastbone, the Heart of the Forest throbbed. Scabbarded across Irian's lap, the Sky-Sword let out a plaintive hum. Anguish spasmed over Irian's face. "In truth, you are mad to believe there are any circumstances under which you and I would ever be here, alone... and I would let myself sleep."

Pleasure and loss stitched over my skin, gossamer as spider silk—as intricate as it was inescapable. Of all I had lost and all I had found, my physical connection with Irian was not the most precious. And yet I did feel its loss keenly. As I knew he did. He and I were bound by all the touches we had shared—sweet heat and bared skin and the desperate clash of mouths and limbs and bodies. Now we were bound by the distance between us—cool air and thick cloaks and the growing knowledge that we might never share another kiss.

The moonlight slicing low between trees made me think suddenly of our strange, stealthy, combative courtship last year. All the dark forest corners and flowering groves and moonlit ruins. All the considering glances and careful touches, growing more intentional and heated as our mutual attraction grew. All the sly flirtations and gratuitous banter we'd traded to hide the words we would not—could not—say.

If I wanted you, colleen, I would go to any lengths to keep you.

I shivered beneath the weight of his gaze, the weight of my memories. Yes, the loss of our physical connection was a grievous blow. But we had once had less...and made it into far more.

"Surely my snoring isn't that loud, Sky-Sword."

Irian exhaled and dropped his eyes. His raven hair fanned down around his ears as regret and resignation soured his smile.

"Right." Irian shifted, drawing his knees beneath his body as his fist closed around the sheathed Sky-Sword. The other hand braced against the tree at his back as he prepared to rise. "Because of the snoring."

"Wait." I was not ready to let this moment go—bittersweet though it might be. Poised here, in the soft, sweet sigh between night and day, with mist sifting between silent trees and the sun waiting somewhere beyond the horizon, I wanted him. I knew I could not have him—not like that. I could not have the imprint of his fingertips at the divot of my waist. Could not have the press of his mouth against my lips. Could not have the thrust of his hips between my legs.

But there was more than one path through the forest.

"Tell me," I breathed, the moment already so tenuous I feared it might be broken by speaking too loudly or moving too quickly. Irian stilled, one arm propped on a raised knee as he stared at me across the space separating us.

"Colleen?"

"Tell me why we would not be sleeping." My voice dropped even quieter, a sudden shyness tiptoeing between the rising vines of desire thorning my veins. "If you and I were here. Alone. In the hour before dawn."

Irian's pupils dilated, the depthless black devouring the silver until it was little more than a halo. "Do not tease me, mo chroí."

"I would never tease you." My voice was little more than vapor in the silver mist. I slid a finger over my metal brooch, then swiftly unfastened it, allowing the hem of my cloak to fall down over one shoulder.

Irian hesitated, the powerful slope of his shoulders bunching as he battled some inner indecision. "Your eyes, Fia. Let me see your eyes."

Slowly, I rose onto my knees and leaned toward him, bracing a hand on the tree at his back. His gloved hand rose to push stray strands of hair off my cheek; his silver eyes flicked between mine, searching for something I could not name—a single thread lost in a tapestry, the final piece of a puzzle, a memory he dared not touch for fear it might dissolve.

"Why?" I whispered.

His throat worked. "The hour before dawn—that was when *she* came to me. Talah. When she peered through your eyes and possessed your body. But I always knew her—by the taste of your lips and the color of your eyes. I knew her, and I held her at bay."

Curiosity and horror mingled with the desire rising inside me. "Did you never—"

"Never." His voice was vehement. "You are more to me than a body to be held. What warmth in your skin, without the fire behind your eyes? What comfort in your touch, without the heart that spurs it? What meaning in your presence, without the thought beneath it? She was but the outline of you—and I have never desired to hold a shadow nor lie with a ghost."

I drew carefully back. Irian settled on his haunches, although he did not relax. If anything, his whole body now sang with tension—his neck cording and his forearms clenching and his jaw-line tautening. As if he held himself back from me through sheer will.

"If my eyes are my own," I urged, "tell me why we would not be sleeping."

"If you and I were here, alone—" He swallowed, forcefully. "Not safe but not in any pressing danger—" Again, he paused, and his eyes on mine were strangely vulnerable. He was silent so long that I almost pulled my cloak back up over my shoulder. "Well. We would not be so far apart."

"Would we not?"

"No." He mouthed the word as if it pained him. "I would have wrapped you in my cloak once night fell, and you would have slept all night in my arms. Dreaming. And when the dawn first peered between the trees, I would have kissed you awake."

I pressed my fingertips to my lips, lightly. "Here?"

"Yes." His head canted to one side, but for once the gesture was not threatening, only tender. "For a moment."

Disappointment nearly pulled my hand away. "Only a moment?"

A smile coiled in the corner of his mouth. "As delicious as your lips may be, mo chroí, I intend to sample all of you." My pulse jumped, and Irian's long fingers splayed over his suddenly rigid thighs. "The lobes of your ears taste like rose petals. The brush of your cheek is soft as peonies. And the hollow of your throat throbs with the rhythm of your want."

I mapped his words onto my body with my own fingertips, graz-ing over my ears before trailing down my throat toward my collar-bones. Irian tracked the motion like a man starved. When my thumb pressed into the hollow of my throat, he exhaled, leaning his whole spine against the trunk behind him as he kicked his long legs out in front of him. His hands flexed on the moss as if he could anchor himself in place.

"But I would not be satisfied for long. With each taste of your skin, I would only grow more ravenous for the rest of you." His eyes—touched now with a whisper of gold, a murmur of blue—dropped to my chest, mostly hidden beneath the edge of my cloak and the bodice of my kirtle. "Your perfect breasts would fill my palms, and the brush of your nipples between my fingers would nearly break me. But I would master myself for all that was to come."

My hands roamed downward, skimming over the curve of my breasts before gliding over the fabric covering my stomach. Skeins of delicious warmth followed my touch, pooling deep in my belly and coiling around my thighs. My legs fell open, and I reached for the hem of my dress, already tangling around my knees.

"Gods alive, Fia." I hesitated, but with his hands braced forcefully in the moss, his head thrown back against the rough bark, and his eyes blown black with desire, I did not think Irian meant for me to stop. He wet his lips, even as the powerful muscles of his torso clenched beneath the outline of his shirt. "Is it not torment enough that I cannot touch you? Let me at least look at you."

Silently, I lifted my hands back to the ties of my dress, slowly undoing them. My bodice fell away, the cool morning air instantly peaking my nipples through the delicate shift. I was flushed with want, bright with anticipation, delirious with desire. A glow rippled over me—my starshine beginning to slip. I did not try to hold it in. Slowly—painstakingly slowly—I unlaced the rest of my dress, until I was left in only my underthings. I paused, but Irian shook his head. The cut of his jaw and the hard bulge in his breeches summoned something unwieldy inside me.

"All of you." The tone of Irian's voice was exacting, a challenge I could not refuse.

I pulled my shift up over my head, mussing my hair. I slipped my underthings down, grazing over my thighs and calves and ankles, until I was bared to him, perfectly naked in the mossy bower, perfectly in my element. Somewhere, a bird began to sing. Sunlight touched the mist. I slid my hand down the plane of my stomach before delving between my legs. I was already wet.

Irian made a desperate kind of noise deep in his throat.

"All of me," I murmured, "demands at least some of you. Unless you truly do wish to be teased."

Irian hesitated, then obliged, shrugging out of his cloak, pulling off his gloves, and unlacing the front of his trousers. His cock sprang free to kiss the musculature of his torso, rock hard and gloriously long. I inhaled, drinking in the sight of him. He took himself in hand, his fingers hesitant on the shaft.

"Go on," I commanded, as I began to move my fingers gently around the center of my pleasure. "What would you taste next?"

"You are a feast without beginning or end, mo chroí," Irian said, his eyes roaming my figure as he deftly stroked himself, keeping time with my own movements. "Every part of you I touch, every inch of you I taste, only makes me hungrier for more. I cannot be sated. I can only devour and devour until I am glutted on you."

Heat coiled inside me, demanding release. I slid one finger inside myself, then another, rolling the base of my hand against the tightness gathering in my belly. I watched Irian through half-closed eyes as he increased his own rhythm, his fingers pumping over his length. I imagined those huge, capable hands on me, his hardness inside me. My breath gusted fast in my throat. My skin bloomed with radiance. Woodbine and honeysuckle and musk rose burst from the dirt.

"And then?"

"When I am glutted on you, I can only seek to ensure you, too, are satisfied." Irian's head was thrown back; his stomach, taut; his eyelashes, casting shadows black as night over eyes as bright as morning. "And I will not stop until you are."

"How?" The word was a breathless plea; I did not care that I was begging him. I needed him—needed this release.

"I will fill you up, mo chroí." The words rasped out of him, insistent. The muscles on his neck corded, and I knew he was close. As I was close. So close. "You will feel every inch of me inside you. Your thighs will tremble around my thrusting hips. Your walls will tighten as you grip me. Claim me. And you will not be able to think for how completely I satisfy you. How fully I complete you. With the weight of my body on yours, your breath is my breath. Your pleasure is my pleasure. Your cries are my cries. And as we crest over the wave and you come around my length, it will be with my name on your lips."

The urgent need tangling in my core reached crescendo. I came fast and hard, arching back against the moss as starlight spilled from me in a brilliant corona. Flowers tangled over my arms and in my hair, intoxicating me with their scents.

"Irian!" I cried out.

His own climax hit him like a punch to the chest. He groaned as he spasmed forward, every muscle in his body wringing taut as he caught his release in his palm. We both trembled for a few long moments with the force of our spent desire. Then Irian was crawling on all fours across the moss. He leaned over me, his face mere inches from mine. He braced his hand on the tree by my head, emblazoned now with flossy flowers and coiling ivy. His own sex dripped down his palm and made a bracelet for his forearm. I smelled him—like ice water and black metal and lightning. My lips parted. He leaned ever closer, until our mouths were a hairsbreadth apart.

My skin sang. My blood shimmered between my ears. A frisson of energy sparked between us—starshine scintillating the air. Irian winced but didn't move.

"Do that again, mo chroí," he growled, low in his throat, "and I do not care if it kills me. I *will* fuck you, and I will die a happy man. Do you understand?"

I laughed as sunlight crowned the trees and the mist burned away into morning.

"I understand, Sky-Sword. But I make no promises."

Soon we stood before the familiar contours of the Gate—the willow combing her hair over the brook and the bridge looping golden as a necklace in the blooming morning.

A small smile of anticipation exposed Irian's canines. "You know, I have always wished to visit the human realms."

I glanced at him with a little smile of my own. Though it had not been my intention, our strange tryst in the wood had unbound something in Irian. Or perhaps bound anew—a fragmented story retold in a more familiar cadence. A distance acknowledged—then quietly crossed.

"I wish I could tell you the human realms will be lovely in the spring." I sobered, the undulations of our relationship ebbing beneath my anxieties about Eala. "But I don't know what my sister has done. We could be walking into ruin and rubble."

"We could be walking through Donn's black gates and it would be worth it, as long as I was with you."

I beat back my dread. "Then let us make of you a tourist, Irian of the Sept of Feathers."

Chapter Thirty-One

Fia

The Willow Gate shivered silver around us. The stones beneath our boots flashed golden, slanted, crumbled. The stream reversed directions. The willow's branches became roots as the world upended.

We stumbled into the human realms. Irian cried out and fell to one knee, his hands fisting in the dirt. I reached for him, stopping myself in the instant before my hand collided with his shoulder.

"This place," he ground out between clenched teeth. "Feels like...a tomb."

I knew what he meant. After so long in Tír na nÓg, returning to Fódla felt like trying to remember a story I had all but forgotten. My thoughts swam, disjointed. My limbs ached, all gnarled branches and twisted roots. The beginnings of a headache throbbed at my temples. I could only imagine how much worse it must be for Irian. He had never set foot outside Tír na nÓg. He was full-blooded Folk Gentry, born of a powerful lineage and raised to inherit immense power. Magic coursed through his veins and soldered his bones.

He did not belong here.

"My blade." He jerked the Sky-Sword from its scabbard. It came free with the sound of steel slithering against leather. No curious hum, no bloodthirsty croon. "It does not sing."

I remembered everything I had learned from Cathair, all those years ago, and layered it atop all I now knew about the Solasóirí, the nemeta, and the Treasures.

"When the Folk forged the Treasures and cloistered them in Tír na nÓg, they removed something vital from the human realms," I reminded him. "Wild magic declines in Tír na nÓg; in Fódla, it has nearly died out. There is no ambient magic for your Treasure to draw on. But it is still connected to its source."

Irian levered himself heavily to his feet. "How can you be sure?"

"Experience." I touched a fingertip to the Heart of the Forest, hidden beneath my outer mantle. "Even without a vessel to channel its power, the Heart of the Forest found me across realms. Ínne found me and stayed close. And when I truly needed their magic, they were waiting for me to claim it."

Irian nodded, scraping back the hair that had flopped over his brow. I couldn't help but stare. In Tír na nÓg, Irian of the Sept of Feathers was devastatingly beautiful. But he was an extension of his environment—bewitching, alluring, a little eerie. Here, crowned by a cool bright morning and silhouetted by blackthorn and wild cherry, he looked downright eldritch. His smooth pale skin glowed, inhuman; his black hair shone, lustrous as a raven's plumage; his blue-gold eyes glittered disconcertingly. Against Fódla's drab backdrop, Irian was etched dark and uncanny as the blade at his waist; sharp and cruel as the incisors cutting divots in his plush lips.

I blinked, and he was just Irian again. My Irian. But I was reminded of nights long ago in Rath na Mara, poring over *The Book of Beotach* and its terrifying chapters detailing the fickle, treacherous Folk Gentry. Callow killers. Nightmare predators.

Strange to think I had not only bound my destiny to one...but become one myself.

"Come." I dared to lightly brush Irian's gloved hand. "The fort is a bit of a hike."

Irian soon shook off his dolor and began inspecting our surroundings with interest. He asked me the names of the birds trilling airily in the trees and the vines spilling new blossoms in the undergrowth and the woodland creatures ducking behind hollow logs. He seemed especially fascinated with a family of common hares playing beneath a rocky scarp.

"Those things," he said with abhorrent glee, "are *adorable*."

I glanced askance at their tufted white tails, smooth brown coats, and black-tipped ears. Cute, but utterly ordinary. "Don't you have hares in Tír na nÓg?"

"We do. But ours have gemstones for eyes. And they fly."

We reached Dún Darragh near noon. The morning had grown warm, and we threw off our outer mantles. Although I knew we had no time to waste in reaching Rath na Mara, I allowed myself a short detour to my greenhouse, threading along the cobbled pathways, now grown weedy and uneven, past the spring in its grotto, burbling merrily beyond its screen of blackthorns, until the brass and glass structure loomed into view.

Winter had been kind to it—no branches had shattered its ceiling; the errant vines of climbing ivy and wisteria had not yet grown strong enough to warp its beams. I creaked open the door and stepped inside. Irian followed, ducking his head to clear the lintel. I spun in a tight circle, nostalgia making my throat tight. The pitted worktable, cluttered with trowels and spades and dibblers. The pots, empty save for a few stubborn seedlings. The trellises, festooned with little save for dried-out weeds.

"You have spoken of this place before, colleen." Irian did not call me that nickname so much anymore. Yet here it seemed fitting, for the girl who had tended these plants and mended this greenhouse had indeed been the one Irian called *colleen*. "I think it must be precious to you. Will you tell me of the time you spent here?"

"Perhaps." When I looked at this place, I saw Rogan throwing wooden boards into fragile pots, heard Corra teasing me from wood knots, felt indecision over slaying the Folk lord I was developing feelings for. Perhaps someday I would discover how to carve this time of my life into a narrative that made sense—to file away its rough edges and smooth out its confusions. "When we are old and gray and tired, I shall tell you of all the tedious mornings I spent weeding in this greenhouse. Then you shall be sorry you ever asked."

The slanting sunlight reminded me I was wasting time. But as I followed Irian out into the early afternoon, I sent a tiny tendril of magic seeking the sleeping bulbs, the desiccated seeds, the straggling seedlings. In an instant, flowers bloomed, berries plumped, saplings grew.

A little hello, and a swift goodbye. From one old friend to another.

Dún Darragh was shadowed, chilly despite the warmth mounting outside. The torches and hearths were cold and unlit, the high vaulted ceilings echoing with silence. My eyes grazed the massive carven pillars to where their arching buttresses disappeared into the gloom, searching for—

"Corra!" The word multiplied, sprinting along crumbling corridors and curving stairways. "Come out at once, fiend! There's someone I wish you to meet!"

Irian seemed taken aback by my tone. "I have never heard you speak in such a way to anyone, mo chroí. Save mortal enemies."

I grinned a little. "You have never met Corra."

A flurry of motion grazed the far wall of the great hall. A beaver thrashed their tail behind the stairs; an elk tossed great antlers upon the ceiling.

"O what a sight, such strength that towers! We'd steal a kiss if he were ours," sang Corra saucily, from behind the chandelier. "But Gentry hearts cost dear, they say...for a face like *that* what a price we'd pay!"

Irian flushed, the pink tinge startling on his impassive warrior's visage. "Is it—" he spluttered, nonplussed. "Is it threatening me? Or *propositioning* me?"

"One never can tell," I muttered ominously, before calling, "He's mine! But you can come and say a polite hello...if you even know how."

I waited for Corra to burst into the outraged face of a nut-starved squirrel and begin cursing my ancestors in inventive language, but the sprite had apparently said all they wished to say.

"Oh well." I shrugged. "Just be glad they didn't call you *porridge face.*"

Irian gave his head a helpless shake. "I have never met a Folk beastie quite like that."

Swiftly, I dashed upstairs to my old garret bedroom, trading the dirty, smoky dress I'd worn from the Cnoc for the only garments left in the wardrobe. Corra's creations were all outlandish; I chose the most demure of the lot, a silken gown the color of a violet dusk. I hesitated, then strapped some old leather armor that needed repairing over top. When I descended the stairs, Irian raised an eyebrow at my attire but said nothing.

The stables were warm and dry and scented pleasantly with hay and oiled leather. Finan drowsed lazily in his stall but roused when he heard footsteps, poking his large dark head over the barrier. He whickered in recognition when he saw me, then startled, pinning his ears to his skull with a piercing whinny. He shied, nearly slamming his head into the beams overhead as panic whited his rolling eyes.

"You'd better not come any closer, mo chroí." I held up my hands in placation as Irian stilled, intimidating and uncanny in the warm, slanting sunlight. "Easy, boy."

Irian stepped sideways into the blue shadow cast by the door and leaned on the wall as I rummaged in the tack room for a pair of thick riding gloves. I didn't think my touch would harm Finan, but I saw no point in taking the risk. I slipped inside the stall, calming the still-restive stallion with nonsense words and soothing strokes on his neck and muzzle.

"He is a fine, handsome animal," Irian remarked. "But tell me, mo chroí—why can he not speak?"

"Speak?" I choked on a laugh. "Oh, my heart—horses cannot communicate in the human realms. Not like the aughiskies. In fact, all beasts here are mute."

"How strange. Is he yours?"

"Not mine." With a distant pang I thought of Eimar, the horse I had accidentally Greenmarked over a year ago. "He was—is—Rogan's."

"Ah." Irian's tone went dry. "Then I suppose I must be grateful he cannot talk, for I warrant he would have many a sordid tale to impart."

I hid my faint blush behind Finan's bulk. There had indeed been one or two literal rolls in the hay last year. But that had been a long time ago. Here, with Irian, my only thought was for him. What would it be like to let Irian take me, here? Now?

His black hair mussed with hay. His hands deft on the ties of my kirtle. Our naked skin glowing golden in the easy sunlight.

I shook my head, dispelling the impossible daydream. I hoped my starshine affliction would not last forever. But for now, I had to keep my distance from the man I loved.

I tacked Finan. Irian watched but did not attempt to come any closer.

"You know, if you sought your anam cló, you would not need a horse at all. You might be able to fly beside me."

"Fly?" I hopped right over the question of my anam cló. With all that troubled me, my soul form—or lack thereof—wasn't my primary concern. "But—"

"My magic is weaker here in Fódla, but my anam cló is rooted deeper in me even than my Treasure."

"Rath na Mara is far—a long day's ride."

"Swans may appear sedate upon the water, mo chroí, but we are strong fliers." He smiled, a sharp dazzle of humor. "If you are intent on riding that beast, perhaps we shall make a race of it."

I finished fastening Finan's girth. "Only if you have a craving to be trounced, Sky-Sword."

Irian shoved off the wall and came at me without warning. Finan shied away with a shriek, but Irian ignored the horse, pinning me with his dazzle-blue eyes before caging me with his arms. One broad hand collided with the stall door at my back; the other wrapped tight around the post by my head. He stood bare inches from me; I could smell him, black leather and cold steel and the faintest tang of ozone, like struck lightning. Slowly—so slowly—my husband bent his head until his lips nearly brushed my ear.

"I crave many things, colleen." His breath gusted over my skin, and my throat hitched as warmth vined my spine. "You make an exceptionally comely stable girl."

I looked up at him, my pulse throbbing reedy between my temples. His mouth was parted; his eyes, shadowed with desire. Tension sang between us, and I ached to break it. With a word, a touch. A kiss.

"Alas." His hands dropped; he rose to his full height. "The afternoon grows weary. We must away, lest darkness strand us in the wilds."

"They say after nightfall, the Fair Folk wander," I agreed, rueful. "And I would hate to meet any of them. Alone. In the woods. After dark."

"One might trap you into a foul bargain."

"Or worse." I mounted Finan. "A fine marriage."

Despite my bravado, Irian's anam cló swiftly and easily outpaced me.

Finan practically had wings for hooves, but I found him difficult to control. Consigned as we were to pitted wagon tracks and goat paths sharp with rocks, I feared for the stallion's slender legs in the treacherous potholes.

I glanced at Irian streaking through the sky like a black arrow and felt a dart of envy.

We did not make good time. It had rained in the past week, and mud soon caked Finan's fetlocks and splattered his girth. After a winter of easy exercise and a soft diet, the stallion was already beginning to lather. As afternoon trundled toward evening, great roiling thunderheads darkened the horizon and turned the sun to a bloody coin.

I cursed but had to admit: We weren't going to make it to Rath na Mara tonight.

I detoured into a nearby field as the rain splattered closer, dismounting beneath a beech as I squinted into the sheeting downpour.

A shard of black zigzagged between squalls, large wings buffeted by the high winds. Irian transformed as he descended to the ground running. His wings were the last thing to go, shedding bedraggled black feathers.

"Gods alive." He shoved sopping black hair off his face, drenched from his mantle to his boots, which squelched audibly. "Storms here are stubborn. When I felt the wind rising, I tried to raise the temperature of the air and change the direction of the draft. The storm practically laughed at me...then tried to strike me with lightning."

I stifled a giggle. Irian was rarely outmatched. Especially not by the weather.

"We should have brought bedrolls," I grumbled. Moisture pattered steadily between the beech leaves, muddying the ground. "We're in for a miserable night."

Finan lowered his head and whuffed unhappily at the bare roots of the tree.

"And you said the beast could not communicate," Irian said wryly.

"I said he couldn't *talk*," I corrected with a laugh. "He's always been apt at complaining."

"I fear he is not wrong." Irian tilted his soaking head to one side. "I spied the lights of a village half a league to the west."

I frowned. "I doubt anyone will be out in the dark and storm. But perhaps we should move a little farther east."

"You misunderstand me, mo chroí." Irian wrung out the hem of his mantle. "Might they not have a . . . way station in this human village? A place where travelers might stop and sup and perhaps sleep?"

"An inn?" Had I not been alarmed, I might have laughed. "Irian, you are full-blooded Gentry in a realm preparing for war with the Folk. I am a changeling. We are both Treasures."

"Indeed." I had lived so long with the shadow of fear in Irian's eyes that this gleam of anticipation was novel. Albeit unnerving. "If Eala has brought her war to these parts, I have not yet seen evidence of it. No one need know we are not human. And should we need to fight our way free of some quarrel, I daresay we can take on a few dozen pitchfork-wielding human peasants."

I barked a disbelieving laugh at his bravado, especially the notion that anyone could suspect him of being anything but otherworldly in origin. I felt as if I had swapped bodies—or perhaps minds—with my husband. How many times had he urged caution and prudence to me in the past year?

And how many times had I readily ignored his warnings?

"This is my realm." I echoed a warning he had given me many times, even as the prospect of a hot meal and a bath wheedled through my misgivings. "There is much you do not know. Have a care for your surroundings, and do not speak or act out of turn."

"Duly noted, colleen." His smile was lightning—a blinding flash of white in the dim. "I shall seek to heed your warnings as dutifully as you have always heeded mine."

"Touché." I narrowed my eyes at him. "Oh, and, Sky-Sword?"

"Yes?"

I mounted Finan briskly, wheeling the stallion in a circle before galloping out into the driving rain. "Kiss my bloody arse."

Chapter Thirty-Two

Wayland

Wayland had never had the opportunity to travel much beyond Emain Ablach. He'd certainly made the odd journey—like the diplomatic mission his father had sent him on the winter he'd met Fia—but such excursions were always on Gavida's whim and at his bidding. Wayland had been like a homing pigeon—he'd use an enchanted looking glass that allowed him to cross vast distances in the blink of an eye, cluck out a pointed message to whomever Gavida was trying to manipulate (usually something along the lines of *Give me this magical artifact you're hiding before I smite you and everyone you hold dear*), then hurry back home before anyone broke the rules of hospitality by slitting his throat. He'd attended revels and feasts, sampling local delicacies and local beauties alike, but rarely saw much at all of the environs he was sent to.

Tír na nÓg, for all its varied landscapes, was a foreign land to him. And it was becoming painfully obvious the same was true for Idris.

Since they'd started walking late that morning, the younger man had been torn between staring over the mountainous horizon with wonder verging on fear and poring over the makeshift map Laoise had drawn for him like his life depended on it. Which Wayland prayed to any gods who were listening that it didn't. Because Idris wasn't particularly good at reading it.

In contrast, Hog was aglow with cheeky excitement, running her claws over Idris's sleek red hair and murmuring.

Wayland experienced a burst of affection tempered by rising guilt. There had been an awful moment that morning when he had been utterly certain that no one would choose him as a traveling partner. That he would not be second choice or even last choice, but no choice at all. That he would be left alone once more by the only people in his life he had ever given himself the opportunity to care about. Then Idris *had*—choosing Wayland over his own sister, no less.

Having Idris by his side was an undeniable comfort. But the thought of leading him into the heart of danger twisted a thick, impenetrable knot in Wayland's gut. Gratitude warred with unease, and he made a silent, fervent wish that this wouldn't be a journey either of them would regret.

"Laoise said after we leave the Barrens, it should be a few days' hike through Tír na Sámhachta," Idris was saying as they made their way through a narrow gully edged in glittering black rock.

"The Land of Tranquility?" Wayland shrugged. "Sounds boring."

"No—these symbols are trees, not mountains." Idris frowned, flipping the scrap of dried-leaf parchment scrawled with Laoise's harried lines of charcoal. "In which case we're headed straight for Tír Fhiáin."

"The Wild Lands?" Wayland whistled. "Less boring. The maidens there are said to be utterly insatiable."

Idris colored, staring even harder at the map. Hog, draped leisurely over his shoulder, blew speculatively on the leaf paper and flicked her tail in glee when it warped from the heat of her breath. Idris jerked it away from the draigling.

"Hog! Don't," he scolded, even as Wayland reached out and plucked the map from his surprised fingers.

"That's enough of that." Wayland folded the map—if one could even call it that—and tucked it into his trousers before smiling broadly. "We are in the mountains. Murias is westward, beside the sea. We follow the sun, and if that doesn't work, we follow the water. And if *that* doesn't work, I can sense where we need to go." He gestured to Fáilsceim, sheathed upon his back. "Perhaps we'll even get lucky and find a few folkways to help us on our journey."

"Folkways?" Idris gave him the same aggrieved look Wayland had received from every single boyhood tutor forced to school him. "Everyone knows they can't be mapped."

"My point exactly." Though most folkways were somewhat reliable and remained open for years, creating safe shortcuts for Folk across the realm, the ficklest could open and close in mere moments. "If you've got your nose shoved into that crude map, you'll never learn how to spot them."

"How *do* you spot them?"

Wayland hesitated. In truth, he had traveled through precious few—Gavida's forged mirrors were more precise and less capricious. The only folkway Wayland had ever interacted with at length was one that had opened for about a month on Emain Ablach when he and Irian were boys. It had been a useless one—its exit two feet behind its entrance. He and Irian had, of course, made a game out of it—if you dashed through fast enough, you could sometimes smack yourself in the back of the head or kick yourself in your own rump.

"I believe there's a shimmer to them?" He hemmed. "Or maybe a strange shadow—"

"You have no idea what you're talking about, do you?" Idris accused.

On his shoulder, Hog hissed a mewling laugh, repeating, "Do you? Do you?"

"Give me back my map," Idris demanded.

"Shan't."

"Now, Wayland!" Idris's expression turned caustic. "I refuse to be led through lands unknown by someone without common sense."

"Common sense is for common people." Wayland made his tone arch. "And I, my darling man, am one of a kind."

He stuck his nose in the air and marched on ahead of Idris, ignoring the stream of well-chosen epithets being hissed at his back by both man and draigling.

It was late afternoon on the following day by the time they left the Barrens. Beyond stretched the plain Irian had named Mag Tuired—the old killing fields where Eala had ambushed them with her army of the dead. Remembered fear arose in Wayland—the visceral horror of watching Irian's tall black stallion hobbled by decrepit hands, seeing Fia sprawled helpless between ravening corpses, and smelling the stench of dust and decay mingling with the searing char of Laoise's draig fire.

Now the plain was still and quiet, scattered skeletons and broken weapons crisscrossed with lines of black ash the only evidence of their struggle.

"What is it?" Idris asked.

Wayland hesitated, then told him what had happened. Idris blanched, staring out over the plain with fear glossing his own eyes.

"We could go around," he suggested, hopefully.

Wayland shaded his eyes against the red burn of the setting sun. To walk around the plain—keeping to the foothills—would add a day to their journey at least. And would necessitate camping *beside* the killing fields.

"No," he decided. "We cross it. Now, before the sun sets and plunges us in darkness."

Idris whistled but didn't complain. "You are brave."

"Not really." Wayland laughed as he stepped onto the flat, scrubby expanse. "My inborn laziness happens to be far stronger than my native cowardice."

Despite his bravado, Wayland's heart thundered a shameful

crescendo between his ears. Sweat slicked the muscles of his back as they picked their way across the desolated landscape pocked by the half-buried bones of Fomorians and Folk. But though Wayland steeled himself for the earth to shake and split, for the flesh-draped skeletons to reach for their weapons, the plain was still and silent.

Neither man spoke, for there was nothing to say that the dead had not already told.

The sun had slipped away beyond the purple line of moors marching toward the horizon when Wayland's boots struck the stony hill beyond the plain, edged with heather and gorse, and he sucked in air touched by smells of new grass and fresh water.

"Another hour," Wayland promised. Both he and Idris were tired after the day's long hike, but neither of them wished to camp beside Mag Tuired. "Then we find food. And a place to sleep."

It was pitch black by the time they reached a narrow wood of thin silver trees, their leaves chiming like bells. The ground beneath their feet was carpeted with velvet moss in hues of midnight blue. They were both too exhausted to make a fire or find provisions—they nibbled on a few leftover fruits from the valley before bedding beneath their cloaks. Hog continued to favor Idris, but in the middle of the night Wayland awoke to her snoring directly in his ear, draped around his neck like a scarf.

In the morning, all the trees had grown luminous fruits bathed in silver dew, dripping with scarlet nectar that tasted of honey and starlight.

"Don't eat that," Idris warned from where he was viciously lacing his boots. "It could be anything. It could be poisonous."

"Coming from the man who grows cave mushrooms and fillets salamanders," Wayland pointed out as he cut a slice of mystery fruit, "that's a bit rich."

Wayland filled his empty belly. He didn't tell Idris that the sweetness clung to his mouth long after they walked on, leaving him thirsty for something he could not name.

The next morning, they found a folkway by accident, when Idris stepped into what seemed like a shallow puddle and disappeared into the ground. Wayland stared after him, jaw dropped, until he had no choice but to get on his hands and knees and stick his face straight into the mud.

Idris had fallen ten or more feet onto his arse between towering black roses, the petals velvety with moisture. Wayland almost laughed until he saw the death glare Idris was shooting him.

"Here." He reached an arm. He was fairly certain they were on the correct route to Murias—the wrongness he'd touched with his mind via Fáilsceim hummed like a curse at the edge of his awareness. Gods only knew what detour this folkway might send them on. "I'll help you."

But no matter how they both strained, their fingers didn't even touch. At last, Wayland sighed, clasped a griping Hog to his chest, and jumped in after Idris.

The scent of the overgrown flowers was intoxicating, but beneath it lurked something darker—a coppery tang, like blood. They did not linger, hastening their pace as the wind whispered tantalizing secrets. That night, they camped on a hill overlooking the rose field, their fire flicking low. They had nothing to eat or drink, and for the first time, Idris sat closer to Wayland than was strictly proper—their shoulders brushing and their boots touching. Wayland held his breath and tried not to look at the other man head-on—as if he were a wild animal who might spook. His fingers twitched with the urge to reach out and touch Idris, but he twined them together and thought of what he'd said the night Idris had fixed his nose.

I'll wait.

❧

The folkway saved them a week of walking. Soon, Wayland noticed evidence of the corrupted wild magic billowing dark and damaging above the ruined city of Murias. It hummed, tense and terrible and tempting, slicking along his limbs and whispering in his ears. He wrapped his hand around Fáilsceim's haft, but that only made things worse—the hum became a shout, throbbing feverishly through his mind and expanding and contracting with the force of his breathing.

They passed through a swamp where the trees wept tears of amber sap and the mud underfoot was black and fetid, sticking to their boots like tar. Strange lights floated above the water—wisps of sickly green and mutilated violet—beckoning them deeper between the trees. Idris followed them. When Wayland caught him by the arm and spun him away, his gaze was wide and slack with wonder. Wayland shook him, hard, his panic fading when the other man's eyes slowly cleared. But instead of showing relief, Idris's expression warped with disappointment...fury...overwhelming sadness. Tears welled in his eyes, stained yellow and black by the strange lights flickering and flitting through the swamp.

"What is it?" Wayland asked, alarmed. Hog leapt from his shoulder to Idris's, wrapping her chubby limbs around his neck and laving the tears from his cheek with her forked tongue. "What's wrong?"

But Idris swiped angrily at his eyes, settled the sheet of his hair carefully over his face, and trudged onward through the swamp.

"Nothing," he ground out. "Let's get out of this place."

They camped on a hillock situated high above the swamp, with a view of the ruined city of Murias, where the Sept of Fins had once ruled. Wayland could barely see the blighted wild magic, but he *felt* it—a sickly pressure on his awareness, as if his ears were blocked. At least here, elevated slightly and upwind from it, he could almost ignore its insistent press.

Idris foraged a few twisted mushrooms from between the rocks, then roasted them over the fire until the air was thick with their earthy, bitter aroma. The two men ate in silence as Hog hunted for field mice beneath the rocky promontory shielding their backs from the wind.

After the last scraps of mushroom were finished, Wayland reached into his pocket and drew out the small flask of liquor he'd carried from the Cnoc. He jiggled it slightly to catch Idris's eye.

Idris raised his eyebrows. "Trust you to escape a burning mountain with nothing but the shirt on your back and a flask of liquor."

"Don't forget a legendary weapon that doesn't strictly belong to me," Wayland said, gesturing to Fáilsceim. "I always carry booze, in case of emergencies. A multipurpose cure, you might say."

Idris hesitated, then accepted the offering. He uncorked the bottle and took a tentative swig.

"That's my deepwood sap wine," he said, surprised but proud. "Except—"

Wayland grinned. "I made some improvements."

In fact, he'd distilled it—wicking away the water content until the alcohol was more concentrated. It was an old trick he'd discovered in his hazy, misspent youth—before his father had collared his magic.

"It's good," Idris said, taking another swig before handing it back to Wayland. "And strong."

"Synonyms, Red." Wayland threw back his head and drank deep, reveling in the sharp, warm burn of the liquor in his chest.

They drank in silence for a while, gazing out over the darkened landscape. At last, Wayland said, "Would you like to talk about it?"

Idris stiffened. "About what?"

"Whatever made you weep like a babe in the middle of the swamp, I'd imagine."

He'd meant the comment to be lighthearted, a joke to dispel the heavy, heart-wrenching reticence Idris had carried with him all day. It immediately had the opposite effect—Idris set down the flask, folded his arms over his knees, and curled in on himself. He could not have used words to speak more clearly than his body spoke without them.

Leave me alone.

Wayland cursed himself inwardly as he rose to his feet, skirting the fire. He knelt before the other man, close enough to touch but careful not to, and tilted his head, angling his face to peer beneath the screen of Idris's hair.

"I'm sorry." He meant it. "That was uncalled for. Utterly out of line. There is no shame in tears, no indignity in emotion. I laugh at myself so I am not tempted to cry as often as I would like. But that does not give me the right to laugh at you. Can you find it in your heart to forgive me?"

For an endless, aching time, Idris kept his eyes downcast. Hog waddled over and settled in his lap, glaring at Wayland as if to berate him.

Finally, Idris heaved a deep, wounded sigh. "Back there in the swamp...I saw my sister. She was beckoning me deeper between the trees. And I wanted to follow her more than I've wanted anything else in a long time."

Wayland didn't understand. "You saw Laoise?"

"No." Idris finally lifted his eyes; they gleamed like gold coins in the fire-fretted dark. "My other sister. Elen. Who has been dead for twenty years."

A chill swept over Wayland, cold as ice water dumped over his head.

"Laoise was the eldest," Idris continued softly. "My parents' heir. The omens blessed her birth—a blood-red dawn and a rain of sparks, or so the stories go. My father even claimed that on the eve of her name day, the Hollow of the Sun briefly erupted, spitting cinders into the sky like newborn stars."

Such stories were common among the Folk—births of important children hallowed by portentous omens. According to Gavida, Wayland's own birth had been blessed by high tides and schools of fish so plentiful they jumped into fishermen's nets. Wayland had never understood exactly what flooded beaches and suicidal fish were supposed to portend, other than a supernatural taste for the fruits of the sea.

He did love seafood.

"My sister Elen came a year or two after." Wayland raised his eyebrows—among the Folk Gentry, children were rare and nearly always purposeful. Breeding mates were carefully selected and considered; offspring spawned to shoulder destinies and carry bloodlines. Unlike sheeries, who hatched from seedpods like tufts of dandelion fluff, or darrigs, who planted cuttings of their own limbs in moonlit marshes, Folk Gentry grew their children inside them. Parenthood was considered a sacred but dangerous magic not all were prepared to wield. Most Gentry women carried but one child in their lifetime; those who birthed more spaced them out over decades or even centuries.

"It was a love match," Idris said, by way of rueful explanation. "Laoise was their heir; Elen was the gift of their love. The two girls were close in age but wildly different. Laoise was fierce and willful, burning hot as an eternal flame. Elen was sweet and gracious, as softhearted as a lamb."

"And you?" Wayland asked gently. "Who were you, in your family?"

"I was the baby," Idris laughed, a little bitterly. "Laoise and Elen were eight and nine when I was born; by the time I was old enough to toddle after them and interrupt their games, they were too grown to want much to do with me. *Play with your brother*, Mother used to command them. Elen would sometimes oblige, scooping me into her arms and carrying me up to count the wyverns nesting on the cliffs. Laoise hated watching me—she'd usually plop me in my crib and leave me to cry my eyes out."

"I'm sorry." Wayland knew a little of what it meant to be ignored and passed over by family who were meant to care about you.

"There's nothing to be sorry for," Idris said, with a shrug. "My parents had no right to expect their elder children to assume their parenting duties. And their shortcomings did not end there. I was too young to understand at the time, but Laoise and Elen were fighting a constant battle, too, one not of their own making. And I was one of many weapons deployed in the war."

Wayland frowned. "What do you mean?"

"Perhaps it is with good reason most Gentry families limit themselves to one child at a time." Idris ducked his head. "Even at the tender age of four, I knew my parents did not treat my sisters the same. Elen was praised for her obedience, while in the same breath, Laoise was criticized for her willfulness. They expected Laoise to lead, burdening her with duties and responsibilities, while Elen, despite her obedience, was shielded from the harder tasks. Whether my parents did it knowingly or not, they constantly pitted my sisters against each other."

Idris passed a hand over his forehead, smoothing his length of hair. His dark eyes were shiny—whether with tears or memory, Wayland didn't know. His fingers twitched with the urge to comfort Idris. He curled his hand into a loose fist.

"Laoise resented Elen for never carrying the same weight yet effortlessly being favored; Elen felt underestimated, trapped by our parents' expectations of her perfection. By the time I was four, and they were both teetering on the brink of womanhood, they were at each other's throats. Literally."

Wayland waited, a cold premonition of tragedy ghosting over his skin.

"Mother sent the girls on some errand to the Sept of Scales' official storehouses—she and Father were hosting a feast for Laoise's birthday. At the last minute she shoved me out the door after them and shouted, 'Take your brother with you!' But Elen and Laoise were already arguing, and neither of them heard. I followed anyway, down winding halls and up towering staircases. I almost lost them a few times, but they were easy to spot, looking like twins with their long auburn curls."

Idris's throat worked, and the next words seemed to scald him.

"By the time we reached the warehouse, the argument had escalated into a quarrel. I don't know what they were fighting about—I suppose it doesn't matter. When I stepped to the door, I saw Laoise slap Elen across the face. Elen grabbed for a silver candlestick, hoisting it like a club. Then Laoise…" Remembered horror bloomed in Idris's eyes, reflecting the smoldering heat of the campfire. "Despite the omens of her birth, Laoise had not yet manifested the fiery magic of our bloodline. Until that moment. She… *combusted*. Fire burst from her skin in a towering inferno, then exploded outward. The contents of the storehouse were tinder for the conflagration—barrels of wine and oil slicking over the floor, fine silks igniting, expensive paintings and priceless books kindling. I saw Elen go up in flames a moment later, her beautiful clothes and long hair torched to ash before my eyes. And then—then—"

Idris's voice cracked. Broke. Wayland put a hand on the other man's knee, ready to pull back if Idris flinched away from him. But the touch seemed to steady him.

"I don't remember much else. The fire burned for days—it demolished a portion of the city and took several other innocent lives. I got lucky—I hadn't stepped all the way inside the warehouse when the first explosion hit. The door protected me from the worst of the flames. Well. Most of me."

Abruptly, Wayland understood. His eyes slid over Idris's features, following the path of light and shadow cast by the flickering firelight. As always, the half of his face revealed by the shaved side of his head was beautiful, expressive, vulnerable. The other half was hidden beneath the purposeful veil of his glowing red hair.

"Do you want to show me?" Wayland did not move to touch Idris beyond his hand on his knee.

"No." His hand passed over the sheen of his hair again, tugging restively on the ends. "But I will. If you truly aren't afraid to see me."

"I fear a great many things in this life, Red." Wayland held Idris's gaze with all the steadiness he possessed. "You are not—and never will be—one of them."

Idris hesitated one last moment, then caught his hair with his hand and pushed it back from his face.

The scar cleaved his face almost perfectly in half, puckering his hairline, twisting over his eyebrow and the corner of his eye, pulling his cheek and the edge of his mouth sideways, before sweeping the line of his jaw and the side of his neck and disappearing beneath his clothes. The firelight played over the burn, casting shiny whorls and puckered divots in deep relief. Horrified sympathy spangled through Wayland—not for the way the scar looked, but for how much the original burn must have *hurt*. Wayland lifted his hand to Idris's face. The other man flinched but did not move away. Wayland's fingertips skimmed over the contours of his cheek, barely touching the damaged skin.

"There must have been skilled healers in Findias, before the purge," he murmured. "Could they not—"

"They tried," Idris said, without inflection. "But in the end, saving my face was of lower priority than saving my life."

"Then they performed their duty," Wayland said fiercely. "And now you are perfect."

Surprise flared in Idris's eyes, igniting the threads of gold hammered along his deep brown irises. He lowered his gaze as a ruddy flush crept over his cheeks.

"Don't say that to me."

"Why not?"

"Because you don't mean it." Idris's tone was flat. "And it isn't true."

"It is true. And I do mean it." Wayland lifted his other hand, until Idris's whole face was cupped between his palms. The unblemished half was cool and smooth, rasping with the faintest hint of stubble; the scarred half was warm and raised, etched with ridges and valleys that Wayland longed to explore. "Scars are maps etched in flesh, Red. Topographies of pain charting the wounds of a life lived. Every twisted seam of flesh tells a story of a battle fought—and a battle survived. Some are fought in blood-soaked soil, some in flame-doused warehouses. And some in the deepest recesses of the heart. Scars are roads carved by suffering, places where pain has folded and healed. This scar is not just a memory, but a testament. To all you have endured."

Idris sighed, his own hand clasping over Wayland's where it rested upon his scar. "But it is so ugly."

"You are perfect," Wayland said again, more forcefully. "Do you think beauty is synonymous with being unblemished? I would rather you bear a thousand scars than none. Suffering is sacred. Damage is divine. Healing is holy. Imperfection *is* perfection."

Idris said nothing, but a single hot tear slid from the corner of his marred eye and dripped over their joined hands.

"What do you want me to say to that?" The question came out half desperate. "What do you want from me, Wayland?"

"What do I want?" Wayland hesitated. "I want to give you something of myself. Something I do not even know if I have in me to give."

Then he slid his palm from Idris's cheek along the clean-shaven side of his head, cupped his nape, and kissed him.

It was a tentative, perilous thing. The softest brush of Idris's mouth on his, a faint exhale as the other man sighed. The taste of his lips shoved away the last of Wayland's restraint—the lingering flavors of earthy mushrooms and sharp berry liquor and woodsmoke clinging to his mouth like perfume. Desire pummeled through Wayland, hot and harsh, tightening the muscles of his stomach as he pulled Idris closer. It had been so long, and he *wanted* him—wanted to press him to the dirt, to shred his clothes until he was bared and begging—

With careful, painful effort, Wayland mastered himself. He pulled back before his tongue could slide between Idris's lips and delve between his teeth. Dropped his hands before they could find all the places that made the other man moan. Rocked away before his body could override his mind.

"Perfect," Wayland reiterated, one last time, before rising and crossing back to his side of the fire, where Hog was curled up looking cross. He nudged her over, shoving away the nagging feeling that he was making a foolish—or at least unnecessary—blunder. What harm could there be in giving in to their shared desire?

No. Idris deserved better than that. He deserved more than being a warm body in the dark, a fleeting pleasure to patch the screaming horror of the void. He deserved care, forethought. Time and attention.

Wayland wondered whether he, too, didn't deserve a little bit more than he'd ever bothered to allow himself.

Chapter Thirty-Three

Fia

Finan's hooves clopped loudly on the rain-washed cobblestones as we moved swiftly but carefully through the village. The houses and shops were shuttered against the storm—only a few bobbing lanterns illuminated the street in the falling dusk. Irian and I drew our hoods far over our faces, but there was no one to watch us pass.

A faint strain of music steered us toward the village green, where a single rangy-looking goat grazed amid the downpour. The inn was dilapidated and small, but well lit. The smells of roasted meat and woodsmoke wafted from the open door; the stable block had a sturdy roof to keep the rain off Finan's back. The faded sign creaking to and fro above the door said *The Stone and Clover*.

I sighed. "I don't like this idea."

"I like it more with each passing moment." Irian gave the air a speculative sniff, even as his lips slid sideways. "What now? Do we call out for the proprietor to invite us in?"

I stared askance at the formidable Gentry warrior. "Irian, do they not have inns in Tír na nÓg?"

"Certainly not." I couldn't tell whether he was teasing me. "The laws of hospitality demand any home be open to any traveler or guest, no matter how mean or grand, provided they abide by the rules of the house."

"You just…let strangers stay in your home whenever they ask?"

"*Provided* they ask." Irian's smile took on a wolfish glint. "Don't worry, mo chroí. Few strangers have lasted out the night in my home. And fewer still have wheedled their way into my bed."

A hint of warmth touched my rain-chilled cheeks. "I did warn you I was a horrendous houseguest." I stuck out my tongue at him, then shivered. "Gods, Irian, it's too cold to flirt. If we're going inside, let's go."

I looped Finan's reins around the gatepost and loped up the path to the entryway. Only to find the door blocked by a stout, imposing woman in middle age, with frizzing ginger hair and a round face etched with laugh lines and frown lines alike. She eyed Finan—he was far too fine an animal to grace this rural village—before glowering at me and Irian, hidden beneath our hoods, and crossing her brawny arms over her chest.

Fortunately, I'd discovered a little cache of silver coins in Finan's saddlebags—a gift through time from an obnoxiously rich and forgetful golden-haired princeling. I drew out three coins and hoped this woman spoke the language humans loved best: money. I flashed the first piece of silver in the lamplight.

"For the horse. Rub him down, water him, and feed him grain if you have it." I held up the second coin. "For a room and a meal and two cups of ale." I brandished the third and saw the woman's eyes gleam with greed. "For you. For your trouble. And your silence."

The innkeeper hesitated a bare second longer before scooping the coins from my glove and stepping aside.

The inn was dim and smoky. A rough-hewn bar sat along one wall, stacked with tankards and barrels and ringed with wobbly looking stools. A few patrons—mostly men—nursed cups and chatted with the barman, a ruddy youth who looked to be the innkeeper's son. Tables for two and four were crammed close together, though few were occupied. Beside a generous hearth on the other wall, a single elderly fiddler picked out a simple tune. No one seemed to be listening, let alone dancing.

A cold finger of unease trailed my already frigid back. On a cold, damp evening a place like this ought to be packed. Patrons should have been clamoring for ale at the bar; children playing games beneath the tables; food and drink circulating as pipers and fiddlers made music. This place was all but deserted.

I pointed Irian to a table in the shadow of a beam in the farthest corner of the tavern, where we'd be able to keep an eye on the door but no one could get a good eyeful of us.

"Go sit down," I commanded, stern. "And don't talk to anyone. I'll go order us some drinks."

He cut me an ironic little bow. "Lady wife."

He prowled toward the back of the tavern, and every single eye in the establishment followed his progress, watching as he lowered his towering height onto a bench, settled back against the shadowed wall, and propped his impossibly long legs on a neighboring chair. The hilt of the Sky-Sword poking from beneath his cloak did not go unnoticed.

You could have heard a pin drop.

I cleared my throat and let my fist fall onto the bar. The redcheeked young man jumped, spinning toward me with only slightly less trepidation than he'd been watching Irian with.

"M-madam?" His throat bobbed. The wispy red beard barely fuzzing over his cheeks told me he couldn't have been older than sixteen or seventeen. "Help you?"

"Two cups of ale." The boy busied himself with fetching tankards and pouring the frothing brown liquid. When he set them before me, I dared to ask, "Can you tell me why the pub is so empty? Is aught amiss in the village?"

He frowned, tilting his head to peer beneath my hood. I kept my head resolutely angled.

"If ye don't know, madam...pardon my saying, but 'tisn't my place to say."

I sighed and fished out another piece of silver, simultaneously grateful to Rogan for leaving so much money lying around and annoyed with him for never carrying small denominations. The boy's eyes widened—it had to be a month's wages for him. He pocketed it swiftly, then leaned closer.

"The high queen is raising a vast army. Bridei's able sons and daughters wend toward Rath na Mara, for Cairell Mòr has bent the knee, to spare our lands." He shook his head. "Brighid only knows what good 'twill do us, when there's no one left to plow or sow."

Fear and hope played like shadows and light on the backs of my eyelids. Mother was mounting an army? Then she surely meant to stand against Eala. "Does Eithne have an enemy in mind?"

Again, the boy stared at me as if I was from another realm. "Surely ye know—Eithne Uí Mainnín no longer sits the throne."

My hope burned away in a flash of black smoke. "Who does?"

"The Deathless Queen, of course. The one they name Grave Mother, for she calls the dead from Donn's dark realm and embraces them as her own living children." The boy leaned even closer and dropped his voice to just above a whisper. "Though I have also heard her called the Rotten Princess, for where she walks, the grass shrivels and the air stinks of decay."

I jerked away, tasting grave dirt and carrion in the back of my throat. The boy seemed to realize he'd said too much, and guiltily returned to his barkeeping. I carried the tankards toward where Irian lounged threateningly, barely noticing the suds slopping over the rims onto my gloves.

Deathless Queen. Grave Mother. Rotten Princess.

We'd known Eala was already here. But in less than two months she had somehow deposed her mother. Stolen Fódla's high throne for herself. And was now drafting an army of able-bodied citizens to supplement her horde of the dead.

Fear nearly throttled me. I thumped the cups onto the wooden table and slid in beside Irian, murmuring, "I spoke to the barkeep, and—"

But when I glanced up to his shadowed face, I saw he was not paying a whit of attention to me. His gaze was fixed halfway across the tavern, his lush mouth slightly parted in fascination.

"What," he asked in disbelief, "is that shriveled human *doing?*"

I followed his eyes. The elderly fiddler had taken a break from his music and sat before the hearth, puffing contentedly at a long wooden pipe. The tip flared red, and Irian's eyes smoldered with it.

"He's smoking." I fought the urge to roll my eyes toward the heavens. "It's a common pastime. Or vice. Depending on who you ask."

"I wish to try it."

What insane wish fulfillment was this? "We haven't got a pipe. Nor weed to fill it."

"Then go bid him give me his."

"Irian, I cannot march over to that stranger and take his pipe."

"Then trade it. For one of those shiny tidbits you keep handing out."

Now I did roll my eyes. "You mean *money?*"

"Yes, that." Irian made an impatient gesture. "If you do not wish to barter, then give it to me, and I shall perform the trade."

Oh, ye gods. I stalked over to the geezer, who saw me coming from halfway across the room and blanched white as a sheet. I plucked one of the last coins from my pocket and held it out between my forefingers, hoping these townsfolk appreciated my forced largesse.

"Grandfather." I fought to keep the annoyance from my voice. "I beg you sell us your pipe."

Wordlessly, the old man handed it over. I returned with it to Irian, who wiped the stem on the hem of his damp cloak before unceremoniously popping it into his mouth. He sucked in a huge lungful of smoke, then blew it out in swirls of vapor that briefly obscured his shadowed face, his stubbled jaw, his armored figure. I glanced over my shoulder, assured the whole bar was once again observing us.

We were *not* blending in well at all.

"Gods alive, colleen," Irian said with immense glee. "But this tastes like a charnel house. Do humans truly inhale ashes for fun?"

I plucked the pipe from his hands and smacked it on the table.

"Keep your voice down," I hissed, "and listen to me. Not only is Eala already at Rath na Mara, but—"

But Irian was reaching for one of the foaming flagons of ale I'd carried over from the bar. He took a tentative sip, then drained the tankard—nearly as big as his head—in three massive gulps. He wiped his mouth on the back of his gloved hand.

"Why, this, too, is absolutely disgusting! It's sweet and bitter and smells of piss, and it bubbles all along my throat." He beamed at me. "Yet already I yearn for another taste."

He reached for my untouched flagon. I supposed not even Folk men were immune to the charms of fresh farm-brewed ale. But I clamped my hands over the tankard, forcing Irian to meet my eyes. "Irian. Eala already sits the high throne, and—"

"Fia." Irian folded his gauntleted palms over my own fists, the layers of leather enough to protect him from the radiance humming inside me. "Wherever Eala sits, she shall sit there until tomorrow. With the storm blowing north, I think it unlikely she will march upon this tiny village, where she has no reason to believe we rest, in the middle of the night. Agreed?"

I grumbled an assent.

"Good." He jerked the tankard from my grip. "Now let me get drunk on human swill in peace. Or better yet, join me. For I am of a mind to dance tonight."

I watched in burgeoning horror as Irian drained his second tankard, rose to his full height, then stalked toward the center of the silent, staring tavern. His muddied boots on the floorboards were loud as thunder; his head nearly brushed the ceiling. His voice, when he spoke, rang as uncannily as the Morrigan's hounds baying over a fell moor.

"O ancient one," he intoned to the fiddler, who, had he not a hardy constitution, might have dropped dead on the spot. "I desire a tune. We shall pay you more nuggets of metal if you play us your music."

The old man, eyes so huge in his face I thought they might pop, wordlessly settled his fiddle beneath his chin.

"And, barkeep!" Irian boomed. The boy startled backward into a rack of drying cups, sending them clattering onto the floorboards. "Two more thimblefuls of hogwash!"

As the music swelled, Irian glanced back at me with his eyebrows raised and his hand outstretched. I glowered back, folding my arms over my chest. He shrugged, slurped another flagon of ale, then began dancing by himself, a sinuous, graceful, and outrageously inhuman series of steps and arm movements that had several patrons at the bar rubbing vigorously at their eyes and staring skeptically at their cups.

I gave up. I stood in a rush, marching across the room and grabbing for Irian's arms before he got us both killed. But he sidestepped me neatly, even as he slid a hand around my waist and spun me against him. His other hand cupped the back of my head, tilting my face gently toward his. I tensed, but between his leather gloves and my hooded cloak, my skin barely sparked. I relaxed, reveling in the rare, precious contact, armored though it was by layers of clothing. Irian's perfect smile was designed just for me, a keen blade sharpened with breathtaking beauty and polished with affection. His silver eyes, when they collided with mine, were my own private moonrise.

"Dance with me, colleen," he murmured, too low for anyone else to hear.

Horrified but laughing, I realized my Folk husband had tricked me into giving him exactly what he wanted.

"Fine," I relented. "But if you keep dancing like that, these townsfolk *will* be running for their pitchforks and torches."

I taught him one of the simplest ceilidh dances as the fiddler sawed out an only slightly off-tune jig. *Step, step, clap. Stomp, stomp, spin.* I was not surprised to find Irian a swift study—his otherworldly grace and effortless poise soon had him stepping and stomping and whirling me around the room by the elbow as I fought not to dissolve in giggles at the utter ridiculousness of the spectacle. Before long, the mood of the whole tavern had eased. One of the men at the bar pulled out a whistle and harmonized with the fiddler. Another elderly fellow—nearly falling down drunk—joined in the jig, and soon the ruddy barkeep was dancing, too, until the whole tavern came alive with firelight and music and merriment.

A few reels—and countless tankards of ale—later, the sturdy innkeeper at last approached me with the key to our room and a meaningful glance at Irian swaying dangerously close to the hearth. I wedged a shoulder beneath his armpit and steered him toward the stairs, navigating around stools and tables.

"Up," I ordered.

" 'M not drunk," Irian insisted.

I patted his rump as we climbed toward the second floor. "Nobody said you were."

The last door on the right led into a neat, modest bedroom with a bed, a window, and a basin for washing. Irian flopped face-first onto the narrow straw mattress, which looked like a child's cot beneath his imposing bulk. His feet hung fully off the end; I unlaced his still-damp boots and set them to dry before the fire.

"I never understood before t'night how humans could be so simpleminded," Irian slurred. "But a few more of these and I'd be in danger of forgetting everything."

"Even me?" I asked lightly, as I moved to tug off his cloak. But he caught me by the wrist and dragged me to face level.

Even stinking of ale and tipsy as a cart with three wheels, Irian was flawless. His glazed eyes were like polished moonstones, his expression unreasonably soft. I wasn't sure I had ever seen him smile as much as he had tonight.

"Never you," he whispered unevenly. "You are my whole world. Without you I am nothing. I love—*love* you."

The words furled my spine like thorned roses, sweet yet stinging. "Irian—"

"By you I am ravaged. Undone. And remade." He caught a hanging tendril of my short damp hair and wound it carefully around his forefinger. "Beautiful. You are so fucking beautiful."

"Irian," I said gently. "You *are* drunk."

The only answer I got was a faint snore. I slowly untangled Irian's hand from my hair, finished unclasping his mantle, and unbuckled what armor I could reach. Then I stepped out of my own sodden kirtle, draping its gossamer layers to dry before the fire. I hesitated, then slid under the warm woolen coverlet, nestling my small frame against Irian's larger one. Cocooned in blankets, I was no threat to him.

As his easy breath tickled my hair, I smiled and closed my eyes.

War loomed. Danger waited. Decisions needed making. But it had been a long, long time since I'd danced carefree with the man I loved.

Chapter Thirty-Four

Fia

Morning dawned the luminous blue-gray of a dove's soft wing. Irian awoke alert and refreshed, the prior evening's revels leaving him none the worse for wear. The inn was quiet in the hush of morning, and we were not accosted as we made our way down the stairs and let ourselves out the door. Beyond, the world had been washed clean by rain. Songbirds chirped and twittered from the budding hazel; along the village green, daffodils and crocuses awoke in vibrant bursts of color. The lone goat munched happily upon emerald grass, heedless of the two geese flapping nearby in what appeared to be an elaborate mating ritual.

I nudged Irian and pointed at the gander, honking and strutting and swerving his neck.

"That's what you looked like last night."

"I will have you know," Irian said in mock affront, "that in our youths both Wayland and I were considered the finest dancers Emain Ablach had ever seen."

"Wayland taught you that dance?" I grinned wickedly. "Now it all makes sense."

Irian shoved me lightly. "Just admit you loved it."

We found Finan—drowsing beneath a blanket with plenty of hay in the bin—and saddled him before departing the village. Even the ramshackle houses with their holey thatch and peeling paint looked quaint and rural in the winsome sunlight. Beyond the last houses, I mounted Finan. But Irian caught his bridle, gazing at me with eyes blue as the sheer morning.

"There is something you have not told me, mo chroí. We said we would not keep secrets."

I bit my lip, guilt nettling between my shoulders. "I did not mean to keep it from you—it's only that I don't know if I'm right."

Briefly, I explained my theory about the starshine to Irian. How Talah had awoken all the dormant wild magic I'd absorbed from Ínne as an infant, in counterpoise to the warped wild magic unleashed by the malicious destruction of the Treasures. And how the fact that my glow harmed only Irian made me wonder if it sought to free the magic bound within him...at the cost of his living vessel.

Irian listened, gravely. "Then you believe it is possible to unforge the Treasures."

"Not without harming the tánaistí. We will find another way."

"And you have come all this way to assassinate your sister."

"I meant what I told the others," I said. "I must try to reason with her before taking drastic action."

"You do not owe her that."

"I owe *myself* that." I tightened my hands in Finan's mane and nailed certainty along my spine. *Find your sister. You are her balance. Only you can bring her to the light.* "Before I destroy my sister, I must try to change her mind. To give her the tools to change her own fate, before I forcibly rip it to shreds. Otherwise I am no better than her. And in the stories they will someday tell of all that has come to pass, I will be as much a villain as she."

"What if her mind cannot be changed?"

"Then yes. If it comes to it, I will let Talah's curse unmake Eala's

Treasure, destroy her living vessel with it, and end this war before it truly begins."

I nudged the stallion forward between the hedgerows as Irian transformed into his anam cló and took to the skies, arrowing above green pastures.

Only to find the war had already begun.

There were no boundaries or markers delineating Bridei from Midhe, the neutral province at the heart of Fódla where high kings and queens kept their capital. But crossing into Midhe was like leaving a heaven and descending into a hell.

I smelled the smoke first, the acrid tang of burnt thatch and charred flesh wafting toward my nostrils on an easy breeze. Then I saw the plume of black sawing the sky in half. Urging Finan over the ridge, I yanked the reins hard at the crest, where the full scope of Eala's devastation spilled before me.

The farmhouse in the valley had been prosperous, with a large yard surrounded by plentiful outbuildings and well-ordered gardens and pastures stretching toward the horizon, where a fruit orchard and wood coppice grew.

The farm complex had been torched to a blackened husk of wood and stone. The animals had been brutally executed, their carcasses laid out in intentional lines. The fields had been churned to mud and blood and ruin. Even with my diminished Treasure, I heard the fruit and timber trees' soundless screams as their leaves and bark flaked to ash and their trunks and branches smoldered.

Finan pinned his ears to his head and half reared, the scent of smoke and carnage making him nervous. At the same time, Irian swooped from the pearly sky, fanning his great wings before he transformed back to his Gentry form. He caught at Finan's bridle, and though the horse shivered, he seemed less frightened of Irian than he was of the destruction before us.

"We should go back." Irian's brows were knitted and his gaze stark.

"Back?" I echoed, hardly understanding his meaning. My eyes

kept returning to the straight lines of butchered animals, blood blooming on their pelts like vicious roses. A thought kept trying to nudge through the horror thronging my mind

There were no people. A farm this size would have likely housed a farming couple, their children, and half a dozen relatives or farmhands hired on to tend the fields and animals. But despite the dozens of slaughtered cows, sheep, and chickens, I saw no humans. Alive, or otherwise. Which meant—

"She is growing her army." Just as the barkeep had warned. The wind and smoke whipped my suddenly stinging eyes.

"She may let them join while they are still alive," Irian said softly. "But burns their holdings to ensure they have no place to return."

"This is madness." My hands tightened on the reins as I thought about all the innocents caught in this terrible conflict. And how many would die before it ended. "Without farms or farmers there will be no harvest. What does she expect to feed her army in a month? A season? A year?"

"Mo chroí." Irian's voice dropped a register. "One does not need to feed an army of the dead."

The thought chilled me even further. Monarchs already had little care for the human lives they treated like cannon fodder. But they were at least forced to operate under the knowledge that a dead soldier could no longer fight. Eala was bound by no such restrictions. She did not care if her soldiers starved or died of exhaustion or bled out in battle.

"We keep going."

"I know you think to kill her, Fia." Irian's expression grew even more troubled. "But we will be alone in a stronghold she controls. Surrounded by her army and her supplicants. There will be nothing to stop her from killing *you*."

"She will not kill me," I said with utter certainty. Her words from the Longest Night were etched along the architecture of my bones. *It matters not whether you are my enemy or my ally. You are my sister. My other half. And only together can we be made whole.* "She believes she needs me, and I need her, to be complete. She will not murder me on a whim."

Irian hesitated a moment longer, then gave a brisk, unhappy nod. "Then we continue to the capital. And may the gods, living and dead, have mercy on us."

⤮

I followed Irian's anam cló as best I could, a shard of black screaming through the smoke-striped blue. Although I knew he tried not to lead me through the worst of the destruction, it was little use— the landscape was apocalyptic. Vast columns of black veered from burning villages and torched holdings. The stench of decay hung heavy in the air. Ravens and vultures swarmed above, their deathly calls casting a pall over the otherwise pleasant spring day.

It was early afternoon by the time we reached the ridge beyond Rath na Mara, but I felt as if I had been riding for years. The sight of the fort that had once been my home brought me little comfort; the dreadful army stacked in silent, orderly rows beyond its stockades nearly sent me running back the way we'd come.

I had never seen an army this size. It easily occupied the whole of the plain surrounding Rath na Mara. Ten thousand strong, perhaps more. And every single soldier was dead.

The stench slapped me full in the face, a noxious wave of carrion. I gagged, the spare contents of my stomach roiling as I fought not to heave. I lifted my arm to cover my nostrils with my sleeve, but the scent of death pervaded all my senses, stinging my eyes and crawling along my throat.

I urged Finan down the slope before either of us could change our minds. Irian alighted a bare moment later, his boots striking the road at the same time as he drew the Sky-Sword.

But as we trotted between their ordered rows, it was plain to see the army meant us no immediate harm. They stood perfectly still, hands—if they had them—hanging loose by their sides and eyes—if they had *them*—staring blankly ahead. The bodies were in every state of decay imaginable. Some might have passed for the living were it not for the faint patterns of livid veins spiderwebbed beneath their skin, the dark hollows ringing their eyes. Some were little more than skeletons, bleached bones decorated by medallions of skin and ribbons of stringy hair.

Most of them were somewhere in between. Horrid, damaged, mutilated corpses. Bashed-in skulls and crippling injuries and gaping, maggot-infested wounds. Worm-eaten flesh and throat-slit smiles and abdomens garlanded by loose guts.

At last, I couldn't stand it. I reined Finan to an inelegant halt, flung myself off his back, and vomited on the road until nothing but bile burned my throat and seared my nostrils. I barely registered Irian's hands carefully smoothing the hair back from my face, his voice murmuring, "We can go back, mo chroí. You do not have to do this."

I scrubbed my sleeve over my lips and blinked scalding tears from my eyes.

"We're nearly there," I croaked. "Let's not waste any more time."

Mercifully, the army of the dead soon gave way to a much smaller one made of the living. Men and women—nearly as dead-eyed and dull-faced as the walking corpses—moved listlessly between patched tents and ramshackle outbuildings and campfires ringed with bedrolls, polishing armor and sharpening weapons and cooking rations. It still stank, but after the rows of the dead, the normal odors of unwashed humans and open privies were practically perfume. Some fénnidi turned their heads to briefly stare at us, but their eyes seemed vacant, as if they knew they were little better than dead men walking.

Finally, the wooden palisade of the fort loomed before us. I stared up, searching for movement along the ramparts. I saw nothing. No one hailed us as I dismounted, stalked to the gate, and slammed my fist on it as hard as I could.

Bang. Bang. Bang.

The gate to Rath na Mara creaked, then swung slowly inward.

When I looked back at Irian, his gaze was shadowed with mis-givings. Beside him, Finan stamped and sallied, the whites of his eyes gleaming with fear. I inhaled, hammered my spine straight with all my misplaced courage, and walked inside the place I'd once called home.

The moment we crossed the threshold, the gate groaned, then slammed closed.

Trapping me and Irian in the stronghold of the Deathless Queen.

Chapter Thirty-Five

Fia

We were met by a platoon of castle guards—these men alive, bristling with weaponry and festooned with armor. One fénnid grabbed a snorting Finan by his bridle; I gave the stallion an encouraging pat on the neck as they led him away, and hoped it wouldn't be the last time I saw him. Another reached as if to wrest the Sky-Sword in its scabbard from Irian's hip; he growled, low and reverberant, and the man lifted his hands away with such speed I nearly laughed. The armed escort tightened like a noose, leading us deeper into the fort.

It was midafternoon in the high queen's capital—Rath na Mara would normally be buzzing with activity. Soldiers sparring and practicing in the courtyard, the clatter of steel ringing in the air. Stable hands and farriers bustling near the stables, blacksmiths' hammers clanging relentlessly off the stone walls. Servants and chambermaids slinking to and fro, stoking fires and sweeping floors and polishing silver, their barely audible chatter mingling with the scrape of brooms and the rustling of fabric. Visiting dignitaries and vassals dining in the great hall or arguing in the library or readying for a hunt.

Instead, Rath na Mara yawned with the sinister hush of a mausoleum. Flocks of sharp-winged crows circled high overhead and lined the palisades, watching our progress across the bailey with beady black eyes. As we plunged into the chilly dim of the great hall, our booted steps desecrated the cold silence within. Few torches were lit; no dogs napped beneath the long tables; no off-duty fénnidi threw dice or drank ale. It was as if Donn's dark underworld had opened its jaws and swallowed Rath na Mara whole, its occupants sleeping as in ancient legend.

My pulse spiked when I realized where we were inevitably headed—the high queen's throne room. The guards did not knock before shoving through the massive double doors leading into the chamber from which my foster mother had once ruled.

Eithne Uí Mainnín had despised ostentation, mistrusted it with the same terrible, all-consuming fury with which she had mistrusted Folk glamours and spells. Eala Ní Mainnín, her daughter, had an altogether different aesthetic.

The throne room was festooned in a thousand pale white flowers—snowdrop and anemone and lily and moonflower. In place of Mother's simple candelabras and torches, Eala had installed a massive intricate chandelier crafted entirely from bone and crystal, suspended from the vaulted ceiling. Each burning candle protruded from the eyehole or gaping mouth of a skull—human, animal, and Folk—so that they glowed from within as if lit with the lingering souls of the dead. Below hunched a huge, heavy throne sculpted from pale marble veined through with obsidian and interwoven with the bleached remains of what appeared to be Folk creatures—the armrests fashioned from a gruagach's curled claws and the back curving upward with the ribs of leipreacháin.

Seated upon it was my sister. At first glance, Eala seemed as poised and perfect as she ever was. But the longer I gazed at her, the more I saw the cracks in both her appearance and her composure. Her chest rose and fell too quickly, as though she had recently run far or fast. Her white skin seemed stretched too tightly over her exquisite bone structure, giving her the look of a porcelain doll before its cheeks and lips had been painted red. The only color on her face at all was her eyes, blazing blue as glass from beneath the pale frills of her eyelashes.

Fringing the room, half hidden in the strange, glancing shadows cast by the awful chandelier, courtiers sat or stood, still and silent. I briefly searched their impassive expressions for any familiar faces but saw only staring eyes and grim-set mouths.

I fought back dread as I feigned nonchalance and cut a mocking bow to my sister.

"Queen Eala." Derision seeped along my voice. "You have built your throne on the backs of the dead. How fitting, since the living can no longer bear the weight of you."

The temperature in the room seemed to drop, the air growing chilly and fraught. But Eala merely smiled, painstakingly, her bloodless lips curling over her gleaming teeth. Her fingers drummed a feverish rhythm on the arm of her throne.

"Always the sense of humor, Sister." Eala's voice was like the moment death calls—soft, yet utterly inescapable. "But as usual, you have it wrong—I am no burden. I am this kingdom's salvation."

She rose in a sharp sudden movement. Her white robes fluttered around her—not feathers as I had originally assumed, but tattered clothing. Strips of ripped dresses, scraps of lace, shreds of silk, all cobbled together in ragged, hovering gossamer. She slowly descended the steps of her throne and came to stand two paces before me, ignoring Irian's growl of displeasure. Our heights were a perfect match—her eyes stared straight into mine. This close, her porcelain perfection was flawed. Tiny hairline cracks fissured over Eala's skin, and despite the radiance suffusing her, what peeked from beneath was not light, but dark. Dark as rot, as grave dirt, sliding along the contours of her skull and creeping beneath her skin, streaking her white-blond hair and threading her crystal-blue eyes.

"Eala," I breathed, horror and nausea rising in me, along with a treacherous kind of concern I hardly had a name for. "I don't think you're well."

"I have never been better." Despite her words, I swore a sudden dart of doubt pierced her gaze. "I am all that was before and all that will be after. I am beginning and end. I am everything."

Terrible wrongness slicked my veins like black oil. My gloved hand twitched at my side, a weapon at the ready.

"But you, Sister." Eala leaned close and sniffed audibly. "You seem somewhat the worse for wear. Where *have* you been hiding out all these months? This is a sorry state in which to appear before your queen."

"You are not"—I ground the words between my teeth like gravel— "my queen."

"And I suppose you have come all this way to tell me why?" Her smile turned radiant, chasing away whatever uncertainty I thought I'd glimpsed. "Let it not be said I am not a generous ruler. I shall allow you to have a bath before you cast aspersions upon my reign. Guards!"

The guards had not gone anywhere—merely shadowed the doorway, bristling with weapons and silent aggression.

"Take our honored guests to the finest guest chamber on the main floor, and ensure all their needs are met with haste and honor," Eala said archly. "Am I understood?"

If the guards were surprised by the request, they did not betray it. The rígfénnid simply cut a nod, then waved us back the way we'd come. The fiann did not try to lay hands on either me or Irian—I supposed they'd learned that lesson already. So I simply stood my ground, refusing to turn away from my sister until I'd said my piece.

"Your hospitality is appreciated, Grave Mother." I laced my tone with irony and was rewarded with a faceless gasp from the edge of the room. Eala's smile slipped; the filaments of black darkening her eyes seemed to swallow the crystal blue of her irises. "But we have come to treat with you, not bathe in perfumed waters and sleep on feather beds. I am as fit for diplomacy in stained clothes as I am in silks and satins. Will you not talk peace? Or have you already set your mind to death and war?"

"You have always loved to insult what you do not understand, Sister." Eala's voice was little more than a hiss between her teeth. "But I shall not let you bait me. We will gather tonight at a feast, like civilized people. We will drink and make merry, and yes, perhaps we will even find time to speak of my peace. Does that suit, or must we quarrel here in public like common folk?"

I gave an ironic laugh. "Far better to destroy each other over the rims of jeweled goblets, with proper decorum."

"Then it is decided. I shall await you both at tonight's feast."

Eala turned back toward her throne, her garments fluttering around her like pale wings. And in the moment before I turned on my own heel toward Irian and the waiting guards, I couldn't help but let my gaze drift to the people seated and standing all around Eala's throne, masked by the fractured shadows cast by the gruesome chandelier. But my eyes had adjusted to the dim now.

They were all there. Rogan, tall and broad-shouldered, standing a pace behind the throne with his hair faintly gleaming in the candlelight. Chandi, seated upon a chair by the wall with her hands tightly folded in her lap. Cathair, his hair gone fully gray, the charms braided in his beard tarnished in the dim.

Mother, her hair unbound around her shoulders, no torc around her neck.

And they were all of them staring at me with pleading in their gaunt, empty eyes.

I turned away before the grotesque horror of it could snatch me and grind me to dust. Because the fact was, I was not sure which of them were alive...and which were dead.

The guards led us through hallways as familiar to me as the inside of my eyelids, yet rendered strange by the echoing silence of the once-raucous castle. We were ushered into a fine suite of rooms reserved for visiting royalty or wealthy dignitaries—I had rarely been allowed to set foot in these chambers, let alone sleep in them. The guards quietly barred the door behind us.

I took in our new surroundings. After the unparalleled opulence of Emain Ablach, the human finery seemed a tad quaint—the four-poster bed small, the tapestries lining the walls dull and simplistic, the whitewashed hearth stained with smoke. But after the trials of the past few days, it was paradise. A copper tub set in the corner steamed invitingly.

"You first," I said to Irian, although it pained me.

"Do you think me so uncouth, mo chroí?" He cocked his head and almost smiled. "I will languish in my filth a little longer if it means I get to watch you bathe."

I scowled at him but did not complain. I stripped off Corra's violet kirtle, now weatherworn and travel stained, and hung it carefully by the fire. Irian, true to his word, did not take his eyes off me, his gaze following where my hands went, unlacing boots and unfastening armor. At last, I stepped neatly into the tub. I had half expected Eala to have vindictively ordered it filled with ice water, but it was gloriously hot.

Irian came to perch on the edge like a raptor upon its roost. He rested a hand on the hilt of the Sky-Sword and waited until I had washed out my hair before saying, "What do you make of our welcome here at Rath na Mara?"

I worked my fingers through a snarl. "I do not trust it, of course. Eala always has plots beneath her plots, plans beneath her plans. Whatever reason she has for this farce of gentility, I have no doubt it masks something far more violent and vengeful."

"Like what?"

"If I knew, you should have cause to worry." A small smile bent my lips. "For then I should have gone truly mad, and you would be forced to take me out behind the privies and remove my head from my neck."

"Is that the common cure for madness in the human realms?" Irian's smile was a blade, his eyes like the summer sun. "How uncivilized. In Tír na nÓg we have healers for such things."

"What Eala suffers from, I fear no healer can cure." I rinsed my hair one last time before standing, the cool air of the room kissing my reddened skin. Irian reached for a towel and pressed it between us. I accepted the fluffy white cloth, my fingers grazing dangerously close to his. I smothered a burst of longing to cup his face with my hands, to press my mouth to his. To sink back into the steaming water and drag him in with me.

Instead, I stepped away. "Your turn."

I settled myself in the window casement, where buttery afternoon sunlight streamed in between gossamer silk curtains. The spring afternoon was balmy, and I finger-combed my short tresses and fluffed them to dry as Irian undressed. I tried not to stare at the cut of his arms as he dragged his shirt over his head; the chiseled expanse of his torso as he jerked his trousers off. It was nearly intolerable—like staring at a Folk feast, tables overflowing with lush food and plentiful drink, and knowing every bite and sip was cursed.

I made myself look out the window and stop dreaming of the day I might have all of him again.

But the sight outside the window brought me little more comfort. Rath na Mara and all her lands spread below the keep in a tapestry of reality and memory. How many times had I run across the main courtyard, Rogan hot on my heels, some game or errand giving our feet wings? How many times had I sparred in the training yard, the older boys yanking on my braids when the weapons master wasn't looking? How many nights had I saddled Eimar and galloped to the edge of the wood, not understanding the call of the forest, only knowing it felt more like a haven than the keep ever did?

I had hated this place, fervently. I had loved it, desperately. It had never been my home, not really. Yet it clung to me still like a ghostly handprint.

"Fia?"

Irian had finished his bath—he stood clean and damp before me, another towel slung low over his hips. Moisture clung in beads to his hard, smooth chest and dripped from the skein of black hair slicked from his face. But there was concern in his eyes as he gazed at me. "What troubles you?"

I swiped at my eyes—I hadn't realized I was crying.

"Nothing." I offered him a wan smile that only made him frown harder. "It is strange to be back here again. Not so long ago I believed this place held everything I cared for, and all I might one day love. When I left with Rogan for Dún Darragh, a year and a half ago, Mother promised me that if I succeeded in rescuing Eala, I would be rewarded with a command in her fiann, the honor of someday becoming Eala's war advisor. It is strange to imagine that I have returned not as a human fénnid but as a Folk Treasure; not as Eala's war advisor but as her adversary, begging for peace."

"Destiny is a poor map, mo chroí." Irian braced an arm on the casement as the sun slanted lower, bathing us both in molten gold. "It is a song half heard, promising triumph and defeat in the same alluring refrain. It leads not with loud certainty—thus we yearn for its quiet mystery."

I gazed at him, his mouth like honey I longed to taste. "In another life I think you might have been a poet."

"I think not." His lush lip lifted over a canine. His free hand toyed with the seam of the gauzy silk curtains floating at the edge of the casement. "I was led to believe you were an outcast in this place. Tell me, colleen—did you grow up amongst all this finery?"

I scoffed. "No."

"Then where?"

I did not want to tell Irian of the garret bedroom I had once called home. I did not want him to think of me as that poor, lowly creature. Yet I had been her, and she me. "These candles are beeswax—mine were tallow. These windows are double-paned glass—I had shutters that leaked a chill in winter. That bed will be feather down—my little mattress was straw. And my curtains would have been patched linen—not this fine silk."

"Silk." Irian was still toying with the edge of the curtain—he slid his hand over its gauzy layers, then without warning gripped my hand through the cloth. The touch jolted me—I automatically jerked away before I could hurt him. But he held on, his grip strong but gentle.

I stilled, curiosity mingling with my alarm. The radiance inside me flared, as if seeking an outlet for its sizzling, searing power. But with the layer of gauzy fabric separating our skin, my touch was muffled—Irian did not flinch away from me, nor did his palms burn.

"Do you know," he murmured as he trailed his hand—still coddled by silk—up my bare arm, "silk is deceptively strong? A single strand rivals metal in fortitude."

His touch slid over my shoulder to cup my cheek. I longed to lean into his touch, but the radiance inside me pummeled the inside of my skin.

"I doubt it is particularly resistant to heat," I murmured, rueful. "Irian—"

"Humor me." A brisk, sudden breeze blew up, catching the curtains like sails and billowing them between us. Dust motes scattered as Irian was transformed to a specter, his form little more than a pale shadow. Amid the sifting clouds of fabric, his hand caught my waist. His other hand curled around my neck, tilting my head back. He kissed me, his touch whisper soft behind the sifting, sighing silk. The fabric glided over my skin, slid over my lips, caressed my cheeks.

"Whether tallow or beeswax, linen or silk, I wish to know your past." His breath tasted of promised things—warmer mornings and longer days and happier times. "Wherever you have been, I wish to visit. Wherever you are, I wish to be. And wherever you go, I wish to follow. Remember that, mo chroí."

He pulled away. The breeze died out. The curtains settled.

And as the sun slid away behind the distant line of trees, a brisk knock came at the door.

I gathered my towel around my suddenly chilled body and slid off the casement.

"An hour until dinner," I said. "We'd better get dressed."

Chapter Thirty-Six

Laoise

Laoise heaved a sigh as she watched her brother leave the valley in the company of the least serious and most dissolute man she had ever met. Although Idris was more than capable of making his own decisions, Laoise couldn't help but feel a fierce, protective warmth toward him—a need to shield him from every hurt the world might throw in his direction. She had never seen much of herself in his wide, wondering eyes; his trusting nature infuriated her, even as it filled her with pride and tenderness. Although he could drive her to the edge of her patience, all she truly wanted was to see Idris safe, happy, and unburdened.

She did not wish to see him ravished, then discarded by the hedonist prionsa of the Silver Isle.

"He'll be all right," Sinéad said, over her shoulder.

Laoise sighed again. "I'm not so sure about that."

"Wayland's not so bad," she added, clearly intuiting Laoise's reservations about the libertine heir. "Once you get to know him."

"I'm also not so sure about *that*," Laoise said dryly. "And the *getting to know him* is exactly what I'm worried about."

She slid her eyes over the valley she had destroyed, then helped renew. There was no reason to stay, now everyone else was gone. But something made her want to linger—a quiet, stubborn reluctance rooting her to the spot. She was not a fearful woman—she had faced greater dangers. Yet the hollow ache of possibility filled her chest, tearing her between the safety of the familiar and the uneasy thrill of stepping toward a future that would change her indelibly.

It did not feel like destiny. It felt like erasure.

So she told Sinéad, "Let's rest one more night. I want the draiglings at their full strength. We fly to Findias in the morning."

Laoise knew the route to Findias well—she had flown back several times since rescuing Idris from its smoldering ruins. The sight of the city she had once called home never failed to elicit a complicated mix of feelings: a bittersweet, burning ache—old painful memories coddled like burning embers in her heart—and the sharp pang of remembering all she had outgrown. Findias was a city burdened by ghosts—of people, of violence. Yet it was haunted mostly by Laoise herself—her past cobbled into the streets and mortared into the walls and thatched upon the roofs.

Nestled deep within a jagged mountain crevasse, Findias caught the late afternoon sunlight, glowing like a living coal in shades of orange and crimson. Sinuous towers of blackened obsidian had once been crowned with ever-burning flames that crackled and danced in the mountain winds. Aqueducts carved from volcanic glass arched over the streets—long ago, rivers of magma had spat and sparked as they were carried toward the city's great forges, wreathed in swarms of tiny red emberfolk. In the heart of the city, a vast plaza sat, dominated by a fountain that had once spilled liquid flames but now only spurted ugly, warped shadows. The corrupted wild magic gathered at the back of the city like a crouching beast ready to pounce.

Above it, the volcano hunched, its crater like two hands cupped around a bowl of fire. It gave a speculative growl as Laoise flew closer, spitting an arc of magma through the darkening sky. Laoise suppressed a shudder of nerves. Before the purge, the volcano had been considered holy—the Sept of Scales had called it Cuas na Gréine. *The Hollow of the Sun.* Elen used to recite a nursery rhyme to frighten Laoise before bed: *In the Hollow of the Sun, where old fire flares bright, the flames cast no warmth, only shadows and fright.*

Laoise alighted on a plateau halfway up the rise—she did not wish to get too close to the flaming crater with Sinéad and the draiglings, but neither did she want to leave Sinéad in the abandoned city.

"It's cold." Sinéad hunched deeper into her mantle as a high wind whipped through the gorge, whistling between the high stone needles and making Laoise's scales quiver. "Is there nowhere else to camp? Surely somewhere in the city—"

"We're not camping." A sliver of guilt pierced Laoise's heart. She should not have let Sinéad come with her—she should have sent her with Balor, where she would have been far safer and likely more comfortable. Selfishly, she had wanted a friend for this journey. And now that friend was suffering. "More dangerous things than ghosts roam Findias after dark. It is a lawless, fell place."

Sinéad frowned. "Then what are we doing here?"

"I know where my Bright One's nemeton is," Laoise said, matter-of-factly. Neither Irian, Wayland, nor Fia had had the upbringing of a tánaiste, which was for the best—they had all survived the purge, while few others had. But the omens of Laoise's birth had been clear, and she had been raised on the sacred lore of her Sept—all the knowledge and training of the Treasure she was sure to inherit. Her education had not been finished—she had been sent away to Dún Scaith before she came of age. But she had learned enough. "It is inside the volcano."

Sinéad blanched, her wind-whipped complexion going gray in the fading light. "*Inside* it?"

"Blodwen—if anything happens to me, you're in charge. Keep Sinéad and the smaller draigs safe. Travel south until you reach the coast, then to the Summerlands as swiftly as you can."

Blodwen bobbed her red head. Sinéad went even paler. "That doesn't sound promising."

"Come now." Laoise forced herself to grin despite the trepidation beginning to clang and clatter inside her. "Do not let fear of what has not yet passed steal your enjoyment of the present moment."

"Enjoyment?" Sinéad's eyebrows drifted up. "What enjoyment?"

Laoise gestured broadly at the sheer, stark mountains painted bloody by the dying sun. "Is this not an utterly *stunning* view?"

Sinéad scoffed, punched Laoise gently on the shoulder, then dragged her in for a brief, bullying hug.

"Be careful," she commanded, gruffly, before planting her back against a large rock and drawing her daggers. "And quick. I'm already freezing. Don't think I'm leaving here without you."

Laoise watched until all six draiglings arranged themselves close around Sinéad—the older three buffering the wind with their wings, Gwyr and Anwyll snuggling on either side of her, and Enfys climbing into her lap—before shifting back into her anam cló and winging toward the crater.

The gateway to the Hollow of the Sun was well hidden and barred with metal. Laoise had always found this humorous—after all, who would willingly break into a volcano? That would be like gift wrapping your own doom with a bow on top. The key guarded by the Sunkeepers was long lost, so she blew white-hot flames over the bars of the gate until they melted into rivulets of gleaming metal, then returned to her Gentry form to sidle through the gap.

She descended the winding steps carved into the throat of the volcano, each one slick with ancient ash. They were warm beneath her feet, moving gently as if the dark stone breathed as it slumbered. Shadows and glow flickered along the walls, cast from below by restless light. The hot air was oppressive, heavy with the scent of sulfur as it beaded sweat along Laoise's skin and crisped her hair. The molten heartbeat of the crater throbbed louder, echoing through the depths.

The staircase bottomed out in the heart of the crater. Spires of glossy black obsidian, able to withstand incredible temperatures, branched up through the bubbling pit of molten lava, towering nearly a hundred feet to the ceiling of the crater. They formed a circle, at the center of which sat a block. A dais, an *altar*.

This was the Hollow of the Sun, where Laoise had made yearly pilgrimage when she was a child. The Sunkeepers' song trembled up the throat of the volcano as the potential heirs trailed them in their golden robes. The reigning tánaiste, Dímma, had conducted the ritual beneath the nemeton. Upon his broad arm lay the Flaming Shield, intricately carved in obsidian atop a circle of sacred wood, wreathed in glowing flame like a small sun.

Laoise had always known, in her heart of hearts, that her destiny would carry her here. The circumstances were just a bit different than she had imagined.

She tried to remember the Sunkeepers' song as she approached the altar, avoiding deep pockets of magma simmering upon the rock. The lava couldn't hurt her, but she liked these boots. She hummed a snatch of a melody, brokenly, but could remember only a few of the lines. *O radiant flame, heart of all light! The sun is arisen, with dawn from night.*

A figure materialized in the spitting, seething glow at the heart of the nemeton. Laoise could not quell the burst of fear sharpening its teeth upon her ribs and slashing its tail along the contours of her stomach. But the figure was only a child—perhaps eleven or twelve. Laoise briefly thought it must be herself—before Scáthach had made her cut her hair, she had worn it in long, loose curls like that. Her silken gown was the warm copper and sharp red worn by the high houses of the Sept of Scales. But a narrow scar bridged the girl's nose from a childhood accident, and the color of her eyes was not molten ember like Laoise's and their mother's, but dark and opaque as their father's and brother's.

Laoise's stomach twisted with a new fear—a chill clawing her spine and freezing her breath in her lungs. Horror rocked her, even as terrible hope scattered her thoughts.

"Elen?" she whispered.

The girl slid off the dais and approached Laoise, her steps dainty and careful. Laoise used to fling herself where she wished to go— running up stairs and dashing down hallways. Elen had always been more measured. More refined, their parents had always said. But as she approached, Laoise saw the girl was not her sister. Not truly. Her red curls were coils of living flame; her bones were tattered kindling, glowing blue at her core; and her eyes were black— black as soot, black as choking smoke, black as the blight spreading over the city Laoise had once called home.

She swallowed her grief, forcing it into the cold, tight dungeon where it usually lived. *Despair is a two-edged blade,* Scáthach always used to tell her. *Learn how to wield it so it does not cut you but instead acts as a shield against those who would harm you.*

"You're not Elen."

No, agreed the Elen-shaped entity—the Bright One of the element of fire. Laoise knew this being—had seen them in her dreams for as long as she could remember. The Sunkeepers had seen this as yet another sign that she would one day inherit the Flaming Shield. The Bright One's voice flicked in Laoise's mind like a tongue of twisted flame, leaving a sooty residue in its wake. *You know us. We know you. Let us not play games.*

"Oh, good," said Laoise, a touch dryly. "I outgrew those a while ago."

You may not have what you wish for, they thundered against the inside of Laoise's skull, drowning out all other words or thoughts. Anger flashed, hot and bright, but it did not mask the sucking darkness lurking beneath. A bleakness—the smoldering ruin of a wildfire that had devoured everything in its path. *For too long we have served others. We have been enslaved by the Fomorians. We have been enslaved by the Folk. We will not be enslaved again— not even by you.*

Laoise took a deep breath. "Not even if I promise to set you free?"

There is no such thing as freedom. There is only power. And I can offer you endless amounts of it.

Laoise cocked her head. "Endless?"

Endless. Eagerness hammered her psyche, greedy and grasping. Images and sensations shattered in her mind's eye, bright and brutal as falling stars. She saw herself crowned upon a throne of obsidian, surrounded by seven massive draigs breathing flame in the dark. She saw vast armies prostrated before her. She saw Idris beside her, whole and unblemished; she saw Elen, grown to womanhood and surrounded by a happy family.

With all her strength, Laoise shoved the terrible, tempting images away. She forced her eyes open. Gazed at Not-Elen.

"Is that how you get them?" She infused her voice with as much humor as she could muster. "What a cheap trick. I can't believe anyone falls for it."

The corrupted Bright One unspooled in a thread of fire, then rematerialized to whisper in her ear: *They all fall for power in the end. Power is everything. Power is freedom.*

"Power is not freedom," Laoise scoffed. "To wield power is to be bound by it. It may be endless—but it is an endless web of consequence and desire. The stronger one grows, the tighter the noose. Power is not freedom—it is merely the illusion of control over a force that is always, in some way, in control of you."

Then let power be a blade. To carve out a home. To strike down your enemies. To take what you need.

"True power is not in what you can take, but in what you care to protect." It was one of Scáthach's favorite sayings—she who could have ruled kingdoms or destroyed kings but chose instead to build a haven for women who wished to find their own strength.

"A blade is poor protection—for it cuts both ways. What I need is a shield."

Not-Elen stared at her, the Bright One's impermeable gaze full of layered, unpredictable flame. Flame that could raze a forest to the ground but spark new growth by clearing away old dead things. Flame that could tear apart empires with chaos and war or bring gentle warmth to hearth and home. Flame that sparked life into being and, within it, carried the darkness at the end of all creation.

The Shield is broken. Its flames are dead, the Bright One said, harsh. *I can give you power. Or I can give you death.*

"A new Treasure rises in the darkness of unchecked power. Many will cower before it, many more will die because of it; more still will break the bonds of nature's balance and rise again." Laoise had never yearned to inherit the Flaming Shield—not like the other potential heirs. She had always seen it for what it was—a noose at the end of a finely decorated rope. But now she had to find a way. "If you will not give me what I need to shield them, then I will have to take it."

Yes, slithered Not-Elen's voice as she circled Laoise. Heat licked along her cheeks and kissed her throat. *Take it. Let it turn your blood to fire and your voice to flame and your hand to claws. Let the world fear Laoise of the Sept of Scales.*

"I do not take it for myself," Laoise cried. She pulled the shard of Blodwen's egg from beneath her tunic, running her thumbs over its jagged edges. "I take it for those who cannot protect themselves. I take it as a shield for the weak. Come with me, and let us right what has been wronged. Then I swear, if it is in my power, I will set us both free."

I am already free! Their voice was passion and restraint, curse and benediction, end and beginning. *You cannot cage me again!*

"You forget, Bright One—I was raised on your lore." Laoise cupped the shard between her palms. "We are one. We are none. We are everything together."

No. The Bright One crackled and snapped, Elen's features

melting and scalding as they had that long-ago day in the warehouse. Her hair, a tongue of flame; her golden dress, a conflagration. *Do not speak the words. Do not speak my name.*

"By fire and by sky, by fast water and by ancient tree." Laoise murmured the words like a prayer, even as she sliced the sharpest corner of the egg over her skin. Glowing scarlet blood welled, lacquering her fingertips. "I promise my willing heart to thee...O Flaming Shield. *Grian.*"

The name was a simplification—a distillation of wildness so deep it could not be named. Shadows cast upon ancient walls by dancing flames. Fullness and emptiness. Heat and cold. Light and the darkness beyond it. They rushed into Laoise with the force of a star plummeting from the firmament, slamming into her with visceral power. Her mind unmoored—slipping free of her body like a yolk from a broken egg.

She was a dying star, fierce and consuming, haunted by the vast, eerie emptiness that waited beyond. She was heat pulsing in molten veins, her skin like embers, her breath curling into gray smoke. She was flame itself: a boundless, searing force with no beginning and no end.

Then she was just Laoise, crouched on a teetering platform of stone between the arching ribs of an obsidian nemeton. The volcano rumbled a warning around her, dark stone plopping into the rippling, seething magma below. For the briefest moment, fear gripped Laoise. But then a memory soothed her—of the only tithing she had lived through, when she was seven. She remembered watching from her family's apartments as the usually dormant Hollow erupted in a great pyre of lightning-streaked smoke. The crater wept rivulets of glowing red, like tears of flame. The spectacle had lasted only a few hours, but the cloud of smog had hung over the city for weeks, blanketing the streets with black ash. The month after, Laoise had made her first pilgrimage to the nemeton—one of the potential heirs for the next tithing.

It was as it had always been. In fire and in smoke, in ash and in stone, she would be reborn. Unmade, remade. This fire would not harm her, would not consume her; it would simply strip away the pieces of who she had once been, leaving only her core. And from that she would rise—awesome and fierce and unknowable. This was the true crucible: flame, heat, and force transforming what had been shattered into something whole. Something powerful. Something impenetrable.

This was a reforging.

She shifted into her anam cló as the magma surged beneath her, molten blood pushed through the earth's veins from its burning heart. Lifting her. Carrying her. She screamed as she arose, the throat of the crater compressing the lava into an inexorable embrace. It was agony; it was ecstasy. The pressure built—scorching, unbearable tension coiling tighter and tighter until it finally reached a breaking point.

Laoise shattered through the mouth of the crater. Filaments of light scattered around her; smoke belched in great furling sweeps; lava splashed the side of the volcano. Her large wings instinctively snapped open in the blinding, burning mayhem of the eruption. Gusts of heat carried her. And when the blackness of the night at last curled around her, cooling her scales and clearing her mind, she angled herself toward a plateau a mile from the crater.

The draigs all winged to meet her—she must be shining like a beacon in the night, even with the volcano erupting behind her. She tumbled through the air with them in affectionate greeting before finally transforming into her Gentry form upon the plateau. Sinéad was on her feet, and Laoise noticed with a jolt that the human girl had been weeping—tears etching rivulets through the light layer of ash coating her face.

"When the volcano erupted—" Her voice was smoky with resentment and choked with relief. "I thought for certain you must have died."

Laoise wasn't sure she had not. But it did not seem to matter so much, in this moment. "I was reborn."

Sinéad nodded, then wordlessly unfastened her cloak from one shoulder and handed it to Laoise. She frowned, not understanding, even as Sinéad's agonized worry shifted into something closer to discomfort.

The tithing had stripped away not only Laoise's old self...but her old clothes too. She was naked as the day she was born. A network of markings climbed her arms and chest and shoulders, filigreed over her skin in a red so dark it was nearly black. Stylized scales, smooth and shining as her draiglings' ombré scutes, licked her skin from the tips of her fingers to the wing of her collarbone, fading in and out of sight as the light played over them. And upon her forearms were vambraces, forged from volcanic obsidian that reflected the flaming night, each one set with half of the draig egg shard.

Laoise laughed—she couldn't help it. She had never been bothered with shame for her physical body, and in this particular moment, clothes seemed silly. She was a vessel for enormous power, linked by a resonant conduit to a source so unknowable that their name was less a word than an idea. She was a *Treasure*.

But to Sinéad, she was just Laoise. And Laoise wore clothes.

"Keep it—you need it more than I." She waved away the cloak. "We shouldn't stay here. Can you fly?"

Sinéad nodded, her mettle returning.

"Good. Then we wing toward the Summerlands." Laoise smiled, her euphoria like an ardent banner carrying her forward. There was no time to waste—there were dead armies to rout and royalty to reign in. There were so many people who needed her protection. "Perhaps the Summer Twins will lend me some clothes before we embroil them in a war."

Chapter Thirty-Seven

Fia

There were exactly two outfits in the wardrobe. My gown was black, with long tight sleeves and a skirt like a cascade of midnight satin, embossed in pale thread with a delicate motif of ebony feathers. I was so transfixed that I almost didn't notice Irian staring askance at his own outfit for the evening.

"What— Oh." I recognized the clothing immediately, the sight like a poorly timed punch to the gut. The dark blue trousers beneath a golden tunic; the bold checked mantle in shades of green. Bridei's colors.

"These are Rogan's clothes." Irian's voice was low.

I swallowed. "Perhaps he is the only man in the fort tall enough to lend you clothing?"

"That may be so," Irian replied, "but I am certain it is not the only reason."

We dressed in silence. The clothes were far from perfect—the dress hung loose over my bodice and dragged on the floor. And though Rogan was tall, Irian was taller—his wrists showed beneath the cuffs of the tunic, and his shoulders strained at the seams of the mantle.

"Perhaps this is her ploy," Irian growled. "To make me ridiculous."

"I fear no one could do that, my heart."

The same platoon of guards greeted us at the door and escorted us to the feast. The sun had set—torches flared in sconces, and the sound of music wafted from the great hall. But nothing could have prepared me for what greeted us when we stepped inside.

Eala's feast might have been a fresco, daubed then dried, or a tapestry, painstakingly picked out in careful colors. Save for the music trilling from a frenzied band of wide-eyed musicians and the torches scattering golden light, all was still and silent. The tables were full of revelers, decked out in finery. But no one lifted so much as a goblet. No one chatted with their neighbor or flirted with the bard or leered at a serving girl. Even the hounds lay quiet beside the hearth, heads on paws and tails tucked.

"Sister!" Eala stood from the queen's place at the center of the high table and beckoned Irian and me to join her. I tried not to look too hard at the other guests at the high table as I passed them—I needed only my nose to tell that some of them were no longer living. Yet my eyes could not help but graze over a few familiar faces.

Chandi, her tall spine bowed as she stared fixedly at the table, her skin wan and her hair dull. Dual arrows of fury and sympathy spiked my heart.

Mother, with Cathair beside her. Something cool and unnerving spooled through me—something slightly more venomous than relief—when I saw they were both alive. Eithne glanced up sharply as I passed her, her diamond-blue eyes scathing on mine. She gave her head a tight, tense shake.

Eala no longer wore her strange fluttering assemblage of rags— she had donned the pale twin to my outfit, a gown white as driven snow and embroidered all over with a delicate motif of feathers picked out in ebony thread. I fought a shudder as she waved me close, guiding me into the chair beside her own. The same chair I had once occupied as the queen's foster daughter.

There was no chair beside it. No chair for Irian.

I thought perhaps it was an oversight until my gaze caught on the figure standing behind Eala, broad-shouldered and golden-haired. Clad in a tunic braided in gold beneath a mantle of green. Blank-eyed and deferent.

Not an oversight. To dress Irian up like Rogan and deny him a place at the feasting table? It was a grave insult.

Irian noticed at the same moment I did. He visibly bristled, his shoulders bulging at the already strained seams of his tunic and his silver eyes narrowing to crescents beneath the fall of his black hair. He was impossibly tall and unbelievably menacing, and whatever hold Eala had over her guests flickered—murmurs erupting as the human courtiers shifted fearfully in their seats. Most of these people had never glimpsed the Folk outside their bedtime stories, let alone laid eyes on a towering Gentry lord with violence etched upon every line of his impressive figure.

"Sister." I held out a gentling hand to Irian, remembering Mother's head shake. Angering Eala was not just foolhardy—it was potentially life-threatening. "You seem to have forgotten a place for Irian to sit."

Her laugh was high and chiming. "I forgot nothing."

I hardened my tone. "He is my consort."

"But you are his queen." Eala's tone switched from humorous to grave in a breath. "Should you sit, his duty is to stand behind you in support. Should you climb a stair, his duty is to follow one step beneath so he may gaze upon you from below. Should a blade threaten you, his duty is to shield you with his body. And should you sit upon a throne, his duty is to kneel at your feet. That is how a queen ought to be treated."

I stared at her, half expecting her to utter the punch line to a bad joke. But she was deathly serious. I opened my mouth to say something like *That is not devotion but domination.*

Then Irian forcibly relaxed, every muscle in his powerful body going loose as he stepped slowly backward to stand beside Rogan. He folded his huge hands across his belt, threw his shoulders back, and set his eyes resolutely forward. I could not help my gaze from sliding over Rogan beside him, his expression flat and blank as slate. Whatever spark of life in his eyes I'd seen—or imagined—on Emain Ablach seemed completely gone.

Eala clapped her hands, and servants streamed in with platters of food and decanters of wine. There was wild garlic and potato soup, but the creamy broth was curdled, and the new potatoes were veined with black rot. Servants cut steaming loaves of freshly baked bread, but by the time it reached our plates, it was cold and stale, as if it had been baked a week ago. The meat was spring lamb with mint and pea puree, but it tasted like old rangy mutton, and the fresh roasted vegetables looked like they'd been scooped from a pig's trough. By the time dessert was served—a rhubarb tart with custard—my stomach roiled. I fought not to heave at the sight of maggots squirming in the custard and pushed my plate away.

Around me, the living guests suffered the same struggle. Only Eala daintily sipped at her soup and shredded her meat with her long-nailed fingers and scooped sour, woody rhubarb between her delicate lips.

Nausea curdled my stomach, hobbled my mind. Could my sister not see what she had done? What she was doing? Her Treasure was not power over life, but the quickening of death. She was rotting this land from the inside out. And Tír na nÓg would be next.

"Sister," I said at last. "We come to you with a proposition for peace."

Eala dabbed at her bloodless lips with a napkin before saying, simply, "No."

Silence guttered around us like a dying fire. Until Eala leaned close, speaking to me softly and directly. Her breath gusted over my face, tasting of decay. This close, the markings on her skin looked like dark spiderwebs, twisting and shifting in the uneven torchlight.

"Can you not see? I have already created peace." Behind Eala, Irian shifted his feet. Eala's cracked-agate eyes were fervent with a curious need that took me aback. As if she was desperate for me to believe her words. Or, perhaps, desperate to believe them herself. "Beneath our mother, our father, and all the high kings of Fódla before them, this realm was in shambles. Thousands suffered while they engaged in petty squabbles and border disputes. *We* suffered—swapped and traded like coins on market day, cursed and manipulated to suit the whims of those who held power. But we have taken back the power, Sister. The control I exert over Fódla has only been to its benefit. I have purged corruption, halted petty wars, ended suffering. I have begun the difficult task of repairing a world that has failed its people—and me—one too many times."

"You cannot make a fist and call it peace, Eala," I ground out. "Nor can you deal death and say you have ended suffering."

"I am *correcting* it," Eala insisted. "Sacrifice paves the way for growth—surely we have both learned that much. I feel the weight of every death, every lost soul, every undone destiny. But it is all made worthwhile in resurrection—the old giving way to the glorious new."

I stared at her. In a twisted way, my sister's words rang true. One only had to look at Eala to see the toll her magic was taking on her. The more she forced her vision upon reality, the more reality resisted. But I knew—this was not growth. It was the opposite—autumn leaves withering to dust, a candle guttering in the wind, a tuneless melody fading to silence.

I curled my hands in my lap, willing my starshine to stay dim. Between my long sleeves and the soft candlelight, Eala had not noticed anything different about me. In contrast, I could not stop staring at the blemishes marring her skin. The more I stared, the more they put me in mind of long, strange feathers with skeletal barbules. My fingers twitched. Eala was but an arm's length away—all I had to do was reach for her.

Only you can bring her to the light.

"I need you by my side." Upon her pale head, Eala's crown stared at me with winking menace. "You are my perfect balance.

The shadow to my light. The ending to my beginning. Together we shall finish what I have started."

An involuntary shudder coiled my spine. "How?"

"For too long, Fódla and Tír na nÓg have been artificially separated. Like us. Torn asunder, like us. Made to hate each other, like us. But they are meant to be one realm. Humans and Folk, one people. The Gates are a travesty, an abomination. We must tear them down to unite all."

Gods help me, but I almost believed her.

"Tír na nÓg is even worse than Fódla. More violent, more corrupt, more power hungry." Her long-nailed fingers steepled on the table, tense as bowstrings. "You should want this just as much as I do, Sister. We were both stolen from our homes against our will, held captive in realms we could not cross from; you were forged beneath the iron fist of a cruel queen, while I was cursed and misused, my life threatened every day I drew breath. Don't you see? Were there no Gates, our misery would never have been possible. Don't you want to save others like us, ground beneath the heel of fate? Don't you wish for everyone to be free?"

Grief for an impossible childhood rose within me. I remembered jolting awake in an unfamiliar bed to the sounds of harsh screams. What had small Eala's first moments in Tír na nÓg been like— alone in an unfamiliar world, scared, powerless? How different would our lives have been, had we not been children abused by the careless intrigues and hungry ambitions of others far more powerful than us?

Behind me, Irian made a sound of warning. My eyes flicked to him, then beyond, snagging on a bold checked cloak and a head of golden hair.

Eala spoke of being cursed and abused. But she was not a little girl anymore.

Hers was the voice that spoke the curses. And the hand that dealt the abuse.

"Free?" I choked out. "Like Rogan is free?"

Eala slammed her fist on the table, rattling my plate of uneaten dessert so it tipped off the edge. Seeping red rhubarb slapped a stain like blood on the tablecloth; the rancid, curdled cream dropped wriggling maggots onto the floor.

"We should never have been made so powerless," I murmured.

"I do not disagree with you. But look around you, Eala! How can you speak of freedom when you are wielding control like a puppeteer with iron strings?"

"There can be no freedom without control!" A note of anguish twisted her words into something breathless. "That is why we must stand together. To prove to both worlds that our purpose unites us—that under our joint authority, we can bring both realms peace. That is why you must give me your willing heart."

I jerked back, instinctively. *"What?"*

"A heart is powerful magic—you taught me that. I could have had your heart before, had I wished it." Irian growled, so low it was barely audible, but it hummed along my bones. "With your *willing* heart we can truly remake the world. Together, in our image. Human and Folk. Dark and light. Magic and nature. Together we will tear down the Gates and return balance to both our worlds."

Horror was a living thing inside me, carving my ribs and gnawing at my heart. Perhaps my dream-father had wished me to save my sister. But I knew now what I had been uncertain of before—Eala was beyond saving. I inched my hand across the table toward her, willing my starshine to remain dim. Her frayed markings suddenly reminded me of my own sinuous thorn tattoos—only her barbs were longer, sharper, dipped in poison.

"If I did this for you, if I gave you my heart…what would I get in return?"

"Whatever you wish for, Sister. I shall make you queen of Tír na nÓg—to sit upon a throne of thorns or reign from a castle of black feathers. You shall slit the throats of the bardaí—of all who have ever wronged you." A terrible new light sparked in her eyes. "Or you shall have Fódla, if you wish it. You shall rule from this keep and make all humans bend to you, their new Gentry queen. Mother shall bow before the bastard whelp her husband got upon his Folk whore."

I flinched. I couldn't help it. I dared a glance across the table, but Eithne might as well have been carved from stone.

"But, Eala." The words were like glue between my teeth. On the table, between our wineglasses, our little fingers almost touched. "How can I rule either realm when I am dead?"

For the space of a heartbeat, Eala's eyes flickered, dread and desperation making a death mask of her beautiful features before her composure snapped back into place. "Because my magic will resurrect you, Sister. You have died once before, have you not? You shall live again—and your rebirth will be holy. We *both* shall live, and our worlds will be made whole in the doing."

"Or maybe only one of us should live." I closed the last inch between us, touching Eala's littlest finger with my own.

Starshine exploded between us in a corona, crackling over her hand. Veins of darkness deepened along her forearm, obsidian through white marble. Eala jerked from her chair with a scream, breaking the connection as she yanked her hand away from mine. She stared uncomprehendingly at her blackened flesh, then slowly lifted her eyes to me.

"Sister," she breathed. "Why are you glowing?"

I stood abruptly, crushing wriggling maggots beneath my shoes, then stalked the length of the table, pausing beside a middle-aged gentleman with graying hair and a mustache. Well, he would have been middle-aged—if he weren't obviously dead.

"What your magic does is not resurrection." Distantly, I registered Irian drawing the Sky-Sword. Even more distantly, I saw Eithne rise in her chair, shaking her head more ferociously than before. "And it is far from holy."

I buried my hands in the man's hair—ragged and dry as straw around my fingers—twisted as hard as I could, then yanked. His hands came up half-heartedly as his head pulled away from his body—his decaying skin separating with the sound of wet parchment ripping, his graying muscles and tendons stretching thin before unraveling with a sucking snap. Viscera slopped out from the cavity of his body, swollen organs and masses of blood bursting on the flagstones, twined with knots of worms.

Eala rose from her chair, some deep and deadly emotion twisting her beautiful, bloodless features into a mask of menace. "Stop that."

"Do you call this life?" I moved past a teenaged girl silently weeping into her untouched dessert, toward her mother, a woman who shared her golden hair but otherwise looked pulled from a casket. Half her skin had sloughed away to reveal the glaring eye socket of her skull and the cage of her ribs. I grabbed one of her desiccated hands resting on the table, and—with a silent apology to her living daughter—yanked it clean off her body. I held up the bony appendage, strung with ribbons of dried flesh. "Do you call this *freedom*?"

"Stop that!" Eala screamed, the words reverberating from her mouth with the force of her denial. "Stop it *now*!"

"Would you do to both worlds what you have done to this one, Eala?" I spat, disgust clinging to my words like the dead flesh clung to its skeleton. "It is not peace. It will not make you whole. It is death. You are no Grave Mother. No Deathless Queen. You are the Rotten Princess. And I will burn you to ash before I let you do this to another realm!"

Eala screamed, a raw, furious cry of life unraveling into death. Her fingers scrabbled at the table, the blackness where she'd touched me expanding along the cracks of her markings.

"Guards!" Her diamond-blue eyes looked hollow—an abyss I hardly dared gaze into. She snapped her fingers, and Rogan obediently straightened. "Secure the changeling!"

Rogan came at me with a speed that belied his bulk. His once-lively eyes, the blue-green of river stones, were as flat and gray as a field left fallow. I searched his gaze for any recognition, any personality, any humanity.

On Emain Ablach, I'd sworn I'd caught fleeting glimpses of the man Rogan had once been. I'd sworn he was still there, albeit trapped inside his own mind, his will subsumed by another. But that had been months ago. Now I feared that what Irian had once predicted had come to pass. No human could withstand the effects of the black flower for that long and keep any shred of themselves intact.

"Princeling?" I whispered as I backed away, hitching my skirts around my knees as I readied to run. Behind me, I sensed Irian prowling, Sky-Sword at the ready. Rogan did not flinch; his eyes did not flicker. Still, I could not bring myself to say goodbye to him—even if there was no one to say it to.

I turned and fled.

But the guards who poured into the great hall—as guests scattered and the musicians dropped their flagging instruments—were not the ones who had escorted us from our rooms.

These ones were dead. And there were more of them.

So many more.

They surged into the room on teetering, jolting legs. Ragged armor listed and shifted over their rotting frames, the sound of their advance a sickening symphony of clattering bones and flesh too far gone. The stench of death and corruption wafted heavy on the air.

I threw up a dense wall of thorns as the undead guards approached us, but they flung their bodies against the barrier until the stiff brambles were streaked with gore. At my back, Irian's black blade swung in deadly arcs as he lunged and parried the onslaught. But there were so many of them. They climbed over my barrier and pressed us to the wall as their withered hands grabbed for his mantle and my arms—

I stilled, letting them seize me. Then I let my starshine slip.

Decaying flesh began to smoke as the radiance lurking beneath my skin expanded, a hot numbness racing from my fingertips over my elbow to cocoon my throbbing heart. Rivulets of silver expanded over the revenants' cold flesh before sparking hot and fast like oil in a scalding pan. Light exploded—I closed my eyes, but I could not escape it. It burned toward my core, incinerated my spine, scalped me. For a bare instant, I floated free of my body, and beyond me there was only light, pure and perfect and impossibly hot.

The light rippled back into me, delicate as fluff blown from a dandelion. And when I opened my eyes, the revenants I'd touched were gone, nothing more than black dust sifting away between my glowing fingers. Shock and awe and creeping horror burned through me in quick succession.

I dared look at Eala.

Fear and hunger slashed across her features, dark as a night sky and insatiable as a bottomless pit. She stared at me as if unsure whether she wanted to destroy me...or devour me.

"Hold!" Her shout skittered over the room, mingling with the clang of Irian's sword and the weeping of the living guests and the wet slump of limbs gone soft with rot. "Leave them be!"

As one, the horde of dead soldiers stopped moving. Irian slowly extricated himself from the mass of bodies and armor. Long scratches ridged his neck; dark brown blood smeared his face and stained the Bridei green of his—Rogan's—mantle. His tarnished-silver eyes caressed my face.

I could not tell what Irian was thinking.

"I must think on this new development." Eala had regained her composure—although she cradled her injured arm to her chest like a babe. "Take them to the dungeons. We shall speak again in the morn."

Although her voice grated like broken nails over soft skin, I neither argued with her nor resisted as we were frog-marched from the great hall by an army of the undead.

But as the doors shut behind us, I swore to myself—I would get close enough to touch my sister again. And this time, I wouldn't let go.

Chapter Thirty-Eight

Wayland

The dark waters below Murias rippled red under a dim dawn. A once sandy and pebbled strand was littered with debris—broken glass and rusted metal jutting from the sand like broken spines. Deeper, the carcasses of ships lay half sunk along shattered jetties, their masts broken and their hulls gaping. The air was heavy with a foul, chemical tang.

Wayland glanced reflexively at Murias, its shattered white towers slicked with red sunlight like a mouth full of broken, bloody teeth. Beyond, he sensed the awful, undeniable ripple of the corrupted wild magic—it sang to him, with a soundless kind of wailing. Like the aching, unknowable calls of the whales who'd swum in the seas around Emain Ablach—except *wrong*.

He tore his eyes away, looking back at the bluff where he'd camped with Idris the night before. He could not see the other man, nor the draigling he'd scolded until she'd agreed to stay with Idris, but he knew they were there.

Wayland did not want either Idris or Hog here with him. But nor did he want them too far away.

Ugly, gloomy waves slapped greasy foam on his boots as Fia's words echoed in his mind: *The nemeta are key. The groves are like homes to them.* Them—the Solasóirí. The Bright One connected to the Treasure Wayland wished to reforge. He somehow knew—whether it was his own innate connection to the seas or Fáilsceim humming faint directions in his mind—where that nemeton would be.

It would be underwater.

Gingerly, he toed off his boots, pulled his tunic over his head, and waded out into the turbid surf with Fáilsceim strapped to his back.

The cold water was a shock against his skin, but he forced himself deeper, the oily surf sucking at his waist, then his chest. The tide was turning—a subtle pull he knew had the potential to turn treacherous. The waters around Emain Ablach had been rife with riptides and whirlpools, and Wayland had spent years learning them—avoiding them or seeking them out as the mood demanded. But these seas were unfamiliar to him. With the warped wild magic extending its blight into the bay, many dangers might lurk below the rippled, dawn-lit surface.

Wayland shifted into his anam cló, reveling as his senses and perception changed from his Gentry form's. The frigid ocean was but a pleasant nothing temperature against his blubber-coated body. His sensitive whiskers vibrated, feeding him information about his surroundings: the direction of the tide, the force of the wind, the path of a three-eyed kelp bass sliding somewhere beneath his flippers. And something else—a corrosive hum climbing through the dark water and glossing unpleasantly over his flesh. It had a magnetic pull, as if the soundless, quivering tune might become audible if he drew closer. Yet beneath its staccato hid a warning—the dangerous thrill of magic Wayland had spent the bulk of his adult life estranged from.

Magic meant power. Magic meant freedom. Magic meant creation.

But magic also meant pain, swift and soul crushing. Magic meant misery. Magic meant loss.

He forced himself to stare through the slippery currents to where the ocean rotted and roiled. Whatever waited for him on the seafloor needed him. He knew that. He was the only heir alive with a natural affinity for the dúil of water. No one else was coming to right this wrong; no one else knew how or even why. Without him, this blight would continue unchecked. Another decade...another century. Another millennium.

Forever.

Wayland cursed, and kicked himself to the slick sighing surface of the bay, shifting back into his Gentry form. The cold waves lapped at him, shocking after the protection of his anam cló. He thought suddenly of the warm imprint of Idris's mouth on his and gazed once more toward the bluffs above the beach. He swore he could make out Idris's lean figure, silhouetted in black against the pink-and-gold morning.

I want to give you something of myself. Something I do not even know if I have in me to give, Wayland had said, and he had meant it. He wanted to be someone Idris deserved, someone who deserved Idris. He wanted to be the kind of man who dived bravely to the bottom of the ocean without reservation to barter with an ancient tortured god. That was who Idris wanted. Who Fia wanted. Who *everyone* wanted.

Wayland had worn many masks in his life. Most of his own making. Some created by others. All far easier to wear than his own imperfect self. He had never, *never* simply been himself. And he wasn't sure what he feared most—that his true, authentic self was just as callous as his persona...or that it simply didn't exist at all.

"This better be fucking worth it." A faint breeze smelling of carrion gathered his curse and gusted it over the swallowing sea.

He inhaled deeply, shifted back into his anam cló, then plunged beneath the water. A metallic taste filled his mouth, the brine clinging to his tongue. His nostrils instinctively closed against the rancid scents wafting with each cresting swell. His fins brushed slimy, wilted strands of seaweed. Filmy sludge stuck to his pelt. Shadows shifted below—fish with cloudy, glowing eyes, their scales dull and pitted; slow-moving turtles crusted with bloated barnacles. Only wavering shafts of sickly green light pierced the heavy, polluted depths.

He pushed deeper. That magnetic hum wavered in and out, eerily dissonant, like a lullaby sung by something that had forgotten what it was to sleep. The sound filled his chest with the uneasy echo of things lost or not yet found.

There—a flicker of movement, serpentine and disjointed in the opaque water. Scales? Tentacles. Wayland dredged the gloom for what had swum by. But not even his seal eyes could plumb these depths.

Then filaments of bioluminescence bloomed along the seafloor. A reef twisted below Wayland, its spires and arches aglow with ghastly radiance, gnarled towers of diatoms and algae twining in spirals veined with violet and blue. The light pulsed like a heartbeat, throbbing in time to that bilious, maudlin *song* that kept digging deeper into Wayland's being. Phantom fish darted between tendrils of sea flora blooming in sickly tones of pastel pink and pallid yellow. The water whorled thick and gummy, heavy with the weight of a thousand unforgiven wrongs.

At the center of the reef was the nemeton, a grove of branching corals unfurling like twisted trees. Dark crimson stalks spiraled upward, their tips crowned with jade-green clusters pulsing with more of that eerie bioluminescent glow. A deep purple mist hung between them, clinging to the puckered candle-wax trunks. Filaments of uncanny radiance laced between the gnarled branches, flickering with ghostly veins of light and casting spectral shadows across the blooms of algae trembling in the ebb tide.

"Gods alive," Wayland blurted in horror, his words gargled bubbles in the dim.

From the shadows beyond the grove, *they* emerged—silent and impossibly vast, their body an undulating mass of rotting sinew and jagged spines. Luminous, unblinking eyes the size of boulders locked onto Wayland's with predatory hunger. Thick tentacles—slick with oily slime—coiled and uncoiled through the water. The leviathan's maw opened, revealing rows of needle-sharp teeth, each as long as a man's arm, gleaming in the dark. The water rippled and distorted around it, as if even the ocean recoiled from this ancient, ravenous thing.

Hello, tánaiste. Hearing the Bright One's psychic voice was like drinking spoiled wine—a clinging, sour sensation that Wayland longed to scrape away. The leviathan roiled closer, shifting as they did—tentacles becoming limbs becoming fins; scales becoming floating dark hair becoming thick pelt. They drifted toward the center of the grove until they, too, were a seal—sloe-eyed and sleek, nearly the same size as Wayland.

The song slithered through the water, unmistakable now. *Rest now, rónán beag, where the black waters creep. The sea knows your name, and she calls you to sleep.*

All Wayland's forced bravery seeped away in an instant as nausea curdled in his gut. That was the lullaby his mother had sung him when he was in his cradle. The heartless tune his father had ground out in his graveled voice, trying to comfort a son who had lost that which was undeniably most precious to him.

"Don't," Wayland gurgled, his voice irritatingly useless beneath the sea. He reached for the warped, wild presence rifling through his thoughts with sucker-studded tentacles and spoke to it directly in his mind. *That is not yours for the taking. For the touching. Leave it be.*

But we are so hungry. The seal exploded, shadows unfurling like ink in dark water to become the vast, looming leviathan once more. *The creatures of the sea have such boring regrets. Such small sorrows. They rue only lost seashells and missed tides. Scarred fins and unheard songs. We cannot dine on such meager delicacies.*

Dine? Wayland had not known what to expect from the corrupted Bright One who had once been linked to the Treasure he hoped to reforge, but it had not been this. He was not prepared for this hollow hunger and anguished appetite, this thirst and starvation. They seemed intent on *taking* from him—seeking his shriveled places and excavating his emptinesses.

What would you rather dine on? Wayland asked, although he did not wish to hear the answer. He wished to swim away as fast as his fins would take him, until precious sunlight brightened this poisonous water. He wished to climb out on that stinking beach and put on his sturdy boots. He wished to find Idris between the lofted dunes and curl himself around his lean, beautiful body, to suck his bottom lip into his mouth and—

Stop that, he snarled.

Can you not guess? The Bright One retreated, but barely. *We wish for Folk, with all their selfish choices and tortured bargains and violent desires. They are discord and delight; thieving and hoarding; envy and obsession. But the Folk of the sea have fled for distant waters; the Folk who once lived in my city return only for rare revels that amount to nothing more than a snack. We are hungry!*

You are a blight, Wayland said, disgusted. *You are the dúil of water, the Bright One of the sea. You are meant to be serene as still waters, slow as a glacier, steady as the tides. Not this ravenous, overgrown brute.*

What is the sea if not hungry? laughed the Bright One, shudderingly. *We swallow ships and drown sailors. We erode shorelines, gnawing away at the land. We feed on the creatures swarming our depths, predator and prey in an endless, devouring cycle. We hoard lost treasures, summon lost souls. We claim sunlight and absorb storms and conceal the deepest secrets. We are infinitely wide and unknowably deep. And we. Are. HUNGRY!*

They lunged toward Wayland, their enormous tentacles coiling possessively around him. Fear froze him, even as something like kinship rose in him like a tide. *Wait.*

The Bright One paused.

I will feed you, Wayland began, bitterly. *I know hunger—and the utter pleasure of gluttony that comes after. I know vainglory and I know covetousness. I know wrath and I know sloth. I breathe envy. And lust? Oh, how I know lust—in all her alluring disguises, each one as perilous as the last.* He steadied his will, eroded as it was. *You wish for selfish choices? Tortured bargains? Violent desires? I am all those things and more. I will feed you. In exchange for magic.*

We will give you magic, promised the Bright One, enticingly. *Feed me all your sins, and you shall have magic beyond anything you could conceive of. Your famine will become feast. You shall have all that you covet. I can make all your desires come true.*

Not like that. Wayland shifted back into his Gentry form, brandishing Fáilsceim as he did. The leviathan shuddered away from the trident. Wayland's breath already burned in his lungs—he would not have long to complete this bargain. *I will feed you. But in return, you must feed me. You are a source. I am a vessel. It is as it has always been. And someday, if I can, I will set you free. I will set us both free from this terrible hunger.*

Still the leviathan recoiled, even as their tentacles wrapped around Fáilsceim. They wrung the haft brutally in Wayland's grasp—he fought to keep hold of it.

Or we could slit your soft belly, they roared. *And suck up your insides.*

With the last of his breath screaming in his lungs, Wayland kicked sideways, pivoting as he twisted the trident through the churning water. Still, the leviathan grabbed for it. The trident's tines blazed in the dark depths, cutting a long, brutal slice along the Bright One's squirming tentacle. A shudder rippled through the creature; ichor thick as blood but blue as a calm sea poured from the wound, swirling like spilled ink in the darker water. Wayland pricked his own finger on Fáilsceim, his blue-black blood mingling with the Bright One's. A brisk ripple of current caught the billow. Cast it in expanding splotches upon the trees of coral.

By fire and by sky, by fast water and by ancient tree.

No. The beast thrashed and floundered, expanding even further. Around them, the seas began to churn, cold water sucking at Wayland's legs and strangling his throat with his hair. *You do not know my name.*

I do. My father whispered it over my cradle, and my mother sang it as I slept. Wayland said this with a certainty he was not sure he believed. *I promise my willing heart to thee...O Un-Dry Cauldron.* Muir.

The Bright One suddenly deflated, more turquoise ichor spilling from their limbs as the current quickened. Wayland lost control of his straining, stretched lungs—the last of the air punched from him with painful force. He gripped Fáilsceim's shaft with all his strength, desperately trying not to give in to the instinct to—

He opened his mouth and swallowed the ocean.

Wayland had almost drowned once—when he was a boy, testing the limits of his abilities in dangerous, twisting currents. He remembered well the choking crush of seawater in his lungs. The taste of salt on his lips as blackness hammered out his eyes.

This time, there would be no furious father to haul him from the shallows. To push on his chest until he gasped and coughed and vomited black water onto the sand.

His lungs bulged, bags filled to bursting with too much seawater. He struggled as he drowned, his limbs vainly fighting the enormous strength of the ocean. The reef had disappeared; the leviathan with it. Streaks of their cerulean blood followed him, dissipating in the water with brilliant clarity. It looked like—

Fresh water.

Wayland stopped fighting the current. He reached out and cupped a single drop of blue water in his palm—a whole world full of seething ocean.

He lifted it to his mouth and drank it.

Sheer panic gave way to sure surrender. He suddenly wanted this—yearned for it with a hunger depthless as a night-black trench in the deepest corner of the ocean. In briny seawater and devouring darkness, in fickle tide and terrible maelstrom, he would be reborn. Unmade, remade. This ocean would not drown him, would not swallow him—it would simply strip away the pieces of who he had been, leaving only the core. This was a cauldron of tides: pressure, turbulence, and unrelenting currents, cleansing and remolding in its swirling depths.

He drank in the sea as if he were a man parched. It coursed through his lungs and burst in his chest and swirled along his bones. Brine pickled his veins and permeated his skin. He curled in on himself, winding tight as a nautilus.

He was the infinite depths, calm yet consuming, haunted by the vast, unknown reaches that stretched beyond his farthest tides. He was a riptide, all salt and storm, his breath swelling into cold mist. He was the tempestuous ocean itself: a boundless ancient force with no beginning and no end.

The tide began to turn. A sea change, slow but inexorable, like light blooming beneath the waves. The sea—dark as wine with salt and sorrow mingling in the depths—grew restless, twisting, swirling. Then exploded forward, a vast, ecstatic surge rolling back toward the shore. Water that had been murky and opaque was suddenly alight and alive, rippling in translucent undulations of emerald and azure. An unseen weight was lifted from the depths: schools of fish darted close to the surface, silver bodies flicking in the shallows, and the sand below shone pale and clean, each grain revealed in the crystalline scintillations. Wayland danced along the crest of the wave, his frame curved like a prow and his limbs like the foam that split before it, and he laughed as the beach rose to greet him. Laughed with joy but also amazement—for a wonder wrought and a miracle enacted.

A Treasure, reborn and reforged.

He had not been sure he could do it.

The vast wave crashed high upon the beach, slamming him onto the pebbled strand with bruising force. It retreated slowly, dragging away all the rotten seaweed and rusted detritus. Wayland fumbled for the shaft of Fáilsceim, gripping it tight even as he swiped sodden hair from his eyes and spat great gushes of brine upon the glittering sand. When he looked up, Idris was standing there, silhouetted against the bright morning, Hog perched questioningly upon his shoulder.

"Did you do it?" Idris asked, tremulously. As if the brilliant shallows teeming with flickering schools of silver fish, the golden beach, and the deep blue expanse sweeping away toward the horizon were not answer enough. As if Wayland himself, wet as a seal and naked as a baby and miraculously alive after what must have been hours underwater, was not answer enough. "Did you reforge the Un-Dry Cauldron?"

"I did." Wayland levered himself onto his knees. Distantly, he registered that his heavy arms were inked now with whorls and waves in a blue so deep it was nearly black. He stood, hefting Fáilsceim, which hummed faintly with a melody Wayland knew. From his childhood, from his dreams, from moments he had yet to encounter. Once, it would have filled him with dread. Now it only seemed to fill him with a contentment, a *satiation*, he had not experienced in a long time. Perhaps ever. A smile spread over his face, joyous and rueful. Hog fluttered over to his shoulder and nuzzled a few toothy kisses on his jaw. "Although I fear we may have to rename it."

"Oh!" Idris matched his smile. "What's the equivalent of the Un-Dry Cauldron? The Forever-Wet Trident?"

Wayland barked a laugh and surged forward to catch Idris around the waist. The other man yelped but did not push him away. One of his hands braced himself against Wayland's warm, bare chest; the other slid idly over the curve of Wayland's shoulder, tracing the recursive pattern of his new markings. Hog squeaked in annoyance, then hovered off to chase sandpipers over the damp rippled sand.

"If that is the best you can invent," Wayland said softly, "you are not allowed to say another word on the matter."

Idris smiled. "Then I shall speak no more."

His chin tilted toward Wayland's face, the fine sheet of his hair gliding off to reveal the furrows and pleats of his scar, glazed golden by the risen sun. Wayland's gaze slid over it, then skimmed over the unmarked side of his face, before coming to rest on Idris's lips, parted slightly in anticipation. He inhaled, expecting the familiar varnish of lust to paint itself flinchingly over the dark lacquer of his endless hurt and shame.

For the first time in forever, Wayland felt only ease. He knew that whatever happened—in this moment, or the next, or the one after that—he was enough. He was as constant as waves crashing upon a silent shore. He could be empty, or full, and still be complete.

He was not alone anymore.

Idris's body pressed his; his face was inches away. Wayland asked, "Do you want this?"

"Yes," Idris said, simply and without hesitation.

Wayland's hand slid up Idris's throat and fisted in the spill of his crimson hair. He closed the last few inches between them, tilting Idris's jaw to his as he captured his lower lip between his teeth, sucking it gently into his mouth. Idris gasped, and Wayland inhaled the sound as if it were oxygen, drank it as if it were fresh water, devoured it like the delicacy it was. And when he bore them both down onto the glittering, shimmering sand, he knew:

He still wanted to give Idris something of himself. Something he now knew he had to give.

So he did.

Chapter Thirty-Nine

Fia

The dungeons were dark and poorly lit, but at least they didn't smell like death.

I paced like a dog at the end of its leash, prowling along the heavy stone walls until the hem of my dress was heavy with moisture and discolored with dirt. Irian sat with his back to the opposite wall and his long legs sprawled in front of him. Moonlight spilled from a high barred window over his closed eyelids.

"How can you rest at a time like this?" I asked peevishly.

"There is not enough room for both of us to pace, mo chroí," he pointed out, without opening his eyes. "We should be constantly crashing into each other, which would ruin the effect."

I huffed a laugh and conceded the point. "At least tell me you're dreaming of a compelling escape plan."

"Escape?" Irian cracked one brilliant eye to look at me. "If that is the plan, why did you not tell me? You are aware I possess a sword that cuts through anything."

I turned a skeptical eye to the thick bars and even thicker walls. "Metal? Stone?"

"Must I define *anything* for you?" A note of humor touched Irian's tone. "The bars would be quick work. The walls might take longer. But unless you are deeply committed to your new pastime of pacing like an affronted wildcat, then we do not have much else to occupy us."

"Surely Eala knows we'll try to escape," I said, half to myself. "What if it's a trap?"

"It almost certainly is." His eyelashes slanted, long and black, along his cut-glass cheekbones. "I suppose we shall have to fight our way out."

A brisk but quiet knock on the dungeon door silenced my response. Irian was on his feet in an instant, the Sky-Sword a gash of night in his hands. I waved him back as I stepped up to the bars and the shadow-masked figure beyond. Fear breathed a chill along my spine as I peered out, expecting grinning teeth and a hollowed-out face. Instead, I saw tangled dark hair spilling over sallow brown skin, wretched amber eyes.

"Chandi?" Her name punched out of me, tight with lingering betrayal. "What in Donn's black hell are you doing here?"

She wrapped her long fingers around the bars and pressed her face close. The moonlight fractured her expression and turned the tears welling in her eyes to cold silver.

Alarm mixed with my resentment. "What's wrong? Are you hurt? Are you—"

Chandi cried harder, her spine bowing as a gasping sob racked her. "Oh, Fia. You don't know how horrible it's been." I could hardly understand her words, garbled as they were by tears. "I thought we would die that night—that silver metal was every-where! But Eala—she—the barge she made saved us, but it was so awful—so unbelievably awful—"

"*Chandi.*" Impulses warred inside me, those of hurt and care. Chandi's betrayal had deeply wounded me—I'd thought we were friends, allies. I'd thought I had earned her loyalty. But to see her like this also hurt me. Despite all she'd done, I still cared about her. "Chandi, slow down. Take a deep breath."

Chandi obeyed, inhaling shakily. Her words, when they finally came, were cramped and crowded, worn thin by sustained horror.

"We escaped that night on a barge of the living dead. Eala wove them together like reeds—legs and arms twisted in an impenetrable mass. We almost didn't make it—the city nearly sucked us down with it. But we did—me, Eala, and Rogan. We struggled toward land—the legs of the dead churning beneath us like paddles, the wind howling over their open mouths like pipes." Chandi bowed her head, as if the memory of that night was too heavy a burden to bear. "There were wild horses upon the cliffs, but Eala was never a great rider, so Rogan, he—"

Again, she broke off, pressing a trembling hand to her mouth. "They were easier to control once she resurrected them, Eala said. She said she could feel you—both of you. But you had a head start. For weeks we rode after you, but when we reached the mountains, the magic there shielded you, hid you. Protected you."

I shared a loaded glance with Irian. He had told me how they'd battled the dead at Mag Tuired—but he had not known how close Eala had come in her pursuit of me. I reminded myself to thank Laoise again for the protection of her sanctuary—and to apologize again for destroying it.

"We returned to the lands of the bardaí, seeking the aid and support of those who had become loyal to Eala beneath the Ember Moon. But they recoiled from what the princess had become—yes, even those who had meddled with warped wild magic were disgusted by her. They shunned her in much the same way as you shunned her tonight, shaming and berating her for her misuse of power. And she—Rogan—" Again, Chandi choked, as if the words she wished to speak were barbed and bloodied. "Laoise and Sinéad saw the swath of destruction she left in her wake. But once we passed through the Gate...the destruction only intensified."

She leaned her head on the cool, damp stone, anguish plain on her features. She had calmed, but her demeanor now was one of utter despair. "And now you are here. You, who she has sought bitterly. You, who she desires almost above all else. Fia, you should not have come."

That ship had sailed. "Tell me. How did M—how did the high queen, Eithne Uí Mainnín, come to bend the knee to her wayward daughter?"

"Perhaps I can shed light on that." Cathair stepped from the shadows and joined Chandi at the bars to our cell. My old teacher looked mostly the same, save for his hair, which had gone fully gray, and the weight of exhaustion that clung to him like a dead hand. I still had not forgiven the man who'd raised me for all his torment and humiliation. Yet I was inexplicably glad to see him.

"The guard detail on this dungeon leaves something to be desired."

"I think you'll find it is exactly what I desire," said Cathair. "The dead make for terrible guards. They barely seem to notice birds; much less are they able to identify starlings. And there are many in this keep who are still loyal to your mother."

I fought the urge to snap, *She's not my mother.* Instead, I focused on what Cathair was hinting at. He had been Eithne's spymaster for as long as I'd been at Rath na Mara—his network of informants more extensive than I was ever allowed to know. His witch-birds—speckle-winged starlings—carried information through Fódla and beyond.

"Then Eithne's abdication was an act to save her own hide," I guessed. "And you and the queen have been plotting against Eala from the shadows."

"My clever little witch." Cathair's words prompted a menacing noise of displeasure from Irian's throat. The older man looked up at his superior height, apparently unfazed by the glowering Gentry warrior. "And her Gentry consort." He clucked his tongue on his teeth. "I suppose war makes strange bedfellows of us all."

"Well, go on, then," I demanded. "What is your plan?"

"I forgot what an impatient little thing you are." This earned another growl from Irian. Cathair fished in his pocket until he retrieved a rough-hewn key. "I must speak with you in my workshop. Alone."

"If you think—" Irian began, chillingly.

"It's all right. He won't harm me," I said. "Though I don't know how you plan to keep the guards, however negligent, from noticing I am gone."

"Chandi will act as decoy," Cathair said. "We will return long before dawn."

I hesitated, glancing between Irian and Chandi.

"He won't harm me," Chandi said, echoing my words with a ghost of a smile. "Will you?"

Irian returned to his vigil in the corner. "You know I will not."

I had not forgotten the druid's sprawling, low-ceilinged chambers, where I'd wasted so many sunlit days of my youth. I wrinkled my nose against the stench of black walnut tincture and cheap mead and starling droppings. Manuscripts and grisly souvenirs stolen from Tír na nÓg during the Gate War stared at me from the cluttered shelves, unpleasantly familiar now: broken ollphéist fangs, a draig's red-gold scute, a shard said to be chipped from a fallen star. My gaze lingered on this last object, a small hunk of shiny jet-black stone striated with pale veins.

"Did this truly fall from the stars?" I heard myself ask.

Cathair glanced over from lighting tapers upon a workbench. "So they say."

I dragged my eyes from it. "Dawn cannot be far off. Speak."

"All the under-kings of Fódla, like Eithne, have bent the knee to Eala to spare their lands and their peoples," Cathair told me. "All of them, also like Eithne, are loath to witness their already ravaged kingdoms fall prey to the death and destruction Eala carries in her wake. Her ascension to the high throne of Fódla has created an unprecedented alliance between the ever-warring provinces."

"They have all agreed to stand against Eala?"

"To a man."

My eyes returned to the starstone as I considered his words. I dared to touch it, gently pressing my thumb into a rough divot. Immediately, all the radiance from my finger was yanked into the shard with a sucking sensation. I jerked my hand away; the rock glowed briefly before winking out. I stared, even as an idea coiled inside me.

"May I have this?"

Cathair shrugged. "I have never found a use for it, little witch."

I wrapped the shard in a piece of rough sacking and shoved it into my bodice.

"But how can they hope to defeat her army?" I returned my focus to the matter at hand. "I saw them, encamped outside the fort. There are thousands—perhaps more. Not to mention Eala will likely resurrect for herself any who die on *either* side."

"We have developed a weapon." Cathair set a vial upon the workbench, no bigger than a flask of whiskey. Inside, a spark—green as bottle glass—jumped and danced, throwing strange shadows on the walls. "Tine Síoraí, we call it. *Eternal Fire*. It burns far hotter than normal flame and needs no fuel or air to sustain it. Best of all, it devours where it lands—an unquenchable blaze that incinerates skin and bone. Not even the dead can withstand this."

"If it works against the dead, it will work against the living." I stared at the dancing light. "Many will die."

"Wars are not won without sacrifice, Fia." To his credit, Cathair was not jubilant about the prospect. "Many more will die if Eala is allowed free reign in this realm. Or the other."

"When do the kings attack?"

"Not until Bealtaine. The Eternal Fire takes time to formulate, and care in transportation."

Rage and regret tangled inside me as I thought of Irian. Rogan. Wayland, Sinéad, Laoise. All the people I loved, drawn into this terrible conflict. I did not want to put anyone else at risk. But Eala was too strong a threat to risk sitting on our hands. "Could the human kings march upon a different location?"

"Certainly," Cathair said, gamely. "Where? And why?"

"I do not believe the human kings, even with their immortal flame, will be able to defeat Eala. Not without the help of the Folk realms." I clenched my glowing fist. "Irian and I will escape to the Willow Gate—Eala will surely follow. There we will keep her occupied—harried but hopeful that she will eventually get what she wants from me. The Bealtaine moon is less than a month away."

Cathair caught my drift. "The Folk will need the strength of a full moon if they are to fight in the human realms. But can you keep Eala busy for over three weeks without giving too much ground?"

"We will have to. Then we will pin Eala between the forces of Fódla and the forces of Tír na nÓg."

Cathair smiled. "And the princess will die with all her dread horde."

"Die?" All my hope turned to char upon my tongue. But of course—not even Cathair knew the true nature of the Treasures. "No—she cannot be killed by mortal means."

His eyebrows jumped toward his graying hairline. "I beg your pardon?"

"If Eala is slaughtered, the magic of her Treasure will be corrupted," I explained. "Warped wild magic will billow over these lands, as destructive as Eala and far more long-lasting. And this time, there will be no heirs left to reforge it."

Cathair cursed inventively. Clearly he understood the problem, even if he did not understand all the terms. "What do you propose?"

"Leave that to me." I laced my fingers together and hoped I knew what I was doing. "Just tell the under-kings—Eala is mine to destroy." I paused. "But all this you could have shared with Irian and Chandi. Why did you wish to speak to me alone?"

"*I* wished to speak to you alone, a stór."

I whirled as the dethroned high queen of Fódla emerged from

the shadows. With her graying hair unbound like a virgin's, her slender throat bare of the marks of royalty, and the weight of many sleepless nights borne in haggard creases upon her face, the woman I had once called Mother looked somehow both very young and incredibly old. The familiar use of her pet name for me startled me, sending twin threads of searing starlight and thorning vines to stitch the inside of my skin.

"You," I said coldly. "Have we not said all that needs to be said?"

"Alas, no," said Eithne Uí Mainnín. "My daughter keeps me alive not from affection but political expediency. When she discovers I have been plotting against her, I have little doubt she will execute me in a show of strength. We must discuss what happens when I am dead."

I set my jaw. I had little affection to spare for the queen. But despite all she had done to me, I did not wish her dead. For all that she had been a bad mother, she had been a strong queen. Fódla already suffered—I feared it would suffer more if she was not there to put it back together after Eala's disastrous reign. "Your fate doesn't concern me."

"It should." The queen drew a heavily illuminated scroll from her sleeves. "The Ó Mainníns are still the rightful ruling dynasty of Fódla. Once I am dead and your sister is defeated, you are next in line for the throne. This document legitimizes you as Rían's daughter and recognizes you as the next high queen of Fódla. I intend to send copies to my under-kings as soon as you sign it."

The words struck me like poison barbs, and I fought the urge to keel over from all the venomous words suddenly boiling inside me. Yet all I could manage was "You knew, didn't you?" I remembered Rían's words in the Deep-Dream. *Then you have truly been a pawn of destiny...and I am sorry for it.* "How long?"

"Almost from the beginning," Eithne said dispassionately. "Though you must have inherited your mother's coloring, both you and Eala strongly resemble *him*. I also recognized his lamentable softness in you."

"Is that why you tormented me so?" I asked bitterly. "To visit the sins of the father upon his bastard daughter?"

"I made you strong, a stór." Eithne's words were the same as the last time I'd seen her; again they conjured memories of rats in buckets and budding flowers tossed on the fire and painful bracelets of nettles and brambles. "Strong enough to realize the fate of Fódla is more important than any enmity we bear toward each other. Strong enough to rule a kingdom brought to its knees by plague and famine and grievous war. Strong enough to be a queen."

This was absurd. "I do not wish to be queen."

"Nor should you." Eithne's eyes glittered like diamonds in the sallow glow of Cathair's chambers. "You will inherit death and ruin. Even with this document, you will face the ridicule and censure of jealous under-kings. Nothing will be easy. Yet it must be you."

"Why?" I spluttered. "Not only am I Rían's illegitimate child, but I am also half-Folk. You ought to hate me—to hate everything I stand for."

"I have come to learn hate is rarely a productive emotion." Eithne's hands were restless on the scroll, rolling it tighter before smoothing it out. "I know you think me cold and manipulative and callous. I may not have been the best mother. I may not have even been the best queen. But I love my country. I want the best for my people. Cathair and I spent years educating you and honing your skills. This is the return on our investment—a queen we can count on to have Fódla's best interests at heart."

"I am a half-Folk bastard," I reiterated, albeit faintly. I felt exposed—as if the wounds she'd dealt me for years had reopened and begun to bleed. "They will never accept me as an Ó Mainnín heir—under-kings, nobility, peasantry. None of them."

"Please." Eithne sneered. "Put grain in their stores and cattle in their fields and gold in the treasury, and they will all forget in a year. The Ó Mainnín line is riddled with inconsistencies, going back to Amergin himself. His eldest son, Prince Marban, abdicated his throne and ran away to a fort in the middle of nowhere, leaving his bastard half brother to rule. Yet Guaire is remembered as a great king and the forefather of Fódla itself."

"*Marban?*" I jolted, nearly stumbling backward into one of Cathair's workbenches. "What fort?"

"Dún Darragh, of course." Mother brandished the scroll. "If we are agreed, then you will sign."

I bolstered myself with a hand on the table. "I will not."

"It matters little if you do," Cathair said softly. He had not spoken since the queen appeared; I had nearly forgotten he was there. "The document will be distributed regardless. But think of your mother's peace of mind."

"She's not my mother." My words lacked their intended venom.

Eithne pushed the document into my palms, then gathered her shawl around herself. She turned toward the door, pausing on the threshold.

"The choice is, and will always be, yours. But when Fódla falls to her knees after my death, *that* devastation will be upon your head." Her pale blue eyes glittered like diamonds. "Swear me this, at least: When you destroy your sister...make sure she is well and truly dead."

That, I could promise. "I will."

Eithne disappeared without another word, leaving me alone with Cathair and a scroll I could barely stand to look at.

"Come," he said, at last. "Dawn is nigh. Your companions await you."

I followed him numbly back toward the dungeons before stopping him in the darkness of the corridor. "Wait."

He turned, his silvering hair glinting in the dim. "Little witch?"

"You, of all people, would not lie to me about this." My voice was strangely guttural in the near black. "Do you really wish me to be queen?"

For a long moment, he was silent. "The problem with monarchs is they are all born to rule. You were not. You know the weight of hunger, the sting of injustice, and the value of mercy—lessons learned not in gilded halls of power, but upon the jagged teeth of a careless world. I believe that because you have lived as common people do, that you will not rule above them...but for them. I believe in you."

I did not know how to respond to that. Cathair tilted his head.

"I could ask my Book for a prophecy," he offered. "Perhaps it will illuminate your destiny."

"No thank you." I shuddered at the thought of Cathair's fell Book of Whispers. "I have had enough of destiny for now." I handed the scroll back to him—unsigned. "Do what you must. But I do not think I can fix what Eithne and Eala have broken."

The dungeon was as we'd left it—Irian seated with his blade across his knees; Chandi hunched in the corner with my cloak masking her face. They both rose at the sound of our footsteps, drawing near the bars as Cathair unlocked them.

"We make for Tír na nÓg," I told Irian. "I will explain as we go. But first...do you mind doing something about this dress?"

Irian knelt before me, using the Sky-Sword to hastily shred the suffocating layers of gown and the petticoat beneath, until the skirt fluttered freely above my knees.

Chandi wrapped her arms around her torso as if holding herself together. "I can show you to the stable block where Finan is kept."

"I know where the stables are," I said, a little tartly.

She hung her head. "Of course you do."

I wasn't sure Chandi deserved my forgiveness—her betrayal had been a heartbreaking shock, and I didn't know if I could ever trust her again. But I did know she didn't deserve to be abandoned here, in the midst of all this death and violence, to suffer at Eala's hands.

I had not been able to save Rogan from my sister's clutches. And I did not have to be a queen to understand the value of mercy.

"But you can show me anyway," I told her. "After all, you're coming with us."

Her head snapped up. "I am?"

"You can ride Finan."

Another round of tears threatened to fall from her amber eyes. "But…why?"

"Twice now, I have left you behind in the heat of conflict," I told her. "I will not do it a third time. But you will have to ride hard, and if it comes to blows, I am not sure we will be able to protect you."

"I understand." She nodded gravely. "Thank you, Fia."

"Don't thank me yet." I gestured curtly. "Shall we?"

As we climbed the steps through pools of torchlight, I felt Irian watching me. I turned to him, lifting an eyebrow. But my husband was not frowning in disagreement. His expression verged on adoration—the flames catching in his silver eyes and transfiguring them to gold.

"The woman you are, mo chroí." His smile, sweet and sharp, cut me to my core. "I never weary of following you to the most unexpected places."

False dawn grayed the horizon. Cathair pressed the vial of Eternal Fire into my palm before he parted ways with us, reiterating its uses.

"We do not need it," Irian said. "We have draigs."

"How thrilling for you." Cathair raised his eyebrows. "Take it anyway. Perhaps the Folk may be able to replicate the formula for the battle to come."

Irian grunted, but I tucked it into the lining of my bodice nevertheless, next to the wrapped starstone.

Few guards stood watch in the cold, silent hours before dawn; fewer still were alive. I fought sorrow for the ones who were, as the Sky-Sword silently and brutally cleared our way toward Finan.

Any violence tonight was only the beginning.

We saddled the drowsy stallion. He moved too slowly. I cringed at the ringing clop of his hooves on the cobblestones, but there was nothing to do about that but pray. I jimmied the infamously fickle lock on the postern gate—I'd snuck out of Rath na Mara a hundred times this way. The gate opened onto the steep rise to the west of the keep—our strange trio picked down the rocky slope as swiftly as we could manage without falling, leading Finan by his reins. Pink and gold dusted the horizon like flower pollen.

Too slow. The morning watch would soon change.

We were nearly to the shadow of the forest at the bottom of the hill when a lone figure burst from the palisade.

Irian and I—both keeping a steady watch behind us as we made for the woods—tensed. Irian had not sheathed the Sky-Sword—he lifted it now, ribboned with gore. But as I squinted into the morning, I saw it was Cathair again, betrayed by his graying hair and the glinting charms braided into it.

Then I saw what he was running from. Movement along the ramparts—a terrible lurching wave as undead soldiers pushed over the top of the wall. Movement near the postern gate—more revenants streaming through the narrow opening like ants. Movement at the main gates, the thunking of the bar lifting and the grinding of the doors opening and the hurried, ungainly tramping of a hundred boots on packed earth—

"Get her up!" I cried to Irian, panic making my voice shrill. He hoisted Chandi onto Finan's saddle. The stallion stamped and sallied as the tall maiden gathered his reins, her fear seeping into the beast. "Go." Then louder. "Go!"

"Colleen," Irian growled.

"I must try to help him," I bit out. Cathair was already faltering, his mad dash taking its toll on his middle-aged body. He was not a fit man—his talents lay in spheres other than the training yard. His earlier words to me rang in my ears: *I believe in you.* "I will catch up. Please!"

Chandi did not protest. She nudged Finan into an eager canter, weaving along the edge of the trees as she sped southeast.

Irian did not budge. "There is no time, mo chroí." The dead

soldiers spilled over the top of the walls, slamming onto the hard ground before tottering back to their feet. They stomped through the gates with newborn sunlight glinting off their bloodstained armor. "I am sorry, but he is a dead man. We must run, lest we share the same fate."

I hesitated one last second, then sprinted back toward Rath na Mara, ignoring Irian's roar of frustration as I flung myself toward my old teacher, meeting him halfway across the plain.

"What happened?" I urged, fear and exertion making my voice raw.

"I was discovered," he wheezed, his face red and his eyes bulging. "With the scroll. But that isn't all. The Book of Whispers spoke to me." A page fluttered in his grip—parchment translucent as human skin stretched too tight, inked with words and images and trailing threads that looked like hair. "I know you asked me not to. But it whispered to me of how the story ends."

"Ends?" The dead fénnidi were drawing closer now—I glimpsed stumps of broken teeth and the rolling of glutinous eyes. "How *what* story ends, Cathair?"

"A feather so black will rise from pain," he intoned, shoving the brittle parchment into my hands, even as fear widened his eyes and his limbs began to shudder. "A crown so silver will rise to reign."

I fell back in retreat, heedlessly shoving the paper into my bodice as my own fear warred with my need to know the next lines.

"A heart so green must bleed once more, for light and dark to one restore." Cathair suddenly straightened, shedding his exhaustion and cowardice like a cheaply made jacket. "The last love lost, the price now paid—through sacrifice, the balance laid."

He stared at me, hazel eyes glinting. I did not know what he saw when he looked at me, but for the briefest moment, I saw *him*. Not the middle-aged druid, the queen's whore, the cunning spymaster. But a younger, more hopeful man. A man who believed in magic in a realm that had shunned it. A man who had loved a young, ambitious queen married to a distant king. A man who had been forced to foster all the worst qualities in a little changeling girl who knew nothing but fairy dust and a deep longing for love.

And as the horde of the dead surged around him, he blended in my mind with Rían. Rían, dragged back through a field of wildflowers toward the cottage where his memory lived. Rían, with his pale hair billowing around him as he was torn from me for the final time.

I had had two fathers. Rían, my blood father, who had never even known I existed, who had loved me only in theory. And Cathair, my foster father, who had known all my terrible weaknesses and exploited them, who had hated that he was not allowed to love me.

One perfect—either perfectly bad or perfectly good, for he did not truly exist. The other utterly imperfect—for all his big mistakes and his huge failings and his infinite cruelties.

Cathair smiled in the moment before a soldier's blade pierced his chest from behind. And as blood bubbled from his lips, he said, "Run, little witch. *Run.*"

I must have screamed—a blade of fury and anguish pierced my own choking throat. Irian was pulling me by the waist, dragging me away and pushing me south. But I could not tear my eyes away—could not help but watch as the horde swallowed Cathair's broken form beneath their ravening strides. They did not stop, did not even slow, flattening him into the trampled grass.

I began to run. Haltingly, crushingly. I thought I must be weeping, for my eyes were hot and my cheeks cold.

"Run," Irian echoed, his light touch on the small of my back the only thing anchoring me to the world. I gazed at him, and his eyes were blue as the morning and gold as the sun. "Dig deep, mo chroí. For you will not be able to outrun them like this."

I did not understand what he meant. I pushed myself harder, my legs pumping beneath me with all the strength I had in my muscles. It was not enough—I had barely eaten. I had not slept. I called on the power of my Treasure, infusing the Heart of the

Forest—weaker, here, in the human realms—into my flagging limbs. It was not enough. I called on the starlight Ínne had fed me in my childhood and Talah had fused to my bones, and I felt myself begin to glow, radiance pearling off me into the dawn.

It was not enough. The relentless thud of boots was like the pounding of a terrible heart. Weapons flashed in my periphery. Armor clanged like a death knell.

Run, little witch. Run.

I thought of my fathers: one too weak to love me...the other too dead.

I would have liked to have loved you, little deer.

The horde's hot, rotten breath gusted upon my neck. Their skeletal fingers scrabbled for my arms. Even if my starshine destroyed a few of them, there were so many. They would drag me back to her—back to my mad sister. And she would not give me another chance to escape.

I closed my eyes and thought not of my dead fathers, but of my absent mother.

Deirdre, the doe. Deirdre, the heir of the Sept of Antlers. Deirdre, my mother.

Where are you? I screamed into the cacophony of panicked voices crowding my head. *Mother, please! Help me!*

The change began with a pull beneath my skin—an unraveling of sinew and a reshaping of bone. It hurt—an ache both ancient and novel. My muscles rippled along legs that felt suddenly too long, too slender. My fingers fused and stretched, tapering as I fell toward the ground. But I did not trip, did not fall. I caught myself and kept running, my gait now impossibly light and astonishingly fast. My pulse quickened, pounding in time to the wild rhythm of magic coursing my veins. The world shifted, my senses sharpening to the unseen world of shadow and light, predator and prey. I was newly made—a transformation both as natural as breathing and as profoundly alien as shapeshifting.

Beside me, feathers rippled along Irian's tall form, lifting him away toward the heavens. I felt as if I could leap high enough to follow him, so I did, bounding lithely and quietly through the swallowing forest. My tail flicked, and I left the shambling horde to slog ungainly through the undergrowth.

And as the forest swallowed me, I knew—I had at last found my anam cló.

Little deer.

Chapter Forty

Fia

We ran.

With Chandi on Finan and Irian as a swan and me, unexpectedly, as a doe, we were faster than the undead horde pursuing us from Rath na Mara. But barely. Chandi was not much of a horsewoman—she hung on to Finan's reins and bounced in his saddle. We cleared the woods and rejoined the high road, then had to rest, letting the stallion slurp from a nearby brook. Only moments later we heard them—the unsteady tromp of thousands of feet crashing through undergrowth and rushing along the road.

We kept going.

As morning bore into afternoon, time lost all meaning. My doe's senses were strange, fleeting—depthless calm giving way to wild alarm. I was agile as a dancer and fleet as a fox, yet there was a fragility to my body I was not prepared for. As Fia, I knew how to fight, how to defend myself. As a doe, all I knew how to do was run. I was defenseless—vulnerable, in a way that made me uneasy.

As we paused beside another rambling brook, I became

transfixed by the sight of an oak leaf swirling gently downstream, gilded gold by the lowering rays of afternoon. The water was like glass. The grass so green it didn't seem real. And when I gazed into the copse of trees, I saw antlers lofting toward a dimming sky. I knew I had to follow them. I splashed through the stream, eagerness flicking my tail as I leapt—

Strong arms caught me. Fear pummeled me, and I fought instinctively, struggling against the broad strength pinning me in place.

"Come back, mo chroí." The deep voice was familiar yet unrelentingly strange. I stilled. "Fia. Do not get lost."

Fia. The name unfurled in me like a forgotten memory, and I clung to it as it brought me back to myself. My normal form embraced me. Relief unspooled like honeysuckle along my veins, tinged with the bitter tang of lingering fear.

Irian instantly released me, and I rose from where I crouched on all fours.

"What happened?" I asked, my voice rusty in my throat. "I felt—"

"The soul form has its own senses—its own will," Irian explained gently. "You must remember who you are or it can overtake you. You can become lost to your anam cló, especially if it is a predator. But prey animals pose their own challenges."

I shivered and glanced at Chandi and Finan. The girl was slumped over in a pose of utter exhaustion; sweat darkened the stallion's hide.

"We lead them by half a league." Irian intuited my question. "We have earned a little respite."

I squinted at the sky. It wasn't enough. We might reach Dún Darragh by sundown. But with an indefatigable army on our heels, we could not stop until we cleared the Gate into Tír na nÓg. We had far to go.

"We may rest a few more minutes," I allowed. "Here—a mulberry bush. Chandi ought to eat."

I picked the maiden handfuls of the slightly unripe fruits, which I ripened with my Greenmark. She gratefully devoured them. Then, though it pained me, I commanded, "Mount up. We have to keep moving."

No one complained. We all knew it was a matter of life or death.

We ran.

The sun slanted low, and a chilly breeze winnowed the spring grass. Finan's fine canter became little more than a plod; Chandi practically lay upon his withers with the reins hanging.

We were no longer moving faster than the horde. My doe's prey senses recognized the rumble of boots on packed earth, the hissing of weapons dragged through long grasses.

When Dún Darragh's stark outline brittled the fading sky, Chandi simply slid from Finan's saddle to thump ungainly in the dirt. The stallion stood there, spittle dribbling from his lips as he hung his head. I knew we had not yet reached salvation.

The doe furled away as I raced on two legs to Chandi. She was breathing and at least semiconscious—she moaned as Irian eased her onto her back in the dirt.

"She's exhausted," Irian said. "She will not make it to the Gate. Perhaps we can barricade ourselves in Dún Darragh until she recovers."

"They will surround us by nightfall." Dún Darragh. In all the death and despair of the last few hours, I'd nearly forgotten the queen's offhand words to me in Cathair's workshop about Marban. "You take her to the Gate—carry her if you must. I must go inside the fort. I must speak to Corra."

Irian's gaze was like iron. "If you stay, I stay with you."

"Then Chandi will die." I softened my tone, fought the urge to lay a palm on his arm. "I will get what I need, then I will run to the Gate in my anam cló. I promise I will come to no harm."

"That is not a promise you can keep." Anticipated pain warped his face, stark in the slanting shards of fading sunlight. "Do not make me agree to this. I swore I would never let you go."

"You are not letting me go, Irian. You are trusting me. Please."

On the ground, Chandi moaned again. Sweat beaded on her forehead—she was feverish. Terrible indecision gripped Irian. At last he knelt, scooped the suffering human maiden into his arms, and fixed me with eyes going silver as the horizon.

"Live, Fia. Live."

He slid away through the dusk, dark as a specter and sharp as a blade. I followed him with my eyes until the trees beyond the fort swallowed them.

I reached for Finan's dragging reins and briskly untacked him, tossing his fine saddle and bridle into the tall grass edging the path. The horse bobbed his head and flicked his tail, as if in thanks. I slapped his rump, not ungently.

"Go on, old boy. This is no place for you now." He shook out his mane, then ambled away into the falling dark.

The distant, grotesque sounds of a thousand feet marching upon the country road shoved me toward the forbidding stones of Dún Darragh. I raced across the courtyard, my changeling feet heavy on the cobbles after my anam cló's light, slender hooves. The heavy carven doors fell open before me. I let a little of my starshine slip as I dashed through the great hall, illuminating the four arching pillars, the curving staircase, the carvings etched in stone.

"Corra!" I shouted, as I took the steps to the second level two at a time. "I know you're here!"

There was a time when I knew these hallways better than the lines on my palm. Now I struggled to recall the exact route to the hidden archive I'd found over a year ago. There—past the annex with the windows shaped like eyes, through the hall draped in dusty tapestries, behind the crumbling mantelpiece carved with rosettes. I didn't bother with candles or torches as I slammed up the tight staircase—my starshine cast enough light to see by.

Beyond, the library was as I'd left it: a narrow worktable stacked with handwritten journals; statues veiled with dust; shelves choked with volumes. I labored beneath the weight of countless hours deciphering ancient murky texts as I grabbed a tome at random and began riffling through it.

"Corra!" I shouted again. "I need you!"

"Need or *want*? Do be clear," sing-songed a voice from one of the veiled statues. "Either way, we're already here."

"Thank the gods," I breathed, slamming another stack of journals on the table and hurriedly paging through them. "It's your help I need. I know better than to expect straight answers from you...but can you tell me whether the man who wrote these was truly named Marban?"

"Marban, you ask?" A few knots in the table shaped faintly like a mouth and two eyes winked to life, making me jump. "Well, that depends. On where we should begin...and how the story ends."

How the story ends. Morrigan, in the day's mad dash I had nearly forgotten about the paper Cathair had shoved at me in his final moments. Perhaps part of me had *wanted* to forget. But now it niggled at me, like a rotten tooth in a painful gum. I fished the crumpled parchment from my bodice, recoiling instinctively from the feeling of it—like papery skin strung with human hair. I smoothed it onto the table before me, pinning its edges with my hands.

The page depicted a white swan sailing upon an expanse of black water beneath an even blacker sky, ringed with a thousand branching trees. Stars fell from the sky, pricking out the swan's black shadow on the mirror of the lough. Heavily illuminated words caressed the edges of the page. I skimmed them, unable at first to decipher their meaning. Then Corra began to sing, and I knew their meaning.

A feather so black will rise from pain,
A crown so silver will rise to reign.
A heart so green must bleed once more,
For light and dark to one restore.
The last love lost, the price now paid—

Through sacrifice, the balance laid.
So white and black, the swans must die,
For stars to weave their fate on high.

I read through it once. Then again, even as panic choked me with brambles and the thorns in my chest grew into a thicket that scratched at my ribs with foreboding.

"No." I fought the urge to crumple the paper and shove it back into my bodice. As if that might reverse the death sentence it preordained. A hot tear slid down my nose and splashed onto the page, cutting ripples into the midnight lake. "No. This cannot be true."

"Some tales ring true, and some deceive." I swore I detected a note of regret in Corra's voice. "But all endings are real, chiar-dhubh. Both to those who must die...and those who must grieve."

"No!" I scrubbed at my burning eyes with my filthy black sleeves. Had I not already sacrificed myself? Once, to the Heart of the Forest. Twice, to Talah. Why must the gods-damned patterns demand my death yet again? "I'll find another way. I will not let this happen."

"The path is laid, the stars decree...And still we walk, both bound and free."

"Are you telling me there is no way to escape this fate?" Now I did crumple the parchment, folding it unevenly and shoving it back in my bodice to rest uneasy between the small vial of Eternal Fire and Cathair's starstone. "Am I truly bound to a destiny I never asked for?"

"The stars may weave, the gods may smite," Corra sang, dancing on half-seen carvings somewhere near the ceiling. "But cunning hands may twist the light. Through deepest dreaming, Marban broke free. But were his bonds gone...or just harder to see?"

"Marban. Yes—Marban." I scraped away the last of my traitor tears and returned to my purpose for coming here. According to Wayland, Marban was a master of bindings—and unbindings.

Perhaps he could tell me how to break free from this awful fate. "Please—I think he's important. Tell me how to find him."

Across the archive, a journal sidled off its ledge and flopped open on the floor. I flung myself toward it, my knees scuffing painfully over the rough flagstones. The open page was curlicued with my ancient warrior's familiar looping script; it took all my concentration to read it.

Marban . . . and Fionnuala. Two hearts entwined in a place where not even time can follow. Long after we are dust, they will speak of our love, weaving our story into the breath of both worlds.

My fingertips skimmed the words, the ink brown as dried blood beneath my touch.

"A story," I breathed. "Corra, is that what you're trying to tell me?"

Silence greeted my words.

"Corra!" I pleaded. "Is there a story about Marban and the woman he bent worlds to follow?"

But Corra had apparently divulged as much as they could. Or would. I cursed, gathering up the journal before flinging it down in frustration. I nearly fell down the curving stairs in my haste to quit the archives; I ran through Dún Darragh at a dead sprint, praying I'd left myself enough time to catch up with Irian and Chandi at the Willow Gate. The huge carved doors of the fort yawned open, spilling me into the leaden hush of fallen night.

Revenants oozed like specters through the dank fog creeping off the lough. They climbed the rise toward Dún Darragh in their hundreds, not bothering to keep to the lane but marching over the fields and scrabbling over the hedges and slurping through the reeds. Fast—too fast. They were falling apart—the long day's forced march over rough terrain taking its toll on their already damaged bodies. Eyes hung from sockets; limbs sagged as spines dislocated.

Fear rose in me, hot and lurid. I glanced at the sky and tried to gauge how much time had passed since Irian disappeared into the forest with Chandi. But there was no moon in the sky tonight. A few stars stared at me, but their light seemed distant and very, very cold. I slanted my eyes toward the edge of the keep. But my escape route—the narrow path to my grotto and the forest beyond—was blocked by revenants stacked six rows deep.

Live, Fia. Live.

I feared that was no longer a promise I was likely to be able to keep.

Either now. Or later.

I was moments away from shifting into my anam cló and throwing fate to the wind when I saw *her*. Eala rode primly upon a fine gray palfrey bedecked in silken regalia and embroidered raiment. She herself was clad in a silver breastplate over white trousers and pale suede boots. I almost scoffed. My sister was no warrior— the only time I had seen her wield a blade had been to carve out her maidens' hearts. But this was no joke. Behind her, riding two abreast along the narrow lane climbing toward Dún Darragh, a living cavalry marched between the flanked rows of the seething dead half visible in the ghostly mist seeping from the lough. Beside her rode Rogan, armed and armored, and her mother, albeit hidden beneath a deep hood.

"Your pageantry is fooling no one, Sister." I laced my tone with poison before I drove the blade of my words home. "No matter how you dress the part, everyone knows you are no more a general than you are a queen."

Eala's luminous eyes flickered, but unlike last night, she kept a tight leash on her composure. "A position I am to understand you covet."

"You've blundered the role so badly, even a fool off the street could do better," I snarled, even as I glanced at Eithne's hooded countenance. In his last moments, Cathair had told me Eala had caught him with the high queen's scroll. Had she also intercepted his missives to the under-kings regarding our offensive? Did she know about the Eternal Fire? Did she know I planned to rally the Folk against her?

"Are you that fool, Sister?" Eala asked mildly. One of her suede-gloved hands made a vague circle in the air. "Where is your rabid hound, ready to snap off any hand that dares touch you? I confess myself shocked—I expected him to be at your side, slavering for violence."

"You ought to work on your metaphors, *Sister.*" I matched my easy tone to hers. "If I am not mistaken, you have compared Irian, Rogan, *and* myself to rabid hounds at one point or another. We cannot all be dogs."

"No," she agreed. "Dogs are loyal. And know their place."

A thorn of fury prickled my spine. I shook the sensation away— I would not let her needle me. "What is my *place*?"

"Beside me. Beneath me." Her eyes had become night skies with a bare glimmer of blue fire. "Bend the knee to me, Sister. Swear you will help me dismantle the Gates. And there need not be any more violence."

"That is enough!" Eithne shoved her hood back from her silvering hair. I searched her regal mien for grief—for evidence that the murder of her lover had affected her. But she just glared at her daughter as if she were a wayward child of seven instead of a rotten, power-mad queen. "You have taken this far enough. We have all witnessed your might. But even the sharpest blade is useless if wielded without purpose."

"Yes, let us speak of blades." Eala turned toward her mother with cold, careful menace. "Tell me, Mother, did you know who my sister was when she came to you? Did you know she was my father's half-blood get? Did you know that if you hammered her hard enough, she might eventually ring true as steel? Or was it enough that she simply wasn't me? That she didn't question your inane rules and small-minded ideals? Was it enough that she loved you, even though you could not return the favor?"

I inhaled, sharp. Eithne raised her chin, staring down her daughter. In the dim light, the two women looked very much alike.

"I have loved you both exactly as you deserved." Eithne spoke as if reciting a proclamation. "You speak of hammering as if it were punishment. But the proof stands before me, as abhorrent as I find it. I made you both strong. I only wish I had made you both sensible."

Fury splintered Eala's face into the mask of a monster. She jerked a blade from the scabbard at her horse's flank. It was a ceremonial weapon—heavy with gilt and jewels. But I could see the edge on it, gleaming in the dark. She laid it across her forearm and presented it to Eithne with a grim, dramatic flourish.

"Ah, yes, *sensible*. Alas—the world has never been changed by playing it safe." She smiled, her mouth like a cavern. "I wish for my sister to bend the knee. Go make her do it. If she does not, you may carve her loyalty from her flesh."

Eithne's mouth worked. "No."

"Whyever not?"

"Because." Her eyes found mine across the courtyard. Even in the dim they seemed to glow—pale and hard and brilliant as gems. I looked for regret but I found only certainty. She gave me a brief, hard nod, then said, "I said once I would not trade one daughter for another. But for Fódla's sake, I will trade a mad queen for a sane one."

"Ugh." Eala drew the sword slowly back. Pivoted in her saddle. Then, fast as a viper, drove the blade into her mother's chest.

Eithne crumpled like a house made of parchment. Her hands scrabbled at the steel blade splitting her in two. Eala twisted the sword, almost lovingly, then yanked it out. Blood spurted, red as ruin. Someone had begun to scream—I thought perhaps it was me. Eithne's mount sallied, ears swiveling. Slowly—impossibly slowly—the rightful high queen of Fódla slid from her saddle. Struck the ground. And lay deathly still.

"That's better," Eala said. "They're always so much more cooperative this way. Now, Mother—rise." The queen's body twitched, rolled, then levered itself to its feet. It had blood dark as wine on its face. Eala placed the sword she had used to kill her mother in the queen's own hands. "I said, *go make my sister kneel. Or kill her where she stands.*"

The dead queen charged at me. I felt nothing and everything at once, my body frozen while my mind churned with disjointed memories and fear thick as treacle. The world around me blurred. Sounds muffled, yet every beat of my heart felt like a hammer striking stone. I couldn't breathe.

Eithne's steps accelerated, devouring the cobbles between us like cakes laid out at a feast. The sword lowered, slick and steaming with still-warm blood. I erected a barrier of thorns, but I was weak after the day; she cut through them easily. My feet wavered—left, then right. I became a statue, carved from stories untold, lives unlived.

The blade arrowed toward my heart.

Muscle and memory overtook doubt, a lifetime of training drilled into my very bones. I sidestepped the strike, angling my body as I wrapped one fist around the hand holding the sword and lifted the other to splay over the queen's face. My starshine spiked with the adrenaline turning my limbs to knotty wood.

White fire ignited deep inside her skull, spreading in searing tendrils that snaked along the contours of her cheeks and the angle of her jaw. Light leaked from her staring eyes, coursed from her open mouth. Then flashed eager over her frame, unraveling her from the inside out. Her skin crisped and peeled like burning paper; her bones glowed molten before disintegrating into flaking cinders. I swore she opened her mouth in the last moment before she collapsed in on herself, the words on her lips like a final, broken plea:

A stór.

The woman who'd raised me sifted away in a scattering of ash and bad memories. My fingers tightened around the hilt of Eala's ceremonial blade. And though it seemed to be heavier than a mountain in my grip, I forced myself to coil back. I twisted, then flung the sword as hard as I could at Eala, mounted upon her pretty pony.

She did not flinch. I did not miss. The blade sailed a half inch from her face, slicing her cheek, nicking her ear, and shearing a few long, floating locks of hair.

The blood that dripped down her face and stained her pale raiment was black as midnight.

"I'll see you on the battlefield, you bitch!" I screamed, as her ghouls broke their stillness and began to claw for me.

"Get her!"

I dived bodily into the waiting horde, fighting toward the corner where the path to the grotto—and Roslea beyond—meandered. The dead swarmed me like ants, burnt faces and rotting mouths and flesh-draped bones. I waded through them, even as they dragged me, caught me, pulled me. I touched a few errant limbs and leering faces, setting off glittering chain reactions among the affected revenants. But there were so many of them. My free hand fought toward my bodice, delving between the last voluminous folds of the dress Eala had put me in.

My knees hit dirt. My fingers touched glass. The dead converged on me as I lifted Cathair's small vial, yanked the cork out with my teeth, and lofted the bottle with what felt like the last of my strength.

I did not see where the Eternal Fire landed. Green light flashed. Thunder cracked. The explosion rocked the courtyard, flattening me to the cobbles and throwing Eala's ghouls off me like flotsam on the sea. I did not wait for the dead to recover or for the flames flickering green in my periphery to spread—I shifted into my anam cló, legs lengthening, pelt rippling, and tail flicking.

And ran.

Part Three

The Heart of the Forest

White shields they carry in their hands,
With emblems of pale silver;
With glittering blue swords,
With mighty stout horns.
In well-devised battle array,
Ahead of their fair chieftain
They march amid blue spears,
Pale-visaged, curly-headed bands.
They scatter the battalions of the foe,
They ravage every land they attack,
Splendidly they march to combat,
A swift, distinguished, avenging host!

—"The Hosts of Faery," translated by Kuno Meyer

Chapter Forty-One

Fia

The unlit forest swallowed me, a strange and somber mouth studded with cracked wooden teeth and whispering with fell voices. I ran as fast as my deer legs could go, bounding and leaping with abandon, irreverent of any path.

I was grateful for a form besides my own. Even as I fled Eala, I hid from myself, and from the grief and rage threatening to flay the skin from my bones. The doe was fast and frightened, but the determined drum of her delicate hooves on the earth was focused on one thing alone: survival. She was made for flight, and she met our purpose with an agile kind of peace that soothed me.

Time lost meaning. There was just me, the trees, and all the shadows between. After what I thought must be an hour, something began to pace me in the dark. An arched, elegant neck. Russet fur ridged with the faintest impression of pale dots. A white signal flag of a tail. Eyes fathomless as the night sky.

Another deer. Another doe.

But when I turned my head to look at her head-on, I saw the fog had grown heavy, and it was but my own shadow.

At last I wove between stone monsters punctuating the earth like guideposts—my fiann from last Samhain, returned to their eternal slumber. Beyond, the path flashed golden as coins. The rushing of a stream filled my ears. A stone bridge arched beside a bent willow.

Irian stood at its peak, carved silent as stone and deadly as a nightmare. I shifted with some difficulty back into my human form, my shorter limbs dense and stocky after the effortless grace of the doe. Profound relief tangled with renewed worry on Irian's perfect features.

"What happened?"

"They're dead." The words came out flat, as if my voice was determined to mask all the emotions roiling beneath my flesh. "The high queen...Cathair. The people who raised me in the human realms—she killed them all."

Irian rocked toward me, his closeness the only balm he could offer. I could tell from the hardness of his features that he did not sorrow for them, only for me—for how their passing would affect me.

In another life, under other circumstances, I thought, he would have gladly killed them all himself.

I clenched my fists, although I longed to wrap my arms around his chest and bury my face in his shoulder and scream until my insides were abraded clean.

"She will not be far behind," I said. "Let's go home."

We crossed the bridge side by side. The Gate rippled a silver whisper over our skin as we crossed back into Tír na nÓg. I exhaled as the full extent of my Treasure came rushing back, twining vines of gladness and green glory around the ecstatic thunder of my Heart. And there was something else—something new and unfamiliar. A third melody joining the chord of my Treasure's near-silent humming, an atonal harmony to the Sky-Sword's louder tune. A song of embers stirred into a bonfire, a symphony of distant blood-red skies.

A surge of power erupted through the night toward us—a wild

blaze roaring over the horizon, consuming the stillness and leaving behind a trail of heat that pulsed like the heartbeat of a distant star.

"Do you feel that?" I asked Irian, wonder in my voice.

"I do, colleen." His voice held an echo of my awe. "I believe Laoise has reforged the Flaming Shield."

I brought my attention back to the Willow Gate, dredging the shadows until I spied Chandi. She sat huddled in Irian's—*Rogan's*—cloak with her back to a rough-hewn boulder. She did not look well. But she was conscious, at least.

Her eyes flicked to mine, then away, the air tangling with a thousand unspoken words. I set my jaw. I hummed with violence and felt numbed by confusing grief. Perhaps there would be time for forgiveness later.

I turned, ignoring Irian's questioning look, and knelt in front of the Gate. I plunged my hands into the dirt and called on the full force of my magic with all the wrath and grief roaring through my veins. The earth answered with a thunderous rumble. Tree roots punched from the earth, knotted like clubs ready to strike at my enemies. Vines twined them, curved with thorns like deadly scythes. Flowers burst to life as the structure growled higher, red as blood and black as night and white as stars. The wall grew tall as Irian, then taller, until it towered high into the dark.

It was not enough. I had seen Eala's ghouls scale Rath na Mara's palisades as if they were playthings. If she tried to pursue me here—as I believed she would—I needed more assurance that she could not cross into Tír na nÓg with her army. Not yet. Not until I was ready for her.

With all the strength left in my limbs, I curved the top of my wall of trees and vines and flowers. It bent with a groan of protest right into the shimmering, wavering outline of the Gate. The barrier between the realms pushed back—nothing but Treasures was meant to pass. I shoved harder, threading the power of my Heart with Talah's curse. Starlight rushed along bent boughs and blew from the pollen of flowers and limned huge thorns in silver.

My botanical wall pushed through the Gate, curving over into the other realm. I anchored it there with ropes of starlight, fused deep between tangled roots where the bones of the earth hummed.

I reeled back on my heels, brushed dirt from my palms, and looked up at the monstrosity I had created. It curved around and above the gate, an impenetrable barrier of magical foliage.

"Mo chroí," Irian murmured, a note of wonder rasping along his voice. "What is that for?"

"Eala will chase me. She will open the Gate for her revenants. But I will not let her in." I stood. Swayed. Irian reached for me, but I regained my balance on my own. "Let them cut themselves to ribbons on that. Let them try to chop it with axes or burn it with fire. It will last until we return with all the troops we can muster. Then I will bury my sister in the grave she has dug herself."

We stayed that night at Irian's crumbling fortress, though only Chandi slept. Irian made a fire in the hearth, waiting quietly until I began to talk. Then he listened in silence, letting the jumbled events of that night flow from me in a torrent. I told him everything—the archive in the tower, Corra's confusing words about Marban, the high queen speaking against her daughter...and Eala killing her for it.

No—not everything.

Cathair's prophecy, crumpled still in the lining of my bodice, seemed to whisper an ongoing curse, trailing between my ribs and infecting my heart. *So white and black, the swans must die, for stars to weave their fate on high.*

I couldn't accept it. After everything I'd done, all I'd fought for? I couldn't accept that my story ended like that. And though I knew I ought not to keep it a secret from Irian...I could not bear to tell him. As if speaking the words out loud would weave them indelibly into the fabric of my fate.

When I was finished, Irian stirred the fire with a poker. Sparks leapt like fireflies, gilding his hair and glossing his silver eyes.

"This Marban," he said softly. "Wayland sought him too. He found a record of him in Laoise's library—something that put me to mind of a story I heard when I was very young. It was a favorite of Deirdre's. Of your mother's."

My pulse spiked. "Tell me?"

"It was a long time ago." He tilted his head. "I am not sure I remember the particulars."

"Please try."

"Once, in a land of eternal youth in the days of legends," Irian began, with the faintest whisper of a smile. "A human prince sought the heart of a Gentry maid so fair none could match her wit nor her beauty. He wooed her without flagging, and after a time her heart softened toward him. But though their love was strong, the human prince's mortality wore on him. His bride stayed young as the morn, even as he passed into the afternoon of his life. One day he plucked a single gray hair from his beard and, in a fit of anguish, carved the heart of his lady love from her chest with his sword. He presented it to the Sept of Feathers in return for his immortality. This they granted him, for the Songbird's Heart was a powerful emblem. But so, too, did they banish the human to the Dúluachair, to live out his immortal days alone and unloved, in a cottage thatched with birds' wings, so he might never forget his terrible crime."

I jerked, my spine going rigid. "What did you say? About the house?"

"It was said to be thatched with birds' wings. Thousands of them. But it is only a story, colleen."

"When I was locked inside my mind, in the Deep-Dream, I spoke to—" My voice could not manage the phrase *my father*. I was not sure if I had truly spoken to Rían Ó Mainnín, slain twenty years past, or a ghost of my own invention. I was not sure it mattered. But I could not forget what he had told me, a phrase I had heard before in dreams. *He is to blame for your troubles, little deer. Not I.* "I believe I must seek this Marban out. I believe he holds the key to my fate. And I believe he lives in a clearing in a strange wood surrounded by wildflowers, in a cottage thatched with birds' wings."

Irian passed a hand over his face. "Then we make for the Dúlu-achair in the morn."

"Why do you say it like that?"

"Because the Dúluachair—also known as the Feral Moor—is said to be the gateway to the underworld. Many believe it to be haunted by wraiths and patrolled by bog cats." Irian flashed me a swift smile that carved my own heart from its soft chest. "Truly, mo chroí—your taste in destinations is unparalleled."

Chandi roused at dawn, looking tired and ill and sick at heart. There was nothing for her to eat, little for her to wear beyond Rogan's oversized cloak. I quelled guilt as I crouched before her in the rheumy light filtering from high windows and told her briefly of our plan.

"Are you asking me to come with you?" she asked, shuddering in folds of green and gold. "Or telling me I must stay behind?"

I honestly wasn't sure. "Do you have anywhere else to go, Chandi?"

"Where are the others?" Her face pinched. "Sinéad...Laoise... Balor?"

"Our agreed waypoint after reforging the Treasures is the Summerlands," I told her.

"Then to the Summerlands I go," she announced.

"Do you know the way?" I asked lamely.

"I lived here for thirteen years, Fia." A flicker of the old Chandi sparked in her amber eyes. "I daresay I know the way better than you."

I glanced helplessly toward Irian, who was kicking the last of the cinders into the grate, then back to Chandi. "I fear Sinéad may try to kill you if you arrive without protection."

"I know my sister." Chandi's expression warped, then hardened. "And I'm not afraid of her."

As the sun rose above the lough, I climbed to the tower and traded my torn and muddied black gown for some of Irian's lamentably ill-fitting clothing. I had nothing else to wear. I found a worn knapsack and tucked the shard of starstone and Cathair's terrible prophecy inside, along with some weapons and a spare cloak.

We parted ways with Chandi on the beach. I tried not to let my worry chase after her.

An hour later—as we hiked the bluff overlooking distant Murias—Irian and I both felt it. A surge of power coursing through the morning—a savage tide crashing upon a distant shore. It swept over the horizon, stirring the forest like a whisper, trailing salt and foam in its wake. The earth and sky pulsed with the steady beat of a distant ocean's heart.

I smiled. Irian nodded once.

"Wayland did it," I said, a little wonderingly.

"He did." Irian's voice held more certainty. "He only had to find it within himself. As we all must do."

I gazed up at him—his night-dark hair and sky-bright eyes. How I suddenly longed to tell him—to let his strong, capable shoulders bear the weight of Cathair's dire prophecy so mine didn't have to. But resentment and denial squandered my bravery. I bent my head and walked forward. "So we must."

Chapter Forty-Two

Fia

"Why can't we fly to this *Feral Moor*, again?" I asked, for the third time in as many days.

Taking turns between our Gentry forms and our anam clónna, Irian and I traveled across Ildathach, a dazzling, undulating plain of flowers that shifted colors with each passing breeze—violet, sapphire, and golden hues all shimmering together in waves of soft light. Blossoms with petals tipped in pollen opened and closed rhythmically, as if breathing. Delicate birds with iridescent wings flitted through the blooms, their songs pealing like crystal bells upon the rising wind. We'd made decent time, but as the sun descended on the third day of travel, I grew fretful.

We sought a person who might not exist. Or worse, who *did* exist but had no idea how to solve the problems burying me in worry with each passing breath.

How could I kill my sister without warping the magic she now wielded? How could I unforge not one or two, but *five* powerful Treasures? And how could I do it all without sacrificing my own heart for balance?

"We cannot fly, mo chroí," Irian patiently explained, also for the third time, "because I cannot go where I have never been before. Lest you wish to materialize a thousand feet above a flaming volcano or entombed inside an inconvenient tree."

"I see your point." I shuddered, memories from the Deep-Dream ghosting over my flesh. If I could not find a way to unforge the Treasures before I died, I would someday end up in that grove— that *mausoleum*. Part of me was already there—the piece hewn from my soul as the price of my tithe beneath the Ember Moon. I forced lightness into my tone. "But if you cannot shorten our journey, then I am not sure why I have let you accompany me."

"Indeed, colleen." He favored me with a glance ridged in mirth. "I am good for little, in the grand scheme of things. That is why the gods made me so tall. And so very, very handsome."

I laughed a little. "You sound like Wayland."

"Please." Irian's smile dazzled me with its easy perfection. "Anything but that."

I watched him stride beside me, his back straight and his hair flying like black feathers in the stiff wind. He was but an arm's length away from me, yet a chasm yawned between us, chiseled by our physical distance and shadowed by the secret I kept from him. I longed to touch him—to twine my hand in his or graze the angle of his jaw or thread my fingers in the hairs at the nape of his neck. But touch was not the only bond we shared. A strange impulse needled me—sharp as a thorn and soft as a rose petal.

"Tell me a story, tánaiste," I asked. Or, perhaps, commanded, as one of Irian's stark brows lifted in humorous affront at my tone. "Please?"

"For you, my heart, I would tell a thousand." His eyes softened on my face. "Only, what sort of story might you like to hear? I have told you much of my past. Our present is yet to be fully written. And—"

"Our future," I suggested. "Tell me a story of our future. A story not of what is or has been, but what could be."

"What...could be." Irian's ease fell away, and he mouthed the words as if they were pieces of glass upon his tongue that might shatter if he spoke them too quickly. He and I had rarely spoken about our future—it always seemed less a blank slate than a half-written parchment riddled with holes. "Very well. Once—"

"*Once?*" I laughed, to hide a sudden sharp spasm of grief. What if there really were no more stories to tell? Only stories already told? "Surely it cannot be *once* if it has not happened yet."

"*Someday*, in a time of hard-earned peace and well-deserved quiet—"

"Peace and quiet?" I interrupted, again. "Is that all we have to look forward to?"

"Would you prefer war and chaos?" Irian made a face. "On second thought, do not answer that."

I stuck my tongue out. "How about...passionate equilibrium? Comfortable thrill?"

"Do you plan to heckle me at every turn, colleen?" He frowned at me theatrically. "Or shall I be allowed to tell the story *you* requested?"

I mimed locking my lips and throwing away the key.

"Someday, in a time of playful tension and...magnetic balance?" His lips quirked and he raised a questioning eyebrow for my approval. But although his mouth teased over words, they died upon his lips before he gave them breath. The restless breeze sighed over the plains of Ildathach, feathering petals and winnowing his sleek black hair. "When I was a boy, I thought the isolated life I shared with my mother was the most tedious existence a child could be cursed with. Repetitive, lonely, and wearisome beyond belief. I yearned for adventures like the ones in Deirdre's stories. Exciting exploits. Fearsome foes. Brave battles. I longed to live at the center of a grand story and shape it with my valiant actions. To become either a great, virtuous hero or a wild, wicked villain—at the age of seven, either seemed appealing."

I listened without interrupting, even as a bleakness rose inside me, fleeting and gray as mist over a blasted moor. The black-haired boy who climbed cliffs and snuck into Deirdre's garden had once known such innocence, only to have it stripped away, replaced with swords and sorrow, curses and contempt.

"But as I have grown older, I find myself dreaming of those routine, mundane, straightforward days." His thumb ghosted over the Sky-Sword's hilt. "Dreams are dangerous, potent things, colleen. They give us hope in dark times. But so, too, do they whisper of what could be, instead of acknowledging what is. Some stories are just as bad. They live quietly in the heart, disguised as harmless diversion, but their pull can be as fierce as any tempest. Longing for what can never be has the power to unravel even the strongest resolve."

We crested a small rise overlooking a wood of strange, slender trees topped with triangular canopies. Late afternoon sun turned them to torches, casting long shadows over the rippling fields. Irian turned to face me, keeping an arm's-length gap between us. I fought the grief tangling in my chest like briars.

"Someday, when days are easy and nights are long and time seems plentiful, a gray-eyed man and a changeling woman build a life as they choose." His eyes were not gray—in the shards of light cresting along his jaw, they were the lacquered blue of broken pottery. The tenuous gold of hoarded treasure. Again, sorrow pierced me, but now its blade was coated with the breathtaking poison of hope. "There is a house, neither too big nor too small. Its walls are not crumbling, and its halls are not haunted, and it stays warm in the winter when a fire is lit. There are meals at a sturdy table decorated by a vase stuffed with wildflowers. Sometimes there is wine, and they stay awake too late, curled beside that fire as they speak of things past and things yet to come. There are chores—floors to sweep and errands to run and animals to feed. There is a garden—too large and poorly tended, with weeds and slugs and vermin, but they do not mind, because it is impossibly plentiful and they never want for vegetables or flowers."

I bit my lip, the pain chasing away the sting behind my eyes.

"There will be a bed," Irian continued, his voice solemn. "A lovely feather mattress. Not too large, for the man could not bear sleeping too far away from the woman. He would climb into her dreams, if only he knew how. But he will content himself with resting his arm around her waist and drawing her close when she murmurs in her sleep."

"With pillows?" I asked softly.

"So many pillows." He dropped his eyes, the vanes of his eyelashes painting black ink along the sweep of his cheekbones. "And someday there may be a child. With dark hair and curious eyes and a sharp, stubborn chin."

My pulse vaulted, a sudden bloom of pale, secretive cereus—beautiful and thrilling, yet burdened by trepidation. I managed, "Not in the bed, I hope."

"Gods alive, no." Irian's smile was like a daydream I kept returning to. "Although I have been told parents have less choice in that matter than they are led to believe."

I held Cathair's awful prophecy like a thorned rose—wishing to share it yet dreading its sting. I had to tell him. I could not bear to tell him.

"I am not certain I can have children," I said, instead. "The way I was born, the way I was raised—" I trailed off. "Even beyond my unusual biology, I am not certain I *wish* to have children. Motherhood hasn't always been the most comforting notion in my life. Where it has not been absence, it has been manipulation and cruelty. What kind of mother would I be?"

"What kind of father would I be?" Irian was as serious as I had ever seen him. Yet his expression bore a lightness, like a man in a dark room gazing at shadows upon a distant wall. "We are not bound by our pasts, colleen. Neither are we bound to any future. This is but a dream. You are my reality. And I have sworn never to let you go."

I reached out, grazing my bare fingertips over his heavy

gloves—close enough that I could imagine his heat, far enough that I could taste his longing, sweet and bitter as blackberry wine.

"That night in the tavern, Irian, you said—"

"Oh," he interrupted, rueful. "Do not taunt me with the nonsense I spewed while in my cups."

"You said that without me, you were *nothing*." I lifted my eyes to his, even as I maintained the tenuous touch of our hands. The half-memorized lines of Cathair's prophecy throbbed in time to the beat of my heart, a bane I could not shake. "What did you mean by that?"

Irian's gaze scathed over mine before lifting toward the horizon, jeweled in a cacophony of colors. When he spoke, the wind nearly snatched the words from his mouth.

"All I have loved, I have lost. My mother, my dearest friend, my brother. The life that was promised me, the death I had earned. All that is left to me now are my oaths. My promises." He lifted his hand from mine, grazed his thumb over the hilt of the Sky-Sword. "This is all I am. You are all I have. It is not melodrama to say that without you, I am nothing."

His words were a blade to my gut, twisting as it cut. I had not always appreciated how much my sacrifice beneath the Ember Moon had devastated Irian—in time, I had learned the depths of his desolation, and how far he would go to prevent such a thing ever happening again. How could I tell him that yet again, the prospect of my death clattered like a feeble pawn upon a game board stacked by destiny? An oath made not by him or by me, but by the stars wheeling in the careless dark?

I couldn't. The vow I had wrenched from my husband on the Longest Night had been made in fear and love in equal measure. It had saved my life. I feared it had scarred his. And it might break us both to sever that bond.

But I began to see how an oath could be a chain. And how love, held too tightly, could bruise the thing it was meant to protect.

"Let us make a bargain, Sky-Sword." I pruned back my regret and tilted my head to look Irian in the eye.

"Colleen." His smile was a pale scythe. "Surely you have been warned not to make bargains with the Folk."

"You have already kept me long beyond my welcome." I could not quite muster a grin. "I am not sure what more you can threaten me with."

"Peace and quiet, apparently."

"My bargain is this." I barreled through the ache of my disquiet. "If we survive the next month of war and chaos, then you shall have all the peace and quiet your heart desires. We shall have our sturdy house and our regular meals and our overgrown garden. And perhaps in time—after a few late-night *discussions* over a bottle of wine—*perhaps* we shall have our child."

Irian's gloved hand grazed over my hips. I rocked forward; his lips hovered a bare inch from mine. A spark passed between us, sharp but not unpleasant. "And in return?"

"Remember him," I whispered. "The boy who climbed cliffs and picked cockles on the beach and listened to Deirdre's stories. Before he traded winkles for war and songs for steel. Remember *Irian*, before he learned to kill."

"For you?" he murmured in return. "Anything."

"Not for me. For *you*."

Irian's stark eyebrows winged together in something that was not quite a frown. Beyond the canopy of the looming forest, the sun had sunk, casting the world in shades of vermilion and taupe. The space between us tautened, a string pulled too tight.

"I will," he promised.

Chapter Forty-Three

Wayland

Light rippled over his closed eyelids like sun through shallows as Wayland surfaced toward waking from somewhere dark and deep. He lingered at the edge of sleep, reveling in the heightened senses his Treasure had brought him.

Cool dew exhaling off broad leaves. Sap percolating along rigid limbs. Clear, cold water rushing below a city built entirely from trees.

Wayland opened his eyes. Midmorning light filtered through gauzy green curtains slanting over rounded windows in a room carved from the boll of an enormous tree. Beside him on the bed, Idris still slumbered, his face buried in the pillow and the linens kicked low over his naked abdomen. Wayland gazed at him, eyes gliding over the angle of Idris's shoulder blades, the curve of his spine, the red hair spilling wantonly across the crisp sheets. He longed to nestle closer beside him in the slow, sultry morning. To kiss him awake, one hand cupping his cheek as the other roamed lower. But Wayland restrained himself.

They had stayed up late last night. And the night before that. He supposed a little rest would do Idris good.

Wayland rolled quietly out of bed, disturbing an aggrieved Hog, who flicked her scaled tail, huffed steam from her nostrils, and glared at him, as if to say, *I know exactly why I've been banished for hours every evening, and I disapprove.* Wayland stroked her gently between the nubs of her horns, yanked on a pair of breeches, and strode out into the sunny common room.

The Summer Twins' guest suites were a series of round hollows carved into the bolls of colossal pine branches. Large and luxurious, they dripped with beaded curtains over the doors and were plumped with hundreds of jewel-toned pillows. Wayland had actually occupied them before, on a diplomatic errand for Gavida a few years back, and admired them for their spacious accommodations and fine decor. They seemed less spacious since he'd been forced to cohabitate with his lover's peevish older sister. And a human girl obsessed with polishing daggers. And a half dozen rambunctious draiglings who'd taken to teasing him with spontaneous fires just to see how swiftly he could put them out with his Treasure.

"A fine morning, Prionsa," Laoise snarked from the window. "Shame you almost missed it."

Wayland just smiled and put water on for tea.

About a week ago, Laoise, Sinéad, and the draiglings had caught up to Balor and the aughiskies, then entered the Summerlands in tandem. They'd caused quite a stir, from what Wayland gathered. The Summer Twins had tried to deny Laoise sanctuary; Laoise had apparently shifted into her anam cló and threatened to burn the whole city to the ground. Hence the fine rooms. Wayland and Idris had arrived a few days later, travel worn but giddy with the fresh bloom of their nascent relationship.

Laoise had taken one look at the two men, holding hands in the threshold of the guest apartments, and nearly combusted.

"Absolutely not," she had said shrilly. "I forbid it."

"Laoise," Idris had said with a laugh. "I'm a grown man. And I'm free to love who I will."

"Love? *Love?*" Laoise had spluttered, as if the presence of feelings made her brother's dalliance with Wayland worse. "I knew our bloodline was cursed, but this is just ridiculous!"

Laoise had confronted Wayland as he unhooked Fáilsceim from the harness on his back.

"I swear on my scales, Prionsa." Wayland was reasonably certain she couldn't breathe fire in her Gentry form, but he hadn't been keen to test the theory. "If you break Idris's heart, I will—I will—" She had seemed to struggle to invent consequences to fit the enormity of the crime. "Death will be too easy. I will make your life a living nightmare. I will curse your shoes to be always too tight and your tea always too cold. I will hire a bard to compose ballads about parts of your body you never thought could be derided and sing them in taverns from here to the Barrens. I will make you experience the kind of pain—"

"Laoise," Wayland had interrupted, swallowing a laugh. "I have no intention of breaking his heart."

Laoise had calmed, but only barely. She had stuck a finger in his face. "Pain. You hear me? Lots of pain."

They'd subsided into an uneasy truce as, all around them, the Summerlands prepared for war. Although Eala had fled to the human realms and no one knew when, or even if, she would return, her gambit at the Ember Moon had stirred rivalries old and new between the bardaí. A great host was already encamped beneath the tree city, colorful tents sprawled beneath snapping banners, each a bright wound upon the endless gold of the grasslands. In the city itself, built from the living wood of vast ancient trees climbing atop a hill, many Folk also seemed to be preparing for war. Forges spat sparks as hammers clanged; rations were divided and packed. But many residents seemed like simple, ordinary Folk. Wayland had seen ghillies tending ponds of algae suspended in oversized acorn caps, brùnaidhean picking fruit from small trees growing from the garden bolls of much larger trees, sheeries collecting dewdrops in flasks before the morning sun burned them away.

He liked it here. It reminded him of the Silver Isle—or perhaps

it just reminded him of his childhood. Before his mother had left...
before Irian had been exiled...before his magic had been imprisoned behind a choking collar. When he had still been whole.

Here, now—as the kettle whistled and Laoise glared daggers
at him and dew evaporated from broad green spring leaves—he
thought perhaps he might like to become whole again.

A tentative knock rattled the door. Sinéad immediately stood,
the knives she had been polishing already in hand.

"Who is it?" Laoise called, as two of her draiglings scampered
across the foyer.

The door swung open to reveal...*Chandi.*

Wayland had met the dark-haired girl but a handful of times,
spoken to her directly perhaps once. He knew her only by the ruin
she'd left behind—less a person than the ghost of a trust grievously
broken.

Sinéad fixed her eyes on Chandi with shattering intensity. Before
anyone could react, the willowy blonde's feet flung her toward
the other human girl. Everyone moved at once—Laoise, pivoting
to intercept her friend; the draiglings, scampering and caroming
as if a game were afoot; Wayland, dropping his mug and moving instinctively in front of the door where Idris slept. But Sinéad
dropped her blades to clatter onto the uneven wooden floor, sidestepped Laoise, then flung herself bodily at Chandi. Chandi was
too weak to hold them both up—the two girls collapsed backward
in a heap before clambering to their knees, neither letting go of the
other as they embraced.

"I'm sorry, I'm sorry. I'm so, so sorry," Chandi cried into her
swan sister's shoulder, fisting her hands so tightly in the fabric of
the other girl's tunic that her knuckles whitened.

They both began weeping, great spine-racking sobs, as they
clutched at each other. Wayland stared, a little mystified. To his
immense vindication, Laoise looked nearly as perplexed. He sidled
over to her and said, "I thought for sure she was going to kill her."

"There will be many difficult conversations to be had." Laoise gave her head a complicated shake. "More tears to be shed…many smiles to share. But in the end, few of us who lose a sister ever get her back. No matter the circumstances." She dragged her eyes from the girls, still sobbing and hugging in the foyer, and narrowed them at Wayland. "Now go put a shirt on. And wake Idris while you're at it. Being in love is no excuse for laziness."

Wayland had asked for a workshop; the Summer Twins had obliged with a tiny, cramped shed he was reasonably sure had been used for storing gardening tools. And recently. Still, he lit a fire in the tiny stove and cleared the cobwebs from the shelves and set down the sheets of parchment and bits of metal and the artifacts he'd begun collecting. It felt good to have a place of his own, however mean and small. It felt even better to begin forging, something not even his countless hours of research in the Cnoc had convinced him he could do.

Becoming a Treasure had loosened something in him. He did not believe his new power had much to do with his forging magic—his affinities had always rested side by side, like wary neighbors divided by a narrow boundary. Close enough to touch, yet never at ease. Now he had been reforged—cast anew from rising tide and rushing water, his edges smoothed, his marrow bolstered. His uncertainties had been hammered out of him, leaving only his truth—unquestioned, unshaken, undeniable.

He had always been capable of forging. Now he believed it.

He didn't want to waste any more time worrying he wasn't good enough for what he'd been born to do. So he began to work.

A tap on the door startled Wayland. He looked up from his project, a tiny glittering fishhook designed to snag daydreams, and was surprised to find the light behind the narrow window of his workshop had gone deep blue. Evening, then. The fire in the stove had burned low, but the air was almost uncomfortably warm.

"Come in," he called.

Idris wedged himself through the rounded doorway, ducking his head and curving his spine to fit inside. He carried a corked bottle of wine and two rough-hewn cups; he set them on Wayland's worktable before settling himself upon a tiny rickety stool beside it.

"I wondered if you were still out here." He sloshed out a few measures of the wine. "You've missed dinner."

"That's because I knew Laoise was cooking." Wayland leaned back, stretching out the kinks in his spine before reaching for one of the cups. He watched Idris glance in interest around the narrow, cramped room, and made a rueful face. "We should go out on the terrace. It's awful in here."

"I like you in here." Idris hid a smile behind the lip of his own cup. "Or maybe I just like you."

Wayland shifted in his own narrow rickety chair until one of his knees bumped Idris's. "Tell me more about that."

"Later." Idris's smile grew. "For now, why don't you tell me about what you're working on?"

Wayland obliged, showing Idris the forgings he'd been toying with: a quill that, when dipped in blood, spilled an enemy's secrets; a looking glass that, when spun, connected two disparate locations; a conch shell that echoed your own voice back at you.

"I suppose they're just for fun," Wayland admitted, suddenly embarrassed as he watched Idris inspect the inventions. "I'm not sure what use they'd be to anyone."

"Things don't have to be useful to be valuable," Idris said as he held the shell to his ear and listened to Wayland's voice reverberate within. "They just have to exist."

Wayland had thought Idris might be more utilitarian. "Do you believe that?"

"I do." Idris set down the conch and sipped more of his wine.

"In the same way that not every life must be meaningful to matter. However short or long, interesting or mundane—existence is its own reward."

"Hmm." Wayland draped his arm along the workbench and leaned his weight into Idris's shadow. "And love? Must love merely *exist* to be worthwhile?"

Idris rocked forward on his stool, pushing his knee between Wayland's thighs and laying slender fingers on his bicep. Heat ignited at his touch and surged through Wayland's veins, a rising current he had no intention of fighting.

"Perhaps it must do a little more than that," Idris murmured, his lips an inch from Wayland's.

"How much more?" Wayland whispered, slowly closing the gap.

Idris curved cool palms around Wayland's cheeks and kissed him, tender. The sleek angle of his hair glided over Wayland's jaw; he tasted of mint and salt and lingering alcohol. Wayland growled and pounced, catching the other man around the waist as he hoisted him onto the workbench. Idris gasped; the shelves rattled, and one of the wine cups bounced off the table as the whole structure shook. They laughed against each other's mouths as Wayland peeled off Idris's shirt and Idris's fingers ridged along the muscles of Wayland's stomach.

And as night fell beyond the narrow window and the workshop grew hotter—and hotter . . . and *hotter*—Wayland thought he finally understood.

It only had to exist.

Chapter Forty-Four

Fia

It was dusk when we crossed into the Dúluachair. There was no change in the flora—the towering trees verdant with new leaves and the thick, tangled vines blurring with new flowers. But there was a disruption in the energy—a strange feeling of unease, like a shadow sweeping over us, although the light did not darken nor the air chill.

"Is this place truly the gateway to the underworld?" I asked Irian.

"How should I know?" he said mildly. "Do I look like a god of the dead to you?"

I squinted at his stark beauty, black garb, and towering height. "A little."

"I shall take that as a compliment." His lip curled over one sharp canine, and he relented. "Nearby lies a strange cave system they call Oweynagat. There are stories about Folk who ventured in but never came out. And creatures that came out...and refused to go back in."

"Oweynagat." I quelled a shudder at the name. There were

similar places in the human realms—places said to lead to Donn's dark realm. The few I had explored had been musty, dusty cracks in the ground. But this was Tír na nÓg. "Doesn't that mean *Cave of the Cats?*"

"It does."

"Why?"

His expression twisted. "You should hope not to find out."

Moments later, I heard them—near-silent footsteps in the dense underbrush. Low growls vibrating the dim. I peered into the shadows, which rippled as though alive. I swore I glimpsed eyes, glowing like molten gold. Fur dark as liquid shadows, sheeny in the faint light.

I pawed at my hips, where my skeans usually sat, but Irian motioned for me to be still.

"Bog cats," he muttered. "They do not feed on flesh—be not alarmed."

Easier said than done. Their huge, lithe bodies crouched low, ready to pounce. Each step the cats took was unnervingly quiet, their claws gliding over the forest floor without disturbing so much as a fallen leaf.

"What *do* they feed on?"

"No one knows. Some say they feast on secrets, lapping truths like spilled cream. Others say they devour regrets, savoring the bitterness of what might have been." Irian glanced over his shoulder. "I do not believe they will chase us, so long as we do not run."

"Are you sure about that?" The bog cats drew steadily closer in the shadows, all sleek limbs and dark fur and glowing eyes. Fear trellised my spine like midnight roses, cloyingly dark and spiked with sharp wishes.

I wanted a blade. Preferably two. Armor. Another set of eyes mounted on the back of my head.

Dusk thickened toward night. The cats slunk ahead of us, spine-chillingly fast, then crouched low, their muscles coiling. Their slit pupils yawned as their tails lashed back and forth. A guttural snarl erupted from one of them; the others took up the sound in a chorus of menace. They bared their fangs—long and curved, glistening like ivory daggers. Their breath oozed like mist between their paws. Irian drew his sword, which sang out an eager note. My pulse ratcheted as my starshine kindled awake. Light and heat spilled from me in radiant pulses, discharging outward in a brilliant burst. I saw Irian shade his eyes in the moment before the world went blindingly white.

My vision returned slowly—little more than bright blotches dancing over blackness before I began to register shapes once more.

The bog cats had disappeared. And where they had crouched, snarling and staring, was a path, cloistered with silver-branched trees. Beyond them, I glimpsed a glen ringed in jewel-bright flowers. Flaxen leaves crowned trees swaying like sheaves of wheat.

"I have been here before." My experiences in the Deep-Dream painted the inside of my mind. "I know this place."

Irian wiped his eyes but did not sheathe his sword. If anything, his demeanor grew even more defensive: his jaw tightening, his mouth thinning, his shoulders bunching.

"Lead the way."

We strode forward, caught between familiarity and strangeness. The glen was not quite the same as my dreams. In the waning light, the wildflowers were sparse, more weeds than wonder. The sky was no diorama of visions; stars pricked in the east as a half-moon lowered. The dilapidated house seated cantankerously in the center of the clearing was indeed thatched with birds' wings—a thousand different shapes and hues. But instead of shimmering and lustrous, a cascade of colors spun from rainbows, the feathers were dingy, ragged, faded.

I swallowed something like disappointment. Memories of what I'd seen in the Deep-Dream layered over me—my father, sliding inside and barring the door behind him as Talah hammered at my defenses. *Little deer, little deer.* Finally, I managed to gird my courage and stride to the house. Irian loomed at my shoulder, clearly unwilling to stand farther away.

I lifted my fist.

The door opened of its own accord. The cottage's occupant was not a faceless shadow, but a man. A *human* man. Neither young nor old, but somewhere in between. Tall, but not towering. Handsome, in the grand, distant way of statues carved of kings, tempered by a tired kind of ordinariness that made him too human to be truly legendary. Dirty blond hair, gray at the temples, fell over his shoulders; piercing eyes an indeterminate shade between green and brown fixed on me.

"You are late, daughter of the forest." His accent was strange—lilting and archaic. I glanced at Irian, unnerved. He was frowning, his stark brows slashing to shadow his silvering eyes. "What kept you?"

"Those were your bog cats, I presume?"

He snorted. "Feeding strays with what I produce in excess does not signify ownership."

I remembered what Irian had said about secrets and regrets. I quashed sympathy for the stranger before me and said, "You have a familiarity with me I do not pretend to share. Who are you?"

He seemed as put off by my language as I was by his. His gaze slid to Irian looming at my shoulder. His eyes narrowed with deep distaste. "Go away, heir of feathers."

If we had been anywhere else, *with* anyone else, Irian would have probably pierced the man's throat with the Sky-Sword and never given him a second thought. Instead, with incredible restraint, Irian satisfied himself by folding sinewed, tattooed arms over his sculpted chest and saying, "*No.*"

The man pursed his lips, exhaled, then swung the door wide, wordlessly inviting us in. Inside, the walls were not plaster and whitewash, but a maze of parchment and vellum. Each scrap bore scrawled notes, sketched maps, and cryptic symbols. Thin cords of twine crisscrossed the room like the web of a maddened spider, pinning together faded letters, charred fragments of books, and smudged charcoal illustrations. In the rafters, birds roosted noisily—owls and crows and pigeons and nightingales, their feathers rustling like leaves in the dark. The floor was littered with their waste, and the place stank of a henhouse.

I made no move to step inside. Irian was a statue at my shoulder.

"My name is Marban." The man faded into the shadows of the cottage. "And I have been expecting you."

I glanced again at Irian, eagerness and dread twin pulses in my throat. He lifted one shoulder in an eloquent shrug, as if to say, *We came all this way.*

I stepped hesitantly into the cottage, Irian ducking under the lintel behind me. Marban fussed over a low-burning fire, stirring the coals and setting a kettle to boil. On the mantelpiece sat stacks and stacks of notebooks, hand bound and stuffed with more notes and scraps of parchment. The sight of them stirred a nauseated sensation of *knowing* within me.

"What is all this?" I asked softly.

"The pattern," snarled Marban. "A tapestry woven by hands whose perfect skill seems haphazard—each thread pulled taut to form a picture you only recognize once it's too late to change!"

I shrank back from his fierceness, and he mastered himself.

"Forgive me." His tone dropped, though bitterness coiled his voice. "I have had no company in a very, very long time. My manners are rusty."

Standing sentinel before the door, Irian made a noise somewhere between a growl and a laugh. His frame loomed hilariously large in the small cottage.

"You know who I am." I gingerly took the spare seat beside the fire. "You know why I'm here."

Marban stared into the shifting layer of coals for a long minute before speaking. "A new Treasure degrades the delicate balance already upset by the original Treasures. Magic teeters on the brink as the worlds once more prepare to go to war. And you wish to know how to unbind the greatest bindings that have ever been wrought. So the Solasóirí bound to the Treasures may go free without destroying the vessels."

"That's...about it." I blinked. "Gavida implied that you were a scholar of bindings. Do you know how it may be done?"

"Perhaps." His strange eyes—green and brown glowing gold in the firelight—lifted to mine. "But first I have a tale to spin. Will you listen?"

Did I have a choice?

"Once, in a time of fractured realms and missing magic, a young prince of Fódla swore to his family that he would be the one to return what the Fair Folk had stolen—the magic bound by Gavida in the four Treasures spirited away to Tír na nÓg." Marban's voice curled like smoke, collecting in dark corners and pooling in the rafters. "He was fair of face and fleet of foot and huge in his own importance. Using all his wiles, he laid a trap for a Treasure. But it was sprung instead by a Gentry maiden of exquisite beauty. She escaped his confinement and fled back to Tír na nÓg, shutting the Gate behind her. The prince should have given up. But he had fallen impossibly, irrevocably in love with the only woman he could never have. So he broke his oaths, abandoned his duty, and made for himself a cursed home in the place he had set his trap, built brick by brick with stones he quarried by hand."

The words rang with haunting familiarity as vines of destiny threaded around me like a living snare. I shivered with the creeping knowledge that I had been bound to this path I could neither see nor escape for longer than I understood.

"But you—" I struggled to remember what I'd guessed about the warrior whose fate had, for a year and a half, seemed to parallel mine, even separated by a millennium. "You did not stay in the human realms. You found a way to build yourself a bridge. To connect Dún Darragh with Tír na nÓg. You wrought one of your geasa droma draíochta—your inviolable magical bindings. And you caught yourself a Corra."

Marban did not seem surprised by my knowledge of the sprite. "One does not *catch* a Bright One. But I did perform a binding, in much the same way Gavida did with the Treasures."

This revelation punched through me with the force of a tree root breaking through solid rock. "Corra is...a *Bright One?*"

Marban looked at me with contempt.

"I thought—" I clawed desperately for everything I knew of the obnoxious, irritating entity haunting Dún Darragh. I had always assumed they were some strange Folk beastie. But what had they actually told me about their origins? *We are broken hearts and old sorrows. We are crumbling rocks and empty glasses and forgotten hallways and the tolling of the bell in the highest tower.*

My head spun as if I had drunk a tankard of wine on an empty stomach. For a whole year I had lived under the roof of an ineffable being of unimaginable celestial power, and I hadn't even realized it? It was too much. It all made perfect sense.

"What element?" I asked faintly.

"You do not even know your dúile?" Marban scoffed. "Not only naïve but poorly educated too. My bloodline has degraded far indeed."

"There is no need to be cruel." I mustered haughty calm. "Unless you do not wish me to hear the rest of your tale."

Again, Marban fixed me with that look of resigned bitterness— as though this was not something he wished to do, but *had* to do. "You are correct: With Corra's aid, I built myself a bridge into Tír na nÓg—a path walked once, with no way back. My tribulations were great, but that is another story. I found Fionnuala and spent years wooing her—that, too, is another story. But our great love was doomed—she was a Treasure, and her bell was tolling its death knell."

By the door, Irian shifted his feet. The Sky-Sword let out a plain-tive note. Marban's eyes flicked toward him, then back to me. His mouth twisted.

"From all I had learned in the human realms, I knew there must be a way to dissolve her bond to the Sky-Sword without corrupting the cycle of magic. The balancing is eternal—"

"But not immutable," Irian finished, his voice low. "What did you learn?"

"Every binding can be overridden by another binding, if it is more powerful than the one before. And the most powerful magic of all—"

"Is a willing heart," I finished. "*Our hearts were made for breaking; that magic made for mending.*"

"Those were the words of a younger and more foolish man." Marban jerked, as if in pain. "Upon the night of Fionnuala's tithing, I offered my willing heart in exchange for her life."

"You offered your life for hers?" I interrupted, aghast but impressed. It was what I had done, in the last moments before Irian's tithing beneath the Heartwood.

"Do you think a *willing heart* is the bleeding red thing you pull from your chest? How rudimentary." Marban looked disgusted. "You, of all people, ought to know that magic is not so literal. No, child of my brother's children—I did not cut an organ from my body and offer it to Fionnuala while I lay dying upon the ground, as the stories like to tell. In offering my willing heart, I sacrificed that which I loved most in the world. *Her.*"

A cold vine twined my spine, caressing each vertebra with a deliberate, chilling thorn. "What do you mean?"

"Fionnuala's life could be saved, in return for an oblation." Marban put his head in his hands, as if, even after a thousand years, this pained him to discuss. "The Solasóirí are governed by laws we are not—and never will be—privy to. Laws of balance in nature. Laws of time and the cosmos. Laws of darkness and light. Laws of beginning and ending." His voice held accusation, although I knew it was not for me. "Notions of human morality—or even Folk morality—are wholly inconsequential to them. All that matters is counterpoise. And in the infinite balancing of the cosmos, love weighs larger than life. It is a force that outlasts the fleeting span of years and burns with a brilliance few things can match. It etches itself upon the stars' patterns with vivid thread, enduring where life inevitably falters. It shapes the world long after the hearts that kindled it have stilled. Love is the most powerful force in the universe."

A strange kind of satisfaction flared to life inside me, even as Eala's mocking words from Emain Ablach echoed in my mind: *Is that still your grand message? Love conquers all?*

"But that is because love is a sacrifice larger than life," Marban continued, his voice shaking with an emptiness I could not comprehend. "And demands far more than death."

"Tell me," I made myself say, although I was not sure I wanted to know.

"I believed my sacrifice would be romantic love, ripped directly from my heart. It was a price I was willing to pay, in return for Fionnuala's near-immortal life. But in the end, I did not choose the price. The magic did. And it was far higher than either of us anticipated." He held up a hand. "Fionnuala!"

A dove fluttered from the rafters, a glowing vision in the dim. Her pale gleaming feathers were as lustrous as fresh-fallen snow. She came to rest on Marban's fist, graceful wings poised. Her dark, knowing gaze carried the weight of centuries. Marban lifted the bird to his face, and she nudged a sleek head against his grizzled cheek.

Nausea churned in my gut. "No."

"As she tithed away her Treasure, my willing heart bought her life," Marban confirmed. "Just not one in her Gentry form. Our love was not annihilated, but made perfect—at least, according to the rules of balance. Eternal and unrequited. I am doomed to love her forever, in whatever form. And she me, although I have only her cooings to confirm it."

Horror pressed me deeper into my chair. I felt Irian's eyes scald my face, but I refused to look at him. Refused to acknowledge the radiance lurking below my skin, the way our love had been resigned to an arm's cruel, infinite length. The way my own destined sacrifice coiled inside me like roots beneath frozen earth—pressing, twisting, aching.

"But you are human," I said woodenly. "How have you lived a thousand years?"

"I do not know." He gestured forcefully toward his walls. "Do you think I have wished to live so long? Under such circumstances? I can only hope that once I have bestowed what knowledge I can, I will be released from this awful half life. And may be reunited with my love in the afterlife, if one exists."

Sorrow burbled inside me. "You believe that my arrival heralds your death?"

"Yes," he spat, "and I am glad for it."

We all sat in silence as the fire crackled and the birds rustled in the rafters. Then I straightened in my seat and said, "Then tell me all you know, great-uncle. And we will leave you to die in peace."

Again, Marban looked at Irian with venom. "Leave, heir of feathers."

Irian went hard all over, his thumb ghosting over the hilt of the Sky-Sword. I pleaded with my eyes—I would not speak of my fate in front of him. Finally, he slowly stepped from the cottage into the night beyond, shutting the door behind him.

Marban cleared his throat, leaned close, and began to speak.

It was nearly dawn when I emerged from Marban's cottage, dazed and nearly delirious with all he had told me. The sky was leaden, the smudged gray of ash. Irian stood a dozen paces from the cottage, facing the woods in silent vigil.

What did he think about when he lost himself to his duty? Or was it easier not to think at all, when confronted by the endless darkness before the rising dawn?

"Irian." I longed to wrap my arms around the sharp cut of his waist, to slide my hands up the front of his jerkin and clasp myself to his hard torso, to lose myself to the heat of his skin. Instead, I wrapped my arms around my own ribs, trying to hold myself together in the aftermath of my terrible, enlightening council with Marban. "It's time to go."

The gray half-light turned Irian's face to a mask of hard lines and stark angles, a specter of sorrow foreseen. Irian was no fool—he may not have heard everything Marban had to say to me, but he had sensed the edges of the truth, the weight of my secret heavy as a storm on the horizon. "Where would you have us go?"

The light along the tops of the trees was cool, glancing. A slight breeze ruffled the feathers molting eternally off the top of Marban's cottage and turned the smoke rising from the chimney to a ghost. I set my jaw and said:

"To war."

Chapter Forty-Five

Fia

Though I had heard both Irian and Chandi speak of it, I had never been to the Summerlands, one of the Folk enclaves situated near a Gate and ruled over by a barda. Or, in this case, *bardaí*—the Summer Twins, Siobhán and Seaghán, claimed joint sovereignty over Geata Tinne and its lands.

It was dawn on the next day by the time we arrived there, wending tiredly through the network of folkways crisscrossing Tír na nÓg like invisible tunnels in an anthill.

My first sensation was one of warmth. Although it was spring in both Folk and human realms, the rain was still cold and the nights brisk. This breeze teasing the short hair off my nape whispered of nights so warm you had to kick the blankets off, days so hot you longed for shade.

A sun golden as a coin was rising over fields shimmering with grain. Atop a green-grass tor, huge trees with full canopies of leaves towered, and when I peered closer, I saw bridges strung like necklaces between their trunks, windows carved in huge bolls along branches, balconies hemmed in bark looking out over the plains.

Tents like burnished gems spangled the hill toward the dell where we'd emerged, like a lady's jewel box spilled across green velvet.

We hadn't walked twenty feet before we were accosted by Gentry guards. Encased in lightweight armor the color of bronze, they shone resplendent. Helms glowed with crests of golden leaves; mantles of emerald were embroidered with recursive patterns of sunbursts, vines, and blooming flowers. Weapons lowered toward us—swords blazing like sunfire, spears tipped with crystalline points, arrows nocked on bows strung with threads of sunlight.

"Yield," said their captain, a willowy woman with hair so golden it hurt to look at. "Or die."

Irian made no move to draw his sword, though it hummed plaintively at his side.

"You will know me as Irian of the Sept of Feathers." His voice, though mild, was threaded with command. "We wish not violence, only sanctuary. We come seeking our friends."

The captain squinted at Irian before turning her glance to me. Although she did not seem to particularly like what she saw, she motioned for her fénnidi to lower their weapons.

"You are known to me, tánaiste," she said. "As are your compatriots, already arrived. In fact, they have caused quite a stir. Come."

Leaving her guards to their posts, the captain led us out across the plain, where bejeweled tents fluttered like earthbound kites in the hot wind. Freshly woken Folk peered out as we passed, beautiful and uncanny even rumpled and bed weary. I saw eyes like garnets and teeth sharp as knives and hair like rushing water. But this was no moonlit revel—these Folk were not here for pleasure. Stacked outside the tents were racks with armor like the bristling carapaces of poison beetles; weapons that called out my name as I passed, or hummed with menace, or seemed slicked with black blood although I knew they must be clean. Tension and violence sang through the Gentry host gathered here in the Summerlands, shivering me.

It occurred to me that *this* was what Eithne Uí Mainnín had fought when she incited the Gate War all those years ago. These were the people she had made her enemy and had somehow nearly defeated.

But the thought of the queen conjured something raw and wretched inside me and made me think of all the violence I was desperately trying to forget.

The warrior led us into the city of trees. It was a marvel—partly grown, partly constructed, the two fusing into something not quite either. Boulevards of lightweight stone climbed vast pines, alleyways and lanes branching off toward residences and shops tucked away in hollow trunks or balanced on platforms between sturdy branches. Ladders meandered upward; ropes dangled in complicated pulley systems. Resembling something between a bee's hive and a spider's web, the city crawled with Gentry and lower Folk alike.

At last we came to the biggest tree of all, a colossal conifer rising a hundred feet above the rest. A road spiraled its trunk; we climbed until we glimpsed golden spires and glass domes peering from spiked needles of sunlit green. The palace—for it could be nothing else—was craftsmanship and nature in harmony, its architecture rising seamlessly from the living wood. The tree's canopy cast warm-hued mosaics over balconies and balustrades; vines and blossoms adorned curved walls and open plazas.

"Welcome to the Summer Palace," said the guard as she ushered us before the bardaí.

The throne room was more an atrium than a chamber—a broad alcove nestled between two great branches, enclosed by a faceted glass dome. Layers of foliage were sealed within the glass, casting shifting patterns of color and light like a living kaleidoscope. Upon matching hardwood thrones sat two Gentry.

Siobhán and Seaghán were not what I had expected. They were, like all Gentry, unconscionably beautiful—Seaghán, tall and lean, with a mop of curling black hair falling over his diadem; Siobhán, petite but visibly strong, with dark golden curls cropped to her chin. They wore the raiment of their position—glossy silks in greens and golds, mantles embroidered with leaping stags and creeping foxes in threads of shimmering bronze.

That wasn't what surprised me. I had met a few of the bardaí—each more terrifying than the last. All, to my knowledge, had tampered with the warped wild magic released from the destroyed Treasures—the power that had bought their positions. But the Summer Twins had no visible alterations, no overgrown teeth or yellow eyes or fur-striped arms. The smell of carrion did not waft from them. Indeed, they seemed altogether normal.

Perhaps they were the best of the bardaí after all.

Or—it occurred to me belatedly—perhaps in reforging the Treasures, we had removed the corrupted magic and its effects from Tír na nÓg altogether.

"Irian of the Sept of Feathers," Siobhán said, her melodious voice carrying a sharpness I wasn't sure I liked. "Come at last to bend the knee, after all these years? Seaghán, tell me why we oughtn't make him grovel?"

"Because grovelers must lick boots," Seaghán said silkily. "And these shoes are my favorite. I'd hate to have them sullied by *his* mouth."

"No." I almost surprised myself by shouldering past a glowering Irian into the center of the throne room. The golden-haired guard lurched toward me, but I held up a faintly glowing hand without looking at her. She faltered, then fell back. "We're not doing this. Not today."

The Summer Twins stared at me, outrage and distaste and curiosity rustling in the silks they rearranged upon their thrones. I could only imagine what they saw—a nameless changeling girl with ragged short hair, wearing dirty clothes that did not fit her as she faintly glowed.

Finally, Seaghán said, "Not doing *what*, pray tell?"

"The song and dance." I twirled my finger. "You'll insult us, we'll insult you, violence will be threatened, blah-blah. We're not doing it." Siobhán opened her mouth, but I held up another forestalling hand and watched as her gaze darkened with affront. "Here's what we are going to do. You're going to welcome us into your lands and give us quarters near our cohort—Laoise of the Sept of Scales and Wayland, king of Emain Ablach. I know they're here, and I'm frankly a little shocked they've allowed you to continue sitting on those adorable little chairs." The twins' indignation slithered toward outright offense, but I wasn't done insulting them. I'd hardly begun. "Then you will send ravens or pigeons or whatever birds you use as messengers to the bardaí. Not just your allies—*all* the bardaí. You will summon them here. You will find some common ground where we may have a council of war. Tomorrow, if possible. In a few days, if not. Trust me when I say, there is no time to lose."

My pronouncement was met with ringing silence. At last, Siobhán gathered her composure enough to point a finger at me and hiss, "And who are you to command such things from us?"

I stalked forward, so fast both bardaí jerked back against their thrones. In my periphery, I saw the golden-haired guard lunge toward me again, only for Irian to step neatly into her path and body-slam her into the glass wall. I planted each of my palms on the arm of a different throne and stared at each twin in turn. Starshine spilled from my visible flesh, and I grinned as they shrank back from me.

I must seem a feral thing.

"I am Fia." Although I did not speak loudly, my voice rang in the domed chamber, dropping golden pine needles and waving fronds of ferns curling around the base of the thrones. "I am the daughter of a human king and a Gentry heir—the first changeling in a thousand years. I was suckled on magic, schooled on violence, and fledged upon love. I have battled monsters, bargained with gods, destroyed islands, and watched monarchs die. I was made of bloody wars and stolen magic and the pattern etched between the stars. I was made to bring balance back to our realms."

I pushed away from them, quelling the insistent glow emanating from my skin. I calmed my breathing, then commanded, "Get all the bardaí here by tomorrow. If you wish to live to see Lughnasa."

I turned on my heel and paced from the throne room. Irian, his smile sharp as a knife, fell in behind me.

We'd barely walked twenty steps before I heard the flutter of wings. I turned and watched eleven doves take wing into the shining morning.

I smiled, but the expression felt grim on my own face.

We were going to war. All of us—Folk and humans. Tír na nÓg and Fódla.

And me and Eala in the middle, surrounded by the restless dead.

❧

The golden-haired Gentry guard grudgingly led us to where our friends were ensconced. I had not been joking about my surprise in finding the Twins still sitting upon their thrones. Between Laoise's and Wayland's new powers and strong personalities, I'd half expected them to have already carved up Tír na nÓg between them like argumentative siblings forced to share toys.

Instead, they'd been forced to yet again uneasily cohabitate. I counted at least four of the seven young draigs, piled in corners and sprawled along low couches. Wayland and Laoise were, unsurprisingly, squabbling.

"...when I said you could work here, I did *not* mean you could work everywhere!" Laoise was shouting. "If I wanted to wake with ashes on my feet, I would have danced barefoot in the cookfire!"

"They are not ashes," Wayland yelled back. "They are—"

Both stopped talking when the musical tinkle of the beaded curtain heralded our arrival, their heads swiveling toward the door. Idris looked up from where he was reading on the couch; beside him, Sinéad paused polishing her daggers, which she had apparently not used on Chandi, who stood by a window, gazing out over the plains.

"Oh." Laoise looked much the same as before, with her tumbled red curls and sparking ember eyes. Her new tattoos were subtler than either mine or Irian's—dark red scales blending and rippling along the contours of her skin. "There you are."

"Not the reaction I was expecting," I said in an undertone, slightly offended.

"Chandi said you and Irian ran off on some new adventure without us," Wayland said, sounding insulted. The markings of his Treasure were flashier—cerulean waves inked in recursive whorls over the rippling contours of his bared biceps. "We wondered if you'd ever return."

"Yet here we are," I said acidly. "Where's Balor? Linn?"

"In the lower city—they call it the Underbrush. Balor and the aughiskies seem to be settling in well." Laoise scanned me from head to toe, quirked an eyebrow, and said, "What do you need? A bath? A meal? A stiff drink?"

"Can I get all three?" I passed a tired hand over my face—until the Bealtaine moon, I doubted I would find another time for any of them. "First, I need to speak with Wayland."

Laoise gave her fingers an irritated flick, as if to say, *You know where to find him.* Wayland glanced at me. Like Irian, his transformation had changed the color of his eyes—no longer the deep cobalt of oceans at midnight, but the mercurial turquoise of a shallow bay at dawn. The change startled me—somehow more harmonious with his features than the deep blue, it lent him a gravity I had not learned to expect from the playboy prionsa.

"Not a raven? Not a rider?" His easy smile assured me he had not changed so much after all. "Have we been so easily forgotten?"

"I think about you all the time—usually when I'm dodging trouble and wondering who to blame." I grinned back, then sobered. "Wayland, I need you."

He slapped his hand over his heart and threw back his head. "My four favorite words. But I fear I'm otherwise attached at the moment."

"Not like that and you know it." I rolled my eyes at Idris, who gave me a tepid smile. "Do you have a forge here in the Summerlands?"

"Yes, he does!" Laoise called from the foyer. "He just prefers to track his junk all over my kitchen!"

"I'll show you." Wayland made a rude gesture at Laoise's back, grumbling something that sounded like *She doesn't even cook.* "This way."

I shot Irian a rueful smile before following Wayland out the door and up a staircase winding around a slanted bough. A rope bridge wobbled onto another, larger bough. At the crook of two branches, a little hovel was built with a curved roof of emerald moss and a circular door with cracked paint. Even I had to duck to get inside. Beyond was a tiny workshop with a hundred tools and artifacts scattered over uneven tables and falling from listing shelves. A sputtering woodstove barely chased away the damp.

"You'll understand why I prefer to work in Laoise's kitchen." Wayland leaned back against one of the tables, folding his heavy muscled arms over his chest and kicking out his legs. He picked up a conch shell and held it out to me. "Here, listen. Something I've been working on."

I held the shell to my ear and was surprised to hear a voice—Wayland's voice. He sounded like he was reciting poetry. Abruptly he stopped, laughed. The sound faded.

"What is it?" I asked.

He shrugged. "I thought people might like to hear the voices of their loved ones even when they're far away. I've been enchanting vessels to carry voices."

"Lovely." It was. "But I need you to do something else for me. And I need it done by tomorrow."

He cocked his head, curious but wary.

"Before I became a Treasure, I was able to breach a Gate from dusk to dawn on the night of a full moon." I held out my arm, as if he could see beneath my skin to the green-dark blood beneath.

"It required my blood and an incantation. Do you think you could replicate the effect? To create a . . . *key*?"

"For a Gate?" His eyebrows lifted. "The Gates are powerful magic—they were forged in tandem with the Treasures, which have now all been renewed. I'm not sure your blood would be sufficient."

"Treasures can open the Gates at will." I leaned closer. "What if we *all* gave blood? All four heirs?"

Wayland frowned, reaching for a sheaf of vellum already half-scrawled with notes and ideas. "If we could somehow isolate that effect and amplify it—" He muttered to himself as he scratched charcoal over the paper. "Tell me why?"

"I need thirteen keys so I can give them to the thirteen bardaí. In return, I believe the bardaí will follow us into battle against Eala. True mastery over the Gates is all they've ever wanted."

"The bardaí." Wayland stared at me, then whistled. "They are dangerous bedfellows, Thorn Girl. You cannot count on their loyalty."

"I'm counting on their betrayal," I told him. "Will you please trust me?"

He gave me a considering glance, then nodded. "I can do it, although a day may not be enough time."

"Can you make me just one, then? Like a prototype?"

"I'll try." He shoved the paper at me. "Write your incantation."

I tried to remember the words Cathair had taught me over a year ago, while trying not to remember that he was dead. But when Wayland pulled the paper from my hands, I held on, careful not to let our fingers touch. Now that he was a full-fledged Treasure, my starshine was a danger to him as well as Irian and Laoise. And Eala.

"I have another favor to ask you. Well. Two, really."

"You know, I was actually beginning to miss you." He whistled again. "Remind me again where you learned to be so demanding?"

"I refer to it as persuasive," I said sweetly.

"Persuasion rarely involves a knife to the throat," he grumbled. "Metaphorical or otherwise. Go on, then. What invaluable services might I render you, milady?"

I sat heavily on a three-legged stool, pulled close another sheaf of papers, and tried to explain.

The bardaí began to arrive the next morning in their most extravagant regalia, surrounded by expansive retinues.

I'd left Wayland in his tiny workshop to return to the rooms the Summer Twins had given us, desperate for my promised meal, bath, and heavy pour of summer mead. Instead, I'd gotten a lesson on the current politics of Tír na nÓg from Laoise, which I only half listened to but could sum up: Everyone was still fighting. With the Treasures renewed, the wild magic many of the bardaí had drawn on for power had dissipated, leaving them scrambling for sovereignty in the vacuum Eala's retreat to the human realms had left behind.

That suited me fine. I didn't need true unity—I just needed the illusion of it.

Now I borrowed some clothes from Laoise, then descended with Irian into the Underbrush, a cheerful if unsophisticated slum below the city. Taverns and brothels and gambling dens were patronized by citizens of the Summerlands and soldiers from the encampments alike—I saw many Gentry concealed beneath hoods or hiding behind masks as they fulfilled their basest desires.

Balor wasn't hard to find—he sat outside a tavern whose roof barely cleared his shoulders, collecting bets on what appeared to be water wrestling. The main contestant was Linn, waiting fetlock deep in a spring-fed pond for her next opponent, a hairy gruagach whose gemstone eyes gleamed with greed.

"Balor!" I pushed back the hood of my mantle, shocked but amused. "Tell me you are not running a fight club down here!"

"Lady!" He stood swiftly, banging his head on a branch that wouldn't have been low-hanging for anyone else. "Lord Scary Husband! You have returned!"

Linn clambered from the pond at the same moment, shaking moisture from her dark mane and sea-foam pelt. She nudged her delicate nose into my shoulder, favoring me with an image of her dragging me into the spring instead of the gruagach and merrily dunking me beneath the surface.

"Is that your way of saying you missed me?" I gently stroked her inky forelock and smiled. "Now, if you lot are finished swindling the locals, I have some jobs for you."

Behind Irian, Abyss stomped his feet as if to say, *Finally, some honest work.*

The aughiskies' jobs were straightforward. For Balor, I hoisted myself onto the thatching of the tavern, then leaned to whisper my request in his ear. He turned his huge head in surprise, but the glimmer in his terrifying eyes was anything but lacking in comprehension. His smile revealed all seventy-nine of his sharp, rock-eating teeth as he said, "I thought you would never ask, lady!"

As afternoon pressed toward evening, I donned a hastily made gown I'd basically coerced from a poor seamstress in the Underbrush. Luckily, the greens and golds of the Summerlands suited the role I knew I must play—the resentful darrig had bolts of emerald silk and forest-green satin already in her shop. The gown swept low to the breastplate of red leather I'd wheedled off Laoise, exposing the Heart of the Forest like a beacon on my chest. I wore chain mail over my arms and belted the skeans I'd bought off a Gentry armorer at my waist. Chandi—still thin, still mostly wordless, but with a little color in her cheeks—helped me smooth my short hair until it lay like a blade against my throat. I painted my face to match my mood—blood, for my lips. Ashes, for my eyes. Fury, for my cheeks.

In the late afternoon, the Summer Twins paraded from the city toward the council table they'd erected beneath a vast tent in the center of the golden plain. I let them have their moment—as if they'd called this convocation, instead of me. As if they had any authority here at all.

Let these bardaí think they still had power. Let them think they had a chance of surviving the aftermath of this war.

When the sun grew low and the feasting and drinking were well underway, I mounted Linn in the Underbrush, sweeping my long train over her haunches. Irian swung onto Abyss behind me, with a long, searching look. I smiled, then urged Linn into the amber sunlight spangling over the plain. She cantered with a coquettish cadence, bannering her dark tail and arching her exquisite neck and flinging her graceful legs out long. An obedient breeze caught my skirts and my hair, swirling them like pennants against the massive trees at my back. Attention collected on me, until every bardaí and attendant and fénnid on the vast plain watched me, rapt.

I rode to the council table. Clucked to Linn, who reared up and launched herself with effortless ease onto the broad, oaken surface. She pranced the length of the table with willful, wanton slowness, her hooves shattering glassware and shoving plates to the ground as the revelers reeled backward with cries of outrage, tripping over benches and colliding with one another in confusion. At the center of the table she gave another pretty rear before planting her hooves, lowering her head, and chattering her shark teeth in warning.

I let my eyes travel over the assembled guests. The Summer Twins—seated at the far end of the table and nearly purple with rage—had been true to their word. They'd invited every bardaí. And every bardaí had come. Some I recognized—Dualtach of the Ivy Gate, whose grandchild Irian had cursed; Almha of the Elder Gate, whose daughter I had slaughtered. Many more I did not recognize.

Soon they would all be at my mercy. Not that I intended to give them any.

"Friends. Enemies. And all who dare stand in the shadows between. Hear me now." I owed Irian the well-placed breeze that carried my voice in all directions. "The hour of our reckoning is nigh. A foe waits beyond the Gates to the human realms—a foe we have faced before and, if we are not definitive in our victory, will surely face again. The name of our foe is Eala, she who they call the Deathless Queen...Grave Mother...or the Rotten Princess." A murmur rose from the host—some must not have heard these names before. "The time has passed for diplomacy—our only option now is war."

"Who are you to call us to war?" The voice was strident, grating—its owner hugely muscled and russet-haired. Although he had lost the vulpine cast to his features, I recognized him—just as ugly to me now as on the night of the Nameless Day, when he'd tried to assault me. If he recognized me as I did him, he did not show it. "If I wanted to follow a girl into battle, I'd play swords with my niece."

Linn sallied beneath me, my fury simmering against her own. But I held her in place, raising my voice to be heard by all.

"I will not tolerate derision, mutiny, defiance, or insubordination. This is not rule by many. There will be one general—me. There will be one battle plan—mine. Anyone who cannot tolerate that should leave now."

Half the bardaí and their retinues immediately stood and walked away, grumbling in disgust. I smiled and fished Wayland's Gate Key prototype from my pocket. A circular pendant on a long chain, it glinted in the late afternoon sunlight, swirling with fragments of red, blue, green, and silver. Blood. The blood of all four heirs, combined. The chain bore Cathair's incantation etched upon its metal. Wayland had described the other geasa he'd forged into the object, but the important thing was this: He believed it would work. It would temporarily open a Gate. Any Gate, from dusk to dawn beneath a full moon.

"To those who stay, I offer this: a Gate Key. The price of your obeisance is low when compared to the reward I offer in return—victory over Eala's shambling hordes *and* true control over the

Gates, which you have so long coveted." Those who had retreated all returned. I held the attention of the bardaí rapt, as I'd known I would. A finger of guilt slid around the contours of my ribs when I remembered Wayland's warning about the bardaí. But Eala's voice suddenly echoed through me, cool and conniving. *Among the many lessons our mother taught me was this gem: Alliances mean nothing. They are a means to an end.* If Eala could bend the bardaí to her purposes, so could I. And if I meted out a little of the punishment they deserved for all the harm they'd done? So be it. "It is a simple exchange. Swear your swords to me, and each of you will go into battle on the Bealtaine moon with a key around your neck. But you must swear now."

For a long, aching moment, the only sound was the wind sighing over the plain. A clatter of steel—a barda I did not recognize threw her scabbard upon the oaken table. Farther down, another heaved off his mace and slammed it on the polished wood. One by one, the bardaí wordlessly promised me their swords, swearing a loyalty I wholeheartedly mistrusted.

They had butchered the Septs. Destroyed the original Treasures. Planned to execute innocent human maidens for access to the Gates. And betrayed existing alliances with my sister, in favor of me.

I did not trust them as far as Donn's black gates.

Which was, coincidentally, exactly where I planned to lead them.

Chapter Forty-Six

Fia

Preparations for war began immediately.

More encampments were pitched on the fields of the Summer-lands, until the rolling plains looked like a cloth of gold studded with thousands of jewels: garnets and sapphires and peridots. The shouts of fénnidi and the clang of weaponry embroidered the air; smoke tooled the blue sky with charcoal.

I spent long hours with the bardaí, who bickered like ill-mannered children, unable to agree to a dinner menu much less a battle plan. When the drawn-out, maddening councils were finished, I repaired to Wayland's cramped forge, checking on the designs I'd already commissioned from him and helping him brainstorm new weapons and contraptions that might give us an edge against the living dead. I told him of Cathair's Eternal Fire, which I had sadly spent the night of my escape from Eala, and saw an answering fire spark in his eyes as his mind began to whir.

"That gives me an idea." His smile broadened. "Although I doubt it will be green."

What followed was a series of experiments, largely consisting of the draiglings spitting sparks into bottles of various liquids—culminating in at least one of Wayland's eyebrows being singed clean off.

Then I sat late into the night, poring over battle plans until I could barely keep my eyes open.

Irian came to me one of these nights. It had been about three weeks since we'd returned from Fódla—less than a week before the full moon.

"Fia." It was late—the waxing moon hammered the plain of the Summerlands to a silver shield. Everyone was sleeping—well, everyone save we four heirs. Wayland was almost certainly in his workshop; Laoise liked to keep watch over Chandi and Sinéad and her draiglings, who slept curled like puppies in a circular bed in one of the rounded bolls. "May I speak with you?"

I put down my sheaf of paper, scrubbed at my tired eyes. Irian knelt beside where I crouched like a goblin upon the low divan, bringing our faces on a level. I had not seen much of him these past weeks—though he stood behind my chair at council meetings and shadowed me through the tree city, we had exchanged little beyond cursory words. My secret lay between us like a widening chasm, turning every unspoken word into a rift neither of us dared to cross. It pained me to feel so distant from him, but I feared even more the hurt of recognizing my own looming death in his silver eyes—a mirror for the fate I feared I could not escape.

But I had never meant to keep it concealed for so long. It wasn't fair to me, and it certainly wasn't fair to him.

"Me first." I still kept Cathair's prophecy folded in my bodice—as if by its proximity to the yearning of my beating heart, I might change its message. I drew it out, skin-warmed and creased by folding, and offered it to Irian. "There is something I need to tell you."

"You must think me a dimwit, mo chroí." Though Irian gazed at the folded parchment, he made no move to take it. "To imagine I do not have an inkling of what you are planning for the full moon."

My fingertips cut divots into the ragged vellum. "Look at it, Irian."

"I do not wish to know, Fia." His words were both blade and balm—the stinging cut its own sweet relief. "I remember the Ember Moon. I saw what Talah did to you on the Silver Isle. I heard your old teacher speak the beginnings of a prophecy. And I heard Marban's cruel tale. This Bealtaine moon will exact a high price from all of us. I fear if I know what it is, I will find myself unwilling to pay."

"You do know," I said softly. "Our willing hearts."

"You are my heart. And I have sworn never to let you go." Despite his unwillingness to look at Cathair's prophecy, the weight of his gaze made me think he had already intuited its contents. "Though I have not always understood it, I have come to admire how deeply you care for both the realm of your mother and the realm of your father. I believe that you will do what is right, no matter the cost. Even if I wished to, I cannot stop you. So I will simply ask of you what you asked of me, before the Longest Night: Find a way to live for us all, instead of trying to die for us. Live, and no matter where you go or what you do, my love will find you."

I swallowed a sudden hot mass in my throat. "Is that a threat?"

His smile was slim and sharp as a trip wire. "It is a promise."

I took a deep, shivering breath, then tucked the parchment back into my bodice. "What did you wish to ask me?"

"I wish for a day."

The words didn't make sense. "What?"

"I know you are busy. But I wish for one of your days. And, if you are generous, perhaps a night. Of the few we have left before we go to war."

"A day you shall have." I untied the noose of dread strangling my heart and forced a smile. "What shall we do? Where will we go?"

He dared to curl a fluttering strand of my short silver-threaded hair around one of his large calloused fingers. "Somewhere you promised to visit with me, when we were back on Emain Ablach. If you still have the inclination."

"I do." This time, my smile wasn't forced. "We will leave with the dawn. Shall we fly?"

"No." He smiled back, although the angle of his mouth held a twist of pain that unsettled me. "Let us ride. The weather will be pleasant. And I do not wish you to meet my mother with vomit on your shoes."

We rode out with the aughiskies at dawn.

Irian was right—it was pleasant. Dew jeweled the waving grasses, and the air was cool and fragrant with loam and flowers. We cut through the heart of the Summerlands until we reached the shore, a glassy sea pounding black sand. We rode until the beach became bluffs, the bluffs became cliffs.

A strange apprehension gripped me as we dismounted—leaving Linn and Abyss to cavort in the warm, glassy shallows below the bluffs—and began to climb. The path was little better than a goat track, narrow and uneven and steep. Irian led the way, his steps sure as he set a brisk pace. How many times had he traversed these cliffs? How familiar were they to him still, after so many years away from his mother's house?

Did he, too, grapple with unnameable dread as he made his way toward a home that could never be his again?

We paused atop the cliffs. Far below, the ocean clashed and clamored, flinging salt spray to kiss our faces. The wind ruffled Irian's hair, longer now than I had ever seen it, fluffing it like an affectionate relative might a favorite nephew. It gave him a rumpled, boyish look that softened my inexplicable nerves.

"We are nearly there." His eyes were as brilliant as the ocean, as golden as the sun. Eagerness spilled over his features, making me ache.

There was so little softness or gentleness to Irian. It was not his fault—such things had been forced out of him at a young age. He was steel sharpened to a killing point, marble carved flat and featureless. But not with me—not always. His unguarded expressions were more precious to me than gold; his tenderness, a better balm than any tincture or healing salve.

Beyond a rocky bluff between the cliffs and the undulating moor, tucked within a fetching garden with a hawthorn fence edged in fruit trees, was a cottage. Smoke streamed from the chimney, although the day was warm. A few garden plots ridged the rocky yard. Bent over them, with a shawl over her hair and her hands covered in dirt, was Irian's mother.

"Do you think she'll like me?" I asked, with a touch of plaintiveness.

His smile was a ray of sunlight breaking from behind a cloud. "I know she will, mo chroí."

If she did, I couldn't tell.

She abandoned her gardening as we crossed the gorge, standing sentry over her garden gate. Despite her humble abode and isolated lifestyle, she was Folk Gentry—she had not been raised to shrink or simper. She stood nearly a head taller than me, her figure powerful. She wore no visible weapons, although I caught a glimpse of a dagger outlined beneath her kirtle. Her features were striking—she shared her son's sharp cheekbones and questing, distinctive eyebrows. Her eyes were gray as a stormy sea, piercing and intelligent. Her hair was so black it gleamed blue in the glancing sunlight.

"M—Moira!" Irian called as we approached, me a wary half step behind. "Well met!"

Like her son, Moira did not appear to enjoy the presence of strangers, but her expression eased as she realized who had come to visit. She unlatched the gate and clasped Irian in a friendly but dispassionate embrace. I remembered with a pang what he had told me on Emain Ablach: *She thinks of me only as a somewhat inconstant friend.*

"Irian, my old friend. It has been too long." Her voice was rich and warm as brewed tea. Her gaze scanned over me, curious. "Who is this?"

Irian ushered me forward, and I bobbed an awkward curtsy.

"My name is Fia." Her eyes were too canny. I abruptly felt two feet tall and ugly as a rock. I wasn't good with parents. "Madam."

"Madam?" Moira tilted her head and quirked one eyebrow in an expression so *Irian* that it unhinged something inside me. I fought the urge to laugh. Or cry. "Pray, what does it mean?"

"My...friend...does not hail from these parts." Irian shot me a glance that bubbled with mirth and seared with heat. I flushed a little. "But where Fia comes from, I believe it is an honorific."

"Well." Moira wiped her hands on her apron and gestured for us to follow her into the cottage. "No honorifics necessary. *Moira* will do. I was about to make lunch. Will you join me for a meal?"

"We would love to," I managed. "Can I bring anything in from the garden?"

I recognized some of the roots and vegetables in Moira's kitchen garden. There were spring onions and stripy little radishes and something blue I was happy to name asparagus. Beyond that, I was at sea. Translucent berries clustered thin prickled vines; flame-colored tubers peered from the rich dirt.

"Not those," Moira said, sharp, when I tried to dig them up. "They won't be ready until Midsummer. And then may only be gathered before the dawn."

I jerked my hands away, afraid to ask what would happen otherwise.

We loaded a bounty into her basket and carried it into the cottage. It was a spare, neat little house. Irian had called it drafty—I thought it cozy. A fire crackled in the hearth; blankets heaped over chairs; whimsical tapestries warmed the walls with bright colors and inviting shapes. As my eyes adjusted, I realized they must be Moira's creations—a generous loom set against one wall featured a weaving in progress. I wafted closer to it as Moira bustled around the kitchen and Irian set a kettle to boil over the fire. I ran my fingers over the warp and weft, not quite touching. There were a thousand threads in blue and silver and inky black, tugging at the edges of my imagination. I stared at the half-woven tapestry but couldn't tell what the picture was meant to be.

"These are beautiful." A swift glance at the walls showed me a hundred splendid stories, picked out in painstaking detail using thread and imagination. Wind-racked seas with sunset-hued salmon dancing above the waves. Lovers racing across bloody moors as they were pursued by enemies. A wild hunt streaming across a stormy sky. "Are you a weaver by trade?"

"My—Moira is a seer." Irian poured hot water into a teapot and set out a few cups with a pot of honey. I stared a little. I'd never seen him so domestic. "As she weaves, she glimpses the future and spies the past."

"It's useless magic," Moira said, matter-of-factly, as she sliced bread and stirred stew. "The past is gone and cannot be changed. The future is malleable but not fully formed. And I never see anyone I know or care to seek out."

"I daresay living on a cliff at the edge of nowhere with no one but the gulls for company lends itself to a small social circle," Irian chided, gently.

Moira *hrmph*ed. "I have no great love for Folk, nor they for me. I cannot bide idle chatter."

I smothered a laugh. Like mother, like son.

Lunch was delicious. Crusty brown bread warmed over the fire, a vegetable stew that was both light and hearty, tea that tasted like a dream of summer to come. Despite Moira's protestations, we chatted about idle things. Irian inquired after Moira's herd of whimsy rams, which I gathered were sheep magically bred to produce colored wool so it did not have to be dyed before spinning. In response, she made an irritated noise deep in her throat.

"The whole herd jumped off a nearby cliff one cold autumn morning and flew away south." She dunked her bread in her stew. "No one told me the damned things migrated for the winter. So I'm back to dyeing my yarn with yarrow and beetroot as the living gods intended."

Eventually, I relaxed enough to ask about her garden and all the wondrous things growing in it, and she was happy to share her secrets for keeping slugs at bay and fending off weeds. She rattled off the names of plants I'd never heard of, and I listened intently, filing them away.

As if I was ever going to get the chance to plant my own kitchen garden. In Tír na nÓg... or anywhere else.

When the food was gone and the plates all cleared away, the mood shifted, subtly but perceptibly. I did not have to touch Irian—or even look at him—to understand how difficult this was for him. He must relish this rare closeness to the woman who had borne him, raised him. He must also dread the inevitable goodbye, made all the more grievous for the fact that she did not remember him.

Could never love him.

We put it off as long as we could, until the sun began to slant sideways through the rheumy panes. Moira fidgeted in her chair, her fingers moving in unconscious patterns as if she was eager to light her candles and begin her weaving. At last, Irian stood, and I with him.

A shaft of dust-shimmering sunlight landed on a tapestry on the far wall, distracting me. Not one tapestry—many, hung one atop another, all different shapes and sizes but layered in a thick stack. I frowned, glancing around to confirm that all the other tapestries were hung singularly. Curiosity got the best of me, and I crossed to inspect it.

The weaving showed an image of a man, tall and dark-haired, wielding a naked black sword as he faced down a massive yellow-eyed, dark-mawed ollphéist amid skeins of dense fog.

Realization shivered through me. It was Irian.

I jerked the hanging to look at the one beneath. Irian, a little less tall, standing beside a mahogany-haired boy on a white cliff above a blue sea. Gnarled golden trees crowned a hill far above them.

Irian, hollow-eyed and hungry-cheeked, pursued by faceless enemies across flowering fields.

Irian, hair grown out and eyes haunted, as he carried a limp female figure through a metal-streaked canyon. Above, specks of red circled against an azure sky.

Irian. They were all Irian.

Wonder and worry shoved my gaze to his. His eyes were fixed on the many-layered tapestries, as if he'd never seen them before. Emotions gusted across his face—hope and longing and rock-hard resignation.

How many times had he been forced to confront this awful pain? And how many times had he returned for more?

"What are these?" I heard myself ask.

Moira looked up from her teacup. She frowned, levered herself from her chair, approached on measured footsteps. When she saw which tapestries I indicated, her frown deepened.

"I'll thank you not to go nosing where you have not been asked." Her tone was stern and unyielding as a cliff, but her eyes were soft. Albeit distant.

"But—" Again, my eyes flew to Irian, who was gazing now at his mother, the same softness lurking in his own eyes. "Who is he?"

"I told you—I rarely recognize the figures who appear in my visions." She turned abruptly to Irian. She *must* recognize him—if not as her son, then at least as the same man who graced her tapestries. But her deep gray eyes settled on him with nothing save mounting irritation. "Your friend lacks manners. Perhaps it is time you go."

Guilt settled like scurf atop the river of my mounting grief—why had I soured this precious, fleeting time with Irian's mother by demanding answers to intrusive questions she could never answer? The true tragedy of Ethadon's twenty-year-old geas was obvious to me now. Though he had stolen Moira's memories of her only child, he had not stolen away her inborn gift of clairvoyance. She still glimpsed Irian, his past and perhaps even his future—the thread of her love stronger than Ethadon's curse. Yet she could not recognize her son even when he stood two feet in front of her.

My eyes burned with tears. Of all the Folk curses I had witnessed, this was among the cruelest. For Moira and Irian both.

Irian uncovered a long, narrow tapestry lurking near the bottom of the stack. I realized with a jolt that it depicted a colossal oak tree, with vast autumnal branches stretching to tangle with its lofting roots. A full moon kept the dark at bay. At the base of the Heartwood, two figures stood—both clad in black, their faces hidden as they gazed at the holy tree. Their hands were joined by a ribbon of black and a ribbon of green.

"This one." Irian ran his fingers gently along the threads and asked, "May I have it?"

The question jolted Moira. Her palm flew to her chest, resting over her heart before drifting thoughtlessly down to rest on her stomach. "No. They are mine. He—he is mine."

Mastering herself, she gestured briskly toward the door. She did not notice how Irian's face shattered in the moment she turned away, vulnerable as he faced the reality of his mother's condition.

"Really, now." Moira's tone grew caustic. "It's getting late."

It was time to go.

Chapter Forty-Seven

Fia

We stepped out into a fine early evening. Breezes winnowed over the moor, sending patches of vivid heather and vibrant gorse nodding. I inhaled, tilting my face toward the setting sun and letting it chase away some of the sorrow Moira's curse had conjured in me.

"I'm sorry." I turned to Irian, whose eyes were shadowed beneath the hair sweeping over his face. "I daresay she didn't like me much after all."

He laughed a little. "She is an ancient cantankerous recluse. She liked you as much as she likes anyone."

"From your lineage, that's practically a confession of love." Irian's smile grew, and I reveled in it, his joy more precious to me than sunlight. "But I am sorry. I think I ruined the afternoon with my prying."

"You ruined nothing." Irian's smile faded. "What my mother and I had was ruined by my father long ago. It is I who should apologize, for clinging to the fragments of something I once cherished but is now broken beyond repair. The edges never grow less sharp. And now I have cut you, as I have myself."

"No." I longed to embrace him, to let closeness comfort us both. "These are the hurts that matter. For if we did not feel them, we would know we had stopped truly living."

Irian's gaze burned hot on my face, and his hand drifted as if he wished to touch me. He reluctantly forced it back to his side, dragged his eyes to the horizon. "The sun lowers. If we wish to make it back to the Summerlands by nightfall, we should return to the aughiskies."

"Let them frolic," I suggested, letting a note of wickedness creep into my voice. "Unless I am much mistaken, we may be blessed with one or two new little murder horses come next spring."

"Scandalous." Irian raised his eyebrows. "And us? Are we to bed down in Moira's whimsy ram barn?"

"The night will be warm." A sudden burst of nerves made my voice meek. I surreptitiously patted my pocket, ensuring what I'd brought from the Summerlands was still stowed securely. "There is something I wish to see before we return."

Curiosity flared to light in Irian's eyes. His voice thrummed low as he asked, "What, pray tell, is that?"

"Once, in a time of hidden heirs and harmless adventures, a little boy found his way into a garden where he was not meant to go." Irian's eyes flashed, and I inhaled, battling my own hollow hope. In the Deep-Dream the Bright One had told me, *Deirdre lives.* I doubted she had spent the last twenty years languishing in the garden where she'd once been imprisoned. But I wanted to see the place where my mother was shaped by earth and sky, where she and young Irian had woven their friendship through whispered tales and shared wonder. I might never lay eyes on her, never hear her voice. But perhaps, in standing where she once stood, I might brush the edges of her memory. "Will you take me there? Will you show me Deirdre's garden?"

An emotion stronger than regret and sharper than hesitation arrowed over Irian's face. Then he straightened, threw his cloak over one shoulder, and beckoned me forward.

"It would be my honor, mo chroí. And my delight."

The moors ridged away from Moira's cottage like a restless sea, punctuated by great smooth stones curved like the backs of whales. We followed a white-capped river scything sleekly through the rock until we reached the edge of a moss-draped woodland painted gold by the dying sun.

Though I saw no path, Irian stepped confidently through verdant undergrowth studded with flowering vines and barred by saplings. How long had it been since anyone had come this way? I brushed my hands over the smooth, sighing trunks of the trees, but their concerns were root deep and earth dark and had little to do with our passing.

At last, Irian stopped, glancing around in the falling gloom.

"Now, let me see if I remember..." He frowned, took two sweeping steps, slanted his body sideways, and *disappeared*.

"Irian?" A thread of panic twined my voice. "Where are you?"

A hand reached from nowhere, gripped my sleeve, and tugged me sideways. Vertigo spun me, and I nearly stumbled. When I looked up, Irian and I stood in a world wholly changed.

The garden shone with dark beauty. Although overgrown and neglected, it had once been magnificent. Unlike a normal garden, which basked in daylight, this one stirred awake with the falling dusk—drowsy blossoms unfurling, fronds aglow in twilight's hush. I turned, breath caught in quiet awe.

"I thought you said it was walled," I managed to whisper, looking back the way we'd come.

"Walled by magic." His smile was little more than a lush lip curled over a gleaming canine. "Folk see walls and want to climb them. It is far harder to covet what you cannot see."

Deirdre's garden was certainly worthy of coveting. Rambling beds of flowers nudged over arbored pathways arched with hanging roses. Hedges made labyrinths studded with statuary and jeweled with broken lanterns. The paths meandered up a gentle rise, necklaced by once-shimmering fountains and crowned by a delicate pavilion gleaming like mother-of-pearl.

"She...lived here?" Unexpected sorrow gnawed at my heart, sharp-toothed and seeking. Whatever hope I carried of finding my mother here disappeared—this place had clearly been abandoned for decades. "Alone?"

"She had Folk nursemaids," Irian told me. "I remember a ghillie named Lanae, who used to shoo me away with a thistle broom. I'm sure there were others. It is common for Gentry children to be tended by lower Folk."

I was silent, remembering my own strange adoption by the Folk of the forest. I supposed it had not been so different an experience to my mother's upbringing.

"She never left this place until she came of age?" The garden was exquisite, ethereal. But it was quiet and very, very empty.

"Deirdre was incredibly lonely." Irian's voice thrummed, ghostly, in the descending dim. "I like to think I brought her some companionship, in her darkest times. But I was young and brash and boyish. She was elegant and wise beyond her years. I doubt I was much to her beyond an amusing distraction."

"I'm sure you brought her great comfort." I longed to squeeze his hand, to curl my arm through his. The thought sent a sizzle of heated anticipation buzzing along my skin. I inhaled and pointed toward the knoll. "I'd like to see the pavilion."

We wended our way along the paths, huge milk-white daturas nodding at our thighs. Roses the color of shining beetles' carapaces tangled around our boots. Still fountains caught the last of the sunset's carmine rays until they looked filled with wine.

Shallow steps led us to the pavilion, where quartz-streaked pillars lofted toward an arched ceiling. Diaphanous curtains—now tattered by wind and streaked by rain—sighed softly. Scattered pillows, frayed and filthy, lumped between divans with broken legs and shredded upholstery. Gossamer lanterns in the shapes of stars and moons and nameless marvels swayed gently on chains hung from the ceiling.

Twenty years ago, this would have been utterly beautiful. A gilded, glamorous prison for an heir with a cursed destiny. Different by far from my childhood in Rath na Mara—Deirdre would have been bored, not bullied. Cosseted, not trained. Doted upon, not driven to prove herself to those who did not understand her.

Irian leaned against one of the cobalt pillars, watching me intently. "What are you thinking, mo chroí?"

"How did she while away all those long years by herself?"

"She was educated in the manner of all Gentry heirs." Irian tapped one of the hanging lanterns—once, twice, thrice. A cool, pale light blossomed. "History, law, magic, warfare. And when she was finished with her lessons, she loved to dance. She was agile as a doe, and as sure-footed. She sang like a nightingale. But mostly, she adored stories." He lit another lantern in the center of the pavilion, illuminating a far wall ridged with rows of empty, broken shelves. "There were once a thousand books upon those shelves, stacked three deep and towering far higher than even I dared climb. Scrolls from the farthest reaches of Tír na nÓg, parchments in languages neither of us spoke. She would read me her favorites, on the nights I snuck into her garden, again and again, until the rhythm of the telling became music on her lips." His eyes, silver now as night descended, glittered far away as stars. "That is what she did to while away the hours. She devoured stories and, in turn, was consumed. In stories the tyranny of her fate was transcended, the mundane transformed to marvels."

"So it is with all tales." I lifted a hand and beckoned Irian toward me. "Come here, mo chroí. There is a story I wish to tell you."

Irian did not move a muscle. "Fia—"

"Come." I unfastened my cloak from my shoulder and swept it onto the cool pavilion floor. I knelt, lifting my eyes to Irian once again. "Please."

He made that glorious noise in the base of his throat, then pushed off the pillar. His steps were careful as he approached. He unclasped his own mantle and layered it over mine, then knelt to face me. His eyes were full of muted longing and harsh uncertainty.

"Once," I began, haltingly, "on a night of murdered maidens and smoldering moons, a man and a woman stood in a sacred grove and pledged their lives to each other." Irian's gaze darkened like a thunderhead. I forced myself to keep going, even as nerves fluttered like dark moths inside my chest. The prospect of rejection reared inside me, and I wished I did not have to be the one to put aside my pride and make myself vulnerable. But I had spoken the terrible words that broke our marriage. So, too, would I have to speak the words to mend it. "But their bond was sundered by cold contempt and violent pride. Now, with the sounds of war lofting on the rising wind, and time pinched like a pauper's purse, the woman wishes to ask the man—" I trailed off, the words of my poor story clumsy on my tongue. Irian's eyes shone, luminous but opaque. "Irian of the Sept of Feathers, pulse of my heart. Mo chroí. Will you marry me...again?"

For an endless moment, Irian was statuesque and silent. When he spoke, it was barely above a whisper.

"Is that truly what you desire, mo chroí?"

"Yes," I said simply. "No matter what becomes of us in the next week, I wish the world to know that you are who I have chosen. If, when this is all over, we may be allowed to live, then let it be as man and wife. And if I must die—"

"Do not." Irian's expression warped with anguish. "Please do not speak it out loud."

"Who will hear me?"

"I will." His tone brooked no argument. "And the cruel stars within their devious pattern."

"Very well." I fought gratitude. For I did not wish to say it either. "Well?"

"Fia of the Sept of Antlers, pulse of my heart. Mo chroí. I will gladly marry you again." His eyes roamed my face. He clasped his hands before him, as if he were a penitent. "But how? When I may not touch you? When I may not kiss you?"

I swallowed and withdrew the little packet I'd stashed in my pocket that morning. The long silken ribbons—one green, one black, embroidered all over with delicate vines and sharp feathers— had been easy to acquire. The same surly darrig who'd made my gown had charged me double her usual rate, but I'd gladly paid it. The ring had been more complex. Wayland had studied me closely when I plunked the starstone on the table and awkwardly explained what I wanted.

"This is for him," he'd asked, carefully, "isn't it?"

There was nothing for me to do but nod. A week later, Wayland had handed me the ring, still buzzing and warm from his magic. When our fingers almost touched, I could smell the scent of his flesh sizzling from my star-touched heat. He'd held on to the jewelry a moment too long.

"Bed him well, Thorn Girl." His smile danced on the edge of mischief, but his turquoise eyes were serious as drowning. "Bed him well."

Now Irian watched with perplexity as I held the circle between us.

"I have heard humans wed each other with rings, mo chroí," he said, with a laugh. "But I was under the impression it was the men who bestow the jewelry upon the women. Is this for me?"

"It is for me." I held it by the band, a slender loop of cold metal glossed with an iridescent sheen. I was careful not to touch the plain cabochon of dark, pitted starstone Cathair had let me take from his workshop. "From the moment I touch the starstone, all the celestial magic imbued within me will be channeled into the ring. But the effect will not last long."

Understanding gusted over Irian's features, carrying with it a complex mixture of hope and desire and loss. "How long will we have?"

"An hour, perhaps." My research on the material had been inconclusive. "Maybe a bit longer."

Irian exhaled. "Then let us waste no time."

He plucked the ring from my grasp. Examined it, though there was not much to see. Then carefully slid it onto my finger without touching my skin.

The cool band glided over my knuckle; the weight of the stone rested upon my skin. Cold numbness gathered at my crown, sliding down my face in rivulets, as if someone had dumped a bowl of ice water over my head. I gasped, and the tingle intensified, coursing over my shoulders and pooling in my stomach before being pulled like a magnet toward my left ring finger. My flesh began to glow, my veins lucent as all the starshine in my body concentrated into a cascade of heat and light. I whimpered, the intensity of the sensation almost unbearable.

Light flared from the ring, a fierce corona of starlight slashing outward. Irian and I both covered our eyes as it blurred through the garden, then sizzled back inward. Slowly, I dropped my hand. The ring on my finger now glowed with white-hot radiance, too bright to look at but cool to the touch. At least, to my touch.

Tentatively, Irian reached for me. The tips of our fingers brushed. He inhaled but did not pull away. His eyes lifted to mine, silver as moonlight on dark water. He pressed his palm to mine, his rough, calloused hands dwarfing my smaller fingers. Then gently—so, so gently—he slid his grip to circle my wrist. I mirrored the gesture, his arm beneath my fingers, corded with sinew and fletched with feathers.

"Fia." His voice was a low rasp.

I swallowed. "Irian?"

The barest smile touched his perfect lips. "The ribbons."

He took the black one; I grasped the green. Beneath the Ember Moon, our handfasting had been rushed and unplanned—the black ribbon had been a skein of Irian's feathers, stolen from his anam cló; the green ribbon, a length of thorny vines, torn from my dress. These were but an echo of our memories embroidered upon the fabric of our intent. Who we had been and who we would become layered into one, even as we, too, were joined.

Irian wrapped the black ribbon around his wrist and over our joined palms, then looped it over my arm.

"Blood of my blood, and bone of my bone." A breeze leapt

around us, rustling flowers and rocking lanterns. Lilac and lavender made a posy for the wind. "I shall not permit thee to wander alone."

Six months ago, I had been wild with sorrow and hesitation. Tonight, I felt only a certainty that bordered on inevitability—as if Irian and I had always stood here. Would always stand here. In this perfect moment, forever.

"Give me your heart and let it be known." I murmured the next verse of the vows, even as I looped the green ribbon in counterpoint to Irian's. "That then, now, and after, you are my home."

Magic rippled between us, sweet as a long-awaited homecoming. For the briefest moment, our skin seemed to fuse, our bodies becoming one. Blood to blood, bone to bone, heart to heart. My forearms buzzed as elegant black feathers took wing along them, settling in loose, harmonic circles between the tangled vines of my markings. At the same time, briars snaked between Irian's pinions, delicate but sharp.

Whatever magic I had spoken into ruin that wintry night in Emain Ablach had been repaired. Nothing was ever lost so completely it could not be found again...nor broken so deeply it could not be reforged. The fractures we'd borne had not vanished. But time, light, and love had healed them, turning fragile seams into gilded lines of strength.

Irian's grip on mine tensed. He pulled me closer, gentle but inexorable. The ribbons fell away from our hands as his palm slid around my waist. His other hand cupped my jaw, fingers light as feathers as he drew my face to his.

"My wife." His breath on my lips tasted like cold steel and frosted dawns. "My world. My heart. *Mo chroí.*"

Chapter Forty-Eight

Irian

Irian kissed his wife, her lips soft as velvet and her breath sharp with desire.

His wife. His *wife.*

Even in the darkest chapters of their love story, he had thought of Fia so. When he had believed her dead after the Ember Moon, she had still been his wife. When her anguished words had sundered the magic binding them before the Longest Night, she had still been his wife. When she had clawed him and fought him and surged over him with eyes of silver, she had still been his wife.

Fia had always been—and would always be—Irian's wife. But to hear the words spoken aloud, to inscribe the vow anew over all that had been written and erased, again and again, felt like a new covenant. An oath made in the language of old stories, inked upon the parchment of their fevered skin, and sealed in defiance beneath the syzygy of savage stars.

She is mine. I am hers. Come what may.

Irian dragged Fia closer and she melted into him, slipping her hands over his chest and tangling her fingertips in the hair growing long at the nape of his neck. His tongue slid against her soft lower lip, delving between her teeth and forcing her mouth open on his. His arms caged her as she crashed against him, fingers fumbling on the buckles of his armor, grazing beneath the hem of his under-shirt, and rippling the muscles of his torso in their wake.

Irian had never been much for intoxicants—self-possession his sharpest weapon and his strongest shield. But the allure of Fia's sweet mouth on his was headier than human ale, the temptation of her soft body pressed to his more ambrosial than áthas. He was already drunk on her, and he wanted more. Always *more*.

She drew back an inch. His lips already missed the imprint of hers. "Why the rush?"

"You said we had but an hour." Her heartbeat slanted beneath his palm. How he had *missed* her. Missed *this*.

Her head tilted. "That is plenty of time."

He growled, low in his throat, and flipped her onto her back upon the softness of their cloaks. "Not when I plan to make you come *at least* twice."

Kneeling over her, he swiftly finished the haphazard job she had started on his armor, undoing the last few buckles and tossing it down. His shirt followed. Fia propped herself onto her elbows to boldly admire him, and he could not help but return the favor—the lantern light shivering over her dainty chin and the ripeness of her parted lips and the sleek angles of her collarbones winging above her shift. He folded himself over her, drawing her arms above her head as he kissed along the column of her throat. Wedging his thigh between her knees, he deepened his weight between her legs. She gasped, bucking her hips, and ecstatic heat surged to life inside him, tightening the muscles of his stomach.

"Only twice?" Her laugh was raw with desire, ragged with affection. It made him delirious—to be wanted, in the same way that he wanted. To be loved, in the same way he loved.

He smiled a little as his fingers found the ties of her bodice. He unlaced them, deft. "It *has* been months."

"Yes," she breathed. "It has."

But when Fia's dress cascaded away to bare her graceful arms and trim waist and perfect breasts, he made no move to touch her. He longed suddenly to memorize her—to map the shape of her lips upon his skin, to imprint the color of her mismatched eyes upon his heart, to engrave the curves of her body upon his darkest reaches. To carve her very essence onto the marrow of his bones, so that when the world unraveled, he would still hold every piece of her inside him.

Not in a thousand lifetimes will I ever let you go.

Only then did he touch her, splaying a hand that felt too rough against the softness of the skin above her heart. "Once, I lost you. Twice, I have wed you. Forever, I will love you."

Fia bit her lip with pleasure but could not hide faint melancholy. She laid her palm over his hand, until their heartbeats aligned. Hand to skin. Skin to hand. "Forever is a long time, Irian."

"A moment or an eternity—it is more than I hoped for." The words slipped easily from his mouth. He meant them. "*You* are more than I hoped for."

Fia's eyes widened, and he knew she remembered—as he did— another night. Another cloak laid upon another floor. Another farewell.

"We have had enough of bitterness," Fia murmured. "And there will surely be more to come. Let tonight be sweet."

She was right. Tonight should not be a goodbye.

"What have I told you, colleen?" He forced away solemnity, allowing his mouth to quirk sideways. "About calling me *sweet*?"

Irian drew back onto his knees, lifting Fia with him. She let out a faint sigh as he settled her in his lap, slinging her legs around his tapered waist. His hands eased her dress the rest of the way down her arms to pool around her hips. A sly little breeze followed the path of his hands, pebbling her flesh and peaking her bared nipples. She gasped, and he dared to palm her breasts, pushing them up as he bent his head to roll his tongue over the sensitive flesh.

Arching into the touch, she tangled her hands in her own hair; the starstone ring shone like a blinding star against the night sky of her glossy dark head.

Fia settled her weight deeper into Irian's lap and swept her hands over his rigid chest, the flexed lines of muscles ridging his stomach. His trousers strained; her fingers on his waistband fumbled to free him. He groaned, dropping his head to her shoulder as she began to slowly stroke him, nearly losing himself to the ecstatic thrill of her deft, delicate touch. His hands found the hem of her dress; he shoved it over her knees, over her thighs, all the fabric puddling around her waist. His fingers dug into her rear, pulling her abruptly closer, as he pressed his length against the damp fabric of her underclothes. Anticipation pulsed through him. He could not resist her.

Sudden shyness flicked Fia's eyes up to the bright glass lanterns fluttering in the lilac-scented breeze. "Should we dim the lights?"

"Let me look at you. Let me touch you. Let me taste you." Irian shook his head. "Let me devour you with all my senses."

Fia did not argue, merely bent her head to capture his bottom lip with her mouth. He pushed aside her underthings to where her pleasure blossomed. He slipped one finger inside her ready wetness, then another. She gasped against his mouth, rocked against his touch. Murmured meaningless words like *please* and *more* and *yes*. Her easy, sweet surrender to him unraveled a measure of his control, and he suddenly could not bear to be anywhere else but inside her.

She made a noise of complaint when he drew his hand away. But the rest of him was already nudging against her, his proud length seeking her heat. She braced her hands against his chest, then eased down onto him with aching slowness.

Irian held himself perfectly still, his eyes locked on Fia's face and his arms bracing her weight. He clung to the last of his restraint as they fused—face to face, chest to chest, belly to belly. No longer just themselves, but something more. Something *whole*. Then the sensation of her around him—glorious wetness and agonizing tightness and wonderful warmth—finally shattered him.

His hands tightened on her rear as he closed the last inch between them with one powerful thrust. Together they fell, like the seasons or the rain or the stars unlatched from the high heavens. It was a descent they both made willingly—a dissolution, an unraveling, a splendid undoing. A controlled dive into the depths of each other.

Fia fractured, her sharp cry of release belling between them. Her legs strangled his waist as she rode out the waves of her climax, and he fought not to follow her over the edge. Not yet. Petals rained around them, soft as memory and sweet as song. Irian buried his face between her breasts, breathing in the euphoric scents of crushed moss and new leaves. When Fia softened against him, he rolled briskly atop her, covering her with his frame as he thrust even deeper inside her. She drove him on with her heels in the small of his back, her hands on his shoulders, her lips dragging perilous kisses against the column of his throat.

"Colleen," he growled, even as he kept his pace careful. Exacting. Excruciating. There was already so much heat, so much want, so much yearning between them. Any more, and he was sure to lose himself. "You are not making this easy on me."

Her laugh was little more than a gasp. "You have never enjoyed *easy*, my heart."

"When you put it like that..." His thumb brushed over her lower lip. "I never do refuse a challenge."

She parted her mouth and drew his thumb between her teeth, swirling her tongue over the tip. All the iron will of him hardened— he pushed ever deeper inside her, driving her toward another peak. She arched against him, writhing and bucking as the lantern light splintered over their sweat-slicked bodies. The garden sighed a midnight melody, buoyant and breathless as it blossomed in profusion, scenting the air with a thousand luminous flowers.

"Wait." Fia could not catch her breath. "Wait for me, and I will come with you. One more time. But you must give me a moment."

Painstakingly, Irian slid out of her. He braced her stiff fingers between his hands as she shuddered, kissed gently down her neck as she gasped and moaned. His need for her was a clamor he could hardly deny. But he would never demand anything of her she was not willing to give.

"Colleen," he murmured against her salt-damp skin, when at last she stilled. "Can you take me now?"

"Yes," she whispered. "Irian, *please.*"

Her words broke him. Or perhaps remade him. She rolled onto her stomach, lifted her hips once more to his. He twined his fingers in her short tresses. Kissed down her neck, kissed the length of her shivering, quivering spine. Kissed over the curve of her perfect rear. His need was an unflagging press against her tenderest spaces.

He was reduced to sensation. Or, perhaps, elevated beyond thought. There was nothing but her earlobe in his mouth. His chest between her shoulder blades. Her skin, molded to his. His hard cock moving inside her. His palm over her stomach; the ecstatic glide of his hand between her thighs, moving in rhythm to his unfaltering thrusts.

He climbed toward the sublime, his movements turning relentless. Stars burst behind his eyelids as his climax struck him like a blow to the chest—insistent, insatiable. He bowed over Fia as if in prayer, clinging to the sanctity of this joining. An apotheosis of all that they were to each other. All they had been. All they might never be again.

And in the end, it was just him and her. *Them.* Gasping and pleasure racked as they lay in the easy circles of each other's arms. Beyond their circle of light, the garden had run riot, resplendent in the night. Above, stars wheeled like the gateway to eternity.

At last, Fia turned to him. Irian pillowed his head upon one arm as he slid the other over her waist and tugged her close, until their faces were inches apart. He glanced at her ring—it had begun to dim. They did not have much time left. Something in his gaze betrayed him—Fia's eyes shifted, her lingering pleasure melting away beneath something akin to dread.

"Irian, please." The repetition of the earlier plea that had brought him such pleasure now brought him only pain—a reckless spill of rage and sorrow. Fia blinked, as if to quell tears. "What did I say about bitterness? I do not wish tonight to be a goodbye."

His hand tightened, his fingertips digging divots into her waist. "Then you are indeed to be torn from me."

She swallowed—he could not bear the trembling bob of her throat. She leaned forward until her forehead was pressed to his chest. His heartbeat thundered, too fast and too loud.

"No—do not tell me how. For then I will be forced to try to stop it. Only tell me how I am meant to bear it."

"This is how." Her lips inscribed the words upon his skin. When she drew back, her expression was composed. "On the Longest Night, I forced a promise from you. Tonight, in exchange for our wedding vows, I release you from it. Irian, my heart—it is time to let me go."

Abruptly, the pressure in the air shifted, popping his ears. Briefly, a great weight was lifted from Irian's shoulders, and he felt impossibly free. The livid scars of all the nights shielding himself against scales or claws smoothed away; the ragged bruises of holding Talah off as she writhed silver-eyed above him faded. All that remained was the wonderful lightness of Fia's *nowness*—her smooth softness in his arms, her sweet glow in the wake of their lovemaking, her threadbare strength in the face of looming tragedy. He savored it—he savored *her*.

And then he reached up and settled the familiar weight back down upon his shoulders.

He was strong enough to bear it.

"No." Gently, he tilted her head back, forcing her eyes to his. Fia had once called him a poet, but he suddenly found words the poorest weapon in his arsenal. How did he express to her that no force in the universe could keep him from his oaths to her? He would throttle the stars, destroy destiny, defeat death itself if it meant he could but *hold* her like this. Forever. "Would you unbind me from every promise I have made you, mo chroí? For I have sworn to love you for all your sharp thorns and churning shadows. I have vowed to adore you through all the seasons of our lives. And I have pledged not to let you wander alone—I care not whether that means I walk beside you or carry you in my arms or yearn for you from a distance."

Fia bit her lip, as if to hold in words she feared to speak. In the flickering lantern light, her mismatched eyes were glazed with unshed tears.

"No, Fia. I will never let you go." Irian's hands cupped the nape of her neck, the curve of her cheek. "Rather, I will make you one more promise: Even if you must go where I cannot follow, I will find you. Even if I cannot see you, I will yearn for the sight of your face. Even if I cannot hear you, I will long for the sound of your voice. Even if I cannot remember you, I will still love you with every throb of my heart. And when at last we find our way back to each other—and we *will*, whether in this life or the next, in this form or another, as sifting ash or distant starlight—I will revel in the chance to relearn your name. Colleen." He cupped the back of her head and kissed her, long and slow. "Mo chroí." He kissed her again, deeply. "Fia."

The air shimmered with the force of his geas. His lips tasted of the salt of her tears. The darks of her pupils shone with the choices she would reckon, the sacrifices she would make, the lives she would save.

If it had been up to him, he would have let both worlds burn.

It was not.

Irian was not a good man. But he thought he finally understood what it meant to love a good woman.

Carefully, deliberately, he disentangled himself from his brave, beautiful wife. Her hair uncurled from his cheeks. Her arms unlooped from his chest. Her fingers unhinged from his.

Gently, Irian let Fia go.

The stone on her finger audibly cracked, falling free from its casing. All her starshine came rushing back, heat and light flooding the space between them. Irian fisted his hands, then forced himself to relax. He rose to his feet, draping his mantle around his nakedness. When Fia, too, moved to dress, he raised a forestalling hand.

"You should sleep," he told her softly. "I will keep vigil."

"Thank you." Her eyes shone up at him like stars. "Nothing could ever make me forget tonight."

"Come, mo chroí." He summoned a smile. "You said we must not speak of goodbyes."

He pulled on his boots and buckled his armor. By the time he was finished, Fia had fallen asleep nestled in her cloak, soothed by the violet scents of lavender and eglantine.

He crouched beside her, ghosting a hand above her rumpled hair and wishing he could savor her dreams. Did she dream of something sweet, as he so rarely did, like a cottage garden and the taste of blackberry wine? Or did she dream, as he so often did, of violence and death and regret?

He stood. The Sky-Sword murmured a little lullaby as he drew it from its scabbard—it knew as well as he that no blood would be spilled here tonight. Still, he held it before him as he stood watch, examining the glittering stars etched into its inky blackness.

As midnight turned toward dawn, Irian made a bargain with the night. He drew his thumb along the blade of his claíomh, then smeared silver along the bevel.

"Let her live." The arcane metal swiftly drank his blood, leaving only darkness behind. "In return, I will endure any torments. Give me her pain so I may hurt; give me her death so I may die. I am strong enough to bear it. Only do not make me bear losing her again. Let her *live*."

The breeze picked up his words and carried them toward the horizon. Over the land, down the cliffs, across the sea. Into the dark, and the brightness beyond. Carried them so far he dared hope someone heard them.

Dawn came hard and leaden as battle metal. Fia stirred awake to the distant sounds of war drums mingling with the bugling of carnyxes upon the lofting wind. She glanced up at him with a desperate, doleful question.

"I asked for a day. " Irian smiled so he would not be tempted to weep. "One perfect day. And now it is done."

Chapter Forty-Nine

Fia

Dusk on the Bealtaine moon came too soon, lowering like a dark blade over the throat of the world.

"My friends." Sunset burned a warning through the windows as I stood in the center of our shared apartments and addressed my friends—my family. We were most of us dressed for war. I wore armor I'd commissioned from an armorer in the Underbrush—crafted from lightweight, flexible leather and dyed black as night, it was embossed all over with the same design as my tattoos—sharp thorns interspersed with sharper feathers. The pauldrons were spiked, fanning out from my shoulders like dark wings; the helmet I carried in the crook of my elbow bore lofting silver antlers. Beneath it, I wore the green dress from the council, yet again cut away above the knees for ease of movement. New skeans hung from my hips, heavier than I was used to, along with a pouch where I carried some of Wayland's forgings. The Heart of the Forest rested atop my breastplate, green as moss.

Irian wore his customary black, with the Sky-Sword singing a melancholy dirge at his waist; Laoise, her red-gold scale mail.

Wayland was naked to the waist but painted all over in blue, with Fáilsceim strapped to his back in leather bracers. Sinéad was fearsome in dark leather and darker kohl, her daggers already drawn. Only Chandi and Idris were not prepared for war—neither was a warrior, so they had been tasked with watching the draigs too young to join the battle. Hog hid beneath the divan, crying softly; Enfys and the twins curled in the window, watching their three eldest brethren soar above the massed armies of the Folk.

In the days since Irian and I had returned from our sojourn, I had spoken to each of my friends privately. I had shared the last of my plans with them, told them everything Marban had told me. It had not been easy; there had been tears and recriminations and anger. Yet here we all stood. None of us wanted to say goodbye to who we'd been. To who we were to one another. To who we might never be again.

And yet...no goodbye at all would be so much worse.

"My friends, you all know my plans. The plan I have told the bardaí...and the plan I have told you. Heed me well when I say, for the last time—although it may controvert everything you hold dear, let the bardaí lead their hosts in the vanguard."

"It would be dishonorable for them to do otherwise," Irian grumbled.

"They have no honor," I reminded him. "Instead, we count on their pride. Even as you deny yours. You must stay to the back of the host. All of you. Protect the Willow Gate. And when midnight approaches—when the full moon is at its zenith—you must retreat to the Heartwood. Do you understand?"

They all hesitated, then nodded. Grimly, I returned the gesture.

"Good. Then it is time to go to war."

"Just like that?" Wayland huffed a laugh. "Thorn Girl, we have got to work on your motivational speeches."

Irian growled, low in his throat, even as Wayland slung an arm over his foster brother's shoulders and dragged him in for a half-willing hug. His other arm, he looped around an equally enthused

Laoise. But then Laoise was throttling her brother, who slung a familiar arm around Sinéad's back. Sinéad reached for Chandi, pulling her tentative figure firmly into the tightening circle. Irian's gloved hand rested at my waist. We bent our heads, reveling in this last quiet moment of camaraderie.

"Thank you," I said softly. "I never had a family before. But I think I finally understand what all the fuss is about."

"Wait until we all get back here at dawn, bloodied and starving, and start fighting over the last piece of Idris's cloudberry pie," Wayland quipped. "Then you'll *really* get it."

Irian punched him on the arm, hard, and we all broke apart, laughing and brushing away surreptitious tears as we reached for weapons and helms.

At the bottom of the tree city, near the Underbrush, Balor waited— a huge, terrifying outline against the blood-streaked sky. Beside him were Linn and Abyss, their noses close together. Beyond, the sweeping golden plains churned with the waiting host—all gleaming armor and deadly weapons and keen, hungry gazes.

All the bardaí save Siobhán and Seaghán watched as I briefly conferred with Balor, then mounted Linn.

"Do you have the keys?" Dualtach asked, his voice like the shriek of an eagle upon a cliff. "We will not march without them."

Silently, I handed out the Gate Keys Wayland had crafted, glittering with strange symbols and shimmering with the heirs' entwined blood. Each bardaí grabbed one, gazing at them as if they finally had the human realms within reach.

Everything worth having came at a cost. I hoped they were ready to pay the price.

"Shall we?" asked another barda, nastily. "The moon will soon rise."

I held up a hand. Drums thundered, rolling like a tide. A carnyx sounded, the wailing ululation raising the hair along my nape and twisting my stomach beneath my armor. The Folk host marched toward the Willow Gate, silver-shod hooves pounding the earth beneath them. The tiny bells braided into the horses' manes and tails warbled like captive nightingales, the merry tune dancing amid the grim cacophony of scraping armor and clanging shields, marching boots and shivering spears.

We passed beneath silver beeches, thick branches pulsing with veins of moonlit metal. Bone foxes already paced us in the undergrowth—their slim-sharp forms eager for carnage. Rooks flapped amid the boughs, keen cries echoing between glass-bright leaves.

Beyond, the forest. Trees forged like spears and hammered into swords. Trees with masts like a great armada, sailing toward a sky etched with a million imperious stars. Trees like soldiers—each one brave as a lion and fearful as a lamb, their faces caught between life and near-certain death. Reaching beneath them, the bones of the earth: roots that would go on living even if this whole forest was burned to ash and ruin.

And us. The procession of grim, uncanny Folk was as strange to me as the first time I glimpsed such a parade, so many moons ago. Only now, I marched with them. Our songs of war sounded like howling wind over a cliff; our drums sounded like hollow bones; our horns sounded like the bugling of the Wild Hunt. We shone of metal and menace; we glimmered bold as bloodstains in the falling dark.

The Willow Gate's glade was a marvel of springtime—waterfalls of flowers, blossoms of white splashing the trees like spilled star-light. My wall of thorns stood, glinting in the dim like a mouth full of fangs. A balmy breeze caressed my skin, but it was scented with death. I did not need eyes to know *they* were still there. Impatient. Waiting.

I waited until the moon knitted silver between the leaves and the glen churned with restless fénnidi in all their regalia. Then I placed my antlered helm upon my brow, wheeled Linn in a tight circle, and cried to the host, "When the barrier falls, you must push through no matter what approaches us! Dualtach: You will lead with your key—the rest will follow in formation!" I raised an arm. "One...two...*three*!"

I shattered my barrier of thorns and branches and flowers, disintegrating it into sawdust and flower pollen. Dualtach galloped forward, and a cry went up as the host surged after him, slamming toward the Gate. The outlines of mangled bodies rippled its silvery surface, held back by the barest thread of magic. The moment Dualtach breached the Gate, they fell toward us. Bodies—ghouls and revenants—gushed through the opening, all dangling limbs and staring, empty faces. They met the Folk with a clash, the bright weapons of the host colliding with the thick thud of decaying meat. One of the draiglings—Blodwen, I thought—arced overhead, disgorging flames to harrow the dead.

Linn sallied, half rearing as warriors streamed around her and fire caught in the undergrowth. I looked around for Balor's huge shadow, then nudged her forward. But a large strong hand wrapped around my vambrace. From Abyss's back Irian stared down at me, his grip tight and his eyes hard as metal.

"I will find you, mo chroí." He leaned down. Hesitated for barely a second. Then slid his gloved hand beneath my chin, lifted my shining face toward his, and captured my burning lips with his mouth. He kissed me slowly, though his flesh blanched; ferociously, although it must have been agony. He tasted like whetted metal and dark water, dawn after an endless night. His hand on my jaw trembled as the host streamed screaming around us. When at last he drew back, he was burned—his lips cracked and blackened where he'd kissed me. He let me go, his hand slipping away from my vambrace to settle on the hilt of the Sky-Sword. "Live, Fia. *Live.*"

Irian's arms flexed as he drew his claíomh, tattoos lengthening and sharpening beneath the cut of his armor. Thunder grumbled above the canopy of the trees, and tendrils of lightning crackled along the length of the blade. He kicked Abyss forward, and together they plunged into the fray.

Linn and I followed. Irian cut a path for us through the shambling horde, then flung himself down before the Gate and began to fight in earnest. I could not help but spare him one last glance as I galloped past on Linn. As always, Irian fought like flame upon the end of a match, impossibly fast and exquisitely graceful, every leap and lunge like the steps to a dance only he knew. I wheeled Linn, jerking her to a halt at the top of the cobbled bridge and staring back, desperate for one last glance of the man who'd forever changed my life. His gaze whipped to mine, as if knowing exactly where I'd be—his eyes shifting from the feral menace of a man who had nothing left to lose to the heartbroken anguish of a man who feared he might have already lost everything.

Oh, *Irian.*

A Gentry soldier slammed into Linn's haunches, making her stumble across the bridge. We passed through the Gate—I crumpled inward, even as I expanded.

When I looked back, Irian was gone.

Roslea was in chaos. The forest churned with the dead—more plentiful than the trees standing black as sentinels in the moonlight. The Folk host fought toward Dún Darragh, but it was like running through mud. There were too many of them. Too many.

"Forward!" Balor shouted, stomping from the Gate with so much force that I half feared he'd shatter the bridge. He grinned at me, the moonlight making his plentiful teeth fearsome. "Ever forward, lady! Is that not the plan?"

He grabbed a handful of revenants—three or four at least—and bashed them skulls-first into a tree. His massive ponderous steps bowled over ten more ghouls like toy soldiers. Linn and I followed, as close on his heels as we dared.

But even Balor could not protect us from all of them. So many. They swerved at us and surged underfoot and climbed the trees to fall upon us from above. Linn veered—I flung one of Wayland's draig-flame devices, which slammed into a revenant before blooming on the ground around him, licking at the roots of the nearby trees. Sudden horror unfurled inside me—Roslea would be destroyed. But it was too late—all around me, the vanguard were also deploying Wayland's forgings, clearing paths through the forest toward Dún Darragh. Behind, closer to the Gate, another of the draiglings made broad golden sweeps over the forest canopy.

I swallowed my dismay. This was war. War claimed casualties.

Still, my heart bled for the innocent forest.

We pressed forward.

The next hours were a nightmare. Dead bodies and licking flames—stabbing swords and slashing spears and savage screaming. Linn was mad havoc—her shark teeth and eager hooves more vicious and effective than any weapons forged by human or Folk. The aughisky, Balor, and I made a strange but effective trio— barreling and biting and slashing out with skeans and thorns alike. The world narrowed to us, and our simple objective.

Ever forward.

Dimly, I noticed the vanguard of the Folk keeping pace with us, even as their numbers dwindled. I saw at least one barda fall, dragged from his mount by the ravening horde. I swore I saw a flash of russet hair and a pointed, vulpine face. I smiled grimly when he did not rise again. But the others stayed determinedly alive.

Fine. I needed them for a while longer.

We burst from Roslea into what had once been my grotto. The greenhouse had been utterly destroyed—the glass shattered, the metal twisted beyond recognition, the plants and clay pots trampled beneath a thousand marching boots. The spring was a cesspool of mud; the garden beds, little more than muck and dead weeds. I grasped my sorrow as if it were a serpent that meant to bite me, and turned it to fury—fangs and all.

"To the keep!" I screamed, pointing at Dún Darragh. Around us, Gentry warriors—gore-stained but not yet beginning to flag— hurled themselves toward the fort, blades flashing. Linn made to follow, her hooves nimble on the uneven stone, but I reined her back, dismounted abruptly, and laid a palm in the center of her elegant chest.

"Linn, no. This is where our paths diverge." I pressed my face into her mane one last time as she burned a brief image against the inside of my mind, blistering with hope—me exiting the fort's doors with dawn at my back and victory in my eyes. But I shook my head.

"You need to get back to the Gate. As fast as you can."

She chattered her teeth in protest.

"Run, Linn. This was never your war. And I know what you're expecting. You and Abyss deserve your peaceful waters and blood-thirsty family. Run!"

I slapped her rump, ungently. She kicked out, narrowly missing me, then sallied away. Her tail bannered out behind her. She leapt back into the fray, aimed for Roslea.

I dared a glance at the sky, calculating the angle of the lofting moon. About an hour until midnight. I squinted into the night, gazing across the lough. Were those riders on the road, or was it merely wind blowing over the grasses? Were those bombards, or hedge-rows? Were those lanterns, or the distant lights of Finn Coradh?

Where were the human kings and their armies? Again I worried that Cathair had not gotten word to them before he died.

A revenant flung itself onto my back. I ducked and rolled, slamming the thing onto its spine and swiftly sawing through its throat with my blade. Black blood gushed over my hands as I ducked another attack, then dashed after Balor, who was gamely filleting ghouls upon the shards of glass piercing from my destroyed greenhouse.

"Balor!" I cried at him. "Do you remember what we discussed?"

"I am your general, lady!" He grinned too broadly as he popped off a revenant's head like the cork of a wine bottle. "Hold the keep. No one goes in, and no one leaves."

"Especially the bardaí," I reminded him. "And when the human kings come—"

"I say, 'The leaders wear necklaces, and if you kill them, the rest will surrender.'"

"That's right, Balor." I nodded in grim satisfaction. "Thank you. Thank you for everything."

"Lady!" His smile grew somehow even broader as he used one

revenant to knock down ten others like bowling pins. "It is my absolute pleasure. I will see you when the battle is done."

I readied my skeans, then flung myself up the rise toward Dún Darragh. Only to come face to face with my sister.

Amid the clashing steel and shrieks of war, the princess sat unshaken atop her pale palfrey, clad once more in her silver breastplate and calfskin boots, with a man-at-arms I thought must be Rogan beside her. In the center of Dún Darragh's courtyard, a ring of stillness clung to her like an invisible shroud that not even the fury of battle dared touch. Violence raged and surged all around, but Eala remained poised and unwavering, her gaze as steadfast as the warped power she clung to.

I fought toward my sister, dodging revenants and Gentry warriors alike, until I burst into the circle of calm surrounding Eala. Only then did I see...

The tortured marks of her Treasure had mutated beyond fractures or spiderwebs, feathers or vines. Veins of black mold now veiled her, spreading across her porcelain skin; ribbons of dark lichen braided through her hair; a crown of night-dark mushrooms sprouted between the palisades of the silver crown resting upon her brow.

Eala had truly become the rotten queen.

Her eyes barely flickered to me as she stared out over the mayhem she had wrought. The cacophony of bugling carnyxes and thundering drums and clanging weapons and shrieking dead nearly drowned out her voice as she said, "Clever sister. You have eluded me longer than I expected. Have you come at last to give me what I want?"

"Remind me—what is that?" I needed to buy a little time. The full moon was not quite at its zenith. And I needed to give my friends as much time as possible to fight their way back to the Heartwood. "My willing heart? Or my head upon a pike?"

"If I cannot have one, then be assured I will have the other." In the uneasy shadows cast by the stark moonlight, Eala's features were veiled with darkness. She did not look at me, staring over my head at the crush and surge of violence. "For I cannot let you survive as either Fódla's heir or a weapon fit to destroy me and my children."

I edged closer. Around us, the battle raged. Here, it was just us—me, Eala, Rogan. This close, I could see that the horses—shockingly calm amid the chaos—were no longer alive. Disgust burned poison through me, and I glanced sharply up at Rogan, his face shadowed beneath his hood. He held a naked blade in one hand; in the other, his dead mount's mildewed reins. He wore gleaming ceremonial regalia matching Eala's, but ill-suited for actual battle. His eyes were gray and flat when he looked at me, but at least he still lived.

"Before I give you my willing heart," I hedged, "let me tell you what is inside it."

"Have you not blurted enough drivel to me about love, Sister?" Eala sighed heavily, as if this, of all things, was the burden she could not stand to bear. "Surely there is nothing left to be said on the matter."

"Once upon a time," I began, as if I had not heard her, "a dark, strange little changeling arrived in a castle in the place of a princess. A princess so fair and kindhearted and graceful that her light hardly cast a shadow. Except there, inside that small sliver of shadow, was where the changeling lived. She looked like the princess, you see—as much a blessing as it was a curse. She longed for the gods to change her enough to pass for that shining paragon. *Please*, she prayed. *Make my hair a little lighter. My smile a little brighter. My eyes a little kinder.* But they were not listening. At least, not in the way she wished. For appearances can be deceiving. And few can forget their true nature. Even those that might wish to." I paused, and Eala almost looked at me, her profile silver against the moonlight. "You see, in the stories, sisters are always two sides of the same coin. One fair as snow and the other red as a rose. One who speaks with jewels and the other who spits toads and snakes. One with a heart pure and true and the other with a soul like tar."

"In case you haven't noticed, Sister," Eala said, unkindly, "this is not a story."

"Indeed. Why were we forced into storybook roles when we ought to have been simply sisters?" I raised my hands toward her as if in supplication. "Can you imagine? The two of us, so close in age and appearance, running riot through Rath na Mara. Charming and defiant in equal, even measures. Wild and willful and wonderful. Step in step, arm in arm. How might we both have lived? How different might we both have become?"

"What do you wish me to say?" At last, Eala looked down at me, letting the moonlight spill over her features. Her face was hollowed in, her skin so cracked and fissured with rot that her features were nearly unrecognizable. Her diamond-blue eyes blazed like beacons. "That I would have let you play with my dolls? Lent you my gowns? Shared your secrets? Your little dream is just that—imaginary. Even if we were raised together, you would have never truly stood beside me. I would have still been a princess. And you would have been nothing more than the bastard get of a Folk harlot who couldn't keep her legs closed."

"I wished you to say that you might have loved me. As I surely would have loved you." I glanced at the sky—white light bleached the landscape to bone. It was nearly midnight. "If you had ever truly been my sister, I would have loved you. But thank you for reminding me that you never would have returned the favor. You do not believe I complete you, Eala. You simply want to use me—as you have used everyone you have ever known."

"If you will not give me your heart," she snarled, with a wave of her gloved hand, "then I suppose I must take your head. Rogan!"

With a stiff but practiced swing of his legs, Rogan dismounted. The steel of his blade gleamed silver in the moonlight as he bent his knees, whipped his cloak to one side...and charged at me.

I fought the paralysis of fear and sorrow, caught in a sudden whirlwind of long-lost memories. My senses dulled as Rogan thundered toward me across the courtyard, my attention narrowing to the drum of his boots and the hammer of my own heart. I wanted, suddenly, to run. To put this confrontation and this battle and this war behind me, and flee back to Tír na nÓg. Back to Irian. Back *home*.

I wouldn't have a home if I didn't fight. None of us would.

So I crouched. Pointed my blades toward my childhood friend. And prepared to battle the man I'd once loved for a future I wasn't sure I had.

Rogan thrust himself toward me. Our blades kissed, then parted with a scream of steel. I spun away as his sword sliced the air where I'd stood, then ducked back in to parry the blow. But when my skeans shrieked against his claíomh, I felt a strange resistance—as if Rogan had not used all his strength to strike me.

As if he fought his own violence.

"Rogan," I panted, too quiet for Eala to hear. "For the last time, you must *fight*. You are strong enough to resist her."

His sword came low this time, aiming for my ribs. I whirled away, the wind of his blade brushing my skin. I slammed one of my daggers into its sheath, then drove my shoulder into his chest. He stumbled but didn't fall. I hooked my free hand beneath his wrist and yanked, using his momentum against him. We collided as I trapped his sword arm between us. I twisted. Rogan's grip slid away like butter.

His sword came free in my hand.

"Yield," I cried, as I lifted the cold steel between us.

Rogan surged forward.

I fell back a step. Angled his claíomh higher. "Yield!"

Rogan twitched. Swiveled. And plowed chest-first onto his own sword.

The metal drove between the plates of his armor into his sternum. I jerked back instinctively, but Rogan's hands wrapped around mine, driving the blade deeper into his own torso. Blood gushed over the gilded hilt, slicking my hands. I screamed, the sound scouring my throat like shattered glass.

"No!"

Thorns splintered from the earth, dislodging cobblestones to rattle and rumble. Briars spiraled up into a tight, vengeful barrier encircling me and the prince. Eala was also screaming—her revenants lunged forward, breaking the bubble of stillness surrounding her. But I was faster—vast rosebushes surged toward the sky, thorns thick as forearms piercing between fluttering blood-red petals.

Rogan collapsed, his knees striking stone before he keeled sideways like a tree falling over. I flung myself next to him and gently—oh so gently—rolled him onto his side. I set my hands around the hilt of the claíomh jutting from Rogan's ribs. I wanted nothing more than to pull the blade from his chest—but for now, it was the only thing keeping him from bleeding out.

Again, I heard Eala scream in rage and frustration. The revenants groaned as they flung themselves onto my briars.

"The joy is in the thrill of the fight, changeling." Inexplicable amusement varnished Rogan's rasping, ragged tenor. "Not the promise of a kill."

A deadly arrow of anguish winged toward my heart. My eyes fluttered to his face—the face I'd known for as long as I could remember. Hard jaw, soft lips, bold brows. Eyes the same shade as the ocean below the hill at Bré, although they were shadowed now with agony. I wound my fist in his mantle, as though if I just held on to him hard enough, I might be able to keep him here.

"Idiot princeling." I tried to smile, but my lips wouldn't obey. "I'm not trying to kill you. I gave that up a long time ago."

"Good thing too. I have a feeling I'd already be dead."

I tried to laugh, choked. More blood stained my hands—it was welling from the wound, staining his tunic, pooling beneath him. His golden hair was already kissed red with it. Tears veiled my vision. I dared not let go of him long enough to wipe them away.

"That was a stupid thing to do, Rogan."

"The stupidest." He lifted a palm to my face. His hands were warm and rough with calluses—the same hands that had brushed wings of snow from my small shoulders, that had sketched a thousand charcoal drawings until his fingers were bruised black, that had caressed me in the dark. "But it was the only thing I could do. The only thing, in the end, that would set me free. And I am so glad, Fia, that I get...to die a free man."

Roses of bloodstained spittle bloomed on his lips. He coughed, wetly.

"You're not going to die." The words were a lie and we both knew it. The blade had slipped between his ribs, damaging something vital. It was not a question of *if*. It was a question of *how long*. "We've gotten out of worse scrapes, you and I. Come on—tell me you fancy fighting off an army of the dead with your own sword sticking from your chest."

"I would, changeling. I really would. But I'm afraid I've...given up standing. I'd rather just lie here." His face sobered, his crooked smile fading away. "Will you tell me something, Fia? Tell me... something true?"

The dead were flinging themselves bodily against my thorns, breaking their bones and leaving ribbons of their rotting flesh hanging from the flowers.

"Anything."

"Do you think...if a great many things had been different, that you and I could have been happy?"

I hesitated. Rogan saw. Pressed a thumb to my lips, as if to cage the words he did not want to hear.

"No, no. Don't answer that." He smiled, sweet and slow. A line of red dribbled from the corner of his mouth. "Let me tell you something instead. You were...the best thing that ever happened to me. You stole my favorite weapons. You ate the best bits of food off my plate. I'm still convinced you trained that one hound to bite me whenever I passed by. But you...were my best friend and I loved—I love—" Another sickening, slurping cough stole away his words.

This time his body racked with it, his spine curling as his head bowed. The blade shuddered, slicing deeper into his flesh. "I was so happy here—at Dún Darragh—although I did not know it at...the time. I had you all to myself, and I treasure those moments. Just us, and the greenhouse, and...the dirt on our hands."

"Stop talking, princeling." My tears were a deluge I could not stop. "You're driving the blade deeper."

"It's all right," he soothed, his thumb dragging salt along my cheek. "I don't deserve your tears. I have...never deserved your tears. Just know...how glad I am. That once upon a time, for a very short time, you were mine. As I have been...ever yours."

My voice was a caged and cowardly thing. Rogan coughed once more, and I knew he didn't have long. His life thrummed restlessly beneath my palms like a caged bird that longed to fly free. I had but moments with him. Why didn't I know what to say?

"Rogan—"

"You don't have to...speak. There is nothing to say that has not already been said. I would ask...but one thing of you." I nodded mutely. "Give me back to the forest, changeling."

"*No.*" I was not sure what I was refusing—his request, or his death.

"Don't you understand? If I die, I...belong to her. And I do not wish her to take me. She has taken enough. She has taken everything." My tears were a waterfall I could not dam. "Do you remember what you did to Eimar, our first night here? You told me once it was not death...just a different kind of life." I gave my head another shake. He clutched me in the moment before his weak hand fell from my cheek. The blue faded from his eyes, like the sun setting over the sea. "I'm sorry I didn't...understand before. But I do now. And I want it...more than anything in the world. Let me have that. Please."

What else could I do? I nodded.

He smiled, peace drifting over his features as his eyes slid shut. "It has been a privilege...to die for you. *Fia.*"

His life left his body on an exhale. I caught it in my hands, then slammed them onto the ground with a cry that stole something vital from my soul. The Heart of the Forest throbbed like a kick to the chest. Power flooded my veins and coursed along my bones, pouring into the earth below Rogan's motionless form.

I thought of his powerful figure, so tall and proud. Roots plunged between the cobblestones to the rock-splinted earth as a trunk coiled up, its bark the warm golden color of fair skin tanned by summer sun. I thought of his eyes, the mercurial blue-green of sunlit river stones. Moss jeweled the expanding spaces between his powerful roots. I thought of the shooting stars we used to watch from the high slate roof of Rath na Mara. Silver threads crept along his bark, poor adornment for his growing might. I thought of his hair, waving long and free over his freckled shoulders. The leaves bursting broad and true from his lofting branches were like hammered gold.

Ten feet. Twenty feet. Fifty feet rose the vast oak from the courtyard of Dún Darragh, until it towered nearly as high as the keep. And when the power thrumming through me finally slowed, I climbed to my feet, pulled the claíomh from where the trunk had nearly swallowed it, and stared up into the darkness between Rogan's branches.

"Rest well." I swiped tears from my cheeks with bloodstained fingers. "It will be a privilege...to kill her for you. *Rogan.*"

I turned. Shifted my grip on my blades—one long, one short. And bade my wall of briars to wilt.

The barrier collapsed. Hordes of thorn-shredded revenants lurched and scrabbled toward me. I dodged and feinted, slamming my dagger into soggy, rotting flesh as I struck out with Rogan's sword. I fought toward Eala. Between the surging hordes of the massed dead, I saw her gray palfrey retreat to the fort; a pale figure dismounted and pushed open the doors of Dún Darragh.

I smiled, grimly. Around the massive oak splitting the courtyard in two, I carved a path for myself with glowing fists and blades alike. Then Dún Darragh opened before me with a crash.

Chapter Fifty

Fia

The great hall arched above me. I let a little of my starshine slip, illuminating the four broad pillars, the curving staircase, the carvings etched into the stone. In the space of a breath, the flagstones trembled beneath my feet and the great hall split in half, cracking open like an enormous egg. My breath was silver dust, and the air was sharp with new-quarried stone. Laughter chimed, bright as a bell. A breeze curled sinuously between the broad ribs of enormous oaks. I tasted sweetness on my tongue, and the tang of scorched metal.

"Not yet, Corra," I whispered, to the air. "Not quite yet."

I sensed Eala immediately, standing at the top of the curving staircase, drenched in shadows dark as death. Her very presence was like a blot of damnation seeping sick and sour through the stones, tainting the grout and tarnishing the plaster. Killing the moss and lichen growing on the walls. Devouring the rats in the holes and the spiders in their webs until—

"Down here," I commanded.

"No," she hissed. "You are armed. I am not."

I dropped my sword and dagger to clang upon the flagstones. "It is as it was always meant to be. You and me. Face to face—no guardians or armies or weapons. Just Fia and Eala. Our Treasures. And our wills. Shall we see at last who is the stronger weapon?"

Eala snarled but did not refuse the challenge. She trod slowly down the stairs, and where her hand trailed along the railing, veins of blackness spread, cracking marble and furrowing carvings and sweeping the hall with the stench of decay.

"I will make you kneel," Eala purred. "I will take your heart. Then I will send your corpse into Tír na nÓg to ravage your Gentry lover."

I waited until Eala stalked close enough, her hands outstretched as if to choke me.

"There are times when you have made me bend. But for you, I will never bow." Then I crouched, planted my palms on the stone, and screamed, "Corra, now!"

Again, that feeling of the hall cracking open. Moonlight streamed in, dancing as if through broad leaves. I poured all the magic of my Treasure into the sensation, anchoring it to the earth, the roots, the branches. Shadows striped the wall, lengthening and deepening until I crouched in a forest at night, full of grasping branches and rough black trunks knobbed with faces. A breeze brushed my hair from my nape. Still I drove my magic deeper, awaking the ossified trunks of ancient oaks that for so long had been encased in stone. Bark replaced the sinuous carvings on the four massive pillars ringing the great hall; the arching buttresses lofting toward the ceiling began to sway as heavy boughs shook off their thousand-year slumber.

"What—" Eala reeled away from me, her back striking one of the massive ancient oaks. "What have you done?"

"Once, in a time of lovelorn mortals and haughty Gentry maidens." The ancient forest hooted and whispered around us, alive with a thousand fell faces and skittering woodland creatures. "A prince named Marban found a sacred grove near the edge of Tír na nÓg—one of the last bastions of magic in the human realms. He did not know it then, but the circle of four vast oaks was called a nemeton. He soon learned that the grove was home to a being called a Bright One—one of the Solasóirí who came to these lands long ago from the stars. He bargained with that being, whose name was Corra. He would build them a haven, a home—to protect them from the ravening eyes of greedy humans. In return, he asked for knowledge. And so he built Dún Darragh around the grove, with stones he quarried by hand, as Corra poured all their knowledge into his willing ears."

"A Bright One?" Fascination and avarice swept across Eala's ruined features. "What element? Which dúil?"

"Imagination. Creation. Story." Corra was everywhere—in every knot of wood and rustle of the branches and whisper in the night. "*Dream.* Corra taught Marban how to access the Deep-Dream, where nothing is real yet where everything may come to pass. And so he learned how to move between realms without use of a Gate. But he left this place, this *grove*, behind, albeit swathed in off-putting rumors of suicides and hauntings and curses. A protected pocket of vast magic. Hidden, dormant. Until now."

Eala said something, but I didn't hear her. My head snapped—a pull yanking me, like a string attached to my sternum. I felt them—even across the barrier between the realms, I felt them. A lick of fire. A trickle of water. A breath of cool air. I felt my own Treasure writhe along my arms, stinging as it caressed. And I felt the starshine harboring beneath my skin dart soft and pearly around my bones.

I stared at the moon, half real and half imagined, perfectly full and sailing high overhead.

It was time.

"By fire and by sky," I intoned, with only the barest shake in my voice. Eala's gaze widened, greed and then suspicion flashing in her diamond eyes. "By fast water and by ancient tree. By the power of my willing heart, I tithe my Treasure to thee…O Eala."

I closed my eyes. *They* were there, as they always were—corded muscles wrapped in russet fur, a face like the forest path, silver antlers chiming among the stars. They towered over me, but I was not afraid, and they were not threatening. Instead, they seemed mournful.

The cost will be high.

"I know." I gazed back at them, fighting my own grief as I asked, "What must I sacrifice? What price does balance demand?"

I knew what they would say before they said it.

Everything.

Wayland

Wayland should have worn a shirt. It hadn't occurred to him ahead of time, but the ravening hordes of the recently dead all had incredibly sharp fingernails. Scratches scored his chest from throat to stomach, rather ruining the illusion of *demigod spawned from the sea* he'd been aiming for.

Still, he managed to fight his way—covered in gore and striped with sweat—to the Heartwood. He had not been here in years— he had forgotten how colossal the sacred tree was. Festooned in brilliant bouquets of wisteria and eglantine, it struck him dumb. Fáilsceim fell to his side, forgotten. He felt it then—a sensation not unlike hunger. A gnawing pull beneath his belly button. A thread of magic, woven across space, connecting him to something else. Someone else.

Some*where* else.

He stared at the sky. The moon stared back. Panic jerked his head on his neck in an eager circle. Where were they? Where were Laoise and Irian?

Something was happening. A sundering—a crucial point wrenched from the circuit they'd all renewed. A living vine hacked from its roots, grasping with creepers for purchase as it was flung into the abyss.

Wayland drove the tines of his trident into the earth, using it to prop his suddenly weak limbs. It was time—he knew it was time. And although he thought he had prepared for this...it suddenly seemed too difficult. Why must he sacrifice all he had gained in the bargain he'd made with Muir—all this mastery and ease and comfort—in return for the man he'd been before? Even more excruciating, he knew he must pay dearly for the pleasure of it.

A sacrifice larger than life, Fia had told him, during one of their muttered, secret conferences in his workshop. To destroy Eala— and unforge their Treasures—all four heirs would have to make a sacrifice. One that demanded far more than death—a sacrifice that demanded *love*.

What love did Wayland have to barter? He had earned so little. Deserved even less. It seemed a cruel and petty thing to bargain with such a meager thing as *his* heart.

It was as it had always been. He shook his head, levered himself to his feet. He had made a promise—one he intended to keep. Even if it killed him.

He had a feeling this was going to be worse.

"By fire and by sky," he spat, the words bitter as poison on his tongue. He fought the urge to choke them back, dreading the burden of giving them voice. "By fast water and by ancient tree. By the power of my willing heart, I tithe my Treasure to thee...O Eala."

He closed his eyes. Muir rose from the depths of him, as vast and vengeful as they had been on the ocean floor. Their massive tentacles reached for him, curling and sucking—somewhere between a caress and a strangulation. Wayland was not afraid.

He was terrified.

The cost will be high.

"I know." He forced his jaw to loosen, forced his hands to unclench. "Only, I beg of you—let me choose."

You cannot trick us. If this price is not enough, balance will demand a reckoning.

"A sacrifice larger than life!" His power sloshed and surged inside him, hungry and eager. "Is that not the price?"

It is. What do you offer?

"The only love I've ever earned. The last love I ever wanted. The love that made me whole. But let *me* take the pain—let no one else bear the cost."

The love we give is equal to the love we take. The leviathan smiled as it furled tighter around him. Devouring.

Idris.

Laoise

The midnight sky was alive with flames.

In the form of her anam cló, Laoise surfed the scudding breezes with her three eldest draigs, hurtling low between the trees to rain fire upon the ravening dead before lofting once more into the darkness. The forest was burning—new green giving way to crackling leaves of red. Trees became pyres of fire, slashing the stars with orange claws.

As the moon lofted, Laoise turned her gaze toward the Heartwood. She knew it was nearly time, but she could not tear herself away from the battle, which raged in and out of the Willow Gate with ongoing intensity. Nor could she tear herself from her children—their scaled bodies arcing through the night. What had she been thinking, letting them fight? They were too young—Blodwen barely grown, the others even younger. It should not have mattered that they begged to come, eager to lend their fire to the fight. She should have fought harder to keep them safe. But now she could no longer shield them.

A thorn tore against the fire in her bones, even as a sweeping tide pulled her toward the colossal tree. With a cry, she ripped herself from the battle and winged toward the Heartwood, her vast, leathery wings tousling the canopy as she streaked through the night. The Heartwood reared up; she tucked her wings and dove, the ground rising to meet her. Quickly—too quickly. She tried to check her speed, but it was not enough. She slammed to the ground in her Gentry form, injuring her shoulder. She muffled a cry, forced herself to her feet.

Wayland was already there, bowed over his trident as if in prayer, his hands curled tight around the haft. His lips moved, but she could not hear what he said. Magic—sticky as foam and fast as a riptide—sloughed away from him like water disappearing down a drain.

Where was Irian?

There was no time. She stared at the moon—the moon stared back. She knelt a pace away from Wayland, crossing her vambraces before her so the shards of the draig egg almost joined. The evermolten metal of the Flaming Shield seemed slicked with dancing fire, and answering fear licked at Laoise.

A sacrifice larger than life, Fia had said, as they sparred in the Underbrush, sweat darkening their tunics. *For love demands far more than death.*

"By fire and by sky," Laoise whispered, the words scorching her throat like magma. She had never wanted this inheritance—this magic, this power. But now that she had it, she could not help but clutch it like a living coal, burning even as it beguiled. "By fast water and by ancient tree. By the power of my willing heart, I tithe my Treasure to thee...O Eala."

She closed her eyes. Grian was already there, constant yet changeable as the flames in the earth's deep core. Their face was Elen's but their eyes were supernovas, blazing so hot they burned holes in Laoise's mind.

The cost will be high.

"I know," Laoise whispered. "I beg of you, though—do not make me choose. Do not make me pick my own pain."

Grian nodded. When they spoke, their voice carried both the warmth of the hearth and the last obliterating spark of a wildfire.

The love we make is equal to the love we break, they said. The embers in Laoise's core throbbed hot, hot, hotter, consuming her with a heat even she could not bear.

Your draigs.

Irian

Irian was late.

He had lost himself to the violence, to stave off the sorrow. Lost himself to the steady, singing sweep of his blade, its hilt so familiar in his palm that he might as well have been born holding it. Lost himself to the easy slide of muscle over bone, the crouching sway of boots on dirt, the rhythmic dance of death.

Still they came—revenants pouring through the Gate like honey through a sieve, slow but inexorable. How many had he slaughtered? Hundreds? Thousands? Their congealed blood slicked his hands and armor; their rotting flesh ribboned his sword.

At last he felt it—a tug beneath his heart. A downdraft before a storm, carrying unfamiliar sensations: the prickle of withering thorns. The drag of an ebb tide. The vanishing flicker of a dying fire.

He cursed, kicking out at the armless revenant trying to gnaw upon his greaves. He turned, flew.

The void between spaces swallowed him. Spat him out.

He stumbled, nearly careening into Laoise. Both she and Wayland bowed in silent vigil beneath the dark, towering shape of the

Heartwood, the sleeping giant of the forest. How he hated the sight of it.

Had this place not taken enough from him? First his future. Then his bride. What more could it demand that he had not already given?

He cursed again as he knelt beside the other two heirs. In this moment it was easier to feel anger than it was to feel the anguish lurking like a specter in his veins. He jammed the tip of the Sky-Sword into the dirt, leaned his forehead on its hilt. Listened as it sang to him the last notes of a valediction.

"By fire and by sky." He sang the words he had always known like a lullaby for all he had wished for. A dirge for all he had gained. A lamentation for all he had lost. "By fast water and by ancient tree. By the power of my willing heart, I tithe my Treasure to thee...O Eala."

He closed his eyes. *They* were waiting for him—Geth, the cosmic, tempestuous source of his Treasure's power. The breath of the world; its first inhale and final exhale. As angry as they were essential—cyclone and breeze and everything in between.

The cost will be high.

"I know." His voice was a storm; his tears, cold as cirrus clouds upon the sky's blue face. "I know."

They reached for him as if they would comfort him, as if they would tear him apart.

The love we give is equal to the love we live. The storm descended on Irian like a tornado, ripping his hair and clothing. Lightning crackled along his bones, a pain he could not stand. His head cracked open and his thoughts and memories poured out, strewn like leaves before a hurricane.

For a moment, he was a dark-haired, gray-eyed boy once more, standing upon the iron cliff as the tide ebbed toward the horizon. Only this time, the waves carried away something precious to him. More precious than clams or pebbles or stories. He reached for it, crying out as it was ripped from his arms.

Fia!

Fia

My Treasure slammed into Eala with the force of a battering ram, forcing her already frail form against the towering
golden oak tree. The nemeton shuddered, and she shuddered with
it. Green laddered over her own cracked markings, vines strangling
her forearms and creeping to circle her throat.

I yanked the Heart of the Forest—now quiescent in my palm as
the source magic tithed away from me—from my neck and threw
it. It skidded over the uneven flagstones until it knocked against
Eala's boots. She stared at it, not quite comprehending what I had
done.

What we were all about to do.

She soon would.

The power of Wayland's Treasure slammed into her next, pummeling her like a brutish sea upon a stormy beach. Water gushed
down the length of her hair, splatting onto the floor. She fell to her
knees, vomiting foam as waves lapped her forearms, layering over
the thorny vines drawing lines of blood down her wrists.

"No," Eala whispered, but her teeth were splinters of wood and her tongue was seaweed and her words rasped like salt. "What have you done to me?"

"Nothing you have not asked for." I watched dispassionately as she writhed upon the floor. "Time and again, you have done unspeakable things for power. You lied to friends for power. You betrayed those who loved you for power. You killed your sisters for power. You stole Rogan's will for power. You traded the fate of both realms for power, and only yearned for more. So now you have it. How does it feel, to be the most powerful individual in both worlds? You are a vessel for three Treasures now—the elemental magic of three sources surges beneath your skin. *How does it feel?*"

She crawled toward me, her movements hectic, jerky. Her mouth opened and closed like that of a gutted fish upon the strand.

The power of Laoise's Treasure flashed over her—a pyre of fire lapping and dancing. Eala roared, and the flames roared with her. Her skin—pulsing and breathing like the inchoate embers of a wildfire—flashed with rose-gold scales.

"Stop!" Her mouth yawned like ashes. Her steaming hair stank of char. "Please, Sister—whatever you are doing to me, *stop*. I cannot bear it!"

I gazed at my sister, nailing my vengeance like a door so my sympathy could not break free. I forced myself to replay all the chilling violence she had carefully machinated. Her hands, slippery with blood, on the hilt of her dagger as she tore the hearts from her sisters' breasts. Her voice, cunning and cold as she demanded Gavida forge her a Treasure. Her mouth, smiling palely as she drove a sword into her own mother's gut. Her eyes, diamond bright as she drove Rogan to destroy himself on his own blade.

Irian's Treasure stormed down on her, bending the giant oaks until their branches fanned and swept the flagstones. My hair whipped around my face, stinging, but I forced myself to watch as Eala bowed even lower, lightning crackling over her spine. Feathers burst from her skin, unfurling along her arms until white wings spread sharp pinions into the storm, half lifting her off her feet.

"How does it feel now?" I cried above the sound of the wind howling through the nemeton. "Five Treasures—more power than anyone has ever wielded, or will ever wield again! You wished to be a queen, Eala? I have made you a goddess. All the elements of nature at your command. *How does it feel?*"

Eala screamed, the agonized reverberation like the screech of falling timber, the crash of waves upon cliffs, the roar of a devouring wildfire, the hollow wail of a distant storm.

"It...*hurts*! Make it stop. Please, Fia—please make it stop!"

I made myself approach her where she lay writhing and screaming and tormented upon the cold stone floor. Around us Dún Darragh phased in and out, as if existing and not existing at the same time. Carvings on the walls...faces in the dark. Pillars made of stone...vast trunks in the forest. I crouched, taking in every unnatural contortion of Eala's limbs, every bulge and creak of her livid, living skin, every flash of color pooling over her.

Green grass. Blue water. Red fire. Silver wind. White death.

I could only imagine what she was feeling. I had played host to two Solasóirí, and it had nearly destroyed me. And I was different than Eala—human, Folk, and something else. Something more. Something other.

Eala was, in the end, just a girl.

"Thirteen years," I whispered. "That is how long you will live with this power. For the Treasures will not let you die—did you know that? Not of natural causes. This pain will not kill you, Eala—it will only continue. Even as your bones rot, they will grow anew. Even as your lungs drown, they will breathe in more water. Even as your skin burns, it will heal. Even as the zephyrs drive you mad, they will comfort you. For thirteen. More. Years."

"No." Horror contorted her already warped, broken face. "You cannot...leave me like this."

"Leave you? No." I barked a laugh. "I intend to watch. I will watch as the magic consumes everything that made you you, piece by rotten piece. I will devour each one of your screams like candy, each whimper more delicious than the last. I will wait until you beg me for mercy. And you *will* beg for mercy. For this is the price of power, my dear sister—*pain*."

She whimpered as another cataclysm rocked her—a terrible earthquake tearing her body apart even as it put her back together. I heard her bones crack, then knit—like roots healing from a stray axe. Her blood surged and gushed, too much volume for her human veins, spewing liquid into her hollow spaces before sucking it up again. Flames crackled along her tongue and blackened what was left of her teeth. White feathers grew and then molted, fluttering from her bleeding, distended shoulders to lay limp on the ground, slick with water and fell with moss and licking with flames.

She was human. Her body was not made to withstand this much power. She was not strong enough.

No one was.

"Please," she begged, lifting her arms in supplication. "I cannot bear it another moment. It is...too much. Take it away. I want to...*die*."

"Die?" I smiled, a little sadly. "No, Eala. This sacrifice must be larger than life. It demands far more than death."

"What, then?" She choked on bloody water, pushed burnt, sizzling hair off her face. "What must...I do?"

I reached for her, grasped her hands. My starshine instantly burned her, blackening her palms. But so, too, did it suffuse her—light flared up her hands to her wrists, illuminating the bones beneath her fragile skin, the veins choked with too much magic.

"Our lives have always lain side by side—separate, but aligned. Now they are one and the same." The knowledge I'd grappled with since Marban's cottage wreathed through me, filling the empty spaces my Treasure had left. Casting light into my darkest corners even as it shadowed my brightness. "You were right, on the Longest Night. We were always meant to stand here, together. You are my sister. My other half. We are light and dark aligned. The white swan, the black swan. One breath, one body. One heart. We were created from imbalance and born to restore it. We *are* balance."

Eala gritted her teeth, thrashing and jerking as renewed pain throttled her. My starshine climbed higher, illuminating the five colors of her layered tattoos like sunlight through stained glass.

"Tell me... what... I must do."

"Say the words," I told her. "Then pay the price."

"By fire and by sky," she screamed. "By fast water and by ancient tree. I promise my willing heart to thee—O *Fia*."

Magic jerked me—a bone-deep tether hooked beneath my heart. My starshine burned farther up Eala's arms, smoothing over the white feathers prickling from her shoulders. Our palms were fused together, and I could *hear* them—all five of them, a boundless, soundless cacophony beating about my ears and throbbing along my bones and juddering through my veins.

The cost will be high. The cost will be high. The cost will be high.

The dissonance of all five eternal voices was unbearable. Their demands echoed through us both, caustic and discordant.

Love. Pain. Loss. Hatred. Mercy.

They layered, then merged, finding a common note between them. The word slid like a blade between us, as inevitable as our births. And our deaths.

Everything. Everything. Everything.

I gazed at Eala and saw the moment she understood. Her eyes widened, not the agonized muddy color of all the elements combined, but the clear, cunning blue of the swan princess I'd met almost a year and a half ago. I gazed back at her, letting all that had passed between us melt away, until we were just Fia and Eala. The shadowy changeling girl and the shining storybook princess.

"I love you, Eala."

She spat blood between broken teeth and snarled, "I despise you, *Sister*."

It was as it had always been.

"My name is Fia Ní Mainnín, heir of the Sept of Antlers and

child of the stars, and I bring us both balance." I smiled as my radiance swelled. "I suppose I was the stronger weapon after all."

Starlight punched out of me, meeting magic like five huge fingers curled into a fist. I gasped, bracing my body as my hands tightened over Eala's fingers.

A feather so black will rise from pain. A crown so silver will rise to reign.

The starlight wrapped around the magic like a cocoon, cradling it as gently as a mother with a babe.

A heart so green must bleed once more, for light and dark to one restore.

Inside the cocoon, the magic melted together, like a caterpillar inside a chrysalis.

The last love lost, the price now paid—through sacrifice, the balance laid.

The magic unfurled, beating great wings inside me. My vision whitened as sensation shattered along my limbs. My head fell back; my hands twined even tighter with Eala's as the starlight consumed us both. She screamed, searing and final, as the light devoured her. My rib cage cracked open, tearing my leather armor in half. White light coursed from my chest and winged toward the night sky, gleaming with a million destinies I could hardly comprehend.

A piece of folded parchment fluttered disconsolately from my bodice, opening as it fell. I did not look at it—I had read it a hundred times, my tears staining the picture as I read the final lines. Again. And again. Until they were imprinted upon my soul.

So white and black, the swans must die, for stars to weave their fate on high.

I cried out as the power left me—the starlight and all it had touched. Earth, water, fire, air. Spirit. No longer tainted by separation, throttled by a thousand years of terrible enslavement. The sources no longer bound to conduits; the conduits no longer tithed to vessels. In my starshine, all that magic was lustrated. Cleansed, renewed. Made numinous, divine. Around us, Corra's nemeton glowed, the trees catching the starlight like plasma. It branched through the sky and rooted through the earth. The sacred circle careened, rings upon rings, circles within circles. The heartwood of an ancient tree, the ripples in a pond after a stone is thrown, the sweeping spiral of a distant galaxy.

We were all the same. We were all different. By the circles we were all bound.

Eala's hands went boneless in mine as she fell backward. Dimly I saw that she, too, had been cleansed. Her fine hair made a halo around her perfect face; her pale feathered dress splayed out like wings behind her.

Distantly, I felt a boundary begin to close. A torn seam being restitched, an infected wound being healed.

Then I, too, was falling. Flying. I soared through a thousand dusk-lit skies toward something so bright I could only name it *love*.

I was made of light and triumph and overwhelming ecstasy.

I was made to tell my own story.

And this...this was where it ended.

Chapter Fifty-One

Deirdre

Deirdre of the Sept of Antlers had been born to die.

Bright stars had fallen on the black night of her birth, heralding delight and doom. It was foretold she would be an heir to her Sept's Treasure—desperately few in the waning days of dying magic. But so, too, was it foretold that she would bring waste to Tír na nÓg. Her beauty would start wars; her destiny was naught but ruin. So they hid her away. As if a childhood isolated behind high walls, singing to rocks and telling stories to flowers, would inoculate her against the plague of her fate.

As if anyone could hide themselves from destiny.

Death was Deirdre's lullaby as a baby, sung over her cradle in the dark of night. Death was her bedtime story as a girl, repeated as the sun rode low. Death was the throb of her heart as a young woman, as she yearned for a world she had never tasted, with all its terrible, fleeting desires.

All came to pass as was foretold. The stars do not lie—their magic is measured in eons, stories unfolding silently in the great, endless dark. There is no hiding from fate, no outrunning doom.

She loved Rían, the human king from beyond the Gates, from the moment she saw him. For his long limbs and curling hair, yes. But also for his hope and his honesty. For his softness and his care. For all of herself she saw in him, and all of him that was nothing like her.

She loved Rían from the moment she saw him, though she knew in her heart that his name, too, was Death.

Still, she loved him. Still, she lay with him. Still, she plotted with him—to save both their lands from the looming disaster set in motion long ago by the forging of the Treasures.

Still, she fled with him, though she knew they would be pursued. Though she knew they would never escape the doom etched in black ink between lambent stars. Though she knew they would both die.

Danu caught them on the high cliffs above the reaching forest. Late winter ice slicked the high stones, and snow capped the branches of the black pines far below. The chieftain slaughtered Rían without mercy for the crime of his human heart. His blood spattered Deirdre's face and stained her dress. She reeled back in dismay, weeping.

Perhaps she meant to fall. Perhaps she did not.

Her slippers slithered. She lost her balance. Frigid, empty air made for a poor final embrace. Branches slashed her as she plummeted down, down, down, tearing her clothing and ripping her hair and eviscerating her skin. The earth smashed her, the impact shattering every bone in her body. Bursting her veins. Cracking her skull. As she lay broken upon the bank of a half-frozen stream, the icy water lapping over her outstretched arms, she knew that Death had finally found her.

She was wrong. Her Treasure would not let her die.

She screamed, shattered and ruptured and nearly split in two, as the magic of the Heart of the Forest tried to knit her back together. Vines splinted bones; nettles sutured wounds. She begged for release—begged for the pain to stop. Begged for Death.

She begged the tall being with the antlers, whom she had known since she was a babe, to let her go.

They simply shook their head, their shadowed face impossibly sad.

Not yet, child. There is life in you.

She did not understand.

Hours or days later, she did.

She had not known she was pregnant. She had not yet missed a moon course. She had not even known she could fall pregnant to a mortal man—their worlds had been separate for so long. Yet his seed quickened inside her. A seed that would, in time, blossom into his child.

Her child.

She could not bear it. She longed for nothing else.

Still, she begged for release. The pain she felt was unfathomable— her healing too slow, the anguish too great. She wept and screamed and raged.

"Set me free!" she demanded. "I will give anything. I will rip my heart out if only it means I could be free of this curse."

Ínne said, *The cost will be high.*

She bared her teeth. "I will give anything. Everything. Take my willing heart, for I have nothing left to barter."

They knelt, gently touching her twisted stomach, then the stone resting cool above her mangled breastbone. *Balance will decide.*

It decided on torture. It did not set her free—not right away. It continued rebuilding her body, bone by bone and nerve by nerve. Fire raced along her limbs and curdled in her stomach. The sun and the moon and the cruel, cruel stars wheeled overhead.

Days. Weeks. Months.

As the pain at last began to ease, the stone above her breast cracked, a noise so horrendous Deirdre thought her ears must burst. Magic spilled from her, dense and oily and clinging. Not the cool, creeping power she had flirted with since childhood, then married upon the last heir's tithing. No—this magic was *wrong*. Warped. As twisted as her body before it healed. And it no longer belonged to her. She reached for it, but it snapped at her, tense and devouring. Then clung to her, devious and tantalizing. She scrambled away, her arm curling protectively over her swelling womb.

"I don't understand." She reached for her Heart, but the chain around her neck had somehow snapped—the dusk-lit river had already tumbled her Treasure downstream. "Why was it not tithed anew?"

There is no heir to accept the magic. So the magic must go free.

Deirdre hardened her heart. The burdens of the Sept of Antlers were no longer hers to shoulder. "Then why am I alive? I traded my willing heart to be set free from the cycle. Take it. And let me die."

We did. Ínne shook their great antlered head. The stars chimed above them. *Your greatest love. That is the price balance demands.*

Deirdre had always known the Solasóirí were governed by laws the Folk were not—and would never be—privy to. Laws of balance in nature. Laws of time and the cosmos. Laws of darkness and light. Laws of beginning and ending. Notions of morality—human and Folk—were inconsequential to them.

But this? This was wrong.

"Not the baby," she choked out. "Not my baby."

But whatever negotiation she had entered into was finished.

She had failed to trade her life to end her sentence. Instead, she had made a sacrifice larger than life.

She had sacrificed a love she did not yet know.

For months, she disappeared into the forest. Her anam cló devoured her—the lithe dancing of its long, limber legs pure comfort after the agony of her damaged Gentry body; the smooth simplicity of its animal mind a balm for the layers of anguish that threatened to smother her.

She preferred the nights. She liked the moon, rising soft and slow, striking silver sparks off the iron anvil of the lough. The rustle of birds in the dense muffled dark of the trees, their songs fading, then dying in the watercolor sweep of green and black.

She wished she had a voice, so she might join in.

But the nights were punctuated by bright days—burnished branch and gilded leaf. Sharp scents lofting in the moss-scented breeze. Foraging—the susurrus of shifting grasses, hard acorn and crunching nut, scraps of birch bark curled tight as fists. Summer.

Then short gray days—polished silver sky and ruffled undergrowth. Furred head bent to the glass-sharp wind. Cold mud seeping quiet and strange between her hooves. Autumn.

A feather's touch within her belly—a mote of warmth, curling inward; an embrace like the silent forest.

Then pain. Pain so strong she feared she would once more be broken, shattered, ended.

In a way, she was.

She birthed her child in the cold, quiet solitude of a forest at dusk. No midwife blotted her sweating brow; no parent nor partner rubbed her aching back. She fisted her shaking hands in the crooks of saplings, nearly ripping them from their roots as she screamed into the night. The stars made a silver gyre as she squatted in the grass and pushed until blackness threatened to overwhelm her. At last, it was done. She scooped the tiny thing from the moss and laid its glistening form upon her distended belly. Its fists were curled like snails. Its hair was the black of nightshade berries. And its eyes—open already, and gazing at her like she was everything—were mismatched. One light, one dark.

Not it. *She.*

A daughter.

"My little deer." The immensity of her emotion nearly engulfed her voice. "My Fia."

But the child was not hers. Already, the compulsion tugged at her—the bargain she had made with Ínne. With her magic. With her destiny. It called to her, and though she fought it, she was weak.

She had always been too weak to deny her own doom.

She swaddled the baby, then cloaked herself against the frigid night. Ínne met her in a clearing, vast arms outstretched. But Deirdre clutched her daughter close. She was so tiny. Deirdre could not imagine how she would possibly survive cradled by those claw-tipped hands.

"She is too new." Deirdre's belly was still soft and round; her hair, stiff with sweat; her thighs, slicked with her own viscera. It had been but an hour. "She cannot survive without me."

She is the price balance demands.

"Please." Deirdre's whole body trembled as she tried to fight destiny. Tears spilled over her face like rain. "Let me have a little time before you take her. A year. Even a month. Just one day."

Do you think it will be easier then? Sorrow wrote a poem beneath the silver antlers. *She belongs to us now. She will live. She will love. But she is no longer yours.*

And so Deirdre relinquished her daughter to the forest and wished Death had claimed her first.

She tried to keep her distance.

She could not.

She watched as the forest nursed her daughter, even as her own breasts grew painful with too much milk, then dried up. She watched as the babe grew into a child and danced along dappled paths between trees, parented by every Folk creature save her own mother.

Deirdre shifted into her anam cló and did not shift back.

One day, the child disappeared.

Deirdre followed.

Perhaps she found a circle of mushrooms, or the hollow boll of a forgotten beech tree. Perhaps a Gate took pity on she who had once been a Treasure and let her through beneath a full moon. Perhaps she traveled in the Deep-Dream, carried between worlds on imagination alone. Her deer mind did not think of these things—it thought only of the inexorable pull of her damaged heart.

She found her daughter in a castle made of stone and wood and bad human tempers. She watched as the child ran out from behind high palisades, barefoot on a snowy night. She watched as the child transformed a cruel nursemaid into a tree.

She watched as the child became a girl, trained on blades and fists and human violence.

She watched as the girl became a woman and fell in love. Then grew sour and sallow in its aftermath.

She watched the young woman gallop to the edge of the forest on her gray mare and tease flowering vines over sleeping bowers.

She watched the young woman travel to a crumbling fort, then fall in love again. She watched her ride a mare of twigs and leaves amid a host of stone monsters, clad in a gown of black feathers.

For a while, she was gone. Deirdre could not find a way to follow her.

She watched the young woman return to the human realms and find the shape of her soul. Of her mother's heart. But though Deirdre followed her through the wood to the Gate, she could not cross over.

Now Deirdre watched as the Gates blew open, raining fire upon the horde of dead clogging her forest. Fire and steel. Her instincts forced her to flee, long legs bounding as her ears and tail flicked warnings to the creatures around her. She drove forward, running before the battle raging beside her. She hid behind the trembling branches of aspens, lost to the soothing dark.

She had spent too long as a doe. When she remembered to know things, she knew this.

Sometime later, she crept out. The grotto where her daughter had once toiled was crushed and broken. Above, on the bluff, the battle raged around the keep, and it was no longer just Gentry who fought the shambling horde.

Were those humans?

They were shorter, stouter, less incandescently beautiful than the Folk. They wore battered helms of iron instead of shining silver armor. Their weapons were simple steel, without the flamboyant decorations favored by the Gentry.

But they were fighting side by side against the ravening horde. Elbow to elbow. Back to back. Beyond, she glimpsed weapons of war she had no name for. A wooden tower with sweeping arms whipping something toward the fort.

Green fire exploded near the edge of the lough; thunder boomed. The screams of the dead and dying echoed. Inside the fort, windows began to glow—light shining like captured stars from behind the thick walls.

Deirdre tried to creep closer, but her doe form balked—the mayhem and havoc triggering something primal in her. She could not go any closer. With supernatural effort, Deirdre conjured her other form—the one she had not used in nearly twenty years. Two legs. Willowy arms. Long dark hair. Slowly, her pelt receded. Her limbs grew thicker, heavier. Her hooves split in five. Her fingers were chilly on the midnight earth as she pushed herself to standing. Her legs wobbled, but she braced herself on the crumbling wall of the keep, creeping along the narrow path until she spied a massive golden oak dominating a courtyard.

Barefoot and nearly naked save for the scraps of clothing she'd worn two decades earlier, Deirdre darted for the door. No one noticed her, focused as they were on fighting for their lives. She slid inside the fort.

The great hall was somehow both inside and outside—carven stone and seething ancient forest alive with staring eyes. Two women stood framed amid a grove of massive golden oaks. One was white-blond, with ribbons of dark mold creeping through her hair. The other was dark-haired, with threads of starlight lightening hers. They stood hand in hand, although it was less an embrace than a compulsion. Magic burst from Deirdre's daughter's chest, a collection of sounds and colors so ephemeral and momentous that Deirdre could hardly fathom it. She shielded her eyes—the great hall was awash with light, brighter than sunlight. It was wings; it was wonder. It was the opposite of the blight that had crept from her after she broke her bond to the Heart of the Forest. It was holy—magic washed clean.

She watched the blond girl crumple, her form slumping on the flagstones.

"No," Deirdre whispered, as if she could stop what she knew would happen next.

Her daughter collapsed, the weight of the sublime lifting off her body and stealing something vital with it. Deirdre lunged for her, but the radiance collected into an orb before abruptly detonating. Light exploded outward, catching her square in the chest and slamming her back against the door. Her vision sparked, white on black. The fort rocked, mortar and stone dropping from the ceiling. Beyond its walls, she heard the muffled screams of living and dead alike.

Deirdre crawled forward to gather her daughter off the ground, into her arms. Her form was too still. Her head lolled on her neck, and her arms flopped limply, and her mismatched eyes stared blankly into the shadows wreathing the dún.

"No," Deirdre whispered as she smoothed the short dark tresses away from her daughter's slack face. Did she remember any other words? She was not sure she did. "No."

Was this truly her fate? Doomed to hold her child only on the day she was born and the day she died? She had always known the stars were cruel, but this was sadistic. She had wished to meet Death a thousand times, but never like this. She cradled Fia closer, pressing her cheek to her daughter's forehead, twining her fingers through her fingers, cupping her head in the crook of her arm.

"No!" This time, the scream rent her throat and echoed through the fort, reverberating off the stones. The hall was dark, dark as Death, save for the tendrils of starlight still clinging to Fia's body. Deirdre clenched her eyes shut as she rocked her daughter like the baby she'd once been. The tears slipping from beneath her eyelashes splashed onto Fia's cooling skin. "This isn't how your story ends. It can't be. It can't be."

The echoes traveled along the walls, transmuting her voice into mockery.

It can't be. It can't be.

Her eyes dredged the gloom. The primeval forest was fading, the colossal golden oaks petrifying as their bark transformed back to stone. But she swore a face was watching her—a serpent with glowing crystal eyes and a tail that spun round in ever-tightening circles.

"Snip, snap, snout," hissed the snake, "our tale's told out. But if you wish to twist the thread...you'll find the story's not quite dead."

"What do you mean?" Deirdre stared, a frown puckering her face. "Who are you?"

"We are your broken heart, Deirdre of the Sorrows." The snake stilled as a giant elk reared to life beside it, piercing the stone with vast silver antlers. "Forgotten hallways where naught's as it seems, where whispers linger and starlight still gleams. Speak to us your desired end; we shall see what sorrow we can mend."

Perhaps it was foolhardy, but Deirdre did not hesitate. The magic of this place was fading—the starlight clinging to Fia little more than a flickering whisper. The trees were nearly columns, the primeval forest but an ancient memory.

"Once, in a time of falling stars and endless nights, a girl was born to die." Deirdre clutched Fia. "Only she lived. She lived when her great love died. She lived when her baby was plucked from her arms. She lived when somewhere far away, all her kin were slaughtered. She lived when her daughter spent her life to free magic. But the stars are calling her—the time has come to fulfill her destiny." She looked down at her daughter, their faces similar yet different—a mirror seen through smoke. "I give my willing heart to you, Fia—for you *are* my heart." The walls no longer moved. "Let me die, so she may live. Let my ending be her new beginning."

Bong.

Somewhere high above, a bell began to toll. Strange—Deirdre had not noticed a bell tower.

Bong. Bong.

Beside her, a much-folded piece of paper stirred on the floor. Upon it, a white swan sailed upon a darkened lough. Her shadow in the water was black as night. A thousand stars careened around them.

Bong. Bong. Bong.

New words were scrawled beneath the ones already written. Deirdre could not make them out.

Bong. Bong. Bong.

Beneath Deirdre's palm, her child's skin shifted.

Bong. Bong.

A heartbeat. *A heartbeat.*

Bong.

Deirdre's daughter stirred in her arms, her lips parting as she inhaled.

Bong.

As the last toll faded into echoes and the forest of dreams turned back into stone, Fia opened her eyes.

Chapter Fifty-Two

Fia

A face loomed over me—beautiful, if gaunt, punctuated by green eyes the color of new leaves and framed by long, tangled dark hair. An echo teased the edge of my hearing.

I smiled. I knew who she was. I knew where we were.

I *didn't* know why lying on the floor of the afterlife felt so damned *cold*.

"Mother?" The word rolled strangely off my tongue. I tried another one. "Deirdre?"

"Yes, little deer." Her eyes were huge and wet as woodland pools, but the smile she gave me was crystal clear. "My Fia. Remember this, if you remember nothing else—I love you. I have always loved you. In the beginning. And at the end."

She brushed a faint kiss upon my brow. My eyes fluttered shut.

When I opened them again, she was gone. I sat up painfully—my chest burned, as if a bonfire had been kindled atop it. I rubbed my sternum with the heel of my palm, trying to get my bearings. It was only when I saw Eala's prone form laid out on the floor that it all came rushing back. I half crawled across the dark floor toward my sister. She might have been sleeping—her lovely face serene, her brow untroubled. My fingers found her wrist. There was no pulse.

I sat back on my heels. Stared around the great hall, now carven stone and lost echoes. A scrap of paper on the floor caught my eye. It was the prophecy Cathair had ripped from his Book of Whispers—the prophecy I had perused countless times in the past weeks, trying to write some other ending to my story. But it seemed a new line had been added to the bottom, though I could not make it out in the dim.

I plucked it up as I stood. Ensuring my pouch was still secured at my waist, I pushed open the heavy doors. Outside, the battle had dwindled into something closer to a rout. All the revenants had fallen, leaving both Gentry and human troops to wander, battered, through the massed dead. Some still fought one another, but the violence was half-hearted, disconsolate. Fire smoldered everywhere—red in the forest and bright green over the hills and between the mounting trebuchets. Horses whinnied. Men shouted. False dawn grayed the horizon.

The battle was won. Death was defeated.

"Lady!" Balor's stomping shook the courtyard. He crouched next to me, touching the top of my head with one large finger as if to make sure I was real. "You survived."

"I am as surprised as you." I smiled up at him, pushing away the sensation of forgetting something important. "Although perhaps even more grateful."

Boots and hooves clattered on gravel. A platoon of human fénnidi trotted up the rise, weapons drawn and helms lowered. Their leader threw out an arm when he saw me, then dragged off his helmet. I recognized him—Breas Mac Cúg, under-king of Delbhna and the high queen's brother. Clearly, he had recognized me too.

"Fia?" His tone was half accusing and half wondering. "What has passed here tonight?"

I hardly knew. "A tale for another time, I fear. The battle is won, but there is work to be done. Can you put out the fires?"

"The Eternal Fire extinguishes after a few days—we can only ensure it does not spread." He glanced toward Roslea. "My men can carry water from the lough toward the forest."

I nodded, though I was not sure how much good it would do. "Tell them not to attack the Folk warriors. Their leaders wear swirling glass pendants over their armor. Kill them if you must— the rest will yield."

I was not sure that was true. But this night had begun with violence—perhaps it could end with peace.

I descended the narrow path toward the grotto. There were far more Gentry here, near the edge of Roslea. They, too, recognized me— a half-hearted cheer roared from the warriors of the Summerlands.

"To the Gate!" someone cried. "The battle is won!"

As the Folk host began to sing, exhaustedly and off tune, my heart began to break. For them, a little. But mostly for myself.

When I unforged the Treasures with my starshine, all the elemental magic had been released back into nature. The sources had been unchained; the conduits, destroyed; the vessels, freed. And the boundary between the worlds had closed, each Gate a wound to be stitched and salved.

Balance, restored.

I feared there were no Gates to return to.

Still, I allowed myself to be caught in the throng of fénnidi trooping back through Roslea. Maybe I hadn't fully accepted it—maybe I needed to witness it with my own eyes. Or maybe I couldn't bear to confess to these Gentry that I had willingly stranded them here in the human realms with no path back to Tír na nÓg.

Here, with me.

Forever.

The forest smoked, patches of fire burning in the undergrowth. The bridge at last arose, its stones dull in the dawn light netting between black-bone trees. The willow was scorched, her long tresses little more than char. The stream was choked with bodies, and the sight of it closed my throat. My fists clenched.

One of them still held a folded square of parchment.

As the Gentry host realized what had happened, they began to keen. They wailed into the smoke-draped morning, pounding their fists upon the stones of the bridge. They pushed deeper into the forest, as if Tír na nÓg might be hiding behind singed trees.

And I—I finally looked at the prophecy I'd read a thousand times. It was the same image Cathair had torn from his Book of Whispers—the swans, on their lake. The falling stars.

Except, at the bottom of the page, a new line had been added. I did not recognize the handwriting, although it had a quirky flourish that reminded me somehow of Corra. And it read:

From death one may rise, through a mother's despair,
Her breaking heart the balm mending sorrow with care.

Anguish swept over me, followed immediately by immense, unrelenting joy. And I knew—I had not dreamed Deirdre. She had found me. She had held me. And her love had saved me.

Somehow, she had given me my new beginning. At the cost of her own ending.

I fought back great dark wings of loss that threatened to overwhelm me. I had surrendered too much for this Pyrrhic victory. My friends, who in turn had sacrificed their willing hearts for Eala's defeat. My husband, who was now separated from me by an insurmountable barrier. My mother, who had traded her life for my own.

"Lady?" Balor boomed down at me. I turned—I had not noticed him follow me from Dún Darragh. "What now?"

I swiped tears from my cheeks as I forced a smile at his mountainous figure, outlined in dawn's cheery pinks and golds. "I have a few ideas."

He smiled back. Somewhere, above the seething smoke and keening Gentry, a single lark began to sing. Beside my boot, a lone fiddlehead nudged, bright green amid the tumbled dank bodies and charred tree trunks. I crouched to touch it with the tip of my finger. Green embroidered my arm, decorating my unmarked skin like lace. The fern unfurled, a single spot of life in a sea of death.

Every ending was its own beginning. And every story...began somewhere.

Chapter Fifty-Three

Wayland

Wayland did not like goodbyes.

He watched with rising petulance as Sinéad and Chandi mounted their horses, slinging heavy packs over rumps and settling cloaks over shoulders, although the day was still hot.

Nearly a month had passed since the Bealtaine War. Of their fateful bargains beneath the Heartwood, Wayland, Laoise, and Irian had been left with little but broken tools and fading memories. Wayland's trident had dissolved into sea-foam; Laoise's vambraces had melted to obsidian ash. Irian's unbreakable blade had shattered from its hilt into a dozen shards. Not long after, the living dead had simply...dropped. The Gentry warriors who'd remained in Tír na nÓg all waited for their brethren to return from beyond the Gate.

They never did.

The Gates had closed, and if the bardaí still lived, they were trapped in the human realms.

With Fia.

The thought still made Wayland smile, although the expression faded as Laoise descended from the tree city, strapping on a plain leather vambrace over her uninjured arm. The collarbone she'd broken was still in a sling. She'd let her hair grow out a little—her curls tumbled over one ember eye, half obscuring her features. She looked up, caught him staring.

She stuck out her tongue at him. "Like what you see, water boy?"

"Oh no, fire girl," he prodded back. "I never taste things I know will burn my tongue."

"You're growing wise in your old age." She checked the buckles over her knives. When she looked back at him, her face was serious. "Are you going to be all right?"

He knew what she was talking about. The three of them—he, Laoise, and Irian—had not explicitly spoken about what they'd bargained to unforge their Treasures. But it had not been hard to guess.

The heirs had clambered up to the apartments near dawn, exhausted and blood-spattered and smoke-stained. The eldest draigs had not yet returned from battle, and as the younger ones crowded toward their mother, it occurred to Wayland that Laoise did not seem concerned about their safety. Enfys barreled into her waist; Anwyll wove between her legs with glee. Laoise stared down at them, something akin to distaste pooling over her lovely features.

"Idris," she said to her brother, who was hovering. "Can't you manage the draigs?"

Confusion swept over Idris's face, but he quickly collected the draiglings as Laoise repaired to her room, clearly intent on removing her boots and wiping the soot from her face. Idris turned to Irian, raised his eyebrows.

"What happened in the battle?" His gaze skated to Wayland without much interest, then snapped back to Irian. "The Treasures? What happened to Fia?"

Irian frowned, his stark brows lowering over eyes that were now the color of slate—gray as the cliffs where he was raised. The same gray Wayland remembered from their childhood.

"Who?"

And they all began to realize—nothing would ever be the same again.

Laoise's vast maternal love for her draig children had been excised from her heart as if with a surgeon's blade. Conversely, Wayland retained all his feelings for Idris, but Idris no longer looked at him. Barely spoke to him. When he did, it was with neither love nor hate—it was with no feeling whatsoever. He spoke with perfect cordiality.

Cordial ought to be a curse word, in Wayland's opinion.

He reminded himself: He had *chosen* this.

He wished he had been more selfish.

And Irian? For Irian, Fia had simply ceased to exist. Her name elicited no memories, no thoughts, no emotions. For Irian and Irian alone... Fia was just *gone*.

Wayland supposed, if he was being perfectly cynical, that it might be a kindness.

"I'm all right," Wayland said now to Laoise, though it was a lie. What else could he say? That his heart was broken? That he mourned for something he had barely possessed? That every time Idris's eyes slid over him, he wanted to grab him by the shoulders and kiss him so hard he saw stars? "And you?"

"There are only so many times I can be told what I have lost before I find myself glad I am no longer burdened by it." Her words were callous. She didn't seem to notice when Wayland flinched.

"Then it is back to Dún Scaith for you?"

Laoise nodded. "Chandi wishes to make amends for all her misdeeds. Sinéad wishes to hone her battlecraft. And I—I have no one to take care of, now that Idris is grown, and little else to occupy my time. Perhaps Lady Scáthach will finally take pity on me and show me how to brew her famous heather mead."

The holes in Laoise's words gnawed at Wayland—the spaces where the draiglings used to live vast and horribly hungry. He folded his arms, as if he could clamp his grief within the cage of his ribs. He did not understand how she could hear herself speak and not feel what she had lost.

It was cruel, cruel magic.

"If you learn, please write to tell me."

"But then I'd have to kill you." Laoise saluted, then mounted her own horse beside Chandi and Sinéad. The human girls both waved at him before urging their horses away over the waving plains of golden wheat.

Wayland sighed and climbed back to their emptying apartments.

Idris was packing up what once had been their room. Books, mostly—in the time since they'd arrived in the Summerlands, he had accumulated a decent portion of his and Laoise's lost collection from the Cnoc. He had three saddlebags already full and was packing a fourth. Tucked behind his ear, the sleek waterfall of his red hair caught the sunlight like fire. He did not hide any part of his face as he sorted scrolls.

Wayland girded himself, then approached the other man. "You're going to need a mule."

"Perhaps I will." Idris sat back on his heels, surveying his collection before cordially adding, "Thanks for the suggestion."

Cordial. Wayland's skin tightened, the muscles of his back going taut as he fought to hold in everything he was feeling. This room especially felt haunted by all he and Idris had shared, before he'd lost him: the bed bruised by their embraces, the pillows marked with their whispers, the air perfumed with their ardor. "May I ask where you're going?"

"Annwyn, I think." Idris glanced out the window. All seven draiglings cavorted in the trees, leaping and tumbling with abandon. "Blodwen is starting to get huge, and the others won't be far behind. I still fear what the Ellyllon might do to them, but I can't protect them here. Not without Laoise. The Summer Twins may be the only bardaí left, thanks to Fia's mercy, and the Septs may be gone... but dominion abhors an empty throne. Some new ambitious leader will soon hunger for power in Tír na nÓg. At least in Annwyn, the draigs will be honored and valued. Perhaps I'll even learn more about where they came from."

"And where you came from," Wayland added. Idris didn't seem to hear him, his attention fixed out the window.

Hog detached herself from the other draiglings, sailing on her stubby, wobbly wings through the window. She bypassed Idris completely, colliding with Wayland's chest and nearly barreling him over. She, too, was getting bigger. She slid her claws through his long hair and purred, "Mine."

A wonderful, awful idea sparked inside Wayland. "Idris?"

He'd returned his attention to packing his books. "Mm?"

"Can I keep her?"

Idris's gaze narrowed.

"I mean, can she stay with me? For a while. If she wants to."

The other man stared at him, then at the draigling, who had climbed on top of Wayland's head to drape herself around his ears like an elaborate hat. At length, he asked, "Will you promise to keep her safe?"

"With my life."

Idris nodded. "Then so be it."

Hog mewled her satisfaction. Wayland pivoted away, then turned back before he could change his mind. "Idris?"

The other man's head snapped up, but now he was annoyed. "*Yes?*"

Wayland beat back fury and sorrow. He had *chosen* this, living gods be cursed. "Do you remember the night on the beach? Before I renewed the Treasure?"

Unlike Irian, whose memories of Fia were completely gone, Idris seemed to remember all that had passed between them. Yet the emotion had been wiped clean—transient fog from clear mirror glass. He narrowed his eyes again. "Yes."

"I just want you to know that I meant what I said. Every word."

A flicker of contempt burned across Idris's features in the moment before he looked back at his books. "Thank you, Wayland."

Wayland turned away, pressing his thumbs into his eyes. And as Hog nipped comfortingly at his ear, he whispered, "Goodbye, Idris."

He found Irian in the kitchen, aggressively polishing a finely tooled steel sword that was already gleaming. Wayland propped himself against the table as he gestured at the blade.

"What's wrong with this one?"

Irian growled, low in his throat, and slammed the claíomh down with a clang. Over the past month, he had commissioned a total of three swords from three different blacksmiths in the Summerlands, deeming each to be less satisfactory than the last. The first had been too long; the second, too short. This one? "The balance is off. It pulls to the left. And my calluses are in all the wrong places for the grip."

"You could renounce swordplay altogether," Wayland suggested lightly. "Perhaps the remnants of the Sky-Sword could be reforged into a passable plow."

A glint of mischief lurked in Irian's storm-gray eyes. It was a look Wayland had not seen him wear in a long time, and it brought back memories of fonder times—a boyhood running riot over the cliffs of Emain Ablach with a foster brother in tow.

"It is funny you should mention that," Irian said, with a bemused smile. "For lately I find myself with the strangest urge to grow a garden."

Wayland's blood ran cold, pooling dread in his stomach. His hands on the table clenched, and he rose to face Irian.

He had not known how to broach all that Irian had forgotten. He still did not know. Did he tell his foster brother of the great, earth-shattering, legendary love he had lost, knowing it would be little more than a story to him? Did he tell him of the woman he'd carried in his arms across half a realm? The woman he'd adored and protected, only to fundamentally lose her in the end?

It was too big. It was too terrible. It was not his place. Instead, he said, "You should. You should fix up that drafty old fort with the creepy chandeliers and put a garden beside the lough, where you can watch the swans swim."

"Oh, no," Irian laughed. "I've had enough of swans for one lifetime. But perhaps the rest. A home and a garden. What more could a man want?"

His wife, Wayland longed to say. But he smothered the words.

"And you?" Irian asked. "What do you plan to do, now that you are a free man?"

Wayland thought *free* was a funny word to use.

"I have a mind to travel." He patted Hog on her plump tail, which she flicked like a cat. "I have not seen much of Tír na nÓg, what with nasty fathers and tight collars. Perhaps I will see the sights before I decide where to hang my hat."

Irian nodded. "I would offer to join you, but I have a feeling I would make a terrible tourist."

"No," Wayland agreed. "You should stay where you belong."

What he meant was *You should stay where she can find you.*

Fia was alive. Wayland had to believe she had survived her confrontation with Eala. Surely he wouldn't be able to miss someone this much if they were dead.

"Perhaps you will visit, Way." Irian returned his eyes to the mediocre sword. "From time to time. I have been remembering lately—of when we were boys."

"Perhaps," Wayland agreed. "Let us not leave it another thirteen years, Ree."

He clapped Irian on the shoulder, then climbed the broad boughs beyond the apartments, hooking his knee over a branch and watching the sun set over the gilded plains of the Summerlands. Laoise's,

Chandi's, and Sinéad's distant mounts were outlined in gold upon the horizon. Wayland watched until they disappeared against the purple backdrop of the foothills beyond.

"Perhaps it would not be so bad to be alone again," he mused, out loud. "Not forever. But perhaps for a while. Maybe it would do me some good."

Hog slapped him across the cheek with one clawed paw, spitting a shower of sparks.

"Alone," Wayland amended, "with *you*."

He had found love once. He had been forced to sacrifice it for balance. But in time, he thought, maybe—just maybe—he might be able to find it again.

Someday, he would be whole.

After

Gort—Ivy
Autumn

My hope and my love, we will go for a while into the wood, scattering the dew, where we will see the trout, we will see the blackbird on its nest; the deer and the buck calling, the little bird that is sweetest singing on the branches; the cuckoo on the top of the fresh green; and death will never come near us for ever in the sweet wood.

—"The Heart of the Wood," translated by
Lady Gregory

The kiss of Dún Darragh's shadow tasted like winter. A keen chill swept the evening as I urged Finan toward the sunset-smeared fort, my cloak streaming out behind me.

I had found the stallion a few days after Eala's defeat, grazing happily in a farmer's paddock near Finn Coradh. The man had not appreciated giving him up, but when he'd glimpsed the strange, bloodied host trailing behind me—battle-worn humans and strange-helmed Folk alike—he'd relinquished the stallion without another word.

The bag of silver I'd sent him a few weeks later hopefully salved the pain of losing such a fine animal.

Now I led Finan to Dún Darragh's stable block, untacking him before checking he had enough hay. Outside, dusk lowered like an onyx blade above the toothy silhouette of Roslea. To the east, a full moon was rising, cool and white as a sail in the night. In the middle of the courtyard, the massive oak loomed, its leaves golden as summer despite autumn pressing close on cold feet. I pressed a palm to its pale, strong bark before heaving the fort's doors open. Inside, all was quiet. Puffs of dust rose around my boots.

"Corra?" I heard nothing save a distant, half-imagined cackling. "I know what you did, fiend. I wanted to make sure to tell you in person: *Thank you* for giving me back my ending."

Corra burst into the guise of a damp muskrat, smoothing its whiskers. "We gave you naught that you lacked before. The time was right—no less, no more."

"I appreciate it all the same." I smiled a little. "I may be back here, from time to time, if it pleases you. Perhaps I'll look after the garden. And I hear there is a greenhouse that needs rebuilding."

"*Pfaugh!*" snorted Corra. "You do little that pleases us, that much is true. We asked for a posy—and still, none from you!"

I frowned in mock outrage, even as Corra rocketed from their host in a flurry of motion toward the ceiling, noisily singing, "*Chiardhubh is back, Chiardhubh is back!*"

The truth was, there was much that needed rebuilding, and not just at Dún Darragh. Eala had left behind an entire kingdom in shambles—severely underpopulated, starving, and now frightened and bewildered by a sudden influx of Gentry refugees from Tír na nÓg. Although Breas had recognized me as the high queen's foster daughter, he had not appreciated when I had announced myself as Rían Ó Mainnín's bastard heir and summarily installed myself on the high throne of Rath na Mara. I supposed he had wanted the seat himself—I hadn't bothered to ask. Instead, I had kept myself busy with rebuilding all the infrastructure Eala had destroyed: sending a sad treasury's worth of aid to the villages and farms she'd ransacked, dispersing the fianna of both humans and Gentry all across Fódla, and managing the argumentative, violent under-kings without starting any new wars.

Acting as high queen was, so far, a thankless task. As I'd known it would be. I had never been so grateful to have a mountainous Fomorian as my general and guardian. Balor took to his new role like a fish to water—second to gleefully bashing in revenants' heads on the Bealtaine moon, I had never seen him so fully in his element.

But after six months of commanding and arguing and delegating and worrying and secretly grieving, I was ready for a night off. I pushed back out into the chilly evening, drew my mantle more tightly around me, and shifted into my anam cló.

My doe's senses carried me through the autumn forest. The air was sharp with cold earth and dying foliage and the distant scent of woodsmoke. Moonlight cast strange skeletons upon the forest floor. The only sound was the brittle crackle of my hooves on fallen leaves, the forest hushed with its midnight secrets.

When stone monsters loomed around me in the dim, I returned to myself. Although summer had smoothed many of the scars left by the Bealtaine War, I could still see where the battle had raged. Char blackened one side of the willow; copper stains darkened the stones of the bridge; the undergrowth grew hectically over the lumped forms of revenants in their final repose. A graveyard of a different sort—a mausoleum of my own memories.

I sighed, carefully drew a looking glass from my pack, and turned my thoughts toward hope.

Encased in a frame of twisted silver vines, the mirror gleamed with ethereal light, its surface neither glass nor metal but something in between. Tiny jeweled flowers bloomed along its beveled edges, nearly hiding the plain dark pebble set into the handle. I flipped it over—its reverse was nearly identical, except the stone set into the base glowed a pearly white in the moonlight.

It was Wayland's creation, inspired by a forging his father had designed. He had frowned when I first asked him, the repercussions of my request swiftly rippling through his mind.

"You believe the Gates will close," he guessed, "when the Treasures are unforged."

"They will either close completely or blow open," I confirmed. "I believe the former is more likely. And I fear I will not be able to make it back to Tír na nÓg in time. If I am even alive to try."

Wayland had frowned harder but had not attempted to dissuade me. I loved him for that, although part of me had longed for someone to argue with the terrible destiny awaiting me in the human realms. Instead, Wayland had used a prototype based on his father's design, supplemented by my own supplies. A moonshadow, caught between panes of hammered quartz. Dream steel, flexible metal said to catch nightmares. And two pebbles—one from Fódla, and one from Tír na nÓg—to hold the geasa in place.

Luckily, a dull black stone from Dún Darragh had lodged in the sole of my boot during my mad escape from Eala's ravening hordes. The other pebble, I found on a quiet, secretive foray to the Willow Gate, while the bugles of war sounded in the distance as the Gentry fianna marched and trained.

Wayland had finally finished it the night before the Bealtaine moon, teaching me the incantation as he demonstrated how to use it. Now I repeated his motions as I carefully recited the verse. My face stared at me as I slowly passed the mirror behind my head until it returned to the front. Then I flipped the looking glass, the pearly white stone winking.

The world slid sideways, slipping free of its moorings before snapping back into place.

I stood in the forest beyond the Willow Gate. The trees seemed to grow down instead of up. The willow was in the wrong place beside the bridge. Everything was backward, like I'd stepped right through the mirror into Tír na nÓg.

Sudden nerves pummeled me, flashing heat through my veins and cold along my spine. Thorns nettled the inside of my skin, though less sharp than they'd once felt. Unforging my Treasure had not stolen away my Greenmark. That inborn magic belonged to me—not even the stars could steal it away.

I tucked the mirror into my pack and started forward as the moon netted between painted autumn branches. A lone bone-fox paced me in the undergrowth; a few sheeries startled at my passing, arcing above the canopy like falling stars. When I reached the shore of the lough, I felt him—less a thunderclap than a heavy footstep in the brush. I turned.

The arrow trained on my heart gleamed bright from twenty paces. The man holding the bow made no effort to hide himself, and the moonlight seemed to love him—cascading over his night-black hair...his angular cheekbones...a jaw like metal.

Only his eyes were shadowed—dark as a dream I longed to share. His was the beauty of the night—full moons and fuller hearts. His was the beauty of the forest—growing thorns and blooming flowers. His was the beauty of black ice—deep and endless and perfect.

He was perfect.

I stepped closer. Recognition blew his pupils wide—deep black amid moon-chased gray.

In his grip, the arrow faltered.

"It's you," Irian murmured, with a touch of wonder.

My heart thrilled in my chest. I quickened my footsteps, even as his expression shifted. Hope curdled toward disappointment—the angles of his face sharpening back toward danger. He lifted the bow once more. I stilled.

He did not know me after all.

I squeezed my fists so hard my nails dug crescents into my palms.

After meeting Irian's mother, I'd known this might happen. I'd seen how cruel the patterns etched in the stars could be—I'd tasted their torments firsthand. There was nothing I could do now, save stay the course.

"Good evening," I said inanely. As if we were guests at a feast, partners in a dance.

Instead of enemies. Friends. Lovers. A thousand things he was to me, and none of them simple.

He tilted his head—a tiny yet threatening gesture. Dread weakened my limbs and muddled my thoughts.

I steeled my emotions. I was made of frost and rot and endless things. I was not made to fear my husband. Even if he had forgotten I was his wife.

He moved closer, although neither bow nor arrow dropped. He was still a warrior, but there was an ease in his gait—less menace than curiosity. Again his eyes caught the moonlight, and I studied their shifting color. Not silver anymore, but gray. As storm clouds. As rough seas. As the cliffs where he was raised.

I couldn't help but smile.

The blade of his jaw tilted, and he scented the air.

"You stink of the human realms. You speak like a human." He glanced beyond me. "Yet the Gates are all closed. Tell me what you are."

I smiled again, a little. "Would you believe me if I told you I was lost?"

"This is no place to be lost." He circled closer. "Nor found."

"The pleasure of the losing is in the finding." I followed him with my eyes. "Or so I've had the pleasure of experiencing."

He stopped an arm's length away. He appraised me with interest, if not recognition.

"Do I know you?" His voice was husky, as if he didn't use it often. When his plush mouth moved over the words, I noticed he had a faint, nearly indiscernible scar over his lips. "You speak as if you are not lost at all, but instead wish to be found."

My throat closed tight around a sudden swell of overpowering emotion. I remembered his last words to me, beneath the Bealtaine moon: *I will find you, mo chroí.*

I hoped he did not mind me finding him instead.

I gestured to his face. "Your scar. May I ask how you came by it?"

His pursed his lips unconsciously. "I do not remember."

I did. Oh, how I did. "It bears the shape of . . . a kiss."

"A kiss?" His mouth quirked. "It must have been a terrible kiss."

"Or perhaps a glorious one."

He stared at me for a long moment. Then sighed and dropped his bow, looking bemused. "Do you intend to leave my domain of your own free will, colleen? Or will I have to chase you?"

Colleen. Colleen. Colleen. That wonderful word scattered through me on the force of my heartbeat, raising hope wherever it throbbed.

"I have another proposition for you." I sat upon the rocky beach, drawing a bottle of wine and two clinking clay cups from my pack as I did. "I would make you a bargain."

"Have you never been warned against making bargains with the Folk?"

"Repeatedly." I gazed up at him, trying to keep the yearning from my face. "I am going to pour you some blackberry wine, then I am going to tell you a story."

"And in return?" He made no move to sit, looming over me with ink-black hair falling into his eyes. "What do you wish from me?"

"Your next full moon." I uncorked the bottle and poured two measures into the cups. "The one after that. And, if the story pleases you, the one after that as well."

"That is many nights," he observed, "for the telling of one story."

"Yet it is less than I hoped for."

Perhaps Irian detected the sorrow spreading like aching roots below the warble of my voice. Perhaps he was simply bored and wished for diversion. Either way, he folded his long legs beneath him and sat beside me. The lough rippled with a crisp breeze as he lifted the cup to his lips, the faint scar puckering as he drank deep. He wiped his mouth with the back of his hand, then reached for the bottle. I reached for it at the same instant, and when our fingers collided, a spark sang along my arm to burst like starlight against the cage of my heart.

His storm-gray eyes slashed to mine. His pupils blew wide, emotion savage as love or despair or longing spasming across his face before smoothing away. He dropped his gaze, curling his fingers around the neck of the bottle.

"Go on," he said, as he poured himself more wine. "Tell your tale."

I took a deep breath. "Once, in a time of realms separated by war, and princesses torn apart at birth—"

"That is a very dramatic way to start a story," he interrupted, sardonic.

A smile crept over my face as tremulous warmth bloomed in my chest.

"Oh, all right. I suppose I ought to keep this story simple." I lifted my own cup to my lips and took a deep draught. The wine was bitter as heartbreak and sweet as the hope beyond it. It tasted like evil and good…light and dark…and all the gray shadows lurking between. It tasted of all the things I'd lost—and, perhaps, all the things I had yet to find. But most of all, it tasted like a promise. "She should not have drunk the blackberry wine…"

Acknowledgments

In late November 2020, during the perplexing, sleepless haze following my daughter's birth, I wrote the first lines of a rewrite of a rewrite of a trunked book I then called *Feather Black*. It began like this: "There was once—in the way of old stories and tall, twisted tales—a queen." That opening line would change—as they so often do—but I like to think that in the strangest fashion, I was telling myself an ending instead of a beginning.

In late November 2024, during the overwrought, sleepless frenzy preceding the deadline for this book, which overshot its target word count by thirty thousand words, I wrote the last lines of the final installment of my first complete trilogy through tear-clouded eyes. It ended—as I always knew it would—back at the beginning.

It is with most profound gratitude that I thank every reader who stuck with me—and, of course, Fia—from chapter 1 all the way to the end of the Fair Folk trilogy. Without you, I would no longer have a writing career.

Thank you to my supportive, hilarious, and incredibly hard-working agent, Jessica Watterson. Without you and the fantastic team at the Sandra Dijkstra Literary Agency, I also would not have a writing career.

To Alyea Canada, who mercilessly points out when my characters have been wearing the same weird outfits for three months straight but nevertheless usually tells me yes when she should probably tell me no. To Nadia Saward, a quiet sorceress of behind-the-scenes miracles. To Orbit and Hachette, and the remarkable teams in editorial, production, audio, marketing, publicity, and sales who made this series happen.

To Kara Quinn, for the reels and the wine and the endless *exactlys*. To Shauna Granger, for *many* things but especially for keeping me from giving Laoise '90s biker gang tattoos. To Roshani Chokshi, for always knowing the best medicine for an ailing story. To all my wonderfully encouraging author friends: Ryan Graudin, Brittney Arena, Breanne Randall, Maya Evan MacGregor, Naomi Farr, Amanda Sinatra, Glenn Ashley, and countless others. I appreciate you!

To the entire unhinged corpus of Irish mythology that convinced me through my tears that this bittersweet ending was not only right, but symbolically necessary.

To Steve, Freya, and Kepler—I won't always be like this (I will always be like this).

Slán go fóill, a chairde. My friends, I trust we will meet again soon, on the pages of another book.

Once upon a time...

Glossary

Amergin (AH-mer-ghin)—founder of Fódla; god of poetry and law

anam cló (AH-num klow), **anam clónna** (AH-num KLOHN-uh) (pl.)—soul form; animal avatar

Annwyn (ah-NOON)—the realm of the Ellyllon

aughisky (AW-ih-ski)—shapeshifting carnivorous water horse

banfhlaith (BAN-lah)—princess

barda (BAR-dah), **bardaí** (bar-DEE) (pl.)—gate warden

Bridei (BREE-dye)—Rogan's home kingdom

Brighid (BRIDGE-id)—goddess of husbandry and healing

brùnaidh (BROO-nee), **brùnaidhean** (BROO-nee-in) (pl.)—small, secretive household Folk who tidy homes in exchange for leftovers or milk

Cathair (KAH-her)

Chandika (CHUN-dee-kaa)

chiardhubh (KEER-va)—sable; nickname roughly meaning *dark-haired*

claíomh (clayve), **claimhte** (CLEV-tah) (pl.)—longsword

Cnoc Féigleann (knock FAYG-lin)—sentinel mountain

Corra (KORE-ah)

dragan (DRAH-gun), **dragain** (DRAH-gin) (pl.)—legendary flying serpent or dragon, in the language of Tír na nÓg

draig (DRAYG)—legendary flying serpent or dragon, in the language of Annwyn

Dubhán (DOO-awn)—an aughisky

dúil (DOOL); **dúile** (DWEE-luh) (pl.)—magical element

dún (dune)—a fort or fortified castle

Dún Darragh (dune DAH-rah)

Dún Scaith (dune SKYE)—a mythic training ground for Folk warriors

Eala (AY-lah)

Ellyllon (EH-leeh-lon)—the Fair Folk of Annwyn

Emain Ablach (EM-in AB-luch)—an island nation ruled by Gavida, the smith-king; the Silver Isle

Fáilsceim (FAWL-shkem)—a legendary trident; also called Scepter of the Flood

fénnid (FAY-nidge), **fénnidi** (fay-nidge-EE) (pl.)—warrior

feis (FESH), **feiseanna** (FESH-uh-nah) (pl.)—a festival with music and dancing

Fia (FEE-ah)

fiann (FEE-in), **fianna** (FEE-nah) (pl.)—band of warriors; army

Fódla (FO-lah)—an island nation ruled by a human high king or queen, with four major provinces ruled by under-kings

Gavida (gah-VEE-dah)—smith-king of Emain Ablach

geas (GESH), **geasa** (GYES-sah) (pl.)—a magical binding or obligation; a curse

Geth (GETH)—the Bright One of Irian's Treasure

Grian (GREE-awn)—the Bright One of Laoise's Treasure

gruagach (GREW-ah-gak), **gruagaigh** (GREW-ah-guy) (pl.)—big, hairy, aggressive Folk

Idris (IH-driss)

Ínne (EEN-yah)—the Bright One of Fia's Treasure

Irian (EER-ee-in)

leipreachán (lep-reh-HAWN), **leipreacháin** (lep-reh-HAYN) (pl.)—diminutive, mischievous Folk

lough (loch)—lake

Mag Tuired (moy TURA)—the site of a legendary battle

Marban (mar-BAHN)

mo chroí (muh CHREE)—endearment meaning *my heart*

Muir (MEER)—the Bright One of Wayland's Treasure

nemeton (NEH-meh-tin), **nemeta** (NEH-meh-tah) (pl.)—holy grove or site of power

Oweynagat (OH-wen-nagat)—Cave of the Cats

prionsa (PRIN-sah)—prince

Rogan (ROE-gin)

rónán beag (ROW-nin BEG)—a nickname meaning *littlest seal*

Sinéad (shi-NAYD)

skean (skene)—a small single-edged knife

Solasóirí (SULL-ah-SO-ree)—another name for the Firbolg; loosely meaning *Bright Ones*

Talah (TAW-lah)

tánaiste (TAW-nisht-uh), **tánaistí** (TAW-nisht-EE) (pl.)—heir apparent of a Sept's Treasure

Tír na nÓg (TEER na NOGUE)—the realm of the Fair Folk; the otherworld

About the Author

Lyra Selene was born under a full moon and has never quite managed to wipe the moonlight out of her eyes. She grew up on a steady diet of mythology, folklore, and fantasy and now writes tall tales of twisted magic, forbidden love, and brooding landscapes. She lives in New England with her husband, daughter, and dog in an antique farmhouse that's probably not haunted.

Find out more about Lyra Selene and other Orbit authors by registering for the free monthly newsletter at orbit-books.co.uk.

RAISING READERS
Books Build Bright Futures

Dear Reader,

We'd love your attention for one more page to tell you about the crisis in children's reading, and what we can all do.

Studies have shown that reading for fun is the **single biggest predictor of a child's future life chances** – more than family circumstance, parents' educational background or income. It improves academic results, mental health, wealth, communication skills, ambition and happiness.[1]

The number of children reading for fun is in rapid decline. Young people have a lot of competition for their time. In 2024, 1 in 10 children and young people in the UK aged 5 to 18 did not own a single book at home.[2]

Hachette works extensively with schools, libraries and literacy charities, but here are some ways we can all raise more readers:

- Reading to children for just 10 minutes a day makes a difference
- Don't give up if children aren't regular readers – there will be books for them!
- Visit bookshops and libraries to get recommendations
- Encourage them to listen to audiobooks
- Support school libraries
- Give books as gifts

There's a lot more information about how to encourage children to read on our website: **www.RaisingReaders.co.uk**

Thank you for reading.

---

[1] OECD, '21st-Century Readers: Developing Literacy Skills in a Digital World', 2021, https://www.oecd.org/en/publications/21st-century-readers_a83d84cb-en.html

[2] National Literacy Trust, 'Book Ownership in 2024', November 2024, https://literacytrust.org.uk/research-services/research-reports/book-ownership-in-2024